HARE TOD

"A wonderful re
mystery humming along. . . . Jessica [illegible] an
attractive and capable sleuth, and the animals in the story provide not only charm but also comic relief in between the more suspenseful portions of the book."
—*Romantic Times*

"A very entertaining series with a menagerie of colorful human and animal characters."
—*Mystery Lovers Bookshop News*

"A neatly crafted mystery, dropping clever clues throughout and giving the reader some fun spooks. Jessica Popper is an entertaining amateur sleuth, supported by a cast of fun, familiar two- and four-legged characters." —*Fresh Fiction*

LEAD A HORSE TO MURDER

"A cleverly constructed mystery chock-full of dysfunctional characters all hiding motives for murder . . . Readers—and particularly pet lovers—[will] savor this delightful cozy."
—*Publishers Weekly*

"*Lead a Horse to Murder* is a good ride, and Baxter's newest novel hits all the right marks. Her characters step out of the pages and into the corral, with plenty of bumps, jumps and lots of horseplay."
—*Horse Directory*

"A pure gold mystery."
—*Midwest Book Review*

"A well-written murder mystery... I enjoyed the glimpses into Jess's personal life as she put the pieces together to solve the murder. Ms. Baxter has created a tale that will delight her fans." —*Fresh Fiction*

PUTTING ON THE DOG

"Dog lovers, rejoice! Baxter is back with a frisky sequel to *Dead Canaries Don't Sing*.... The tale moves smoothly as Jess mingles with the film industry's hottest stars, tracking down clues, but readers will derive the most pleasure from the antics of Jess's canine companions, Max and Lou, the author's behind-the-scenes look at dog shows and the sprinkling of information she provides on each breed." —*Publishers Weekly*

"In a similar vein to that of Susan Conant, Ms. Baxter does an excellent job of creating hysterical characters and providing plenty of descriptions of their four-legged companions. An extremely quick read, *Putting On the Dog* is a wonderful mystery that packs a lot of action and red herrings into a slim volume that avoids the pitfalls of pretentious punning. This is a great book to read while curled on the couch with your own four-legged friends."
—TheBestReviews.com

"Cynthia Baxter has done it once again, and created an extremely enjoyable, laugh-out-loud-funny mystery that would please anyone.... Loaded with tons of pop culture references, as well as an exclusive peek at how the rich live, this is sure to be an absolute hit with all."
—*California Community Bugle*

"Baxter excels at the telling detail: Her dogs wake up in the morning as if they've 'already hit the espresso pot,' and a scene with Jessica dancing with the movie heartthrob of the moment is so real it offers a vicarious fantasy." —*Romantic Times*

"A light read when you totally want to tune out the educational stuff. Two paws up."
—*Cleveland Plain Dealer*

"A fun romp through Long Island's east end . . . well crafted and moves at a fast pace. It's an easy and enjoyable read. . . . A real page-turner. If you love good mysteries or love animals or mysteries with animals, you'll love Baxter's *Putting On the Dog*."
—*Long Island Times-Herald*

DEAD CANARIES DON'T SING

"Clever, fast-paced and well-plotted, *Dead Canaries Don't Sing* stars an appealing heroine and furry sidekicks sure to enchant pet lovers."
—Carolyn Hart, Agatha, Anthony and Macavity Awards winner

"Dead canaries don't sing, but you will after reading this terrific mystery!"
—Rita Mae Brown, *New York Times* bestselling author

"A little bird told me to read this mystery, which is awfully good. For the record, I would shred any canary who insulted me."
—Sneaky Pie Brown, *New York Times* bestselling cat

"*Dead Canaries Don't Sing* is top dog, the cat's pajamas, and the paws that refresh all rolled into one un-furr-gettable mystery entertainment."
—Sarah Graves

"Loads of fun! Baxter's veterinary sleuth and her menagerie of animal companions are a great way to spend an afternoon. So pull up a chair and dive in."
—T. J. MacGregor, Edgar Award winner and author of *Category Five*

"An auspicious debut . . . Messages, murder and a menagerie of odd animals are along for the fun."
—*Mystery Scene*

"Baxter's lighthearted, enjoyable mystery is an entertaining debut featuring a likable menagerie of characters, a few surprising plot twists and a touch of romance." —*Lansing State Journal*

"Charmingly humorous . . . [Baxter is] funny without being fussy. Along with lovable Jessica and her menagerie, the author has created a subtle yet creepy antagonist whose unmasking is as intense as it is surprising." —*Romantic Times*

"A truly refreshing read that moved the plot right along. I'm looking forward to more in this new series." —*Rendezvous*

"Should be on your [summer reading list]."
—*Newsday*

Also by Cynthia Baxter

DEAD CANARIES DON'T SING

PUTTING ON THE DOG

LEAD A HORSE TO MURDER

HARE TODAY, DEAD TOMORROW

Right from the Gecko

A *Reigning Cats & Dogs* Mystery

Cynthia Baxter

BANTAM BOOKS

RIGHT FROM THE GECKO
A Bantam Book / April 2007

Published by Bantam Dell
A Division of Random House, Inc.
New York, New York

This is a work of fiction. Names, characters, places, and incidents either are the product of the author's imagination or are used fictitiously. Any resemblance to actual persons, living or dead, events, or locales is entirely coincidental.

Cover design by Marietta Anastassatos

ISBN 978-0-553-58844-6

Printed in the United States of America
Published simultaneously in Canada

www.bantamdell.com

OPM 10 9 8 7 6 5 4 3 2 1

To Rachel

Acknowledgments

As always, in researching this book, I was amazed by how generous the experts I consulted were with their knowledge, their time, and their creativity. I would like to thank Abraham D. Krikorian, Vitaly Citovsky, and Dale Deutsch of Stony Brook University's Biochemistry Department, as well as Greenhouse Curator Michael Axelrod, for unraveling some of the mysteries of botany.

I would also like to thank Bill Stephens and Sara Sue Hoklotubbe, both of whom are lucky enough to live on Maui, for the information they provided about their beautiful island. Thanks also to the Joplin Humane Society in Joplin, Missouri.

And as always, thanks to Faith and Caitlin.

Right from the Gecko

Chapter 1

"When a cat adopts you there is nothing to be done about it except put up with it until the wind changes."

—T. S. Eliot

"Ladies and gentlemen, the captain has turned on the seat-belt sign. Please return to your seats and fasten your seat belts, as we expect to encounter some turbulence. . . ."

I looped my thumb under my seat belt to double-check it, then glanced over at Nick, who was crammed into the seat beside me. Even the flight attendant's warning hadn't motivated him to look up from his guidebook. Then again, he'd pretty much buried his nose in the fat paperback the moment our plane had taken off from Los Angeles. The only time he'd come up for air had been complimentary beverage time, when he'd ordered pineapple juice after expressing his extreme disappointment that mango juice wasn't on the menu.

"*The Penny-Pinching Traveler's Guide to Maui* says there's a great snorkeling spot right behind the Royal Banyan Hotel," he announced, passing along his eighteen-hundredth travel tip since we'd boarded the plane four and a half hours earlier. "And you can go on a sunrise bike ride on Haleakala, the volcanic crater, that's a thirty-eight-mile ride downhill—"

"Sir?" the flight attendant interrupted. "Please fasten your seat belt. We're expecting things to get a bit rocky."

"Sorry." Nick pulled his seat belt low and tight across his lap, nestling it between a pair of khaki cargo pants and a black T-shirt he'd assured me would be replaced by the brightest, most outrageous Hawaiian shirt he could find as soon as we landed.

"I'm glad you're so excited about this trip," I commented.

"Are you kidding?" Nick exclaimed. "Ten days in Hawaii is the best possible antidote to law school. After the total nightmare of exam week, I *need* a few days of snorkeling on some fabulous beach with a mai tai in one hand and a papaya in the other."

I didn't bother to point out that drinking mai tais and snorkeling at the same time probably wouldn't work all that well. Or that, complaining aside, Nick had managed an A in every one of the courses he'd taken during his first semester at the Brookside University School of Law. Not when I was as happy as he was to be embarking on a ten-day vacation on the Hawaiian island of Maui, combining the American Veterinary Medical Association's annual conference with what I hoped would be a romantic getaway.

I was equally pleased that I'd come up with the idea of giving him a plane ticket for Christmas. True, flying nearly six thousand miles from Long Island to Maui was a bit of a luxury, one that not every vet I knew had opted to indulge in. Suzanne Fox, for example, a close friend from vet school whose practice was on the island's East End. Of course, she was still recovering from a brush with the law she'd had a few months earlier. Frankly, I didn't blame her for needing time to get over the trauma of having the police peg her as their number-one suspect in the murder of her ex-husband's fiancée.

Another local vet I knew, Marcus Scruggs, wasn't going either. He had the distinction of being Suzanne's boyfriend for a while—an episode in Suzanne's life I still considered incomprehensible. In fact, given the messy way their relationship had ended, I wondered if they'd both decided to skip the conference because they were afraid of running into each other.

But I was convinced that Nick and I deserved to splurge. Taking a real vacation was my way of saying, *Let's celebrate the fact that we* both *made it through your first semester of law school.* Of course, his return to studenthood after years of a successful career as a private investigator was in addition to me running my busy veterinary practice, tooling around Long Island in my twenty-six-foot clinic on wheels with the words REIGNING CATS AND DOGS: MOBILE VETERINARY SERVICES, LARGE AND SMALL ANIMALS stenciled on the side.

On top of that, for the past few months I'd been hosting a weekly TV spot on a Long Island cable station, discussing various aspects of pet care and answering callers' questions during a phone-in segment. Then there was Suzanne's brush with the law: I'd helped figure out who really murdered her ex-husband's fiancée and had almost been shoved off a cliff by the killer. So a vacation-for-two was long overdue, and I was absolutely ecstatic about this trip.

Unfortunately, ecstasy wasn't the only emotion I was experiencing.

Deep down in the pit of my stomach—an inch or two below the tingle of ecstasy—lurked a low-level feeling of anxiety. Sure, I was looking forward to our vacation in paradise, everything from gorging on coconut-flavored shave ice to watching tacky hula shows to taking those long walks on the beach that people in search of romance are always talking about.

What I *wasn't* looking forward to was returning to the scene of the crime.

Not a real crime. More like a crime of the heart. Almost a year and a half earlier, Nick and I had flown to Maui for our first real vacation together. And it was wonderful, until I found out he'd planned an activity I hadn't seen listed in any guidebook: proposing marriage on an isolated stretch of beach as the sun was just about ready to dip below the horizon.

It turned into one of the biggest fiascos of my entire life.

In fact, the results were so devastating that they had torn us apart. It took a murder investigation to bring us back together—but that's another story. Nick and I finally managed to patch up our relationship after spending nearly three months apart, but not until Ms. Commitmentphobe here was able to admit both to him and to myself that I didn't want to live without him.

I'd made major progress since then. He and I had just finished a three-month trial period living together in my tiny cottage in Joshua's Hollow. And I had to admit that having Nick as a roommate and live-in lover went a lot better than I'd expected. Once I got over the initial shock of having another person around all the time—which, it turns out, is very different from living with two crazed yet severely codependent dogs, an aging feline with arthritis, a tiger kitten who thinks she's Marie Antoinette, an ever-silent Jackson's chameleon with amazingly expressive eyes, and a mouthy blue and gold macaw who has the colorful vocabulary of a sailor—I actually enjoyed it.

Still, the anguish caused by what had happened the last time Nick and I went Hawaiian hadn't been forgotten. In fact, it hovered above us as we flew the five and a half hours from New York's JFK Airport to LAX in Los Angeles, then continued on a second five-hour leg to Maui. It was as much a presence as the overhead luggage compartment that Nick banged his head against every time he stood up to let me go to the bathroom.

But we were determined to make the best of it. Or ignore it. Or at least work around it. At any rate, despite whatever worries may have lingered from our last trip, I was looking forward to a long, leisurely break filled with sun, surf, and sand, with a little intellectual stimulation thrown in courtesy of the veterinary conference.

And hopefully as little turbulence as possible.

• • •

As Nick and I emerged from Kahului Airport, I felt like Dorothy stepping out of Auntie Em's house after the tornado dropped it in the Land of Oz. Gone were the dreary gray skies of the New York winter, the piles of slushy snow sprinkled with black soot, and the icy winds that stung any and all exposed flesh without mercy.

Instead, the landscape was lush and inviting. All around us were palm trees topped with long, spiky fronds and bright pink, red, and yellow flowers with ridiculously huge blossoms. The giant yellow blob of a sun was so wonderfully warm that I immediately tore off the sweater that had seemed so inadequate back on Long Island. Even the air smelled different, sweet and wonderfully fresh.

As if he'd read my mind, Nick said in an awed whisper, "We're not in Kansas anymore."

I just smiled. And then I whipped out my brand-new digital camera, Nick's Christmas present to me. I snapped at least a dozen photos before tucking it back into the small flowered backpack that was serving as my pocketbook on this trip.

The same feeling—that we'd just received a mandate to relax—permeated the lobby of the Royal Banyan Hotel. The fact that it had no walls to speak of helped, as did the tremendous bouquets of tropical flowers and the old-fashioned Hawaiian ukulele music piping in from hidden speakers. Two women sat at a long table, one making leis by stringing together fragrant flowers and one weaving hats and baskets out of grass. Behind them hung a display of Hawaiian quilts in pastel colors. Next to the hotel bar, the White Orchid, was a sign advertising a poolside demonstration of Polynesian music and dance every evening at six. A second sign advertised the hotel's luau, claiming it was *Maui's Finest*.

"Aloha," the dark-haired woman at the front desk greeted us. She was dressed in a loose-fitting muumuu made of deep-purple fabric splashed with big white flowers, and she'd tucked a white hibiscus into her hair. "Welcome to the Royal Banyan."

As she punched the keys of her computer, Nick commented, "Everybody's so friendly here."

The woman smiled. "It's what we call 'aloha spirit.' " Then she added, "That's a term that refers to the warmth and sincerity of the Hawaiian people, which comes from coordinating the mind and the heart. We try to think good thoughts and convey good feelings."

"I remember that term from the last time we were here," I said.

"Maybe we can bring a little back to New York," Nick commented. "As in, 'Yo! How about showin' a little aloha spirit over here?' "

Laughing, the woman said, "To fully understand it, you have to experience the magic of the Hawaiian Islands." She handed us our key cards, saying, "*Mahalo*. That's Hawaiian for thank you."

"Yo, and *mahalo* to you too!"

I jabbed Nick in the ribs with my elbow, but lightly, because I wanted to show him that I had already mastered the aloha spirit concept.

"Chill, bro," I told him. "You're in Hawaii now."

"Don't I know it," he returned. "Let's check out our room and then hit the shops. Somewhere out there is an extremely loud shirt with my name on it."

Like the lobby, our room had a relaxing tropical feel. Sliding glass doors opened onto a balcony, which the Hawaiians called a lanai, with a view of both the hotel's lush gardens and the ocean just beyond. The large room's turquoise and purple decor brought the same intoxicating feeling inside, even though it had all the modern conveniences like a minifridge, a hair dryer, and an iron.

We stayed just long enough to pull our clothes out of our suitcases in what could loosely be interpreted as unpacking. I threw the beige canvas tote bag I'd used as my carry-on into the closet, figuring that at some point it could double as a beach bag. Then, as soon as we changed into shorts and sandals and I pulled my dark-blond hair back into a ponytail, we headed downstairs. I was anxious to check in at the AVMA conference and get my badge, program, and all the other essentials for the five-day event.

But first, my shopaholic traveling companion needed a quick fix.

"Hey, check these out!" Nick darted into the hotel

gift shop and pounced upon a rack of boxy aloha shirts in loud, colorful prints that featured, in various combinations, palm trees, exotic-looking flowers, parrots, outrigger canoes, and 1950s-era station wagons with surfboards mounted on the roof. He pulled out the loudest one and held it up to his chest. It was splashed with hot-pink hibiscus and orange parrots, neither of which bore the slightest resemblance to any flora or fauna actually found in nature. "How do I look?"

"Like Don Ho on dress-down Friday," I replied. "But somehow, it suits you."

He grinned. "I'll go try this on. D'you mind?"

"Be my guest. And see if they have a matching muumuu for me."

Actually, the idea of doing some shopping of my own was pretty tempting. I wanted to get something for my dear friend and landlady Betty Vandervoort, perhaps a colorful sundress or some unusual shell jewelry. Even though Betty's last birthday cake had had more than seventy candles on it, she'd never outgrown her love of dressing flamboyantly. I planned to bring back a souvenir for Suzanne too, although I had a feeling her taste ran more to a Hunks of Hawaii calendar. I also wanted to stock up on coffee beans, since Hawaiian coffees, especially Kona coffee, were among the finest in the world.

But I figured all that could wait, especially since I'd just gotten here. Glancing across the lobby, I added, "I'm going to see if I can register before the line gets too long."

Fortunately, registration for the conference had just begun, enabling me to walk right up and give my name without waiting in line.

"Popper, Popper . . . Jessica Popper?" the man running the show asked.

"That's me."

He gave me my laminated badge, a thick conference program listing the topics and speakers for all the sessions, and a forest-green canvas bag printed with the name of the conference and the organization's logo. I figured I was all set, but then he handed me a bulky brown envelope so stuffed with goodies it was stapled shut to keep them all from falling out.

"Here's everything you need," he announced. "Enjoy the conference."

"Thanks." I stuck the badge and the program in my backpack. As for the envelope, I'd been to enough of these conferences to know it contained the usual assortment of booklets advertising medications and other items of interest to veterinarians. No doubt it was also packed with freebies from the drug companies, promotional items like pens, refrigerator magnets, coasters, rubber chewy toys in bright colors, and pads of Post-its, all emblazoned with the names of the drugs they manufactured.

This one also had a hard plastic item in it that felt like an audiocassette. I'd gotten these before too. They invariably turned out to be a recording of some James Herriot wannabe reading from a book he'd written, hoping this free sample would entice all of us to buy his masterpiece and put him that much closer to *The New York Times* best-seller list.

I tucked the envelope inside the green bag, figuring I'd sort through the contents later. At the moment, I wasn't quite ready to focus on my day job. Instead, I luxuriated in the simple act of wandering through the open-air lobby, breathing in the soothingly warm air that was lightly scented with flowers. A nice side effect of all those huge bouquets of exotic flowers, I realized. Even the couches and chairs fit into the tropical feeling. They were made of bamboo and covered in bright floral fabrics.

As I strode by the front door of the hotel, however, I saw that the scene right outside the hotel was definitely lacking in aloha spirit. Crammed near the entrance were trucks from what looked like every one of the island's television stations. They were emblazoned with the call letters of what I assumed were affiliates of the major networks: KHNL, KGMB, KITV, KHON.

"What's going on?" I asked aloud, even though nobody was around to answer.

The presence of a caravan of limousines told me that whatever it was, it was bigger than the luau chef making off with the roast pig.

At the far end of the lobby, I noticed a small group of people hurrying toward a set of double doors. They looked authoritative, not only because they clutched notebooks but also because they were decked out in Hawaii's version of business clothes: neatly pressed aloha shirts worn with light-colored pants for the men, pretty flowered dresses for the women. Figuring they were somehow connected to whatever all the fuss was about, I followed.

As I neared the double doors, I heard loud singing. But this was no hula show.

"For he's a jolly good fel-low . . ."

The singing grew even louder when someone flung open the doors. As the group filed through, I made a quick detour back to the friendly woman at the front desk who'd checked in Nick and me.

"Excuse me, what's going on?" I asked.

Glancing toward the double doors, she replied, "Governor Wickham. He's holding a press conference. I think he's announcing the official opening of some big company that's setting up its headquarters here on the island."

"Thank you." I glanced back at the gift shop long enough to spot Nick, who was wearing the hot-pink and orange aloha shirt, its tags still hanging, as he examined every single shirt that remained on the rack. And then, hesitating for only a second or two, I made a beeline for the double doors and pushed my way through.

I blinked at the sight of hundreds of people crowded into a large ballroom, exuding so much enthusiasm it could have been New Year's Eve. Most of them faced the stage that was set up at one end, a platform framed by clusters of red, white, and blue crepe-paper streamers and backed with a huge Hawaiian state flag. My eyes were automatically drawn to the man at the center of it all, who stood beneath a canopy of red, white, and blue helium balloons.

Governor Wickham, I surmised. The guy with the most expensive-looking suit and the best haircut.

And a very clever haircut at that, I realized. His hair reminded me of Nick's, the way it kept falling across his forehead, giving him an energetic, almost boyish look that was an interesting contrast to its silvery-white color. In fact, his locks gleamed almost as brightly as the two rows of straight, even teeth he never stopped flashing.

A man as comfortable in the public eye as J-Lo, I thought wryly.

". . . Which no-bo-dy can de-ny!"

At the end of the song, the crowd burst into loud cheering.

"Thank you so much for your support," the governor boomed, leaning forward to make sure the microphone carried his voice throughout the room. "I'm extremely pleased to announce the arrival of an innovative new biotech firm on the island. FloraTech has performed conclusive research about the hibiscus plant's curative powers—powers that no one else has ever tapped. Their plan is to grow them on the island in massive quantities for medicinal purposes, providing not only a boon to the island's agricultural sector but also to its industrial economy. This marks a major, positive step for the people of this island. Here's to a bigger and brighter future for our beloved state of Hawaii!"

His final words elicited bursts of loud cheering and applause. Waving and smiling, Governor Wickham stepped off the stage and into the crowd. He was flanked by two men in suits that looked almost as expensive as his. I assumed they were aides, although given the almost manic vigilance with which the tall one with the dark-red hair scanned the room, he could have doubled as a bodyguard.

As the three men made their way through the ballroom toward the exit, people moved aside to clear an irregular path. So I was startled when a small group suddenly stepped forward a few yards in front of where I stood.

The press, I realized, recognizing a few of them as the notebook-bearing crowd I'd noticed earlier. The group also included photographers, some of them snapping pictures while others balanced huge video cameras on their shoulders. As the governor drew close, they swarmed around him.

"Governor Wickham," one of the reporters called out. "Nan Higginson from the *Honolulu Star-Bulletin*. Have you made a decision yet about whether you'll run for reelection in November?"

Flashing those perfect teeth that were an orthodontist's dream, he answered, "Let's just say it's not out of the question."

The entire room trembled from the whistles and cheers that followed.

"Governor, what will your platform be if you decide to run?" a woman clutching a KITV microphone asked.

The tall, silver-haired politician frowned as if he were giving her question careful consideration. And then, his eyes shining merrily, he replied, "That I'll continue doing the same good work for the people of Hawaii that I've been doing all along!"

This guy must spend hours practicing in front of a mirror, I thought, shaking my head.

I'd suddenly had enough of politics. Shopping for aloha shirts was beginning to sound much more appealing. In fact, I'd just turned away from the action, intending to slink out of the ballroom to find Nick, when I noticed a tiny young woman with large blue eyes and short, spiky light-brown hair that gave her a pixieish look. She was dressed in a dark blue miniskirt and a white T-shirt, with a distinctive string of multicolored beads around her neck. An oversize black canvas tote bag that looked heavy enough to contain a bowling ball was slung over one shoulder.

I would have thought she was a teenager who'd wandered into the wrong part of the hotel if it hadn't been for the small tape recorder in her hand. I watched her make her way toward the governor with a fierce determination that reminded me of my terrier, Max. Especially when she planted herself directly in front of him.

"Governor Wickham, Marnie Burton, *Maui Dispatch*. Do you feel the arrival of a big biotech firm on an island that most people consider paradise could be seen as a major step in the wrong direction?"

I noticed that the governor's smile faltered for the first time since I'd entered the room. But only for a moment. He turned away, suddenly absorbed in waving to the people behind him.

As he and his entourage strode by, the aide on his left, the one with the red hair, passed right in front of the reporter who'd asked the troublesome question. As he did, I noticed a sudden movement. Before I had a chance to figure out what was happening, I saw the reporter lose her balance. The tape recorder flew out of her hand. She let out a startled shriek as she fell backward toward a huge potted plant.

"Oh, no!" I cried as I watched the back of her head hit the sharp edge of the metal pot. The necklace she was wearing broke from the impact, sending dozens of beads flying into the air like fireworks.

A few people gasped, but I was the only one who rushed over to help. "Are you all right?" I demanded.

She let out a moan. "Ooh! My head!" As she started to stand, she muttered, "That jerk!"

"Don't move," I instructed. "I'll get security."

"Jeez, no! Don't do that!"

"Then maybe I can help. Here, let me take a look." Gently, I moved the young woman's hand away from her head. She flinched as I touched an area that was quickly swelling to the size of a small snowball.

"You've got yourself quite a bump," I informed her.

I glanced around, still expecting someone else to come forward to help. No one did. In fact, the rest of the crowd was already streaming toward the double doors and out of the ballroom.

"You've got to get some ice on that."

"Thanks, but I'm fine. Really. I should follow him—" As she tried to stand up, she swayed uncertainly.

"I don't think so," I replied, grabbing her under the arms. "You might have a concussion. I'll find someone to take you to the hospital."

"No way! I'll get stuck in the emergency room for

hours, and I've got to write my article. It's not every day I get a chance to do a big story like this."

"In that case, why don't you come up to my room so we can put some ice on that bump? At least you can lie down for a few minutes."

"That's really nice of you," Marnie replied, grabbing her black bag and stuffing her tape recorder into it. "I guess I probably should. But just for, like, five minutes."

As we crossed the lobby, I spotted Nick in the gift shop. After sitting Marnie down on one of the bamboo couches, I scurried over. Not only did he have three Hawaiian shirts draped across his arm, their tags fluttering like butterflies, but he'd moved on to the display of macadamia nuts.

"Cinnamon macadamia nuts," he greeted me. "Does that sound like something we could get addicted to?"

"Definitely," I replied. "But right now I've got a bit of a disaster to deal with. A reporter I just met—her name is Marnie Burton—tripped and got bonked on the head. I'm going to bring her up to our room and get her some ice."

"Whoa. Anything I can do?"

"Thanks, but I think I can handle it."

"In that case, I'll be up soon."

Ten minutes later, Marnie Burton was stretched across the king-size bed in my hotel room with her shoes off and a plastic bag of ice resting on the back of her head. I was about to suggest the hospital one more time when she mumbled, "I've got to get out of here. Mr. C is counting on me."

"Mr. C?"

"Mr. Carrera, my editor. He really needs me to get this story in by tonight. Our staff is pretty lean, so it's not as if there's anybody else who could fill in for me."

Sounding apologetic, she added, "The *Maui Dispatch* is kind of a small newspaper. Number two to the *Maui News*."

"Sounds like a great place to learn the business, though," I offered encouragingly.

From the grateful look on Marnie's face, I realized I'd said just the right thing. "That's exactly what I thought!" Readjusting the ice pack, she said, "You're being so kind. Who are you, anyway, my guardian angel?"

"Sorry. Guess I forgot to introduce myself. My name is Jessica Popper. I'm here for the veterinary conference."

"The AVMA, right? I noticed the sign in the lobby."

"That's the one."

"So you're a vet? Cool."

"I like it." In fact, I loved it. But I didn't take the time to go into details, since Marnie and I were still in a fact-finding mode.

"Do you have, like, a million pets?" she asked.

I laughed. "It sure feels like it sometimes. But actually, I only have two dogs, two cats, a blue and gold macaw, and a chameleon. At least, at the moment."

"That's great. Personally, I've always been a cat person." She suddenly laughed self-consciously. "Here I am, telling you my life story, practically, and I realize I haven't even told you my name. I'm Marnie Burton from the *Maui Dispatch*—" She stopped herself. "Sorry. Habit. That's what happens when you're working your butt off, trying to live out your lifelong dream of becoming a reporter. Although at the moment, I'm wondering if I should have followed my mother's advice and stayed in Ellensburg, Washington, and become a nursery-school teacher instead. Especially since I never planned on someplace as far away and exotic as Hawaii. But when I found the job on Monster dot-com, I figured what the heck."

"How long ago was that?"

"Two years."

"And how do your parents back in Ellensburg, Washington, feel about that?"

She made a face. "Not exactly supportive. In fact, they haven't talked to me since I left. Not even a birthday card. They're, like, totally the opposite of me. They've never been anywhere, and they have no interest in going anywhere. I guess they figure they can change my mind by freezing me out. Heck, I bet they don't even know my address. I keep writing to them, sending them long letters about how well I'm doing, but for all I know, they just throw them out without even opening them."

"You must feel awful about that."

She shrugged. "I'm still hoping they'll come around once they find out what a success I've become." Grinning, she added, "That is, once I actually manage to *become* a success. In the meantime, at least I've got my boyfriend, Ace, to keep me from getting too lonely."

"*Ace?* Are you serious?" I hadn't meant to sound stuffy, but somehow the words just popped out that way.

Fortunately, she laughed. "I get the same reaction from everybody. It's not as if he's some card shark or something. Actually, he has his own business. Bodywork. He's really good at it. The best on Maui, in fact. And his real name is Ashton—Ashton Atwood. But when that actor got so famous, he couldn't stand being teased anymore, so he started telling people his name was Ace. Of course, it turns out he gets teased just as much."

An expression of alarm suddenly crossed her face. "What time is it?"

I glanced at my watch. "Almost six."

"Oh, no! Ace is gonna kill me!" Quickly she added, "Not that he's not absolutely crazy about me, but he's got a bit of a temper. I'm supposed to meet him for dinner tonight, and he goes ballistic if I'm even, like, five minutes late."

I raised my eyebrows but kept my opinions to myself.

"I've got to rush home to shower and change," she went on. "Ace picked a really romantic restaurant, this quiet, out-of-the-way place in Kula he really likes. We go there all the time. He said he has something important to talk to me about tonight." She grinned impishly. "I think I can guess what it might be."

If this boyfriend of yours pops the question, I thought, I hope you handle it a lot better than I did.

She stood up, then grimaced and sat down again, as if she'd been hit with an unexpected jolt of pain. She reached up and gingerly touched the back of her head. "Ugh, my head feels like a volcano that's about to erupt."

"Can I get you anything?" I asked anxiously.

"I've got some Advil in my bag—if you don't mind looking through all my stuff to find it. It's in a little cosmetics bag with flowers on it."

I looked at her black canvas tote bag and grimaced. It was so big that finding anything in there was guaranteed to be a challenge. But I rummaged around until I found the small flowered bag, hidden beneath her tape recorder, cell phone, pens, makeup, notebooks, manila file folders, Band-Aids, and chewing-gum wrappers.

"Thanks." Dutifully, she downed the two Advil I retrieved for her, gulping down the entire glass of water. "Boy, I can't believe that idiot John Irwin actually decked me. Jeez, what a creep! You'd think a governor's aide would be a little more civilized!"

"I'm sure it was an accident," I assured her.

Marnie's blue eyes widened. "I'm not."

I tried to hide my confusion. "Surely you don't think someone from the governor's office would do something like that on purpose!"

"Are you kidding? One of the first lessons I learned in the newspaper business is that things are rarely what they seem," she insisted. "Especially in Hawaii."

As if she'd suddenly remembered something, she raised her hand to her throat. "Oh, great."

"What's wrong?"

"My favorite necklace. It's gone!"

"I saw it break when you fell. Beads went flying everywhere."

"They weren't beads. The necklace was made of little shells, dyed these really cool colors. A native woman who lives out in the middle of nowhere makes them. They sell them in Lahaina in a shop that specializes in crafts made by local artists. That necklace was one of the first things I bought myself when I got here. Darn!"

"I noticed you wearing it," I commented, sharing her regret. "It was really pretty."

"It matched these earrings—see?" She pointed at the cluster of tiny shells, dyed pastel colors, bobbing below her earlobes. "Oh, well. Maybe I can get her to make me another one. Whenever I get the money, that is."

She began rummaging through her big black bag, pulling out one thing after another before finally retrieving her tape recorder. It wasn't much larger than the palm of her hand. "I hope this stupid thing fared better," she muttered, grimacing. "I've been having enough trouble with it lately, even before I dropped it.

I finally figured out I have to check it each time to make sure it's behaving."

She flicked a button and the sound of her own voice emerged from the tiny machine. "*. . . feel the arrival of a big biotech firm on an island that most people consider paradise could be seen as a major step in the wrong direction?*"

She clicked it off and stuck it back in her bag, muttering, "I got the question on tape. Too bad I didn't get an answer. But at least this stupid thing is working. I'm supposed to meet with my secret source later on tonight."

"Secret source?" I repeated, not sure if she was serious.

Apparently she was. "Cool, huh?" she replied, grinning. "It turns out that's something reporters really do. Just like in the movies!

"Anyhow," she said as she stood, smoothing her skirt and running her fingers through her short, spiky hair, "I've got to get out of here."

I had to admit, she looked a lot better than she had twenty minutes earlier.

"I owe you," Marnie said. "If there's anything I can do for you while you're here . . ."

"I think I'm set, but you should try to take it easy for a few hours."

"Thanks. Maybe I could take you on a tour later this week," she offered. "You know, give you an insider's look at Maui that most tourists don't get to see."

"That sounds great," I told her sincerely. "Let me talk to my boyfriend, Nick. Between the conference and what's supposed to be a romantic vacation for the two of us, we've got a lot of activities to squeeze in over the next few days. But it would be fun if we could work something out."

"Here's my card," she said, reaching into her purse. "It's got all my phone numbers on it."

The business card she handed me read, *Marnie Burton, Reporter, Maui Dispatch,* followed by the newspaper's Kaohu Street address, phone number, and, in the lower left corner, her cell phone number. I stuck it into my pocket, then gave her one of mine.

"Thanks." As she dropped my card into her giant tote bag, she caught sight of her watch and cried, "Now I've *really* got to get out of here. 'Bye, Jessica. Thanks for everything. It was great meeting you. And I can't wait to show you around Maui!"

The room seemed strangely silent after she left. I realized that Marnie Burton was one of those people who was always surrounded by a whirlwind of energy. Just talking to her was exhausting.

Still, Nick's arrival five minutes later, his eyes glowing in a way that can only come from a shopping victory, immediately reenergized me. That, and the colors in his flashy aloha shirt.

"Is this shirt cool or what?" he asked, holding out his arms to model it for me.

"Way cool. The other law students will love it."

Wearing a satisfied smile, he flopped down on the bed, his arms folded beneath his head. "Right now, law school feels very far away. I'm much more interested in the *wahine* standing in front of me. That would be you."

"*Wahine,* huh?" I countered. "Have I just been insulted?"

"It's the Hawaiian word for woman."

"In that case, I'm guilty as charged. Come here. You're too far away, you . . . you . . . What's the Hawaiian word for man?"

"Kane."

As I sat down on the bed next to him, he rolled away to make room. And promptly let out a yelp.

"Ouch! Hey, what's this?" Nick asked. From underneath his khaki-covered butt, he pulled out a brown mailing envelope. The initials *MB* were handwritten in pencil on the front.

"Oh, no. That's probably Marnie's," I said. "She must have left it here by accident. It probably fell out of her giant tote bag, either while she was going through it or when I was scrounging around for Advil."

As I took the envelope from him, I saw it was sealed. It felt as if there was an audiocassette tape inside, but I wasn't about to violate Marnie's privacy by opening it to check. Whatever was in that envelope certainly wasn't any of my business. "It might be important. I'd better call her and tell her she left it here."

"How's her head? Is she okay?"

"She's fine. In fact, I have a feeling her forgetfulness has more to do with her personality than her head injury."

I retrieved her business card from my pocket and dialed her cell phone number from my cell phone. According to my calculations, she'd barely had time to leave the hotel. So I was surprised that I got her voice mail.

"Hey, Marnie, it's Jessie Popper," I recorded after the beep. "You left a brown envelope in my room. I didn't open it, but it feels like there's something plastic in it—maybe an audiotape. When you get this message, call me at the Royal Banyan Hotel or on my cell phone. The number's on the card I gave you. I can get it back to you whenever we get together—or if you need it sooner, just stop by the room and knock. It's room six twenty-six. Catch you later!"

After I ended the call, I looked around, trying to

find a safe place to put the envelope. The room was already pretty chaotic, between our clothes, guidebooks, snorkeling equipment, and the two bags of cinnamon macadamia nuts Nick had bought. I finally put it in the night-table drawer, right on top of the phone book that was stashed there.

"Now, where were we?" I murmured. I draped myself across the bed and nestled beside Nick. I had to admit that he looked pretty darned terrific in his Hawaiian shirt.

As far as I was concerned, it was time to get this romantic getaway under way.

• • •

By the next morning, I had made major inroads into reaching the highest possible level of aloha spirit. As I sat on the lanai in a pair of shorts and a tank top, scarfing down the coconut syrup–slathered macadamia nut waffles Nick and I had ordered from room service, concepts like worry and tension and hurrying seemed far away. Like Polarfleece, hot chocolate, and ice scrapers, they simply didn't belong here.

The setting also happened to be wonderfully romantic. There we were, just the two of us, sitting on a balcony overlooking a lush tropical garden. The golden sun was warm, and the balmy air was softened by a refreshing sea breeze. Birds chirped sweetly, and we spotted the occasional gecko basking in the sun or darting up the side of a palm tree. If this wasn't a genuine Adam and Eve moment, I didn't know what was.

Still, there were practicalities to consider.

I skimmed the conference catalog, trying to remind myself I was here in my capacity as a medical professional, rather than a beach bunny, by deciding which of the day's sessions to attend.

"There are some great talks scheduled today," I

said thoughtfully, "starting with one on feline AIDS this morning at nine. Hey, this one on exotics sounds really interesting. The afternoon has some good ones too. One on diabetic ketoacidosis, one on canine pancreatitis . . . look, here's one on inflammatory bowel disease. In fact, if you wouldn't mind occupying yourself pretty much all day, I'd be happy to go from one session to the next."

I glanced over at Nick, who was wearing one of the fluffy white terry-cloth robes that came with the room.

He didn't seem to be listening. He was much too absorbed in the complimentary copy of the *Honolulu Star-Bulletin* we'd found outside our door.

"Maybe you could hit the beach," I suggested. "Didn't your guidebook say there was good snorkeling right behind the hotel? You could—"

"Jess," he interrupted, his tone strained, "isn't Marnie Burton the name of that reporter you met yesterday?"

"That's her," I replied. "Why? What about her?"

"Whoa," Nick breathed. "Bad news."

He held up the newspaper so I could see the headlines. I gasped loudly as I read, REPORTER FOUND MURDERED.

Chapter 2

"The silent dog is the first to bite."

—German proverb

Let me see that!" I cried, grabbing the newspaper out of Nick's hands. My head was spinning as I stared at the headline, trying to digest the meaning of the words.

I wasn't doing very well. So I forced myself to read the front-page article, hoping to make sense of it.

> Kahului Bay, Maui, Hawaii——The body of Marnie Burton, a reporter for the *Maui Dispatch*, was discovered late last night on a remote stretch of beach on Kahului Bay, west of Kanaha Beach Park. The cause of death is not known at this time.
>
> According to Detective Peter Paleka of the Maui Police Department's Homicide Squad, the victim was identified by her driver's license. Richard Carrera, Managing Editor of the *Maui Dispatch*, verified Burton's identity.
>
> Burton, 24, was a native of Ellensburg, Washington. She moved to Maui two years ago

after earning a B.A. in Journalism from Central Washington University. She resided in the village of Paia.

"Marnie was a good kid and a fine reporter," Carrera said. "This is an unbelievable tragedy."

An investigation is ongoing, and anyone with any information is asked to contact the Maui Police Department's Homicide Squad at 555-5000.

"Wow, that's awful," Nick said, shaking his head. "Imagine, you just met her yesterday and today she's on the front page."

I didn't answer. I was too busy trying to stop the buzzing in my head.

And fighting the knot that had formed in my stomach. I felt sickened by the news. Marnie Burton had struck me as an enthusiastic, energetic young woman who was so full of life she seemed ready to burst. It was difficult to believe that anyone could want her dead.

Nick reached across the table and took my hand. "Are you okay, Jess?"

"I will be, as soon as I get over the shock."

"Maybe I should forget about the beach today. I could stay around here and—"

"No, go ahead. And I'll go to the conference, the way we planned." I forced a sad smile. "It's not as if there's anything we can do. Besides, I barely knew Marnie."

I wasn't really in the mood to throw myself into learning about new developments in veterinary medicine. But I figured going to a few sessions would provide a good distraction. And at the moment, a good distraction was exactly what I longed for.

• • •

It turned out that spending the day thinking about medicine really was the perfect cure. I started with the session on feline AIDS, then moved on to the talk on treating exotic animals. As soon as I started taking notes, I realized the whole issue of exotics would make a terrific topic for *Pet People,* the television show I'd recently started hosting on a Long Island cable TV station. While a lot of people consider adopting animals like iguanas, monkeys, flying squirrels, ferrets, and even poison dart frogs, the reality is that it's not a very good idea to keep them as pets.

The speaker reinforced what I already knew: that exotics don't generally do well living among people, because it's invariably difficult to meet all their needs. Those that do survive tend to live long lives, and if their owners tire of them, there's no good place to bring them. The most common "solution," setting them loose, is cruel to the animal and dangerous to the community. Another negative is that exotics often carry bacteria that are harmful to humans and can transmit chlamydia, hepatitis A, ringworm, and even tuberculosis. Then there's the simple fact that owning certain exotics is illegal. I took pages of notes, pleased that I'd be able to spread the speaker's message far beyond the walls of the room.

Over lunch, I caught up with a bunch of people I'd gone to vet school with and hadn't seen since graduating. It was fun filling one another in on the details of our lives over the past decade and exchanging news about other classmates we'd kept in touch with.

The afternoon was filled with more sessions, back to back. Yet through it all, the terrible thing that had happened to Marnie Burton was never far from my mind. A despondent feeling hung over me like a headache I just couldn't shake.

By the end of the day, I was ready for a break. The

last session ended a bit early, which gave me time to shower before Nick got back from the beach.

I stood beneath the spray of steaming water, relishing the sensation of my muscles relaxing. It was as if all the tensions of the day were gurgling down the drain. I stayed in much longer than I needed to, reluctant to leave such a welcome refuge.

As I stepped out and began drying off, I was already looking forward to the evening ahead. I pictured Nick and me at a beachside restaurant, holding hands and gazing out past the flickering tiki torches at the dramatic Maui sunset. . . .

And then, *bang*. I was so startled by the noise that I smashed my shinbone against the edge of the tub. But from the way the wall behind the sink vibrated, I realized it was nothing more threatening than the door of the hotel room slamming shut.

"Nick?" I called, wrapping a big white towel around me. I opened the bathroom door and poked my head out. "Nick, is that you?"

Silence. Puzzled, I stepped out into the foyer—and immediately felt a rush of fear.

Someone's been in here, I thought, my heartbeat racing.

I surveyed the room, anxious to make certain the intruder was gone. Nobody was there.

Next, I went over to the door and debated whether or not to open it. I finally did—about two inches. No one stood lurking outside the room, at least as far as I could tell. I opened the door further and looked up and down the corridor.

Empty. Not a soul in sight. Not even a cleaning cart.

You're imagining this, I thought, closing the door firmly, because of what happened to Marnie.

But I still didn't manage to convince myself. I walked around the room slowly, studying each detail and trying to decide whether my impression that something was out of sorts was valid—or simply the result of being edgy because of the murder.

The closet door is open, but you probably left it that way yourself, I thought, determined to convince myself that I was imagining things. The same went for those two dresser drawers. And Nick must have dragged the suitcase and my beige canvas tote bag out of the closet before he left this morning and I just didn't notice it before.

Even so, I searched the room. The fact that I still wasn't sure if I was just imagining things made me all the more anxious to figure out if anything was missing. The contents of my pocketbook appeared to be intact. All my cash was still in my wallet, along with my credit cards and driver's license.

Nick's wallet, which he'd left in the back pocket of the jeans lying at the bottom of the closet, was also untouched. The little bit of jewelry I'd brought along was safe in the top drawer of the dresser. The same went for my watch, which was still sitting on the night table.

And then I focused on the top of the dresser. Or more accurately, I realized that something was *missing* from the top of the dresser.

The sealed brown envelope that contained my conference materials.

I stood frozen, staring at the big empty space where it should have been, since that was precisely the spot in which I'd deposited it the day before. In fact, I remembered noticing it as I undressed for my shower. I'd tossed my T-shirt next to it on the dresser, thinking I really should take five minutes to look through it, decide how much of its contents was worth lugging home, and throw the rest out.

The T-shirt was now lying on the floor in a heap.

A sick feeling lodged itself in the pit of my stomach

as the entire scenario began to unfold in my mind. While I was in the shower, someone had broken in, taken the envelope, and hightailed it out of there, slamming the door on the way out.

But I was also confused. Why on earth would somebody want to steal my registration packet?

As the most likely answer came to me, a wave of heat traveled through my entire body. Within seconds, the room began feeling uncomfortably warm, even though the air-conditioning was turned way up.

The missing envelope looked a lot like the one Marnie had left behind—and it clearly contained an audiotape, just as Marnie's did. What if the intruder had taken what he or she thought was the envelope the eager young reporter had left here in my hotel room?

That's crazy! I insisted to myself. You're *really* getting carried away this time.

But in my head, I replayed the voice-mail message I'd left on Marnie's cell phone shortly before she was murdered. In it, I said she'd left a brown envelope behind, mentioned that I thought there was an audiocassette inside, and given the name of my hotel and the number of my hotel room.

I'd practically left a road map for anyone who was interested in getting hold of the cassette that was in Marnie's envelope.

I dashed over to the night table and pulled open the drawer. Sure enough, Marnie's envelope was exactly where I'd left it, right on top of the phone book. I took it out and, holding my breath, slit open the top with the plastic pen I found next to the phone. Just as I'd suspected, there was an audiocassette inside. And nothing else.

I sank onto the edge of the bed, clutching my towel tightly around me. My thoughts raced as I tried to cling to the idea that I was simply imagining the whole thing. Frankly, I wasn't having much success.

When I heard a key card being inserted into the lock, my heart began to pound wildly.

"Nick?" I called hopefully.

"One and the same," he replied as he tromped in, his damp hair matted around his face and his mask and fins tucked under his arm. Instead of the skintight Speedo he'd worn the last time he and I were on Maui—a garment I'd teased him about nonstop—he was wearing a baggy boxer-style jobbie that, if you used your imagination, made him look like a surfer dude. It wasn't much more dignified, but at least it was considerably more modest. "The guidebook was right. The snorkeling behind the hotel is fabulous! I had a terrific day on the beach. But I've got to take a shower before we—"

His expression suddenly changed. "What's wrong, Jess? Your face is almost as white as that towel."

Somberly, I said, "Something really awful just happened. While I was in the shower, somebody broke into our room."

"Oh, my God!" he cried. "Are you okay?"

"I'm fine," I assured him.

"What did they take? Our cash? Our credit cards?"

"Our money and credit cards are untouched. So is my jewelry."

Nick glanced around the room and frowned. "If your cash and credit cards are safe, how can you be sure somebody even broke in? I mean, look at what a mess this place is. We weren't exactly careful about unpacking. We just threw our shirts and underwear into a couple of drawers."

"Because something *is* missing: the packet of booklets I got when I registered for the veterinary conference."

He looked at me as if I'd just sprung a couple of additional heads. "Why would anybody take that?"

"A very good question, and there's only one answer: because they *thought* they were taking the envelope Marnie Burton left here yesterday. Especially since both envelopes had an audiocassette inside. You didn't even have to open mine to know that, since it was so stuffed you could feel the tape from the outside. Whoever took it must have grabbed the envelope, felt the tape, and run off without bothering to check inside."

Nick now looked as if I'd sprung five or six more heads. "Jess, I don't know where this business about Marnie Burton and the envelope she left here is coming from. No offense, but it sounds kind of off-the-wall. That aside, I'm sure if you explain to the people at the registration desk that you misplaced the conference materials they gave you, they'd be happy to—"

"But I *didn't* misplace them! Somebody broke into our hotel room and took that envelope! And once they figure out that they didn't get what they wanted, they might be back."

By this point, Nick's expression made it clear that he was exercising all the patience he possessed—and that he was on the verge of running out. "Look, it sounds as if you really believe that's what happened. But think about it, Jess. How likely is it that someone would go to all the trouble of breaking into a hotel room—in broad daylight, no less, while somebody was clearly in the bathroom, taking a shower—then steal nothing besides an envelope? You said yourself that our cash and other valuables were untouched."

I didn't answer. I was too busy ruminating about the obvious answer: because there was something on Marnie's audiotape that somebody wanted to keep a secret.

Maybe even something worth killing over.

"I'm going to stop at the front desk and have our room changed," I told Nick soberly. "And then I think I'd better talk to the police."

"And tell them what? That you—" He stopped himself. "Okay. Here's my cell phone."

I cleared my throat, bracing myself for the reaction I knew my next statement was going to elicit. "Actually, I think I'd like to go down to the police station and talk to them in person."

Nick threw out his arms in exasperation. "Jessie, are you *kidding*? You're honestly telling me that you plan to waste the rest of the afternoon talking to the police about a missing envelope that you're not even sure was taken?"

I didn't point out that *I* was sure. *He* was the one who wasn't sure.

Instead, I simply replied, "That's right."

"And how do you propose to get to the police station, assuming you even know where it is?"

"You and I talked about renting a car after the conference so we could see the rest of the island," I told him in a calm voice. "I'll just move the reservation up a few days."

"Jess-ie . . ." he said, not even trying to hide his frustration.

"Nick," I interjected before he could go on, "I already feel involved in what happened to Marnie, just because I was probably one of the last people to see her alive. One of the very last conversations she had before she was murdered was with me! But now that someone actually broke into our hotel room and stole something they believed belonged to her—while I was alone in the shower, no less—I can't simply stand around and do nothing! Especially since the intruder is undoubtedly going to think the tape is still in my possession. They'll probably be back!"

"So you're going to trek all the way over to the police station?"

"It won't take that long," I assured him. "And I should turn over Marnie's tape to them anyway." But I didn't sound very convincing, not even to me.

Nick sighed. "Jess, what happened to that reporter is horrific, and I understand that it shook you up. But I thought coming to Maui for your veterinary conference was supposed to give us an excuse to take a vacation together. *Not* for you to get involved in something as dangerous as a murder!"

I opened my mouth to argue my case further, then realized there was no point. "Tell you what. After I get our room changed, I'll run over to the police station and talk to them about what happened, and then you and I can meet back here at the hotel at six o'clock for the poolside Polynesian dance show."

Nick thought for a few seconds. As he did, I searched his face for a crack in his stoniness. And then: "Will there be umbrella drinks?"

I laughed, relieved that he was finally coming around. "Plenty of umbrella drinks. Mai tais, piña coladas, you name it."

"And dinner afterward—with mahimahi and pupu platters?"

"Enough for our own private luau."

"Okay. Six o'clock." He cast me a wary look, just to make sure I knew he thought I was making a volcanic mountain out of a molehill.

"This is just one of the many reasons I love you," I told him, sprinting across the room and kissing him on the cheek.

In less than a minute, I'd pulled on shorts and a T-shirt, grabbed the canvas sun hat I'd brought, tucked

Marnie's tape into my backpack, and dashed out. I was suddenly in a hurry to get out of that hotel room, a place that just minutes before had been occupied by some unwelcome visitor, and settle into a different room in some other part of the hotel.

But I was also in a hurry to talk to the Maui police. And while I hadn't managed to convince Nick that something was very wrong, I hoped I'd manage to do a much better job with the cops.

• • •

The good news was that the Royal Banyan Hotel had a car rental service right on the premises, reachable by a stairwell that was accessible through the lobby. The even better news was that its inventory of available cars included a nifty dark blue Jeep Wrangler that came equipped with something called Command-Trac four-wheel drive. I didn't know exactly what that meant, but from the way it looked, the sturdy little vehicle could have made it through the Haleakala crater, zipping along the forbidding terrain as if it were no more challenging than a few irritating speed bumps. Daredevil antics aside, scuttling around a tropical island in a Jeep was undoubtedly going to be more fun than lumbering around Long Island in a veterinary clinic on wheels, or even in my beloved red VW Beetle.

But I hadn't come to the fun part of the vacation yet. I still had some nasty business to take care of.

Before leaving the immense underground parking garage that sprawled beneath the Royal Banyan, I tried out all the Jeep's buttons, levers, and other technological toys, wanting to make sure I wouldn't encounter any surprises once I got it out on the road. As I fumbled around for the seat adjustment, my hand made contact with something plastic. I pulled the mystery item out from underneath the seat and discovered I was the proud new owner of a pair of sunglasses.

Unfortunately, they were so badly scratched that they'd outlived their usefulness. The fact that one of the earpieces was also pretty wobbly didn't help.

So much for doing a crackerjack job of cleaning out the rental cars, I thought with annoyance, looking around for a garbage can. Since none was in sight, I tossed the shades into the glove compartment.

I did a quick search for other leftovers. Then, once I was sure any additional clutter that accumulated in the car would be the result of my own carelessness, I took off for police headquarters in Wailuku.

Guided by the map I'd picked up at the car rental counter, I headed south along Honoapiilani Highway. As I traveled along Maui's scenic western coast, I tried to think positive. My hope was that this Detective Peter Paleka who was mentioned in the newspaper, or whoever else I managed to speak with at police headquarters in Wailuku, would put the whole incident of the missing envelope and how it might be related to Marnie's murder into perspective. Or maybe he'd simply do a better job than Nick had of convincing me that I'd imagined the whole thing.

I was still trying to convince myself of that possibility when my stomach suddenly lurched, an annoying phenomenon that seemed to occur pretty much every time an unsavory thought popped into my mind. I instinctively grasped the steering wheel more tightly to make sure I didn't veer off the road.

What if whoever wanted that cassette badly enough to break into my hotel room thinks *I* know something? I thought. What if he assumes I know what was on the tape he was so desperate to get his hands on?

And what would happen once he realized he'd snatched the wrong tape? I wondered. Sooner or later, he was bound to discover that the one he grabbed out of my hotel room contained nothing more interesting than some jovial veterinarian relating amusing anecdotes about the zany antics of his clients and their pets. Would he come back, determined to get hold of the right one?

For all I knew, just being in the wrong place at the wrong time had put me in serious danger. Maybe even as much danger as Marnie.

I took a few deep breaths, trying to calm down. I told myself that Detective Paleka would help me sort it all out. Meanwhile, I attempted to distract myself by rolling down the windows, breathing in the sweet, warm air, and taking in my surroundings.

I could see that this part of the island didn't cater to tourists. There were no humongous hotels here, no dense complexes of condos. Instead, this was where the real residents lived. I knew from Nick's guidebook that Wailuku had its share of attractions to lure visitors: antiques shops, an old theater, a very old church, and a museum of Hawaiian history inside the nineteenth-century home of a sugar plantation owner. But as I drove through, I was inundated with signs of modern-day life. I passed low-rise office buildings occupied by doctors, lawyers, and accountants, video stores and supermarkets, and a few national chain stores that were guaranteed to cure any tourist who might be suffering pangs of homesickness.

The Maui police station on Mahalani Street was a modern two-story building with lush trees decorating the front lawn. To the east was a dramatic view of the ocean. As I pulled into the parking lot, I was still trying to convince myself that I was simply letting my paranoia run away with me. The idea that I had inadvertently become involved in whatever Marnie Burton was involved in—a situation that had led to her murder—was almost too much to process. I'd come to Maui to learn about the latest developments in veterinary medicine, strengthen my relationship with Nick, and do something I rarely had time for at home: relax. Even I recognized that letting my overly active imagination get in the way of these three noble causes would be a major mistake.

I pulled open the glass doors of the station, hoping that by the time I left, I'd be laughing about how silly I'd been.

But I wasn't there yet. I squared my shoulders and approached the uniformed officer sitting at the front desk. He was wearing a dark blue shirt emblazoned with a shield-shaped patch. In the middle was an eagle, printed with the words *Maui County Police—Hawaii.*

"I'd like to talk to someone who's involved with the investigation of Marnie Burton's murder," I told him.

I braced myself for an argument, or at least a smirk. After all, that was certainly a typical response from the Norfolk County Homicide Department back at home. Instead, the police officer picked up his phone.

"I'll see if Detective Paleka is available. Your name, please?"

Nick was right, I thought, amazed. People really are friendlier in Hawaii—even though I wouldn't expect a police station to be a bastion of aloha spirit. I only hoped the warmth and mellowness that seemed to pervade every aspect of life on Hawaii would carry through my meeting with the police.

Fortunately, that meeting was with the man at the top. "Afternoon, Ms. Popper," Detective Peter Paleka greeted me with a curt nod as I entered his small, cluttered office. "Thanks for coming in."

I studied the stocky middle-aged man with dark brown eyes, jet black hair, and an expressionless face. He sat up straight in his chair, his back rigid and his hands placed palms down on the surface of his large metal desk. The red-and-blue-striped necktie he wore with his short-sleeved white shirt was held firmly in place with a tie tack so that it formed a perfectly straight line. His militaristic demeanor served as a startling contrast to his Hawaiian-American features, which I'd already come to associate with a relaxed island attitude.

He struck me as someone who was about as approachable as another Chief of Homicide I'd been forced to deal with: Lieutenant Anthony Falcone, who ran the Norfolk County Homicide Department back on Long Island. Falcone also had dark eyes that bore into me with such intensity that I frequently ended up squirming.

And he had that same stiff demeanor that invariably made me feel I was wasting his time. While Falcone had no qualms about coming right out and saying as much, Detective Paleka seemed much more polite. Still, aside from the governor and his entourage, I gave this man the award for the most uptight individual I'd encountered so far on the laid-back island of Maui.

As I studied him, I got the distinct feeling he was studying me too.

"I understand you have some information about Marnie Burton's murder," he said, staring at me with disconcerting intensity.

"Not information, exactly." I shifted in my chair uncomfortably. Now that I was sitting in the hot seat, I wished I'd put more thought into how this conversation was likely to go. "But given the timing of her death, I believe I was one of the last people to speak to her."

Interest flickered in his dark eyes. "And did she say anything about where she was going or who she was meeting?"

"She said she was meeting someone she referred to as a 'secret source' later that night."

I searched his face for a reaction, expecting him to be impressed. If he was, he didn't show it.

"The two of you were close friends?" he asked in the same even voice.

"Not exactly. I just met her once." In response to his look of surprise, I added, "I've only been here a day."

The flicker of interest had vanished. "You're a tourist," he said flatly.

I got the feeling he didn't mean it as a compliment. Sitting up a little straighter in my seat, I said, "Not exactly. I'm here for the veterinary conference at the Royal Banyan." A technicality, I knew, but still something I felt was worth pointing out.

"I see. So you're Dr. Popper, not Ms. Popper."

"Either is fine." I appreciated the show of respect, even though the wary look on his face was already clueing me in to the fact that my revelation about Marnie's "secret source" hadn't made quite the impact I'd expected.

Detective Paleka folded his hands together. "Look, Dr. Popper," he said, "I'm sorry about your friend, but I'm afraid there's not much of a mystery here. I just got off the phone with a witness who saw her coming out of a bar near the airport, the Purple Mango, at approximately nine-forty last night. She was accompanied by a man who's most likely the person who killed her. We'll be looking into whether she had a boyfriend, but this incident is probably the result of your friend picking up the wrong guy. Unfortunately, young women do it all the time. I can promise you we'll find out his identity. At this point, we don't have any reason to believe that what happened is any more complicated than that."

I took a deep breath. "How was she killed?"

"We don't have the autopsy report in yet, but it looks like strangulation. Afterward, whoever killed her deposited her body in the bay."

I suddenly felt sick to my stomach. I took a couple of seconds to get past that horrifying bit of news before I reminded myself that I'd come here with some important information of my own. "I don't suppose you found her cell phone when you discovered her body, did you?"

"No, as a matter of fact." He looked surprised. "Why do you ask?"

"Because I think there's a lot more to Marnie Burton's murder than the scenario you just described," I replied. "And the fact that her cell phone was missing is part of it."

"Really?" He raised his eyebrows about a millimeter. "And why is that?"

In a low, even voice, I related all the events of the past twenty-four hours. Meeting Marnie after the governor's aide pushed her—at least, according to Marnie. Talking to her in my hotel room, when she'd mentioned, among other things, that she was on her way to meet with an informant. Discovering that she'd accidentally left an audiocassette in my room, no doubt because it had fallen out of her chaotic, overstuffed tote bag. Leaving a message on her cell phone that anyone—including her murderer—could have listened to, saying I had the tape and giving the name of my hotel and the room number. Then, soon after she was murdered, having an intruder break in to my hotel room and steal only one thing: an envelope that looked very similar to the one containing Marnie's tape.

After I finished, I watched the police detective's face expectantly. I was certain that this time I'd witness an explosive reaction.

Instead, he calmly asked, "And what exactly is on this cassette?"

"I don't know." I tried to come across as forceful, but my words sounded pretty wishy-washy, even to me. "I haven't actually listened to it, since I don't have access to a tape recorder."

"I do. Did you bring the tape with you?" He pressed a button on his phone and asked whoever answered to bring in a tape recorder. Within seconds, he was popping the cassette into the machine.

Detective Paleka and I sat in silence as it began to play. My heart pounded so loudly I hoped it wouldn't block out the sound. I was certain we were about to hear something that would incriminate Marnie Burton's murderer—or at least put the cops one giant step closer to knowing who had killed her and why.

I listened, motionless, to the sound of static. Then more static. Then even more.

"There's nothing on this tape," Detective Paleka announced, looking more puzzled than annoyed.

"Maybe later on? Or on the other side?" I tried hopefully. "We didn't listen to all of it."

A deep crease had appeared in his forehead. "I'll have someone play the whole tape, but so far, the only thing I can conclude is that you've been wasting my time."

Aha. So he *was* annoyed. He was just better than some people at hiding it—probably the secret behind aloha spirit.

In a voice that came out sounding much meeker than I'd intended, I said, "Marnie mentioned she'd been having problems with her tape recorder, so maybe—"

"Let me make sure I understand all this correctly," the detective interrupted, his voice suddenly loud and obviously strained. "You've come all the way into the station to tell me that you may have been one of the last people who saw Marnie Burton alive. But you literally meant *see* her. You didn't have any meaningful conversations, you didn't notice that she expressed any fear or apprehension, and she didn't give you any indication of who she was going to meet, aside from her boyfriend and some unnamed person she referred to as a 'secret source.' In fact, you barely knew her. And then, shortly after she was murdered, you discovered that you'd misplaced the registration packet from the conference you're attending. Is that pretty much it, Dr. Popper?"

I glowered at him, wondering what the odds were that a Hawaiian police detective on the Maui police force could manage to look and sound so much like the Italian-American Chief of Homicide I was used to dealing with at home. Was it possible that Anthony Falcone and Peter Paleka were twins who had somehow been separated at birth?

"Look," the Hawaiian half of the duo continued tersely, "I suggest that you go back to your hotel, find a comfortable spot on the beach, and enjoy the rest of your vacation. The most sensible thing you can do is leave this investigation to the professionals."

I could feel my blood starting to boil. "But don't you see?" I protested. "I'm already involved in this! I left that message about the tape's whereabouts on Marnie's cell phone right before she was killed. Don't you think it's more than coincidence that her phone is now missing—and that hours after she was murdered, somebody came to the exact spot I described, looking for the tape? And don't you think it's likely that whoever stole the envelope out of my hotel room thinks I heard what was on it? That he thinks I know whatever it is they're so anxious to keep quiet?"

"There's nothing on the tape," he pointed out.

"But they don't know that!" I insisted, trying not to sound as frustrated as I felt. "There was *supposed* to be something on it. Even Marnie thought there was. Don't you see? I could be in danger!"

The expression on the detective's face told me he didn't see at all. That, like Nick, he thought the business about the stolen envelope with the audiocassette inside was all in my head.

"I'll tell you what, Dr. Popper," he said, his voice once again calm and unflappable. "I'll call you if we need you. Or if we come up with anything new on the case.

"As for your alleged hotel-room theft," he continued, "I don't know that there's much we can do. According to what you told me, the only thing that was taken from your room was an envelope full of conference booklets. I suggest that you file a report with the hotel—and that you ask the nice folks at the conference to get you a replacement.

"My other piece of advice," he added, "is to forget all about Marnie Burton and the terrible thing that happened to her."

He stood up, a sure sign that, as far as he was concerned, this meeting was over.

• • •

"So much for putting all this into perspective," I grumbled as I turned the key in the Jeep's ignition and pulled out of the police station parking lot.

I told myself that, given Nick's reaction, I probably shouldn't have been surprised Detective Paleka didn't believe the envelope containing the tape had been stolen from my hotel room as part of some cover-up related to Marnie's murder. Or that I was now involved because I'd had the bad luck to end up with her audiocassette.

Even though the tape had turned out to have absolutely nothing on it.

But the police detective's skepticism hadn't done a thing to convince me that I was wrong. And his assurances aside, I was scared. Maybe he was convinced that Marnie's murder had been the simple result of a rendezvous with the wrong guy, either a man she already knew or someone she met at the bar. But I believed there was more to it.

In fact, I was still ruminating about what I should do about the rumbling of fear in the pit of my stomach when I instinctively stepped on the brakes. I'd just spotted a sign that read *Kaohu Street,* a name I recognized from Marnie's business card.

Still driving slowly, I glanced at my watch. My mind raced as I did some quick calculations. It was already well past five, meaning I didn't have much time before I was supposed to meet Nick. Still, the hotel was only twenty minutes away . . .

Don't forget that you have to change your clothes and take other dramatic measures to make yourself presentable, a voice inside my head insisted.

But you're right here! a second voice interrupted.

Nick is expecting you back at the Royal Banyan, the first voice reminded me, sounding very practical and very firm. You don't have time for any detours. Go back to the hotel, put on a sexy sundress, and concentrate on spending a romantic evening with your beau.

I continued debating for about three more seconds. Then I eased into the right lane, made a quick turn, and scanned the signs on the buildings I passed, trying to find the one that read *Maui Dispatch*.

Chapter 3

"When a man's best friend is his dog, that dog has a problem."

—Edward Abbey

The *Maui Dispatch* office was easy to locate. I'd been expecting something grand—if not a towering office building, then at least a modern, important-looking one with fountains and a formal lobby. Instead, a series of signs that looked as if they'd been printed on someone's computer indicated it was around the back of a low, warehouse-style building that housed a title company, a macadamia-nut wholesaler, and a surfboard distributor.

The door was locked, but the receptionist who could see me through the glass window set into it buzzed me in. Even though she was on the phone, she gave me a distracted wave. Waiting in the small entrance area gave me a chance to look around.

I didn't know what I'd expected to find. The entire staff in a frenzy, maybe, making phone calls and trying to answer the question of who had killed Marnie Burton. Or maybe I thought I'd find the whole office closed down for a few days of mourning.

Instead, it looked like business as usual.

The receptionist sat at a metal desk, collecting faxes in addition to fielding phone calls. She was probably in her forties, dressed in a yellow blouse that was as plain as her navy blue pants. Her light brown hair was held in place with a headband. I peered over her shoulder and watched the most recent fax come in. From what I could see, it was an announcement of an upcoming boat race.

Behind the receptionist's desk was a small office. While the door was closed, the top half of its front walls were made of frosted glass, enabling me to make out the silhouette of the person sitting inside. According to the plaque on the door, inscribed with RICHARD CARRERA, MANAGING EDITOR, that silhouette belonged to Marnie's boss.

To the right was a large narrow space that stretched to the back of the building, with fake-wood paneling, well-worn gray wall-to-wall carpeting, and, at the very end, a small kitchen. It was furnished with four metal desks, each one outfitted with a computer. Two were pushed up against the wall, while the other two faced the windows that ran along the side of the building.

The only desk that was occupied was one of the two that offered a first-rate view of the parking lot. I decided the man sitting at it was most likely a reporter, since his desk was a sea of paper. Even from where I stood, I could see that most of the sheets were covered with neatly printed text and not-so-neat handwritten red scribbles. Whether those were his markings or the editor's, I couldn't say.

The man, probably in his thirties, was clearly someone who put a lot of effort into his appearance. He wore a crisp white shirt with wrinkle-free beige pants, and his dark hair looked carefully styled. He stood in sharp contrast to most of the other young men I'd seen in Hawaii, who looked as if they were no more likely to own an iron than they were to own a snowblower. Even though his attention was fixed on his computer screen and all I got were occasional glimpses of his profile, he struck me as unusually good-looking.

I figured that one of the other desks must have belonged to Marnie. Not the front desk on the left, since I surmised that one belonged to the newspaper's photographer. More than a dozen photographs that had been torn out of the newspaper were tacked haphazardly on the bulletin board above the desk. His best work, I figured, displayed either to inspire him or to impress the rest of the staff.

As for the desk next to the photographer's, it was meticulously neat, with stacks of perfectly aligned papers and a row of pens carefully lined up. The papers and personal photographs tacked onto the bulletin board above it had clearly been arranged with care.

There was no way that one was Marnie's. Hers had to have been the desk next to the reporter's, which, at the moment, was completely bare except for a lone pencil mug and a few stray paper clips scattered about. The sight of it made my heart wrench.

I focused my attention back on the receptionist, just in time to hear her instruct her caller, "Okay, send us a fax with the details like the time and place and the correct spellings of everyone's names. I'll make sure it gets into the next edition. . . . Just write *Attention: Karen Nelson* on top to make sure I get it. Have a great day."

As she hung up, she looked at me and smiled. "Sorry about the wait. What can I do for you?"

"I wondered if I could have a word with Mr. Carrera."

"I'll see if he's available. Is he expecting you?"

"Not exactly." I hesitated. "My name is Jessica Popper. I'd like to speak to him about Marnie Burton."

"But you don't have an appointment?"

"No." I stood straighter, hoping to give the impression I actually belonged there.

"Does he know you?"

This time, I held my chin up a bit higher. "No."

She just nodded. "Hold on. I'll see if he's free." She disappeared into the office behind her desk for a few seconds. I had just about braced myself for rejection when she reappeared and said, "Go right in."

"Thanks." I took a deep breath as I made my way toward the frosted glass–enclosed space, surprised at how easily I'd gotten in to see Marnie's boss. Unfortunately, I still wasn't sure exactly what I hoped to learn from him. Maybe something that would reassure me that Detective Paleka was right, that Marnie's death had nothing to do with the audiotape I still feared could be putting me in danger.

"Mr. Carrera?" I asked politely as I strode into his office.

He stood up as I entered. Even though Richard Carrera was the head of this operation, he was barely over five feet tall. And he was as slight as he was short. I had a feeling I could have wrestled him to the ground without too much trouble. Just like the other man in the office, the one I'd pegged as a reporter, he wore a crisp white shirt. But he had on a necktie, one that was covered with palm trees but held in place with an expensive-looking gold clasp. An interesting combination of Hawaiian casual and no-nonsense business, I decided.

But his features made it clear his roots were not Polynesian. True, his neatly cut hair was as black as coal and his eyes were such a dark brown that they, too, were almost the same shade. But his features, like his name, struck me as Hispanic in origin. Especially his eyebrows, which were the thickest, blackest, and bushiest I'd ever seen in my life.

"Jessica Popper, right?" he greeted me. "Come in and have a seat."

Even with those few words, I saw that Mr. Carrera's way of speaking involved moving his lips but keeping his two rows of white, even teeth tightly clenched. That was an idiosyncrasy I couldn't affix to any particular ethnicity.

It also made him a little hard to hear—and to understand. I wondered if it was more than coincidence that he'd ended up in a career that focused on the printed word.

"Thanks for taking the time to speak with me, Mr. Carrera," I said as I took him up on his offer and lowered myself onto one of the two metal folding chairs that faced his desk.

Unlike the reporter who worked for him, Richard Carrera kept his desk perfectly clear of paper. Unless, of course, he had made a point of straightening up before opening his office to a stranger. My suspicious side wondered if he had something to hide, while my practical side told me he was probably just one of those people who prefers a neat working environment.

"What can I do for you?" he asked. At least, I was pretty sure that was what he asked. Given the fact that his words came out sounding like, "Whahdoferyou?" I had to rely a lot on context.

"I was hoping you'd be willing to talk to me about Marnie Burton." Before he had a chance to mumble an obvious question like, "Why should I?" or "Who are you?"—or at least something that sounded like that—I volunteered, "I was a friend of Marnie's. Needless to say, I've been frantic ever since I heard the news, and I've been desperate to find out anything I can about what happened. I even stopped at the police station earlier today and talked to someone named Detective Paleka, but he wasn't all that helpful about the details. I was hoping you might know something."

He sat perfectly still, his dark eyes burning into mine in a truly unnerving way. I couldn't tell if he was angry or surprised or if this was simply the way he looked all the time. "Why would I know any more than the police?" he finally said, his teeth still clamped together.

"Because you were Marnie's boss. And because you're the person the police called in to identify her last night.

"Besides," I continued, "you're a newspaperman. It's your job to find out things other people don't know and to find them out first. That's your area of expertise."

One thing I'd learned being in business for myself was that it never hurt to butter people up a little. Especially people of the male persuasion.

And it seemed to be working. I could have just been imagining things, but the tension in the room seemed to decrease just a little.

"I suppose that's true," he remarked.

"There's another reason too," I went on, feeling bolder. "Marnie mentioned you the last time she and I talked. That was just a few hours before she was killed."

He tensed his forehead, moving his caterpillarlike eyebrows a little closer to each other. "What did she say?"

"That you were the editor of the newspaper she worked for and that you were counting on her to meet the deadline for an article she was writing on the governor's press conference." Figuring that slathering on a little more dairy fat would grease the wheels even further, I added, "From the way she spoke, I could tell she had a lot of respect for you. It was obvious that what you thought of her and her work really mattered to her."

The muscles in his face relaxed. In fact, his whole demeanor shifted from wary to sorrowful. "Marnie was a good kid," he commented. "I enjoyed having her on my staff. She was so committed. So passionate."

Shaking his head slowly, he added, "And so energetic. Intense, in fact. That girl had big plans, and she was in a hurry to get to where she wanted to be. Seems to me she was on her way too. I'm sure she told you about the award she won."

"Of course," I said without missing a beat. Even though what I really meant was, *Of course not.*

"It's a pretty big deal, being honored by the Association of Professional Journalists like that," Mr. Carrera noted. "Even though she won it in the category for reporters who've been working in the field for three years or less, she's still one of the youngest people to ever win it. Her series on illegal immigrants on Maui was very thoroughly researched. Insightful and well written too.

"To make it as a newspaper reporter," he continued, "there are two things you need. Curiosity and pushiness. As I'm sure you know, Marnie had plenty of both. As a result, she could sometimes rub people the wrong way. But she was basically a sweet kid, and I think most of the people she came across could pretty much see that in her."

Sweet, but intense. Marnie's editor's description of her was completely consistent with the impression I'd gotten.

"She did seem like she had a certain innocence," I observed conversationally. "Maybe it was because she came from a small town. But that girl also had a real sense of adventure. I always thought she was pretty brave, coming all the way to Hawaii from Washington State."

"Actually, we get a lot of people coming through here who grew up somewhere else. That's not at all unusual in Hawaii."

"How about you?" I asked in the same chatty tone. I hoped we were bonding, at least enough for him to tell me something useful about Marnie. "Where are you from?"

"Born and raised right here on this island," he replied. "Actually, my family's been here for generations."

I was so used to thinking of Hawaii as either a tourist destination or a place people moved to because they wanted to get away from the real world that it hadn't occurred to me that, for some people, it *was* the real world.

"One of my ancestors," Mr. Carrera went on, "that is, my great-great-great-grandfather—or however many 'greats' there should be—was a *paniolo.*"

"Really?" I didn't mind showing how impressed I was. I'd read all about the *paniolos*—Hawaiian cowboys—in Nick's guidebook. Back in the late 1700s, a British sea captain named George Vancouver, the namesake of the city of Vancouver, Canada, presented the leader of the Hawaiian Islands, King Kamehameha, with some Mexican longhorn cattle as a token of friendship. Kamehameha allowed them to roam free, and within a few decades there were thousands of them all over the island. Cattle handlers from Mexico were brought over to teach the locals how to deal with them. They were called *españols*, meaning Spanish. Somehow, the word evolved into *paniolos*.

Ranching still took place on Maui, and the term *paniolos* was still used to refer to Hawaiian cowboys who worked on the cattle ranches. These days, most of them were of mixed heritage, every ethnic background imaginable from Portuguese to Japanese to Caucasian.

"From the research I've done," he continued, "combined with family lore, I've learned I'm descended from one of the original *vaqueros*. A man named Juan Carrera, one of the first of the Mexican cowboys to come over in the mid-1800s."

By the way he told the story, it was clear this wasn't the first time he'd related this bit of family history. It was equally clear that he was darned proud of it.

"Marnie never told me about any of that," I told him, realizing that Richard Carrera's revelation about his roots provided me with the perfect opportunity to ask about the rest of the people she worked with. "In fact, even though she worked crazy hours and was really dedicated to her job, she never told me much about the other people at the paper. She mentioned them in passing, of course, but she was always much more interested in talking about the stories she was working on."

"There aren't many of us to talk about," he replied. "We're a pretty lean organization."

"What about the other reporters on the staff?" I asked.

"There's only one. Bryce Bolt."

"Were he and Marnie close?" I asked.

He hesitated before replying. "Not really. Actually, the two of them were pretty competitive with each other. I guess that's not surprising, since they were both ambitious. They were similar in other ways too. He's another one who never stops talking, although what he talks about ninety-nine percent of the time is himself. Everybody in this office knows everything there is to know about him. His social life, his apartment, his passion for windsurfing—you name it. Oh, his car too. Can't leave that out. He's always talking about his flashy silver BMW. He bought it used, but still, I'm sure it's a financial burden." He snorted. "I guess maintaining his image matters to him more than the struggle of keeping up with the monthly payments, but that's Bryce for you. A real show-off."

I made a mental note to try to corner him while I was at the office, since I suspected he might be a good source of information about what was going on in Marnie's life. Especially her professional life, which at the moment was what interested me most.

"Is there a photographer on staff too?" I asked, curious about the person who sat at the desk with the photos tacked up above it.

"We use a freelance photographer," Mr. Carrera replied. "He also does the layouts. He's in and out all the time, does some of the work from home. Then there's Peggy Ehrhart, who handles advertising. The classified ads too. Real estate, help wanted, used cars. But she's only part-time. Most of our advertisers are regulars who put ads in every week, so Peggy's job is pretty routine. The only other person here is Karen Nelson, our receptionist. You spoke with her when you came in."

Leaning forward in my chair, I asked earnestly, "Mr. Carrera, do you think it's possible any of the people Marnie worked with had anything to do with what happened?"

"I sincerely doubt that," he replied, sounding a bit defensive. "We're a family here. When you work with such a small group, you become very close in a very short time. There's no way anybody at the *Dispatch* wished her any harm."

I suddenly had another idea. "What about the person who found her on the beach?" I asked. "Do you know who it was and whether the police consider that person a suspect?"

Mr. Carrera shook his head. "I can't imagine they'd suspect Alice. She's not the type to give anybody any serious trouble."

"'Alice'?" I repeated. He'd already given me more information than I'd hoped for.

"Alice Feeley. Kind of a burned-out hippie who moved here from California ages ago. Wild hair, funny clothes, occasionally does a little ranting and raving. Nobody really knows how she gets by, but she's a regular on the beaches after hours. She uses one of those metal detectors to find valuables that poor unsuspecting tourists lose in the sand. Jewelry, mostly, but also money. Probably picks up cans too and brings them back to the market for the deposit. She may be eccentric, but she's perfectly harmless."

Perhaps she's harmless, I thought, but she might be able to tell me something that nobody else can, some detail or even an impression she got when she discovered a young woman's body washed up on the beach—something even the police weren't aware of that would help identify the killer. I made a mental note to try to track her down.

I also decided to try out the theory that had been haunting me ever since my conference packet was stolen from my hotel room.

"Mr. Carrera," I said, trying to sound matter-of-fact, "I can't help wondering if maybe the reason Marnie was killed had something to do with one of the stories she was working on."

His bushy eyebrows flew upward. "Why would you think that?" He was back to sounding guarded again, and his teeth were clenched together more tightly than ever. "The police are convinced she was strangled by a man she was seen coming out of a bar with, and I'm afraid they're probably right. As sad as it is, young women get killed by strangers like that all the time. In fact, that's the story we're running with in the next edition."

"But what if there's more to it?" I insisted. "What if her murder was the result of her being in the newspaper business? Like maybe she was investigating something that somehow got her into trouble . . . ?"

Mr. Carrera made a strange hiccuping noise that I had to assume was his version of a laugh. "I think you've read too many novels, Ms. Popper. And to be fair, that theory might make sense if Marnie worked at some big-city newspaper. But here on Maui, the biggest stories we get are tourists having their cameras stolen off the backseat of their unlocked rental cars and the occasional entrepreneur getting caught growing pot in his backyard."

I just nodded, since pretending to agree seemed like the most graceful way of getting out of what had somehow become an uncomfortable moment.

Mr. Carrera also seemed happy to move on. "Since you were a friend of Marnie's," he said, "I suppose you've been in contact with her family."

"Actually, I haven't," I replied, smiling ruefully. "Even Marnie wasn't in contact with her family. It seems they didn't agree with her decision to move so far away from home just for her career. According to her, her parents pretty much cut her off. So I'm leaving it up to the police to take care of that end of things."

"Probably wise," he agreed, nodding. "Since her parents might not be around for a while, then maybe you'd do me a favor. Would you be willing to fill a couple of boxes with her personal possessions and move them out of here? I've already taken care of her files and all her work-related stuff. But when it comes to the rest, like the mug she always drank her coffee out of and all the other junk she stashed in her desk that we always used to tease her about, I don't think any of us could stomach it."

I tried not to look too surprised. "I would have thought the police would take her possessions as possible evidence. They have been here, haven't they?"

"Sure. That homicide detective you mentioned you'd spoken to, Paleka, came by first thing this morning. He's the same guy who called me last night, asking me to come in and identify the . . . identify Marnie." He swallowed hard, then took a deep breath before continuing. "He asked the usual questions and looked through her desk, but Detective Paleka wasn't all that interested in what he found there. Especially since he seems pretty sold on the idea that Marnie was killed by the guy she was seen with coming out of that bar near the airport. The one they're still working on identifying."

"I'd be happy to clean out Marnie's desk," I told Mr. Carrera, pleased that I'd be getting the opportunity to look through the personal items Marnie had left behind. While my main concern was that there might be someone out there who thought I had Marnie's tape, I was also trying to find everything I could about someone who died just hours after I met her. My hope was that this little cleanup job would tell me a little more about her life. Maybe even her death.

"Thanks." He sounded relieved. "You'll find some cartons in the kitchen, way in back. If you need any help, just ask Karen."

"I will. By the way," I couldn't resist asking, "did you ever meet Marnie's boyfriend, Mr. Carrera?"

He looked surprised. "I didn't even know she had one. I figured all that girl ever did was work. I'd come in here at seven in the morning and she'd be working. I'd come in at eleven at night to pick up something I forgot and she'd be working. How any guy would ever put up with that is beyond me."

I wasn't about to admit that I was a little curious about Marnie's social life myself. But that would have to wait until later.

At the moment, I was much more concerned with the fact that my interview with Marnie's boss was coming to a close. He glanced at his watch, the sides of his mouth twitching downward.

I decided to go for broke.

Desperately hoping he couldn't hear how loudly my heart was pounding, I said, "Mr. Carrera, one of the things I wanted to ask you about was a tape Marnie recently made. I can't help wondering if it had anything to do with her murder."

"A tape?" The hardness I'd perceived on Mr. Carrera's face when I first walked into his office returned, fast and furious. His eyes blazing with suspicion, he insisted, "I don't know anything about a tape." I noticed he was suddenly enunciating quite clearly. "Why don't you tell me what *you* know?"

I began to feel extremely uncomfortable. And the fact that I'd come here to find out what he knew, not to tell him what I knew, was only partly responsible. From the way he reacted, I got the distinct feeling he knew exactly what tape I was talking about. "Nothing, really. It was just something she mentioned."

"Tell me what she said," he insisted.

Instead, I plastered on an innocent-looking smile. "My mistake," I said with a shrug. "When Marnie and I last spoke, she said something about a tape, that's all. I thought it might have meant something, but I was obviously wrong. For all I know, she was referring to the latest Green Day CD." I laughed, trying to make light of a subject I wished I hadn't brought up in the first place.

I told myself I was probably misinterpreting his reaction. After all, I hardly knew the man, and he certainly didn't seem to be someone who openly displayed his emotions. It was possible that he had some policy about his reporters not taping interviews, or . . . or maybe as the managing editor, he insisted upon being made aware of every tape his staff members made. Who knew how things worked in the newspaper business?

"Well, I know you're busy, so I guess I'll get started cleaning out Marnie's desk," I announced abruptly, popping out of my seat like a jack-in-the-box. "Thanks for your time."

I hightailed it out of there, wondering if perhaps in addition to changing his mood, the mention of Marnie's tape had also prompted Mr. Carrera to change his mind about electing me to go through Marnie's personal things. But I wasn't about to let him rescind his offer.

I wasn't about to linger at the *Dispatch*'s offices any longer than I had to either. Not when I got the feeling that even though I'd only been on Maui for a little over twenty-four hours, I already seemed to be making myself pretty darned unpopular.

• • •

I found a lot more than a stack of abandoned cardboard boxes in the newspaper office's small kitchen. I also found Marnie's counterpart, Bryce Bolt, downing a couple of donuts and a cup of black coffee he'd poured into a ceramic mug. The fact that he hadn't bothered to sit down while doing so may have explained why he had such a lean, muscular frame despite his obvious weakness for dough fried in grease and saturated in sugar.

"Bryce, right?" I greeted him. Actually, I felt pretty confident about holding my own with reporters, even though they were in the habit of being the ones asking the questions. Thanks to my penchant for getting involved in murder investigations, I'd gotten to know a newspaper reporter on Long Island—strictly on a professional basis, of course—named Forrester Sloan. Even though he had a tendency to be cocky, the fact that I'd outshone him a few times when it came to getting the scoop had won his respect, enough that on more than one occasion he'd actually suggested that I follow in his journalistic footsteps.

"You found me." Bryce looked me up and down in a way that was all too familiar. For a minute there, I thought I really was talking to Forrester. He too was an incredible flirt. With me, anyway. As much as I hated to admit it, there was definitely chemistry—however minimal—between Forrester and me.

But chemistry is one thing. Biology is something else altogether—and with Bryce, I got the feeling his interest in me was determined by something much more basic, not to mention more base. He was clearly trying to decide whether or not this particular female was worth his time.

I guess I measured up to his standards, because he cocked his head and grinned. "Which means this must be my lucky day."

"Too bad we can't say the same for Marnie Burton," I replied curtly.

His engaging grin was gone in a flash.

"I was a friend of Marnie's," I said, figuring that even though I disliked the guy on sight, I owed him an explanation. Especially since Mr. Carrera's claim that Bryce had worked closely with Marnie made me anxious to pump him for as much information as I could. "I came by today to see if anybody here at the paper had any inside information on the horrible thing that happened last night. I was just talking to Mr. Carrera."

"Really?" Now that Bryce realized I hadn't followed him into the kitchen to admire his charms, he was suddenly standoffish. "And was Dickie-boy helpful?"

I raised my eyebrows. If this guy's rude enough to say insulting things about his boss to a complete stranger, I thought, he should at least have the grace to do it out of earshot.

"I think it's still too early for anyone to know much more than what was already in the paper this morning," I replied politely.

"Right. I saw that piece in the *Star-Bulletin*. I applied there too." Smirking, Bryce added, "I guess those guys on Oahu are just too dense to recognize real talent when they see it."

I made a point of not responding. Especially since being sincere about my reaction to Marnie's colleague would have demanded that at least some of the coffee in his mug end up on his head.

"So you must be freakin' out," he went on coolly. "Having one of your friends end up in Kahului Bay like that and all."

Whether he was going out of his way to be offensive or if this was just his personality, I couldn't tell. But this guy made Forrester Sloan look like Mr. Rogers.

"I guess I'm still in shock," I finally replied. I glanced around, adding, "Although now that I'm here, I'm finding it kind of a surreal experience, seeing Marnie's office and meeting some of the people she worked with day in and day out. But who knows? Maybe being in the middle of her work environment like this will help me come to grips with her murder."

"I suppose you're looking for 'closure,'" Bryce

sneered, meanwhile making that annoying quotations gesture in the air with two fingers of each hand. "To be honest, I'm not the best person to help you with that. Marnie and I were both reporters, but that's where our connection ends. Even though we worked in the same place, I never got to know her all that well. For one thing, I never felt there was a lot of potential for a warm, fuzzy relationship between the two of us, given her personality. For another thing, I've only been here at the *Dispatch* a few months." He paused to stuff a large part of his second donut into his mouth, chewing and swallowing it with amazing speed.

"I didn't realize you'd been here such a short time," I commented. "Was there someone you replaced, someone who might have known Marnie longer than you did?"

He looked annoyed, perhaps because he preferred being the one who asked all the questions. "My predecessor's name was Holly Gruen. But for all I know, she's left Maui by now."

His answer surprised me. "Why would she have left the island?"

He shrugged. "She just didn't seem to fit in here. On Maui, I mean. She was too . . . tense. Not that I knew her that well either," he added quickly. "She was gone by the time I started. But she used to stop in at the office every once in a while."

"To visit, you mean?"

"Look, I never paid that much attention to either Holly or Marnie, okay?" Bryce insisted impatiently. "But there is one thing I can tell you about Marnie. She was a real know-it-all. A lot of people found her extremely irritating."

Talk about the pot calling the kettle black, I thought with annoyance. Still, thanks to her boss's comments, I knew Bryce wasn't alone in that perception.

"Maybe that was just a front," I suggested. "To convince people she was on top of things. After all, she was pretty ambitious."

"No kidding," he replied with a contemptuous snort. "She thought she was the next Woodward and Bernstein. Y'know, those guys who uncovered the Watergate scandal during the seventies?"

"Yes, I think I've heard of them," I replied. And I managed not to sound the least bit sarcastic.

"Trouble was, most of the stuff she came up with was out of Fantasyland."

"Meaning . . . ?"

Bryce made an annoying boy-was-that-a-dumb-question face. "Meaning she saw scandal and intrigue and corruption everywhere she looked. Dickie-boy would send her out to cover . . . I don't know, the Girl Scout jamboree, and she'd come back convinced that the leader was embezzling the cookie money." He shook his head disapprovingly. "I mean, it's one thing to sniff out news. But Marnie was pretty wacky, the way she was always convinced she'd just uncovered the hottest story of the century."

"Maybe she was just passionate about what she did."

"More like desperate to make a name for herself. She was ambitious, all right." Glancing around, he lowered his voice conspiratorially before adding, "In fact, our little punk-haired friend wasn't above kissing up to Dickie-boy to get the big stories. Or at least the stories she was sure were gonna turn out to be big."

"Like FloraTech?"

He looked startled. "How did you know about that?"

I shrugged. "I just remember her mentioning that it was something she was working on."

He looked satisfied with my answer. "Okay, then,

perfect example. Here's this really positive thing that's happening on Maui—an innovative new company, bringing in high-tech jobs in the biomedical field—and good old Marnie had to go and find something negative about it."

"Which was . . . ?"

Bryce snorted again. "That it was ruining the ambience of our tropical paradise or something. Like we're still living in the days of grass huts and outrigger canoes! I mean, get real! There is such a thing as progress, y'know? We are in the twenty-first century. Isn't it time to get with the program? Instead, she wants to pit people against each other about whether it's a good thing or a bad thing."

"I guess controversy sells newspapers," I offered.

"Right," he grumbled. "And makes a name for the people who stir it up."

O-kay, I thought. I think I've had about enough of Bryce Bolt.

And I hadn't even learned very much, aside from the fact that he had clearly disliked Marnie. Whether his reaction to her was rooted in sexism, professional jealousy, or something much more personal, I couldn't say.

"I'm curious, Bryce," I said, casually bringing up a question that had just occurred to me. "What were you doing before you came to the *Maui Dispatch*?"

He narrowed his eyes. "You sure ask a lot of questions. What do you think you are, a reporter?"

"Actually, I'm a veterinarian," I told him with a big smile. "But I'm interested in everything and anything that has to do with Marnie's life, including the people she worked with."

Still eyeing me warily, he replied, "I worked for a couple of papers on the mainland."

I noticed he didn't volunteer their names, or even

the cities he'd lived in, which made me wonder if there was a story there.

But Bryce was already heading out of the kitchen, brushing powdered sugar and cinnamon off his fingertips. I grabbed an empty cardboard carton and made a beeline for Marnie's desk.

Chapter 4

"An animal's eyes have the power to speak a great language."

—Martin Buber

I quickly got busy cleaning out Marnie's desk, starting with the drawers. And I immediately learned that our eager young reporter had been prepared for everything.

Almost everything, I thought regretfully. Too bad she didn't consider carrying a can of Mace in her purse standard operating procedure.

But she'd thought of just about everything else. In addition to a coffee mug, her desk was crammed with tissues, Tampax, a large tube of sunblock, a hairbrush and comb, several packs of chewing gum, half a dozen protein bars, Advil and Tylenol, Band-Aids, a toothbrush and toothpaste, a flashlight, several books of matches, and, for some reason, a pair of socks. She also kept a sweater and a pair of dressy shoes in the bottom drawer.

Handling each item as if it were made of very breakable glass, I packed them into the carton I'd found in the kitchen. As I surveyed them, a wave of despondency rushed over me.

How sad, I thought, that the most important aspect of this woman's life, her career as a reporter, could be reduced to a cardboard box of things that meant practically nothing to anybody else.

When I'd finished, I did a final check, opening each drawer one last time to make sure I'd gotten everything. In the bottom drawer, pushed way toward the back, I found a badly wrinkled electric bill dated seven months earlier. I tossed that into the box too, since printed on top was Marnie's home address. I suspected that checking out her apartment was going to end up on my to-do list.

I carried the carton toward the door, discovering that, while it wasn't heavy, it was fairly awkward. Even so, I made a point of stopping at the receptionist's desk.

"Excuse me," I said politely. "It's Karen, isn't it?"

"That's right," she replied pleasantly. "What can I do for you?"

"I don't suppose you have a phone number for Holly Gruen, do you? The reporter who used to work here?"

"As a matter of fact, I do." She clicked a few keys on her keyboard, then peered at her computer screen. "I can jot down her cell phone number for you. Will that do?"

"Perfect," I told her, already knowing who was next on my list of people to contact.

As she handed me a Post-it with a local phone number written on it, Karen glanced around nervously, as if checking to see if anyone was listening. I automatically did the same. At the moment, Bryce Bolt was hunched over his keyboard, typing away madly. Richard Carrera, the only other person in the office, was talking on the phone.

"I don't mean to pry," she said in a soft voice, "but I thought I heard you asking questions about Marnie."

"That's right."

"And now it sounds like you're planning on calling Holly. Is that also to talk about Marnie?"

"I thought I might do that."

Karen hesitated for a few moments, then looked around the office one more time. "Maybe you and I should walk out to your car together," she suggested.

"Sure. I could use the help." I tried not to let on how intrigued I was.

Standing abruptly, she said in a voice that was slightly too loud, "Here, let me help you with that box." Then, with a flourish, she opened the door of the office so I could pass through it, box and all.

Once we were outside in the parking lot, she led me to the corner of the building. It afforded some shade, thanks to the overhanging roof. It also afforded a place to sit, courtesy of a yard-high ledge around what was supposed to be an area for planting flowers. Instead, it contained nothing but a few scraggly weeds and an empty Mountain Dew can.

"Since you don't know Holly, I thought it might be useful for you to be aware of a few things before you ask her about Marnie," Karen began. "I don't usually like to talk about people behind their back, but this is kind of a special situation, don't you think?"

"It definitely is," I agreed.

"Mint?" she offered, reaching into her pants pocket and pulling out a metal box of Altoids. "They're wintergreen."

"No, thanks."

She nodded, then picked out a tiny mint and popped

it into her mouth. "When it came to Marnie, Holly was a little bit . . . strange."

"In what way?" I asked.

"At first, it was little things, the kind of things the guys in the office probably wouldn't have noticed. But I did. Peggy too. We used to talk about it all the time."

"Little things like what?" I prompted.

"Well, you know the way Marnie wore her hair, right? Kind of spiky-looking? The way she put gel in it or whatever to make it come to points?"

"What about it?"

Karen sighed. "After Holly had been working here for a few weeks, one Monday morning she came in wearing her hair the exact same way."

"Maybe she thought it was cute," I suggested. "Or that it would be flattering."

Eyeing me warily, Karen said, "I think you'll have a better idea of what I'm talking about after you've met Holly. It's just that . . . it wasn't really a good look for her."

"Okay," I said, trying to reserve judgment.

"Then there were the clothes. Again, it was the same kind of thing."

"The same how?"

"Holly started imitating Marnie. Marnie dressed kind of crazy sometimes. And she could carry it off, since she weighed about a hundred pounds and she had this pixie thing going for her. She'd show up in one of those short flouncy skirts, or maybe one of those little sweaters—shrugs, I think they're called—and she'd look great. But then, a few days later, Holly would show up in the same style garment."

"They say imitation is the sincerest form of flattery," I remarked.

Karen shook her head. "I think it was more than that. It was almost like Holly wanted to *be* Marnie.

And there were other things besides the clothes. Like she'd order whatever Marnie was having for lunch. And she started using the same expressions Marnie used. And then she began keeping track of wherever Marnie went and who she went with."

Maybe Holly was just lonely, I thought. But the fact that her behavior had made Karen so uncomfortable made me wonder if it could be explained away so easily.

"Of course," she continued, "that was only up until a few months ago, when Marnie won that award. As soon as that happened, everything changed."

"Changed how?" I asked.

Karen stuck her hand into her pants pocket and began jiggling the box of Altoids. I didn't think she was even aware of what she was doing. "Holly got kind of . . . mean. It was clear she'd idolized Marnie, but Holly was also a very competitive person. She was sure she was going to get that award, and she wasn't at all happy about the fact that Marnie won it."

"How do you know Holly thought she'd get it?"

"I overheard her talking to someone on her cell phone about it right before they announced the winners," she replied. "I couldn't tell who it was. Her mother, maybe. But she sounded all excited about it, as if she was sure she was a shoo-in. See, she'd just done a big article on a new plant Hawaii Power and Light was trying to build. It never happened, since there was such a strong public outcry. But she'd done a great job of covering the story. Even Mr. Carrera thought so."

"But then Marnie won the award instead."

"Exactly. And after that, everything was different. It was like Holly froze Marnie out completely. She wouldn't even talk to her unless she absolutely had to. You know, about job-related things. But it wasn't just

Marnie. She began acting oddly toward all of us. She became . . . withdrawn. Sulking all the time, not saying much, that kind of thing."

With a shrug, she added, "And then, a few weeks later, Holly just upped and quit. Completely out of the blue. I sure didn't see it coming. I don't think any of us did."

Glancing back at the building, Karen said, "I should get back. The phone's probably been ringing off the hook. Mr. Carrera will have a fit."

"Thank you, Karen. For filling me in, I mean."

She grimaced. "Well, if you were going to go looking for Holly, I figured you should know that Marnie wasn't exactly at the top of her A-list. At least, not anymore."

• • •

Once the cardboard box was settled beside me on the front seat of the Jeep, I checked the Post-it Karen had handed me, the one with Holly Gruen's cell phone number. When I'd first gotten it, I couldn't wait to call her. Now, after what I'd learned, I felt as if I was treading in dangerous waters.

Yet there was no way I could walk away. Not when I hadn't learned anything that convinced me I wasn't in the same danger Marnie had been. I had no choice but to keep going.

Still, I wasn't very encouraged when a sullen female voice answered, "Hello?"

"I'm trying to reach Holly Gruen."

"Speaking," she replied. Then, sounding wary, she added, "Who's this?"

"My name is Jessica Popper. I understand you used to work at the *Maui Dispatch*." I hesitated before saying, "I was a friend of Marnie Burton's, and I was wondering if you and I could get together."

There was a long silence at the other end of the line. I was about to ask if she was still there when I heard, "What for?"

I was desperately trying to come up with an answer when my eyes lit on the box of Marnie's personal possessions. "I, uh, have something I'd like to give you, something that belonged to her. It's, uh, an award. She won it for"—I grabbed a three-inch square of marble with an engraved gold-colored metal plaque affixed to one side—"for her coverage of the Maui Special Olympics."

As soon as I got the words out, I kicked myself for latching on to the first thing I found. An award, of all things. "Anyway," I went on quickly, "I thought you might like to have something to remember her by. And since you were both reporters, I figured this award would be fitting."

"Yeah, I remember when she got that," Holly admitted grudgingly. "Even though that paperweight thing they gave her is kind of hokey, she was pretty excited about it."

"I'd really like you to have it," I replied. "I'm sure she would too. When can we meet?"

"I'm kind of busy," Holly said, still showing about as much animation as a tree slug. "I'm also pretty upset about what happened to Marnie. I'm not exactly in the mood for socializing."

"Me either," I assured her. "But I'm not asking for much time. Fifteen minutes. Ten, even. I just have a feeling that Marnie would have liked it if everybody she worked with got something that meant a lot to her.

"Besides," I added, "maybe it would make us both feel better. You know, just to talk."

It took five more minutes of cajoling before she finally agreed to meet me at a coffee shop in Lahaina the following afternoon at two. I seemed to remember that a particularly intriguing conference session on hyper-lipidemia—a potentially dangerous elevation of lipids like cholesterol and triglycerides in the blood—was scheduled around then, but now that I'd managed to pin Holly down, I wasn't about to let her go.

"The Bean Scene is a pretty out-of-the-way place," she assured me as her parting words. "Nobody's likely to see us there."

As I hung up, I wondered if her interest in privacy was simply a result of her reporter's instincts. At any rate, I hoped that the following day she'd be more open with me than she'd been on the phone.

• • •

"Oh, no," I breathed, glancing at my watch as I put the car in gear. It was after six—well past the time I'd sworn I'd meet Nick.

After racing back to the Royal Banyan and parking the Jeep in the garage, I dashed up two flights of stairs to the hotel. Any thoughts I'd had of getting gussied up for my evening out with my special guy had already flown out the window.

As I sprinted across the lobby's tiled floor, thankful for the traction my rubber-soled sandals provided, I flashed back to the painful memory of our last trip to Maui. Then I'd also let Nick down, big-time. Funny how a marriage proposal gone bad will do that, especially one that's made on an isolated stretch of beach at sunset, beneath swaying palms and a sky streaked with pink, orange, and lavender.

What happened the last time Nick and I were here wasn't Hawaii's fault. Nick's either. It was *me* that was the problem. The moment I found out the reason Nick had become flustered and tongue-tied wasn't that he was about to confess he'd lost his credit card or left the snorkeling gear at the beach or some other similarly harmless catastrophe, I was swamped with a wave of anxiety unlike any I'd ever experienced before. And that included the time I'd held a sealed envelope from the Cornell University College of Veterinary Medicine in my hands, knowing that opening it would tell me whether or not I was about to embark on my lifelong dream of becoming a veterinarian. By comparison, that experience was the proverbial piece of cake.

As I stared at the engagement ring Nick had whipped out of his pocket, as red-faced as if he'd spent the entire day in the sun without wearing any sunblock, an intense rushing noise rose up inside my head. It felt as if I'd just leaped into twenty feet of turbulent ocean waves. The whole beach started to spin—really, really fast—and I felt as if the soft white beach had turned into quicksand that was greedily sucking me downward.

Even the hopeful look on Nick's face and the bright anticipation in his hazel eyes hadn't been enough to bring me back.

Getting my mouth to work had been an iffy proposition. But somehow, for better or for worse, I'd managed to do it.

"I—I'm sorry, Nick," I muttered. "I can't do this." I stood up and began running blindly, so desperate to get away that I didn't even look back to see the expression on his face.

Not exactly my finest moment.

The trip had gone downhill from there. Fortunately, we had only two days left. Nick spent most of the remaining hours snorkeling—alone—while I took long walks on the beach—also alone—or wandered around shops and pretended I was actually looking at the coral necklaces and splashy aloha shirts instead of berating myself for being such a commitmentphobe. Of course, part of me was also congratulating myself on having escaped giving up my independence.

The two of us had flown home in silence, sitting side by side and making only the minimum of polite conversation. The fact that our relationship was over was understood. When we got back home, we divided up the CDs and all the other possessions we'd acquired as a couple, agreeing that Nick would keep Leilani, the Jackson's chameleon we'd shanghaied and brought home from Maui in a sock.

And then we'd gone our separate ways.

• • •

My heart sank when I reached the hotel pool area and saw that the Polynesian dance show was already under way. A small, low stage was set up at one end, with the blue-green Pacific Ocean and orange-streaked sky of the Maui sunset serving as a backdrop. Five middle-aged men wearing matching aloha shirts and playing ukuleles, Hawaiian guitars, and drums stood off to one side.

But the focus was the dancers. Three angry-looking Maori—or else some local men who'd taken a few dance lessons and were unusually good sports—were stamping their feet and grunting furiously as they did a sort of war dance. At least, that was what I assumed it was. I couldn't imagine painting one's face with all those elaborate designs for anything short of a bloody, no-holds-barred battle.

The entire seating area was packed solid. Hundreds of plastic chairs were crammed around the pool, and each and every one appeared to be occupied by a tourist juggling a digital camera and a plastic cup containing a brightly colored beverage. Some of them sat so close to the edge of the pool that I desperately hoped a couple of those Maori warriors had some life-saving training—especially since it looked as if all the regular lifeguards had gone home for the day.

I was agonizing over how I'd ever find Nick in this crowd when I noticed a bunch of orange parrots and hot pink hibiscus in the front row, over by the diving board. It took me only a moment to realize that wasn't just any jungle scene. It was Nick's chest.

I hurried over, crouching down as I wove among the seats in an attempt to minimize my obstruction of the angry-yet-agile performers.

"Nick?" I called in a hoarse whisper.

As he glanced up, I braced myself for a tirade. Instead, he simply cast me a look that was somewhere between scathing and woeful. Frankly, I would have preferred the tirade.

I sank into the seat that he'd graciously saved for me, no doubt having to fight off hordes of tourists at least as angry as those Maori on stage.

"I'm sorry," I told him. "I lost track of the time—"

"This is yours," he grumbled, handing me a plastic cup. In it was a watered-down mai tai, at least if its pale color was any indication. "I saved it for you. Why don't we just watch the show?"

"Good idea."

I glanced at the stage and saw that the Maori were gone. Instead, two large, muscular hunks wearing nothing but loincloths and excellent tans were twirling flaming batons. I had to admit, they put those Miss America contestants to shame. Drums pounded with such a powerful, primitive beat that I hoped they weren't getting ready to sacrifice somebody.

I watched in silence, meanwhile gulping down half my mai tai. I was determined to show Nick what a party girl I could be once I set my mind to it. At first, I was pretty tense. Not only was Nick emitting anger rays; watching two young men toss around incendiary devices without any extinguishers in sight was a bit unnerving.

But slowly but surely I could feel myself relaxing. Maybe it was the exquisite sunset, maybe it was the balmy air . . . or maybe it was just the rum in my watery mai tai kicking in. At any rate, I whooped and hollered with the best of them when the emcee, a pretty, dark-haired woman wearing a traditional hula costume, commanded, "Give it up for the Samoan fire dancers!"

"Not bad," I commented, leaning over to Nick. "I wonder if you could do that."

His response was to mutter, "This was supposed to be a chance for us to do something really fun together. But you couldn't even get here on time. I didn't even know if you were going to make it."

So much for aloha spirit. "I'm here now," I offered feebly.

"Right. But between working on my third mai tai and suffering from severe jet lag, I can hardly keep my eyes open."

"Maybe we can get you some coffee."

I scanned the pool area desperately, wondering if all the waiters had carpooled home with the lifeguards. At the moment, it looked as if the only hotel staff members who hadn't punched out for the day were the gyrating, half-dressed members of the Polynesian dance troupe.

"Thanks, I'm all right," Nick insisted, not sounding all right at all.

I'd always believed that nobody was supposed to have a bad time in paradise. But it seemed like it was all I ever managed to do.

Before I had a chance to ask myself what else could possibly go wrong, I noticed that the emcee in the grass skirt was weaving through the aisles, heading straight in our direction with a fierce look of determination in her brown eyes.

Run! a little voice inside my head commanded. But I was stuck to my chair—no doubt the result of either my horror over what was about to happen or that devil rum hidden amid the melted ice cubes.

"Ladies and gentlemen, let's give this happy couple a big round of applause as they join us up on stage!" the hula dancer cried loudly enough for all to hear. Apparently she had a microphone tucked away in her coconut bra.

"Um, no, thank you," I told her. "We're not much for—"

"Where are you two from?"

I had no idea hula dancers could be so pushy. "No, really," I insisted amid the loud clapping that erupted all around me. "We're not the ones you want."

"Don't tell me, the East Coast, right?" our Polynesian princess continued. "I can tell because you're both so pale. I'm thinking New York, Philadelphia, Boston . . . someplace where there's lots of snow."

"Uh, New York," I croaked. "Outside of New York. Long Island."

"Welcome! But you're not in the Big Apple anymore. It's time for you both to experience a little Polynesian-style fun."

Frantically I glanced over at Nick. As I'd expected, he had the same deer-in-the-headlights expression on his face that I was certain was on mine. But even he was no match for the dark-haired waif wearing someone else's lawn around her hips. Before you could say "pupu platter," she grabbed him by the arm and dragged him toward the stage.

I had no choice but to follow.

On stage, I stood frozen, staring out at the audience

and blinking. The Marine-drill-sergeant-turned-hula-dancer hadn't even put our leis on yet, and I was already overwhelmed by the tiki torches, the pounding drums, and the sea of faces I could see gaping at me through my mai tai–induced fog. By this point, I really hoped human sacrifice wasn't on the program.

"I'm Lokelani," she chirped into her bra. "And you are . . . ?"

"Jessie," I replied, doing my best to smile.

"And who's your handsome friend?"

"Nick," he grunted.

"Great!" Draping a lei over each of us, she added, "Welcome, Jessie and Nick, and thanks for volunteering."

"We didn't exactly—"

Before I could finish that thought, Lokelani exclaimed, "You two are going to demonstrate to our audience how easy it is to learn the hula!"

"I don't think we're the best people for the job," Nick protested.

"You see, we have no actual Polynesian dance experience," I added lamely.

But I knew I was wasting my breath. We were already part of the show. There was no turning back now.

Besides, Lokelani had put her hands on Nick's hips and was grinding them back and forth in a swaying motion.

"Now bend your knees and move in time to the music," she instructed. "There you go! You're a natural!"

"You're doing great, Nick," I added encouragingly as I copied his movements.

"Our first vacation in years," he whispered loudly, "a romantic getaway in paradise, and you have to spoil it by throwing yourself into the investigation of the murder of somebody you barely knew!"

"Now raise your arms and move them like the graceful leaves of a palm tree!" Lokelani cried.

"It's not as if I planned any of this!" I whispered back. Fortunately, the music was loud enough that no one in the audience could hear us.

"Now move your feet," Lokelani instructed. "And pretend your fingers are drops of rain. . . . Go for it, you two! You're doing great!"

"You can't let it go, just this once?" Nick persisted, talking through clenched teeth even as he moved his arms like the graceful leaves of a palm tree.

"A young woman has been murdered!" I countered, turning around slowly and making fluttering movements with my fingers. "And her murderer thinks I have something he wants! Do you really expect me to ignore all that?"

"Yes! That's exactly what I expect!" he shot back. "Because even though I try to be supportive, I think this time you've got some serious delusions about your role in this whole—"

"Keep those feet moving!" Lokelani interrupted. "Now you two face each other. . . . You're both doing a terrific job!"

"Then you're just not getting it!" I told Nick as we stood eye to eye, our hips swaying and our fingers fluttering. "Not to mention the fact that you're cold and heartless!"

"What I am is somebody who's supposed to be enjoying a relaxing and well-deserved vacation!"

"Come on, you two!" Lokelani urged. "Put a little more sway into those hips!"

"Maybe you can stand by without doing anything," I whispered impatiently, "but I can't."

"Then don't expect me to sit around and wait for you while you're off indulging your Nancy Drew fantasies," Nick returned. "I plan to have fun while I'm in Hawaii!"

"Don't let me stop you."

"Believe me, I won't!"

"All *right*!" Lokelani exclaimed happily. "Great job, you two! Let's have one more round of applause for Jessie and Nick!"

I glared at him. He glowered back.

"And because the two of you were such good sports," Lokelani continued with just as much enthusiasm, "here are four free tickets to the Royal Banyan Hotel's luau, any night you choose. *Mahalo,* and enjoy your stay!"

How could we not? I thought grimly, aware that this Hawaiian vacation of ours was starting to feel an awful lot like instant replay.

As Nick and I shuffled back to our seats, everybody else in the audience applauded loudly. A few let out yelps of appreciation. No doubt they were all demonstrating how grateful they were that *they* weren't the ones who'd been dragged up on stage and publicly humiliated.

Once we sat down, our fifteen minutes of fame already old news, I turned to him and said, "At least we got free tickets to a luau. We can even go twice."

Nick just grunted, his way of signifying that he'd heard what I'd said but had absolutely no intention of responding to it.

Terrific, I thought sullenly, rearranging my lei to keep it from scratching the back of my neck. Here I am on a romantic getaway in paradise, and my significant other isn't even speaking to me.

True, I felt bad. But at the same time, I was already switching my focus to the next step in my unofficial investigation of Marnie Burton's murder. My interest in finding her killer was as strong as ever, not only because of my desire to see justice done but even more because I still believed that I wouldn't be completely safe until the murderer had been caught.

I only hoped her boyfriend would be more willing to talk to me than my own boyfriend was.

Chapter 5

"The clever cat eats cheese and breathes down rat holes with bated breath."

—W. C. Fields

It was after nine by the time Nick and I settled into our new hotel room, one that looked identical to our first room but was a few floors higher up. Getting the manager to move us turned out to be harder than I'd anticipated. While at first he'd seemed quite concerned about the break-in, his attitude changed when I told him that the only thing that was taken was an envelope filled with booklets from the veterinary conference. He gave me a form to fill out, one I suspected would get stuck in some file folder, then begrudgingly handed me a new set of key cards.

Since Nick and I were still not officially on speaking terms, as we unpacked we limited our communications to simple questions and curt responses. We topped off the evening by flopping into bed and falling asleep without any of our body parts touching.

By the next morning, the air still hadn't cleared. I was glad Nick decided to take advantage of the hotel's free windsurfing lesson. I, meanwhile, had a task of my own: tracking down Marnie's boyfriend and trying to decide whether he was someone who deserved a spot on my list of suspects.

Thank heaven for the yellow pages, I thought after Nick took off, leaving me alone in our room. I ran my finger along the page with the heading *Auto Body and Collision Repair* and stopped when it collided with *Ace's Auto Artists.*

The Plastic Surgeons of Car Bodies! the subheading read. But I was much more interested in Ace's address, which was printed below the drawing of a sleek automobile with an even sleeker woman draped across it. She had more curves than a Rolls Royce.

Ace's Auto Artists was located near the airport. In fact, as I drove toward it with my trusty map in tow, I passed the Purple Mango, the bar I remembered Detective Paleka mentioning as the place where Marnie was last seen. Startled, I stepped on the brake to get a better look. I don't know what I hoped to find out, but I didn't learn anything besides the fact that the Purple Mango looked like a seedy bar that I, for one, would be nervous about patronizing. Just riding past it gave me the creeps. It was a terrific reminder of why I was pursuing this investigation with such determination—as if I needed one.

Compared to the Purple Mango, Ace's establishment, two blocks away, was a breath of fresh air. It looked positively ordinary: a low concrete-block building with a black and white sign informing me that this was the place. Through the open garage doors I could see a couple of car-filled bays.

In fact, as I strode inside with a confidence I didn't actually feel, I saw that everything at Ace's was related to cars. Big metal tools, paint, oil, noise, brawny men. The place practically reeked of testosterone. The only reminder that the planet was also inhabited by women came in the form of the Babes of Hawaii calendar hanging over a cluttered desk.

I spotted the man himself as he strutted into the office from the back, wiping his hands on a greasy towel and thrusting his pelvis out as if he was cruisin' for chicks. Given the way he'd billed himself in the yellow pages, I half-expected him to be wearing scrubs and a surgical mask. Instead, he was dressed in tight jeans and a navy blue T-shirt with the name *Ace* printed in white on the front and *Ace's Auto Artists* across the back. The shirt looked as if it was at least one size too small, given the way the stretchy fabric pulled against his exaggerated muscles.

He stopped abruptly in front of a small plastic-framed mirror that hung on the side of a tall metal file cabinet. It looked like one of those mirrors designed for hormonally challenged high-school students to stick inside their lockers to facilitate frequent zit counts. Even though Ace was well past the bad skin years, he stopped and peered into it, taking a comb out of his pocket and running it through his straight black hair. It was already perfectly styled, thanks to a shiny substance that looked as greasy as the tattered rag he'd stuck in his belt.

But I was looking for something beyond the obvious. I was trying to evaluate his attractiveness to the opposite sex. Frankly, at first glance I couldn't figure out what Marnie had seen in him. His preening aside, his face had the leathery look of someone who'd spent too much time in the sun as a young man and, as a middle-aged man, discovered it was prematurely turning him into an old man.

But one thing that was definitely in his favor was that he had the bluest eyes I'd ever seen. In fact, they were as blue as the Pacific Ocean. I could see how a young woman who wasn't a very seasoned swimmer could drown in them.

I was still studying him when he suddenly flashed a grin at the mirror. At first, I gave him the benefit of the doubt, assuming he was checking his teeth for sesame seeds or taking care of some other form of personal housecleaning. Then I realized he was simply admiring his own reflection.

Overcome with embarrassment, I cleared my throat loudly.

He snapped his head in my direction. "Hey, how ya doing?" he called, looking completely unfazed. He swaggered toward me, still carrying himself as if he was king of the hill—or cock of the walk. "Drive around the side so I can take a look."

"Actually, I'm not here about my car," I told him. In a gentle voice, I added, "I'm here about Marnie Burton."

I braced myself for his reaction. Frankly, I didn't know what to expect, but I figured there was a good chance I was about to see a grown man cry.

Instead, he jutted out his chin defensively and demanded, "You a cop?"

"No, I was a friend of Marnie's." Trying not to show my surprise over his unexpected reaction, I said, "I'm trying to get some sense of closure, or maybe even some understanding, by talking to other people she knew. I thought it might help to meet you, since the two of you were so close."

His eyebrows jumped up so high they nearly overshot his hairline. "Is that what she told you?"

"Yes, that's right."

"No way," Ace insisted, his voice suddenly sharp. "Listen, Marnie Burton and I had a business relationship, and that's it. She became a regular customer after she came in with some dings on her Honda."

And you've been dinging her ever since, I thought wryly.

"As far as I know, she didn't even have a boyfriend," he went on, sounding annoyingly confident. "I don't think romance was very high on her list of priorities, y'know? She was too busy with her career. Yeah, that was real important to her. She was always going on and on about the newspaper business. She loved everything about it, even the weird people she was always talking to as part of her job."

He must have realized suddenly that most of us don't discuss our dreams and desires with the guy who smooths out our chassis, because he quickly added, "I mean, I think I remember her sayin' something about that once. We were, y'know, making small talk."

"So it sounds as if you've know Marnie for a while," I commented. "I guess you met when she first moved here."

He shrugged. "I don't remember . . . maybe a year ago? After that, she ended up bringing her car in here every couple of months, since she was always banging it up. She wasn't that great a driver, if you know what I mean. But there's no way she was anything more than a good customer."

I couldn't help noticing that the longer he spoke, the more agitated he became. He kept slicking back his hair with one hand, and his left eye twitched, just a little. "Okay, so *maybe* you could say we were friends. It's my policy to go out of my way to establish a good relationship with my regular customers, you know? It's good business. But that's it. If she told you we were anything besides friends, it was just because she had things twisted up in her head."

Right, I thought wryly. Friends. Somehow, I didn't see Ace as the kind of guy who had a lot of buddies of the female variety, even if they were steady customers.

My main clue was Miss January, who, behind his right shoulder, was romping in the surf in nothing more than a lei, a seductive smile, and a few well-placed grains of sand.

I put on my "confused" expression. "So Marnie wasn't telling the truth when she and I talked Sunday afternoon and she mentioned that she was meeting you for dinner later that night."

Ace's eyebrows shot up. "She said that?" he squawked.

I just nodded.

"No way," he insisted. His left eye gave another little twitch. "You must have me confused with somebody else. Besides, Sunday night I was at Scores, havin' a beer."

I guess my face registered my surprise, because he quickly added, "It's a sports bar. Y'know, scores? Like sports scores?"

I'm sure it's an extremely wholesome place, I thought disdainfully. "So you were out with friends?"

"Actually, I was alone." He reached into his pocket and began rattling a set of keys or something else metallic. Once again, his left eye got busy. "Sometimes I just like to relax by myself, y'know?" he said, sounding more than a little defensive. "So I get a table in back, alone, and watch the TV that's over the bar. It gives me a chance to think."

If I ever heard a weak alibi, I thought, that's it. If the bartender can't remember him being there, Ace can always blame the fact that he's a shy, retiring guy who likes to be alone with his thoughts, no doubt pondering the great mysteries of the universe. And the latest sports scores, of course.

"I must have misunderstood what Marnie said." I hoped I sounded as if I was actually buying all this. "And I certainly understand that in your line of work, you must need some serious downtime. It can't be easy, spending all day dealing with cranky customers who come in upset because their cars are smashed up."

"Yeah, well," he said, smirking, "it's not like I intend to do this for the rest of my life."

Aromatherapist? I guessed. Yoga instructor? Kindergarten teacher?

"I'm gonna sell this place and get me one of those cushy nine-to-five jobs," Ace went on, exhibiting more passion than I'd seen since I walked into his fine establishment. "One that comes with a steady paycheck and a ni-i-ice long lunch hour."

Frankly, while there was definitely something to be said for having a reliable income, having a desk that one was expected to be seated at promptly at nine every Monday through Friday had never appealed to me. I much preferred making my own schedule, even if it usually ended up extending from very early in the morning until very late at night, Monday through Sunday, twelve months a year.

"So being your own boss isn't all it's cracked up to be?" I asked.

"It's not that so much." He hesitated before adding, "Let's just say I've had a better offer."

I wasn't particularly interested in Ace's career plans. I found his insistence that he and Marnie had been "just friends" much more intriguing. It left me with two possibilities to consider. One was that Marnie's claim that she and Ace were boyfriend and girlfriend and that he was on the verge of popping the question had simply been a manifestation of her tendency to exaggerate or even to see things that weren't there.

But I found that explanation hard to accept. Maybe some of the people who'd worked with her found her likely to exaggerate, but the starry-eyed way she'd spoken about him—and the pride she'd exhibited in his professional abilities—convinced me that Ace was the one whose story was out of alignment, not her.

Which brought me to the other possibility: that my pal Ace here was lying through his teeth.

Of course, I understood perfectly why he would feel compelled to do exactly that. After all, he must have been aware that whenever a woman was murdered, her husband or boyfriend immediately became a prime suspect.

But from what Marnie had told me, Ace had also been secretive about their relationship while she was alive. Maybe she had been lovestruck enough to interpret his preference for quiet, out-of-the-way restaurants as a sign that he was a hopeless romantic, but frankly, now that I'd met the man, I didn't buy that explanation at all.

Nevertheless, I nodded, acting as if I believed him as much as I believed the sign behind him that read, *All Our Work Is 100% Guaranteed.*

"Ace, you mentioned before that Marnie was totally involved in her career—so much so that she had no time for romance."

"Ri-i-ight," he agreed uncertainly, as if he wasn't sure where I was going with this.

"Did she ever mention any of the stories she was working on?"

He just stared at me.

"Or the fact that she was getting information from a secret source?" I continued. "How about a tape she'd been carrying around, one that might have been a recording of an interview she'd conducted recently?"

"You're thinkin' maybe her job got her killed."

So Ace had a few brain cells in that swelled head of his after all. "I think it's a possibility," I ventured.

"Yeah, she did talk to me about that, as a matter of fact. She mentioned she was working on something really dangerous." The more he talked, the more animated he became. "Yeah, now I remember. *Dangerous*—that was the exact word she used."

I wasn't sure whether or not to believe him, mainly because his sudden claim that Marnie was worried about a "dangerous" story she was pursuing went a long way in relieving him of guilt.

"What was it?" I asked.

"She, uh, didn't say." I could see his defenses springing up so clearly I felt I was watching a movie about a castle under attack. "Like I told you, we weren't exactly best friends."

"Ri-i-ight," I agreed with the same level of certainty he'd just expressed.

"Listen, I got stuff to do, so is there anything else you wanted to talk to me about?" Ace asked abruptly. "Aside from this misunderstanding about what the nature of my relationship with Marnie is? I mean, was?"

"Actually, there is. There's something I wanted to give you." I unbuckled my flowered backpack and took out the framed photograph I'd found in Marnie's desk at the *Dispatch*. It was a picture of Marnie and Ace, sitting at a table in what looked like one of those quiet, out-of-the-way restaurants he seemed so fond of. They had their arms slung around each other's shoulders and they were both grinning at the camera.

As soon as Ace glanced at it, all the blood drained out of his face. "Where'd you get that?" he demanded hoarsely.

"Marnie's desk. At work."

"She kept that thing on her desk?" he croaked. In fact, I suspected he sounded the way he had when he was a teenager and his voice started changing.

"In her desk, not on it," I assured him. "I found it in a drawer."

"Oh." He looked relieved. But I could practically

hear the wheels turning in his head. "I guess that picture must have been taken on, uh, Customer Appreciation Day."

"I see," I replied dryly. Ace was turning out to be a lot faster on his feet than I would have expected. Fast, but not particularly skillful. "Anyway, I'm sure she would have liked you to have this. As a token, I mean. Something to remember her by."

"There's not much to remember," he insisted, still unwilling to touch it.

"In that case, maybe I should hang on to this—"

"No!" A lightbulb must have suddenly gone off in Ace's head, because he grabbed the photograph out of my hand. Maybe he wasn't the sharpest tack on the bulletin board, but he knew a piece of incriminating evidence when he saw it. Somehow, I had a feeling this photo wasn't going to end up posted on the wall next to Miss January and her rash-inducing outfit.

"Well, I should probably let you go," I said, figuring my work at Ace's art studio was done. I hadn't known what I'd learn, but I'd learned plenty. "I can see how busy you are. Thanks for your time."

"Sure," he said, turning away. "And, uh, thanks for the picture. Catch ya later."

You know it, I thought. When it came to Ace Atwood, I'd say he ranked pretty high on the list of suspects.

Yet what his motive for murdering his girlfriend might have been, I had yet to determine.

• • •

I continued puzzling over the bizarrely different reports Marnie and Ace had given me after I went back to the hotel. Even though the late morning conference session on traditional Chinese acupuncture that I attended was fascinating, I couldn't keep from pondering the true nature of Marnie and Ace's relationship.

After wolfing down a buffet lunch provided by a pharmaceutical firm, I headed up to the hotel room. I assumed that Nick was still windsurfing or brooding or however he'd chosen to spend the day.

Instead, I found him sitting on the bed, his cheerful Hawaiian shirt a jarring contradiction to his forlorn expression.

"I miss you," he announced sheepishly.

"Oh, Nick. I miss you too." We both ran toward each other, collapsing in each other's arms somewhere between the closet and the luggage rack. "I'm sorry I got so wrapped up in Marnie Burton's murder."

"And I'm sorry if I sounded coldhearted last night. You're right about her murder being a terrible thing, and I don't blame you for wanting to help."

"Let's start again, okay?" I suggested hopefully. "Can we pretend none of this other stuff even happened?"

"Okay by me."

To commemorate our decision to turn over a new leaf, we fell onto the bed, still wrapped in each other's arms.

"At last," Nick said, doing his best to leer. "I've finally got you in my clutches."

"Oh, yeah?" I murmured. "Now that I'm in these clutches of yours, what are you going to do?"

"Clutch you, for one thing."

"Is that all?"

"Nope." Nick's tone had softened. "I'm going to do this . . ."

He reached down and gently pulled my hair away from my neck, tickling me as the strands swept across my skin.

"And this . . ." He leaned over, lightly brushing his lips against my neck.

"And this . . ." He clasped his mouth against mine in a kiss that was more like the kind I was used to encountering in the movies than in real life.

There's definitely something to be said for this romantic-getaway business, I thought, kissing him back.

As Nick and I wriggled out of our clothes, I was only vaguely aware of a soft pounding in the background. So it took me a few seconds to realize it wasn't just my heart.

"Nick," I murmured, "somebody's at the door."

"Hmm?"

"The door. Somebody's knocking."

"Must be room service," Nick murmured.

"I didn't call room service," I told him.

"I did." In response to my puzzled look, he replied, "Champagne. I thought it would be a nice change from all those mai tais. Kind of romantic too, especially in the middle of the day."

I jumped up, pulled on a fluffy white bathrobe, and opened the door.

"Surprise!" two cheerful voices cried excitedly.

That was an understatement. I'd been expecting a waiter pushing a cart with two glasses and a bottle of Moët & Chandon, not two pale, suitcase-bearing tourists decked out in straw hats, flip-flops, and gaudy Hawaiian shirts, their faces aglow with excitement and jet lag.

"Betty? Winston?" I gasped, blinking. "What are *you* doing here?"

"See, Win?" Betty said triumphantly. "I told you she'd be surprised!"

"She certainly looks surprised," Winston observed

in his dignified English accent. "I imagine we're the last people you expected to see in Hawaii, aren't we?"

"Uh, you could say that," I gasped, still trying to catch my breath.

Betty Vandervoort was one of my dearest friends, as well as my landlady. She lived in the mansion on the Joshua's Hollow estate that was also the site of the cozy little cottage I rented from her. Even our age difference of forty-odd years didn't get in the way of our friendship, and I enjoyed stopping in for tea and advice whenever I was in need of either.

I was also fond of her new beau, Winston Farnsworth, who had said good-bye to seventy long ago as well. The dignified Englishman had brought a wonderful new luster to Betty's already sparkly sapphire blue eyes. The fact that the two of them were struggling to make a go of living together, just as Nick and I were, had brought the four of us even closer.

But I thought I'd left all my friends back on the mainland.

"Betty? Winston?" Nick had come up behind me. He too had had the presence of mind to put something on. Only instead of a bathrobe, the bottom half of him was wrapped in a sheet. "What are *you* doing here?"

"You two are beginning to sound like Prometheus," Betty replied gaily, referring to my blue and gold macaw, "the way you keep parroting each other."

"Perhaps they're *too* surprised," Winston said, sounding uneasy. "Maybe we should have telephoned instead of just dropping in on them like this."

"Nonsense," Betty insisted. "I'm sure they're thrilled to see us."

"Thrilled," I assured her. "And surprised."

"Definitely surprised," Nick mumbled behind me. "How did you know which room we were in?"

"You should have seen Betty flirting with the hotel clerk," Winston said proudly. "Our own Mata Hari!"

Betty's cheeks, which were already red from a bit too much blush, grew flushed. "I know it's kind of crazy, the two of us just showing up like this. But right after you left, Winston and I were talking about what a wonderful idea it was for the two of you to vacation in Maui. I said I hadn't been to Hawaii in years—decades, actually—and he said he'd never been here. I told him that one of these days, we had to remedy that. Before we knew it, we were on the phone, making reservations!" She spoke so animatedly that her hot-pink flamingo-shaped earrings swayed wildly from side to side.

"Who's taking care of my animals?" I asked. "Max and Lou and Cat—"

"They're fine!" Betty assured me. "You don't think I'd do anything to endanger those sweeties, do you? I called your veterinarian friend Suzanne, and she picked them all up and brought them straight to her house. By the way, she sends her best. She also said to tell you she hopes you're having a blast."

"At least the animals are in good hands," Nick noted, glancing at me. Turning back to our unexpected guests, he asked, "Uh, where are you two staying?"

"Right here!" Betty replied brightly.

"In this very same hotel!" Winston chimed in.

"That's great," I said in a slightly choked voice.

"So, uh, how *long* are you staying?" Nick asked.

"As long as you two are." Betty was positively glowing.

"And to get things rolling," Winston interjected in a jovial voice, "we thought you might both like to help us kick off our vacation in paradise by joining us down at the beach."

"This hotel has a beautiful beach," Betty added.

"Don't you two need time to unpack?" I asked, trying to sound practical instead of hopeful.

"Oh, pshaw." Betty waved her hand in the air dismissively. "Who has time for that? Besides, what's a few wrinkles in our clothes? At our age, wrinkles are a way of life!"

"We don't want to waste a single minute," Winston piped up. "Not when we've come all this way for sun and fun!"

I opened my mouth, hoping a convincing excuse would magically come out of it. Fortunately, Nick came to my rescue.

"Gee, the beach sounds great. But Jessie has to go to a talk in about five minutes. Something on feline . . . uh, canine . . . chicken pox, isn't it?"

"Yes! Yes, I do!" I told them. "I'm really sorry, but the veterinary convention has to come first. It is the main reason I came to Maui, after all."

"Then you must join us, Nick," Winston insisted. "We'll keep you occupied while Jessica is busy with her conference."

"Sounds great," Nick said heartily, "but, uh, I'm signed up for a scuba-diving lesson." Quickly, he added, "A *private* lesson."

"Too bad," Betty cooed.

"But we'll definitely catch up with you later," Winston said.

"Later," Nick agreed. "Definitely."

"This is going to be such a kick!" Betty cried. "Think of all the fun we'll have, just the four of us!"

Funny, I thought gloomily, glancing over at Nick. And here I'd been thinking about all the fun the *two* of us would be having.

• • •

As soon as we closed the door behind Betty and Winston—after promising to get together as soon as possible for either sunset mai tais, which was our idea, or a surfing lesson, which was Betty's—I turned to Nick and sighed.

"Thanks for getting us out of going to the beach," I told him. "It's not that I don't adore Betty and Winston . . . but here? Now? This was supposed to be a romantic getaway for just the two of us!"

"We'll figure out a way to enjoy their company but still have plenty of time alone together," Nick said. He let his sheet drop to the floor. "Like right now."

I happened to catch sight of my watch. Instantly a jolt of adrenaline shot through me, one that had nothing to do with the glint in his eyes. "Now?" I squawked.

"Now, where were we?" he murmured, gently tugging at the belt of my bathrobe.

I clamped my hands around it, bracing myself for his reaction when I told him that wherever we were before, we weren't about to go there again. At least, not right now.

"Nick, I have to go." Before he had a chance to utter the words that matched the confused look on his face, I explained, "There really is someplace I have to be in about twenty minutes. I'm already running late."

His expression changed immediately. He looked as forlorn as Lou, my Dalmatian, whenever he watched me leave the house, car keys in hand, without inviting him to join me. "But room service hasn't even brought our champagne yet! Besides, I thought you said you weren't planning to go to any lectures this afternoon."

"It's not about the conference." I hesitated. "It's about Marnie Burton's murder."

I braced myself for all the fury of the Mauna Loa volcano. And that's exactly what I got.

"Why did you bother to bring me all this way if it wasn't to spend at least a little time with me?" he demanded, grabbing his sheet off the floor and holding it in front of him like a giant three-hundred-thread-count fig leaf. "I thought this was our chance to get away together. Instead, you're totally obsessed with this Marnie person that you only met once—"

"I know I only met her once. But I'm involved, Nick! Whether you believe me or not, whoever killed her thinks I have something he's after!"

"What about the Maui Police Department?" Nick demanded. "Isn't this supposed to be their job?"

"I know it's their job, and of course they're working on it. But aside from the horror of what happened to that poor young woman, *I* could be in danger. *You* could be in danger!"

Nick cast me a look that qualified him to be the poster boy for skepticism.

"I thought you understood!" I cried.

"I do—up to a point. I know you've gotten involved in murder investigations before. I can't say I completely understand it, other than that being in the wrong place at the wrong time happens to be a quirk of yours. But I don't understand why you have to run off right now, just as you and I were about to—"

"Okay, here's why: because I have an appointment with someone who knew her. Someone who worked with her, in fact. Because she might help me figure out who killed Marnie and what they wanted so badly that they broke into our hotel room to get their hands on it. Because at this very moment, she's probably sitting in a coffee shop in Lahaina—and from the way she sounded on the phone, looking for a reason not to wait for me."

"Fine," Nick retorted. "If you keep insisting that the fact that you misplaced that stupid conference packet means you're next on some crazed murderer's hit list, fine. If that's how you want to spend your vacation on Maui, then fine. But don't expect me to sit around waiting for you while you live out your Miss Marple fantasies!" He grabbed a bathing suit, his snorkel and fins, and a towel, then strode toward the door.

"Then don't!" I exclaimed. "That's fine with me."

"Fine!" he cried.

"Fine!" I shot back.

But as I heard him slam the door on his way out, I didn't feel even close to fine.

Chapter 6

"If a dog jumps in your lap, it is because he is fond of you; but if a cat does the same thing, it is because your lap is warmer."

—Alfred North Whitehead

Despite being a Mecca for tourists, the town of Lahaina managed to retain the quaint, old-fashioned feeling of the whaling center it became a few decades after the missionaries arrived and forced the natives out of their grass skirts and loincloths and into muumuus and aloha shirts. Its main thoroughfare, Front Street, was lined with weatherworn wooden buildings that gave the impression that some enterprising individual with a deeply rooted Walt Disney complex had transported an entire nineteenth-century whaling town all the way from New England.

According to Nick's guidebook, the picturesque port was the home of Seamen's Cemetery, Seamen's Hospital, and a prison that had undoubtedly gotten a lot of use during the town's raucous thar-she-blows days. Even Herman Melville had dropped in for some wild partying, 1800s-style, during his stint as a sailor.

These days, free-spirited natives and fun-seeking

sailors had been replaced by free-spirited, fun-seeking tourists. The low, flat-roofed buildings housed art galleries, jewelry stores, clothing boutiques, and restaurants, and the narrow sidewalks were crowded with out-of-town visitors strolling around the lively streets of the charming downtown area.

I, however, was in no mood for strolling. Not when I was frantic over the possibility that Holly Gruen might have already bolted. I half-jogged toward the coffee shop she had chosen as our meeting place, jostling a few surprised-looking tourists and trying to make up for it by muttering "Sorry" and "Excuse me" every time I took a breath.

I turned a corner and spotted the Bean Scene. I was overcome with relief, although that feeling pretty much vanished as soon as I glanced at my watch and saw that I was more than fifteen minutes late.

I pushed open the door, cringing at the blast of air-conditioning that assaulted me. Scanning the coffee shop, I saw that only two or three of the Formica tables were in use. The small eatery appeared to be more popular with locals than tourists—although in the middle of the afternoon, it clearly wasn't particularly popular with anyone.

Only one of the tables was occupied by a young woman sitting alone. Even though she'd pulled out one of the laminated menus wedged between the plastic ketchup and mustard bottles and left it open in front of her, she kept glancing around furtively.

"Holly?" I asked as I neared the table. When she nodded, I added, "Sorry I'm late."

What struck me most about Holly Gruen was that, physically, she was the exact opposite of Marnie. While Marnie had a tiny frame that gave her the appearance of a wood sprite, the other female reporter who had worked at the *Maui Dispatch* had a stocky build. Her straight, dark-brown hair was cut chin-length and tucked behind her ears, with no signs of the punky style Karen Nelson claimed she had once adopted.

She wore eyeglasses with black plastic frames, their severity surpassed only by the color of the black cotton blouse she was wearing. The shirt was huge, probably a man's size. I suspected its primary function was to conceal as much of her as possible.

As for the color, I couldn't remember having seen anybody else on Maui dressed in black. Somehow, it didn't fit in. Not when all the lush, fragrant hibiscus and palm trees made it practically impossible not to grab the first brightly colored garment you saw and put it on.

I suddenly understood why Karen Nelson had become alarmed when Holly started showing up at the *Dispatch* with spiked hair and short flouncy skirts.

"I was halfway out the door," she announced petulantly as I took a seat opposite her. She sat hunched over the table, barely raising her head as she spoke to me. "I was counting down from one hundred. If you didn't show up by the time I got to zero, I was going to leave."

"What number were you down to?"

"Twelve."

Yikes, I thought. "In that case, I'm *really* sorry I'm late."

I was already concluding that Holly was Marnie's opposite in other ways besides physical appearance. While Marnie had possessed enough energy and optimism to be considered practically manic, Holly in person was as lethargic and downbeat as she had sounded on the phone. No doubt another reason her idolization of Marnie had been so jarring to the people who'd known them both.

First thing, I reached into my backpack and pulled out the marble paperweight with the gold plaque. "Here's that award we talked about on the phone," I said as I handed it over. "I think Marnie would have wanted you to have it."

"Thanks," she said sullenly. Without even bothering to look at it, she tucked it away in her oversize black leather pocketbook. I was surprised by her lack of interest—especially given what Karen Nelson had told me about Holly's response to Marnie winning the Association of Professional Journalists' award. Then again, this was small potatoes in comparison.

Holly leaned back in her chair, studying me suspiciously. "So who are you, anyway?" she asked. "I know you said you were friends with Marnie, but why should I believe you? How do I know you're not with the police? Or a private investigator?"

"I'm neither, Holly. I really was just a friend." As if to prove I had nothing to do with the cops, I handed her my business card. "See? I'm a veterinarian. I live on Long Island, outside New York City."

As she glanced at my card, her mouth twitched downward. "I don't remember Marnie ever mentioning you," she said as she stuck it into her shirt pocket. She appeared to have no more interest in it than she'd had in Marnie's award. "Not that I knew her all that well. Outside of the office, I mean."

"I used to live in Ellensburg, where she grew up," I explained, hoping I was doing a convincing job of rewriting history. "But I've lived on the East Coast for a long time now. Over the years, Marnie and I grew apart in a lot of ways, but we still stayed in touch. Christmas cards, the occasional e-mail, that kind of thing. So I looked her up when I came to Maui for the veterinary conference that's going on right now at the Royal Banyan Hotel. We got together on Sunday afternoon and had a great time reminiscing about the old days. And then this terrible thing happened."

I searched her face for a reaction. There was none.

"Actually, I'm probably one of the last people who saw her alive," I continued. "And I'm still in shock. I mean, she was killed just a few hours after I talked to her."

"It's awful, isn't it?" Holly's face sagged. For the first time, I got a sense that somewhere in there was an empathetic creature. And that maybe she was starting to let down her guard a bit.

Just then our waitress wandered over. "What can I get you girls?" she asked cheerfully, pulling a well-chewed pencil out from behind her ear.

"I'll just have iced tea," Holly replied without glancing up at her.

"Order whatever you want," I urged. "I'm taking you out."

"Really?" The brightness that momentarily appeared in her eyes told me I'd just said the magic words. "In that case, I'll have a mahi sandwich—no, make that a shrimp salad sandwich—with onion rings. And fries."

"I'll stick with iced tea," I told the waitress.

"Gotcha."

"I'm really hungry," Holly told me, her cheeks flushed and her tone defensive. "I haven't had lunch yet. Besides, I hardly ever get to eat out. I couldn't really afford it on what the *Dispatch* paid, and now that I'm not working, I pretty much stick to peanut butter and jelly."

"Not exactly what people expect when they fantasize about living in Hawaii," I observed.

She grimaced. "The problem is that it's so darned expensive here. They have to bring everything over by boat or plane, so anything you buy costs way more than on the mainland."

"Where are you from?"

"Florida. So I guess that makes me one of the few people who didn't come for the weather."

"What did bring you here, then?" I asked.

"A few things," she replied with a little shrug. "The lifestyle. The ocean, although I'm not a big fan of sun-worshipping on the beach. Not with these thighs. Adventure too, I guess. You know, the romance of picking up and coming to an exotic new place."

"So you had different motivations than Marnie," I observed. "She told me she came here because of the job. She was determined to make a name for herself as a reporter."

"Yeah, that sounds like Marnie," she agreed. Disapprovingly, she added, "I mean, there aren't many people who would move three thousand miles away from home just for a job."

"But that's just because she was ambitious," I pointed out. I was anxious to bring the conversation back to Holly's feelings about Marnie. The report Karen Nelson had given about the relationship between the two women was chilling, and I was hoping to get a sense of just how accurate it was.

"That's an understatement." Holly let out an odd little laugh, then added, "Believe me, everybody who ever came into contact with her knew that. It was her nature. That girl was the type who wouldn't stop at anything. I mean, I'm as competitive as the next person, but she was in another category altogether."

My eyebrows shot up. "Of course I knew she was a go-getter, but you make her sound really extreme."

"She *was* extreme," she said simply. "I mean, you knew her for a long time, right? So you must have had a sense that she was one of those people who don't understand limits."

I pretended to think for a few seconds. "It's true that she had a few problems with the way she interacted with other people . . ."

Holly snorted. "That girl had problems understanding limits in terms of everything she did. And that definitely included her job. Whatever story she was working on was always the hottest story of the decade. Whoever she'd just interviewed was the most fascinating interview of her entire life. She was just so intense in the way she approached things."

Intense. That same word I kept hearing over and over again.

"And talk about being a workaholic," Holly continued, rolling her eyes. "I mean, she'd get into work before Mr. Carrera even, and she'd still be working into the wee hours. I remember once I stopped by the office pretty late because I'd forgotten something I wanted to bring home with me. Notes for something I was covering first thing the next morning. It was probably close to eleven. But there she was, still working away. She was the only one there, in fact.

"But that doesn't mean she didn't spend plenty of time out of the office too, covering stories," she added. "The paper has a really small staff. When I was there, it was just Marnie and me reporting the news. So we were always pretty busy."

We stopped talking as our waitress deposited our iced teas on the table. I was still emptying a packet of sugar into mine as Holly poured in two packets of her own, then sucked up a full third of her drink through a straw without coming up for air.

I took only a small sip, wanting to make sure I had enough time to ask all the questions I wanted before Holly's food disappeared and Holly disappeared with it. "Marnie always had such big plans," I commented. "That was true even when she was a kid."

"*Oh,* yeah." Holly frowned. "To hear her talk, she was destined to become the next Christiane Amanpour. Y'know, we were friends, kind of, since we worked together and all, and in a way I hate to say this. Especially since when I first met her, I kind of admired her, you know? But then I got to know her better, and believe me, I ended up having serious doubts about whether she could ever have made it."

"Really?" My surprise was genuine. "Why?"

"Marnie had kind of a strange way of looking at things. I mean, she saw the worst in every situation. She was always convinced there was scandal and corruption and all kinds of evil stuff everywhere. It got to be such a thing with her that you started wondering if she was paranoid."

The exact same assessment Bryce Bolt made, I noted. I wondered if that particular personality trait could have been what turned Holly off in the end, rather than her competitiveness toward Marnie. I wondered if it was what had gotten Marnie murdered too.

"But is it possible she uncovered an important story that would have caused somebody embarrassment—or had even worse ramifications?" I persisted. "An exposé that would have made her a few enemies?"

Holly shook her head. "Nope. At least, not while I was working there."

"How can you be sure?"

"Believe me, if there was anything that interesting going on, we'd all have known about it," she replied, sounding scornful of my naïveté. "Maui is like a small town. Everybody knows everybody else's business. And nobody had any secrets at the *Dispatch* office. You've been there, right? You can hear everyone else's phone calls and you can see what's on everybody else's computer screen. If Marnie was working on something like that, I'd have known about it."

Unless she talked on a cell phone in some other location, I reflected. And recorded what she learned on tapes instead of on the office computer.

I decided to try a different approach.

"What stories was Marnie working on?" I asked. "I don't mean car accidents and ribbon-cutting ceremonies. I'm talking about big stories, like your Hawaii Power and Light story."

She looked startled. "I don't think that's any of your business." Realizing she'd sounded a bit harsh, she added, "I mean, I don't think Richard Carrera would appreciate it if his reporters and his ex-reporters went around blabbing about insider stuff like that."

I couldn't help wondering if Holly was really that loyal—or if she had something to hide.

"Would you say she acted the same way in her personal life too?" I asked. "Intense? Extreme?"

Holly hesitated, staring at her iced tea.

"Look, like I already told you, I didn't know her all that well, okay? I mean, if you knew her since you were both kids, I'm sure you have a better sense of what she was all about than I ever did. We were just work friends.

"But she definitely had some weird stuff going on where her social life was concerned," she continued, measuring her words. "There was this one time, just a few weeks ago, when she called me out of the blue. She said she was meeting this guy she'd been seeing for a drink after work, and she insisted that I come along. I mean, she wouldn't take no for an answer."

"Why do you think it mattered to her so much?"

She shrugged. "Got me. It was just the way Marnie was. From what I could see, everything she did was just turned up to a higher speed than everybody else. Anyway, from the way she'd been going on about this guy, I figured the two of them were practically engaged or something. But when I saw them together, it was like they hardly even knew each other. You would have thought they were on a blind date or something. One that wasn't going particularly well."

"No chemistry?"

"That was part of it. But the guy—he had a goofy name . . ."

"Ace?"

"That's it, Ace. He didn't seem all that into her, y'know? She was all giggly and flirty, and he was practically a stone wall. He seemed like kind of a creep too. Frankly, I couldn't figure out what she saw in him. But the one thing that really stands out in my mind about that night is that she kept touching him—you know, grabbing his hand or putting her arm around him—and he kept shrugging her off. I never once saw him touch her. You know, the way a guy will put his hand on his girlfriend's back or let his arm brush against hers, really casual like it's the kind of thing he's used to doing all the time. The other thing I remember is that he hardly spent any time talking to us. He kept getting calls on his cell phone, and he seemed much more interested in talking to whoever was calling him than to Marnie."

"Do you have any idea who he was talking to? Friends? Business associates . . . ?"

She shook her head. "Nope. Every time he got a call, he just got up and went to another part of the bar. Besides, it was pretty noisy in there."

We paused as our waitress laid out the various plates that contained Holly's lunch. I found it difficult to believe she was going to be able to consume all that food. That is, until I saw her inhale half her shrimp salad sandwich in three seconds flat.

"So Ace wasn't exactly the love of her life," I said, anxious to keep our conversation going. "But that sounds so typical of Marnie, doesn't it? The way she tended to see things differently from the way they really were?"

"I guess so." Holly thought for a few seconds, meanwhile smothering her fries with salt. I got the impression she'd never really thought about Marnie Burton in exactly those terms before. "Yeah, that sounds about right."

By that point, I figured I'd pretty much gotten everything I was likely to get out of Holly. Even though she and Marnie hadn't been close, she seemed more than eager to tell me whatever she knew, including her most negative impressions. I decided it was time to move on to other possibly relevant topics—like Holly Gruen herself.

"Holly," I asked gently, "if you don't mind me asking, why did you leave the *Dispatch*?"

I was trying to be sensitive to the possibility that she'd been fired—or that she'd resigned because she was on the verge of being let go. But I wasn't prepared for the look of alarm that crossed her face.

"Why?" she demanded, showing more fire than I'd seen since I sat down at the table. "What did you hear?"

"Nothing," I replied, struggling not to react.

In a strained voice, she replied, "It was just time for me to move on. That's all."

Right, I thought. With no other job to go to. And with your finances in such bad shape that the only food groups you can afford to make part of your diet are the Peanut Butter Group and the Jelly Group.

"But I guess we should eat, right?" Holly said with

an air of finality, as if she'd decided she'd told me enough. Grabbing the other half of her sandwich, she added, "I'm sorry I haven't been more helpful, but I really don't know very much. In fact, I don't even know why you bothered to track me down."

It was true that Holly hadn't given me much useful information about Marnie, aside from confirming that she was intent on uncovering scandal as a means of advancing her career and that her relationship with Ace hadn't been as solid as she seemed to think it was.

But I was struck by the strange way Holly had reacted to my question about why she'd left the paper. For the price of a sandwich and a couple of sides, I'd learned something valuable: that Marnie wasn't the only *Dispatch* reporter with secrets.

• • •

It was nearly four by the time I got back to the hotel. I was still ruminating about my conversation with Holly as I pulled into the parking garage. She had admitted to having "admired" Marnie back when they first met, as well as changing the way she felt about her over time. That was certainly consistent with what Karen Nelson had told me about their relationship. I also found it interesting that she had agreed with the *Dispatch*'s other reporter, Bryce Bolt, about Marnie being intense as well as determined to find scandal everywhere she looked. In addition, Holly had picked up on the fact that there was something peculiar about Marnie's relationship with Ace.

But what I found most interesting was the fact that Holly had left the paper so abruptly—without having another job lined up. While the operation had looked innocent enough during my brief behind-the-scenes peek, the fact that one of their reporters had chosen to flee left me wondering if I'd misjudged it.

As I crossed the lobby, I spotted a crowd of veterinarians streaming out of a meeting room. The sight was a harsh reminder that I wasn't doing a very good job of balancing my murder investigation with the conference that had brought me here in the first place.

Which forced me to focus on something else that was off-balance: my relationship with my traveling companion. As far as I knew, Nick was still pretty angry with me.

I stood in the lobby, trying to muster up the courage or energy or whatever was required to go up to our room, where I was more than likely to run into him. As I procrastinated, I noticed a sign outside the White Orchid that read, HAPPY HOUR—4:00 TO 7:00. ALL DRINKS HALF-PRICE!

Even though I wasn't feeling particularly happy, I figured that enjoying a little Hawaiian culture—or at least a little Hawaiian tourist culture—might push me a little further in that direction. Besides, indulging in happy hour offered me a really convenient way to delay confronting Nick. In a somewhat pathetic attempt at putting myself into a partying mood, I pulled a hibiscus out of one of the lobby's over-the-top flower arrangements and stuck it behind my ear. Then I headed inside.

I wasn't the only one who'd been lured in by the promise of cheap drinks. Every table in the dark, bamboo-walled bar was full. The comfortable armchairs, also made of bamboo, appeared to be occupied mainly by tourists. Young Japanese couples poring over guidebooks and sipping cool drinks in tall cylindrical glasses sat side by side with senior citizens, college kids on break, and middle-aged American couples in Bermuda shorts and splashy shirts I bet they wouldn't be caught dead in at home. I also spotted a few veterinarians sitting in clusters, still sporting their convention name tags, but I wasn't in the mood to talk shop.

Instead, I dropped onto a bar stool and ordered a mai tai. Before the bartender even had a chance to slap a cocktail napkin in front of me, a tall ponytailed gentleman slid onto the stool next to me. Even though he was probably well past forty, he was dressed like a surfer dude in denim cutoffs, battered leather sandals, and an extremely faded Hanauma Bay T-shirt that looked as if one more encounter with a clothes dryer was guaranteed to reduce it to shreds.

Glancing over at me, he said, "Hey."

"Hey," I mumbled, not wanting to appear rude even though I craved nothing more than solitude.

He didn't take the hint. "I haven't seen you here before."

I grimaced. "Can't you come up with a better line than that?"

"It's not a line," he returned, sounding a bit indignant. He brushed away a strand of dark-blond hair that had fallen over his face. "It's an honest observation."

"At least it's accurate," I replied crisply. "I haven't been here before."

I always thought part of the appeal of travel was that it enabled you to leave some of the less savory aspects of your life behind. Yet even though I'd traveled nearly six thousand miles to paradise, someone who could be a clone of Marcus Scruggs, one of my least favorite people in the world, ended up sitting on the bar stool next to mine.

I first met Marcus when I was applying to veterinary school. I'd hoped he'd be able to offer me some good advice. Instead, I spent our first meeting ignoring his off-color questions and suggestive comments. And just a couple of months ago, when my friend Suzanne Fox actually found him attractive for some inexplicable reason, I was forced to socialize with him on several occasions. When they finally split up, I didn't know who was happier, Suzanne or me.

Yet here I was again, fighting off the unwelcome attentions of a sleazeball who looked like a survivor from a deserted island and acted just as desperate.

"Tourist?"

"Not exactly." I looked around, suddenly wishing Nick would magically appear—even if it was just to scowl at me.

"Ah. Conventioneer."

"Something like that."

"Don't tell me—you're a veterinarian."

I shrugged. "Okay. I won't tell you."

He chuckled appreciatively. As annoying as he was, at least he had a sense of humor. "Can I get you a drink, Dr. Dolittle? Maybe one of those fruity ones that come with a paper umbrella or a real flower in it?"

"Thanks, but I'm waiting for someone," I lied. "I can't imagine what's keeping him. Besides, I already ordered a drink."

Just then my mai tai arrived. I flinched when I saw that the tall, slender glass was decorated with both a flower *and* a tiny yellow paper umbrella.

Smirking, he told the bartender, "Bring me a Scotch. Neat."

"You got it," the bartender assured him.

Mr. Ponytail turned his attention back to me. "So, where do you hail from?"

"Look," I returned evenly, "I'm sure you mean well, but frankly I'm not in the mood for conversation. I had kind of a bad day."

"A bad day? In paradise?" He pretended to be shocked. "Impossible!"

I smiled despite myself. I also looked him fully in the face for the first time. He had exceptionally high cheekbones, pale, deep-set gray eyes, and the same weathered look that so many locals seemed to have. Just one more individual paying the price of sun-worshipping, I mused.

"Yeah, that's what I thought too," I commented. "Turns out that old saying about bringing your own baggage wherever you go is true."

"No kidding." He shook his head slowly, as if he understood what I was talking about only too well. "And I should know. Believe it or not, I actually live here."

"Really?"

"That's right." He paused while the bartender brought him his drink, then took a long, slow sip. "I bet I'm the first person you've met who's a bona fide resident."

Funny: Bona fide residents were practically the only people I'd had a chance to talk to.

"Aside from hotel employees and waiters and people like that, I mean," he continued. "A lot of people in the service industry were probably born here. But I'm a transplant. I'd had enough of L.A., and I figured there'd be less traffic and less smog on a tropical island. So a few years ago I packed up all my worldly possessions and moved here."

"What do you do, job-wise, that gives you so much flexibility?" I asked.

"Oh, a little of this, a little of that. Actually, I was premed myself, back in college. Before I came to my senses, that is."

I had a feeling he'd dropped that little tidbit in there to impress me, maybe because he knew I was a science jock myself. The maneuver struck me as something right out of *Marcus Scruggs's Guide to Picking Up*

Babes. Ordinarily, I wouldn't have given a guy like this the satisfaction of sounding impressed or even interested. But it turns out those pretty pink drinks with the paper umbrellas do a lot more than quench a person's thirst.

"A jack-of-all-trades, huh?" I commented.

"I manage," he replied, grinning. "But, hey, I don't want to talk about work. It's after hours. Let's talk about all the fun things you plan on doing while you're on Maui."

I glanced at my watch. As if on cue, the bartender appeared. "Another drink?" he asked me.

"No, thanks. I've got to be going." Finding myself shooting the breeze with a strange man in a bar was an indication that one drink was more than enough.

"So soon?" My date looked genuinely disappointed. "What about the person you said you were waiting for?"

"He's probably so busy snorkeling he lost track of the time."

"But you haven't even told me your name."

I hesitated. "Jessica."

"Jessica," he repeated. "Pretty name for a pretty lady. And I'm Graham. Graham Warner." Solemnly he stuck out his hand, and I shook it. "Pleased to meet you. And I hope it's not for the last time."

"It probably is." Sliding off my bar stool, I pointedly told him, "My boyfriend and I will be pretty busy while we're here, between the convention and all the touristy things we plan to do."

"Ah. A boyfriend." He pondered the fact that I was already attached for about three seconds before saying, "I'm really good at working around boyfriends."

That was my wake-up call, especially since, once again, it sounded exactly like something Marcus would say. What are you doing wasting your time on this creep? I thought. Especially when Nick is probably upstairs in the room at this very moment, waiting for you with champagne and an apology?

My blood was suddenly boiling, despite the cooling effects of the mai tai. "I see that when you packed up your computer and your textbooks, you also brought along your sleaziness."

He just laughed. "Touché. But before you run off, let me give you some advice."

I looked at him coolly.

"That flower in your hair?"

Automatically I reached up and touched the fragile blossom. "What about it?"

"It's on the wrong side," he said with a crooked half smile.

"Excuse me?"

"If you're already taken, you're supposed to wear it on the left side of your head. If you're in the market, you wear it on your right." Grinning, he added, "Can't blame a guy for hitting on you when you're blatantly advertising your availability."

"Thanks for the lesson in Polynesian culture," I returned. I yanked the flower out of my hair and dropped it into his drink. "Enjoy."

Much to my annoyance, I could hear him snickering as I stalked off.

• • •

As I crossed the lobby and headed toward the elevators, I chastised myself for talking to strangers, especially in a bar. What were you thinking? I asked myself, wondering why on earth I'd wasted my time talking to a jerk like that.

I had almost reached the bank of elevators across from the front desk when a loud voice interrupted my self-flagellation. "You've got to be kidding!" someone shouted. "You *charged* us for that?"

I turned to see what was going on. Me and just about everybody else in the cavernous lobby.

I was surprised to see that the outraged voice belonged to someone I knew, or at least recognized. I moved closer to the front desk, where John Irwin, Governor Wickham's redheaded aide, stood. He was decked out in a suit and tie and shiny black shoes. The man on the other side of the desk, the person he was arguing with, was a distraught-looking older gentleman in an aloha shirt.

"Okay, okay, so that's a legitimate expense," John Irwin grumbled. "But what about this one, down here? You're charging us for bottled water? We told you up front we didn't need any."

"Mr. Irwin, I have your original order right here," the hotel employee said in a strained but polite voice. "If you'd just take a moment to look it over, you'll see that every item you were charged for is something you specifically requested."

I hovered near the front desk, listening as Irwin begrudgingly let himself be convinced that he hadn't been ripped off at the press conference here at the hotel two days earlier. When he finally turned to leave, I planted myself in front of him.

"Mr. Irwin?" I began.

He peered at me suspiciously. "Do I know you?"

"I was a friend of Marnie Burton's."

"Who?"

"The reporter from the *Maui Dispatch* who was murdered."

"Oh, yeah. Tough break."

He brushed past me, walking away so quickly I had to jog to keep up with him.

"Mr. Irwin?" I called after him.

"What now?"

He cast me an icy look, but at least he slowed down enough that I was able to walk next to him.

"Could I talk to you about Marnie for just a minute?"

"What for?" he replied impatiently. "I barely knew her."

I took a deep breath, gearing up for something I hoped wouldn't turn out to be a huge mistake. "She seemed to think you had it out for her."

"Ridiculous," he returned, barely glancing in my direction. "Like I just said, I hardly knew her."

The wall he'd put up was so thick I practically needed X-ray vision to make eye contact with the man. A tidal wave of anger rose up inside me, the result of his dismissive attitude.

I decided to challenge him, just to see what kind of reaction I'd get.

"She claimed you pushed her at the governor's press conference here the other day."

That got his attention. He stopped and turned to face me, his steely blue-gray eyes boring into mine. "*What?*" he demanded angrily.

"I was with her at the press conference that was held here at the hotel a few hours before she was murdered," I said, struggling to keep my voice calm. "She fell and hit her head on a flowerpot, and she told me it was because you shoved her. Right afterward, I brought her to my room to put ice on her bruise. It was pretty severe. In fact, I was afraid she'd gotten a concussion."

He suddenly loomed so close that his nose was nearly touching mine. "Are you saying you think I had something to do with that kid's murder?"

I didn't flinch. Instead, I stared right back at him, eye to eye. "I'm saying she said you shoved her the day she was killed. She and I talked about it afterward. She told me your name. That's how I knew who you were."

He stepped back suddenly, almost as if he were performing a dance step. But any semblance to anything the least bit lighthearted was canceled out by the way he pointed at me menacingly with one finger.

"Listen to me. I don't know who the hell you think you are, but you'd better be careful about making accusations. Maybe you're too dumb to know it, but you're playing with fire."

"Are you speaking personally or as the governor's spokesperson?" I shot back.

"Just watch it," he hissed, leaning forward so that I could feel his hot breath on my ear. "If I were you, I'd mind my own business."

He turned and stalked away, his expensive-looking shoes squeaking against the tile floor.

Nice guy, I thought, following him with my eyes until he passed through the front entrance and disappeared.

I told myself I'd done the right thing by testing his reaction when I mentioned Marnie Burton's name, as well as the incident that had occurred here in the hotel. And his reaction—a threat—had been pretty revealing.

You got what you wanted, I told myself.

But as I strode toward the elevators with my head held high, I felt anything but satisfied.

In my head, I replayed Marnie's claim that John Irwin had purposely knocked her over. At the time, I'd thought she was imagining things.

Yet now that I'd seen for myself what kind of person he was, I wondered if there might be some history between them that had caused him to react to her so strongly. I felt a wave of frustration that there was so much I didn't know—and that, as an outsider, I was guaranteed to have a hard time understanding. But I suddenly felt as if I couldn't rule out the possibility that the governor's aide might have had something to do with her murder.

Which was probably the reason that, as I pressed the up button, my hand was shaking.

• • •

"Nick?" I called as I let myself into my hotel room with my key card.

I desperately hoped I'd find him in the room. It didn't matter to me in the least that, at last report, he and I were barely speaking. After my unpleasant exchange with John Irwin, I needed him.

Unfortunately, my fantasy that he was waiting for me, prepared to eat crow and drink champagne, turned out to be nothing more than that: a fantasy. The room was empty.

I sank onto the bed, suddenly exhausted and overwhelmed. Too much had happened that day, and none of it had put me any closer to understanding why Marnie Burton was murdered—and by who.

When the phone rang, I jumped up and grabbed it.

"Nick?" I cried, anxious to hear his voice and know that at least I wasn't alone.

I didn't hear anything.

"Nick?" I repeated.

Still nothing.

"Hello. *Hello?*"

When I heard a rush of air, a noise that sounded like someone breathing, I didn't know whether to feel relieved or perturbed.

And then, *click*.

The phone suddenly felt like a hot potato. I dropped it on the bed, my heart thumping in my chest and my dry mouth suddenly tasting of metal.

Somebody is trying to find out if I'm here in the room.

I froze at the barely audible sound of scratching at the door. It took me a few seconds to realize that someone was struggling with the lock, trying to get in.

Oh, my God! I thought, my mind racing wildly. The intruder! He's back!

Fighting the wave of panic that was quickly rushing over me, I whipped my head around, desperately searching for a weapon. Surely a fully equipped luxury hotel room had to come with something more treacherous than a fluffy white robe or a tiny plastic bottle of hibiscus-scented shampoo.

And then I spotted it, tucked away discreetly on the closet shelf. A harsh reminder of the demands of real life, the kind of thing a tourist hotel in a tourist destination would want to keep out of sight unless it was really, truly needed.

An iron.

It was metal, it was heavy, and it was capable of causing a lot of damage if used properly. I grabbed it off the shelf, gripped it tightly in both hands.

I positioned myself right inside the door, holding the iron high above my head, ready to strike. Then I held my breath as the door to the room finally swung open.

Chapter 7

"What counts is not necessarily the size of the dog in the fight—it's the size of the fight in the dog."

—Dwight D. Eisenhower

Hi-yah-ah-ah!" I screamed, brandishing the iron.

"Ar-ar-argh!" the intruder yelled, ducking and throwing both arms over his head.

Fortunately, it took me only a fraction of a second to realize that the dangerous prowler who'd broken into my room was Nick, which was just enough time to keep me from assaulting him with a deadly home appliance.

"Nick! It's you!" I cried, lowering the iron.

"Of course it's me!" he squawked. "Who else would it be?" He backed away, his stance protective and his eyes wild with fear. Or at least confusion.

"I'm so sorry!" I told him. "I didn't know—I thought it was—"

"You could have killed me!" he exclaimed.

I stood up straighter, suddenly indignant. "I wasn't going to hit you—or whoever came through that door—without making sure of the intruder's identity first."

"Good thing I didn't have sunblock all over my face," he replied, still keeping a safe distance away. "If you hadn't recognized me, I might have ended up with *General Electric* branded on my forehead!"

"This iron isn't hot," I informed him, still feeling a tad defensive. Actually, the main reason for that was there hadn't been time to plug it in, but I thought it best to leave that piece of information out.

Nick took a few deep breaths. "Okay. That weird little episode is over. Now will you please tell me what's going on?"

I put the iron down on the dresser. "I guess I overreacted," I admitted. Suddenly, all my indignation was gone. Instead, I just felt silly.

In a gentle, understanding voice, he asked, "Exactly what were you overreacting to, Jess?"

I was pleased he'd put aside the argument we'd been having—ever since we landed on Maui, it seemed. "I just got a very weird phone call."

"What do you mean?" Nick stooped over to deposit the snorkeling equipment he'd been carrying. When he stood up again, his forehead was tensed and his eyes were clouded.

"The phone rang just now," I explained in an even voice, "and when I picked it up, no one said anything."

He stared at me for a second or two before saying, "Excuse me?"

"Don't you see?" I cried. "Somebody was trying to find out if the room was occupied!"

"Or realized they got a wrong number."

"How often does that happen?" I shot back, feeling my blood start to boil so rapidly I could have cooked pasta in it. "Whether you're willing to look at what's going on here or not, the bottom line is that through a stroke of extremely bad luck, I seem to have found myself in the middle of a murder—"

Nick sighed impatiently. "Jessie, when are you going to let this go? This—this obsession of yours? This paranoia?" He sank onto the edge of the bed, holding his arms out in despair.

"It's not paranoia!" I insisted. "Somebody wanted that tape of Marnie's badly enough to break into our hotel room. For all I know, it's the same person who killed her. I'm hoping the fact that we changed rooms—and that it's under your name now, not mine—will make it harder to track us down, but as soon as he figures out he has the wrong tape, he's going to come back looking for it. Or maybe even do something worse, since he probably thinks I know whatever it is he's so desperate to keep under wraps!"

"Look, I know you really believe that's what's going on," Nick said. He sounded so frustrated I almost felt sorry for him. Then I remembered he wasn't the only one around here who was experiencing megalevels of frustration. "But step back a minute. Isn't there at least a chance that you're reading things into the situation that aren't there? I mean, you told me yourself that that homicide cop, whatever his name was—"

"Paleka," I informed him. I tossed my head, hoping I looked self-assured. "Peter Paleka."

"Okay, didn't this Detective Paleka say Marnie was most likely killed by the man she was seen leaving that bar with late that night? And didn't he tell you himself that your theory about the missing envelope and the tape was probably bogus?"

He had, indeed. But that didn't mean he was right. And frankly, hearing Nick say the same thing didn't exactly do much to lower my blood from boil to simmer either.

"Okay, so you've talked to a few people about the

reporter who was killed," he finally said. "Don't you think it's time to let it go? Maybe even spend a little time going to the conference you flew six thousand miles to attend?"

"Actually, I think the exact opposite," I countered. "That given the fact that I'm very much involved in this, I have no choice but to continue."

But that was only part of my reason for being so insistent. It was true I believed I could well be in danger. But I also happen to possess a stubborn streak that, on occasion, has been known to motivate me to do the opposite of what other people want me to do. Maybe it's a statement about my independence, or maybe there's just a screw loose. Whatever it is, the more involved I become in something, the more determined I become to see it through to the end. That particular personality had served me well in life thus far, so I wasn't going to change now.

"Before you say another word," I went on before he had a chance to come up with some new argument, "I want you to listen to what I've learned so far. Will you at least do that much for me?"

Nick opened his mouth to protest, then shut it quickly enough that I could see he recognized a losing battle when he was confronted with one. I decided to take advantage of his sudden cooperative spirit, no matter how grudging it may have been.

I lowered myself onto the bed next to him, then spent the next ten minutes filling him in on all the interactions I'd had over the past two days. I told him about Marnie's editor and fellow staff members at the *Maui Dispatch,* her alleged boyfriend Ace, former reporter Holly Gruen, and even John Irwin, the charming man whom she'd been certain had decked her the afternoon of the governor's press conference.

As I spoke, I could tell he was trying to remain expressionless. But I knew him well enough that I could practically hear what he was thinking.

So I wasn't surprised that when I finally finished my report, Nick opened his mouth—no doubt to go back to trying to convince me that chasing down a killer, no matter what my reasons, was not the best way to spend a vacation in paradise.

He never got a chance. The sharp rapping at the door interrupted him.

"I'd better get that," I said, hopping off the bed.

"Aren't you afraid it's the cat burglar?" Nick asked wryly.

I didn't deign to answer him. I did check the peephole, however, before flinging open the door.

"Betty and Winston!" I announced. "What a lovely surprise!"

This time, I meant it.

"Hello, hello!" Betty cried, waltzing into the room. She was dressed in a fetching yellow bathing suit, her bottom half modestly covered by an orange and yellow batik pareo, a Polynesian-style sarong. Underneath the wide brim of her straw sun hat, her damp hair clung to her neck in curls, and the large, limp hotel towel draped over her arm was sprinkled with sand. Her nose couldn't have been redder and her smile couldn't have been wider.

"Winston and I had such a fabulous afternoon on the beach!" she exclaimed. "I can hardly believe that just yesterday, we were driving on the Long Island Expressway, watching the sleet hit the windshield and wondering if our plane would take off!"

Winston came in right behind her. He, too, was wearing a bathing suit, a baggy, knee-length jobbie covered with lime green geckos. His nose was streaked with white sunblock, and dangling from a chain on his neck was one of those pink plastic plugs that keeps water from going up your nose.

"We're still a bit jet-lagged," he said jovially, "but we weren't about to let that get in our way. In fact, we thought we'd shower and then find a place in our guidebook that has both dinner and dancing. Care to join us?"

I glanced at Nick woefully. "Thanks, but I think we'll pass. Besides, I'm sure you two would rather be alone."

"On the contrary!" Winston boomed. "The more, the merrier!"

"Next time," Nick promised. "Right now, Jessie and I have a few things to sort out."

Betty's sunny smile faded. "Oh, my. That doesn't sound good."

"It's nothing," I said quickly. "We're just, uh, trying to decide how to spend the next few days. Between the conference and everything else."

"It's the 'everything else' part that sounds dangerous," Betty commented. "In that case, let's take a rain check. I'm sure we'll have plenty of other chances."

"Tell them about the luau," Winston prompted.

She immediately brightened. "I almost forgot! There's a luau right here at the hotel that's supposed to be one of the best on the island. I was thinking it might be fun for all of us to go one night."

"As a matter of fact, we have four free tickets," I told them. "Nick and I won them at a Polynesian dance show."

"Actually, we earned them," he corrected me. "And in the process made total fools of ourselves."

"I don't know about that," I remarked, unable to resist a little teasing. "You turned out to be pretty good at moving your arms with the grace of a palm tree. You've got excellent hip motion too."

"Aw, shucks," he said with a smile. "Let's go to that luau tomorrow night, then. The four of us. Does that sound okay, Jess?"

"I'm there," I agreed.

"Marvelous," Betty said, beaming. "It starts at eight. I'll make a reservation and we can all meet at the restaurant."

"In the meantime, perhaps we'd better leave you two to sort out whatever it is that needs sorting," Winston suggested diplomatically.

"But we'll have plenty of time to enjoy one another's company tomorrow," Betty said gaily. "I'm already looking forward to it!"

By the time they toddled off to shower and dress for a romantic night of cha-cha'ing and bossa-nova'ing and whatever else was on their agenda, the air in the room had definitely cleared. In fact, I was beginning to accept the fact that I really had overreacted to my silent phone caller. I supposed that maybe, just maybe, it was possible Nick was right, that it really could have been nothing more ominous than a wrong number.

I turned to him and took both his hands in mine. "Nick," I said solemnly, "I don't want to argue."

"I don't either," he agreed. "Believe me, that's the last thing I want."

"In that case, why don't we spend the evening doing what we came to Maui to do?" I suggested. "Let's find a romantic seaside restaurant, one with tiki torches and a great view of the sunset, and just hold hands and gaze at the ocean and all that corny stuff."

I held my breath as I waited for his answer. Fortunately, it took only about two seconds for his stony expression to melt.

"Sounds good to me," he replied.

I leaned over and kissed him lightly. "And I promise

I won't talk about murder. In fact, I guarantee that tonight is all about fun."

"Mmm," he replied, taking me in his arms. "I'm already having fun."

Frankly, I felt as if a little fun was something both of us needed.

• • •

The hotel's Oceanview Terrace restaurant delivered exactly what it promised: a magnificent view of the ocean. It also had the requisite tiki torches, an extensive selection of umbrella drinks, and soft Hawaiian music playing in the background. Even our waiter helped set the scene for the perfect island fantasy. Not only were both of his bulging biceps tattooed with what looked like authentic Polynesian motifs; he was dressed in a dark blue pareo batiked with starfish and sea horses and other sea life I had to assume actually lived in the Pacific Ocean.

"Now this is what a vacation in Maui is supposed to be like," Nick said with a satisfied grin. "Sitting by the ocean and watching the sunset with my best girl." He reached across the table to take my hand, deftly bypassing the plate of coconut shrimp sitting between us.

"I had no idea you were such a romantic," I replied teasingly.

"Are you kidding? I'm totally romantic."

"Okay, then here's my three-question romance test. First question: Did you cry at the end of *Titanic*?"

"No, but I felt really, really sad."

"Second question: How many Jane Austen novels have you read?"

"All of them," he replied. "I was an English major, remember?"

"You're doing very well," I told him. "But the third question is the killer: Would you rather walk along a beach hand in hand at sunset or watch wrestling on TV?"

He frowned, pretending he was mulling that one over. "Are the wrestlers male or female?"

I let out a whoop. "I think you just failed!" I said, laughing.

"Hey, female wrestling can be extremely erotic. And erotic is close to romantic."

"Not close enough!" I insisted. "I'm sorry, but you didn't win the trip to Acapulco."

Even though I was kidding, Nick suddenly grew serious. "That's okay," he said earnestly, his hazel eyes boring into mine. "I'm happy with this trip. Maui is very romantic, even if we haven't had a chance to walk on the beach hand in hand yet."

Even though he hadn't said anything particularly controversial, the mood instantly shifted. I suddenly felt myself growing uncomfortable. We were getting dangerously close to the one topic I'd been avoiding since I first learned about the location of this year's AVMA conference—our *other* visit to Maui.

And then, before I could change the subject or spill my drink or do something else that would counteract the heaviness hanging over us, Nick said, "I think you and I are in a totally different place, compared to where we were when we took our last trip to Maui. Don't you agree?"

I suddenly felt dizzy. But instead of seeing spots before my eyes, I was seeing rice—the kind that's thrown on the front steps of churches. I blinked a few times, fixing my gaze on the tables behind Nick and taking deep breaths.

"I think the two of us living together for these past three months has brought us much closer together," he went on. "I know you kind of got roped into it, since I was thrown out of my apartment and all. But it's worked out great, the two of us sharing your place and splitting the expenses and acting like . . . well, like a real couple."

I glanced around frantically, wondering who'd turned off the air-conditioning. Then I remembered that we were sitting outside. Where on earth had that lovely sea breeze gone? How was it possible that I suddenly felt as if I were choking from the stifling air? Even noticing that nobody else who was dining on the terrace seemed to be having the least bit of difficulty didn't help me catch my breath.

"But I've really enjoyed the experience." Nick sounded remarkably cheerful for someone whose dinner companion was about to pass out. Then again, maybe he was so caught up in what he was saying that he didn't notice. "And I'm really glad that taking our relationship to the next level has worked out so well. In fact, I'm sure that you've thought of the possibility of—"

"Who gets the macadamia-encrusted mahimahi?"

I was so relieved when our waiter showed up with two steaming plates that I nearly threw my arms around him. Of course, he was naked from the waist up, since he was wearing nothing but a big piece of fabric, albeit an exceptionally modest and extremely tasteful one. Even in my advanced state of anxiety, I knew that hugging strange men who looked completely qualified to pose for the Hunks of Hawaii calender wasn't exactly a recipe for a successful romantic evening.

Fortunately, our dinner entrees turned out to be enough of a distraction that Nick seemed to forget all about the unfortunate direction in which our conversation had been heading. In fact, all through dinner and into dessert, I managed to keep the conversation focused on exactly which activities we planned to squeeze into our vacation.

It wasn't until we'd both tasted the dessert we'd agreed to split that I picked up on the fact that the conversation was veering back into dangerous waters again. And here I'd been so happy in the wonderfully safe, clear blue waters of the Pacific that were so perfect for swimming, snorkeling, surfing, and a dozen other activities that caused neither shortness of breath nor heart palpitations.

"You know, Jess," Nick said, taking my hand once again, "there's something important I've wanted to talk to you about all evening. I've just been waiting for the right moment."

The coconut shrimp, macadamia nut–encrusted fish, and all the other delicious food that had been sitting in my stomach so happily suddenly felt like lead. Extremely thick layers of it.

What on earth makes you think this is the right moment? I wanted to demand. *Here we've been having such a nice time, scarfing down fabulous food and sipping sweet, fruity drinks that look as if they've been decorated by a professional florist and listening to wonderfully tacky Hawaiian music . . . Why ruin it?*

"But it's so late!" I cried. "And . . . and we have this extremely huge macadamia nut ice cream concoction to finish."

"We really need to have this talk," he insisted, stroking my hand.

I desperately wanted to curl said hand around a spoon and focus on much more immediate and considerably less stressful pastimes.

But before I had a chance to point out that our ice cream was melting, Nick gave my hand a squeeze, then held it even more tightly. "Jessie," he said slowly, "I've been thinking about Marnie Burton's murder."

Is *that* all, I thought, feeling all the air rush out of my lungs in a sudden burst of relief. And here I'd been afraid he was talking about something really frightening, like the *other* M word that had done such a fine job of ruining our last trip to Hawaii.

"And this . . . this compulsion you have to investigate murders," he continued.

I suppose it was his use of the word *compulsion*, but the air between us suddenly felt colder than the dessert in front of me. I'd had no idea the weather in Hawaii was so changeable.

It's true I have a little something invested in Marnie Burton's murder, I thought. Especially since I'm convinced I could be the murderer's next target. But excuse me for being *compulsive* about it. . . .

"What about it?" I said calmly, deciding to act like a grown-up, or at least give my best imitation of one.

Nick sighed. "I realize that when it comes to that particular subject, I may have come across as kind of an ogre in the past. Especially on this trip." Wearing a lopsided grin, he pushed up the hair on both sides of his head, right over his ears. "Take a look. Have I sprouted those funny-shaped horn things?"

"I've definitely seen signs of horniness," I replied seriously, "but not on your head."

"Good. At least things haven't gotten that far." He dropped his arms to his sides and sighed. "Look, Jess, it's not that I don't want to support you in anything you decide to do. I admire your strength and your initiative and your intelligence and . . . and all those other things that make me love you.

"But, honestly, murder?" he continued. "Is there anything more dangerous? I mean, you've gotten involved in three or four investigations over the last year or so, and each time you've come really close to getting seriously hurt—or worse. Do you have any idea how it makes me feel, knowing that you keep getting into such horrific situations and that you're bringing it all on yourself?"

I could feel my defensiveness slipping away. Logic like that was hard to argue with. Nick was absolutely right. When it came to murder, I did seem to have a knack for being in the wrong place at the wrong time. And more than once, I'd found myself in a life-threatening situation. I had no one to blame but myself—and my dogged determination to find out who had committed such heinous crimes.

Nick reached over and took my hand again. "Jess, just think of how you'd react if Max or Cat or Prometheus, or let's say a friend like Betty, ever got into a situation like some of the scrapes you've been in—"

"Stop!" I cried. He was right. The very idea of someone I really loved, be it a human, canine, feline, or avian friend, becoming involved in any of the nightmare-inducing scenarios I'd found myself in over the past fourteen months was enough to freeze every drop of blood in my body.

"You're right, Nick," I said, squeezing his hand. "I never really stopped to think about how all this affects you."

He took a deep breath. "That said, I've decided that you are who you are. And that I should stop making things even more difficult for you and do whatever I can to support you. And to help you. After all, you have to do what you think is right. I know I'll never be able to keep myself from worrying about you—or wishing you'd stop—but I can work a little harder at helping you." Grinning, he added, "Or at least supply you with all the Chinese food you need to recharge after a long, trying day."

I blinked, still half-expecting a punch line that

would totally contradict what he'd just said. None came.

"Thanks, Nick," I finally said. My voice sounded oddly husky. "That means a lot to me. And I want you to know that I never intended to spoil our vacation. I really wanted it to be great."

"And it's *been* great," he replied. "I mean, come on: Hawaii? How could that not be great? Besides, it's time for one of the best parts of every vacation."

"What's that?" I asked, puzzled.

"It's time to go to bed."

Finally, the two of us were on the same page.

Chapter 8

"There are two means of refuge from the misery of life—music and cats."

—Albert Schweitzer

"Are you sure you don't want me to come with you?" Nick offered early the next morning. "I don't want you to think I didn't mean what I said last night, about being helpful."

The two of us were lounging on our hotel room's lanai, sipping Hawaiian coffee and gorging on fluffy banana pancakes doused with the wonderfully ubiquitous coconut syrup I feared I was becoming addicted to. Of course, I was fully aware that I was also becoming addicted to smelling sweet, fragrant flowers wherever I went, wearing footwear that allowed my toes along with the rest of my body to enjoy the breeze, and basking in the sunshine even though the calendar insisted it was January—all dangerous habits for someone whose real life was based in the Northeast.

"Thanks, but I really think I have a better chance of pulling this off if I'm alone," I told him. While I was fairly confident about my acting abilities, my mission for that morning—pretending to be Marnie's sister in an attempt to gain access to her apartment—struck me as something that would be easier without an audience.

"In that case," Nick asked, "do you mind if I do some hiking in the Haleakala crater today, the way I planned?"

"Nope. Go for it. We can meet back here in the room later this afternoon." I hesitated before adding, "Nick? Thanks."

"Just be safe, okay?" He took me in his arms and held me for a very long time.

Knowing I could count on him for support as I forged ahead with my investigation of Marnie Burton's murder gave me a newfound sense of strength, not to mention determination. As soon as I kissed him goodbye and sent him on his way, armed with a hat, hiking shoes, drinking water and a large bottle of sunblock, I set to work preparing for my morning's outing. I folded up my canvas tote bag so I could carry it into Marnie's place without anyone noticing. Then I stopped at the front desk to ask directions to the address I'd found on the electric bill in her desk, climbed into my rented Jeep, and took off for Paia, a former sugar town on the island's northern coast that had also been Marnie's home here on Maui.

When I checked the map beside me on the front seat, I saw that Paia was located just east of Kahului Airport. It was also near Kanaha Beach Park, where Marnie's body had been found. Still, as I coasted into town, I tried to think about the time she had spent living here, not the fact that she had died just a few miles away.

I was instantly charmed. Paia's few streets housed an eclectic mix of the old and the new. I spotted a health-food store, an Internet café, an arts-and-crafts cooperative, and a store specializing in products made with hemp. I also saw a mom-and-pop grocery store, a fish market, and a hardware store that looked as if it hadn't updated its inventory since 1973.

While Marnie's personality hadn't exactly fit in with the town's mellowness, I could understand why she had chosen to live here. Paia offered all the conveniences of life in the twenty-first century, but its one- and two-story wooden buildings still reflected its origins—even though many of the facades had been painted bright colors like purple, orange, and turquoise.

The small apartment complex in which she'd lived, Palm Breezes Court, was at the end of a quiet residential street at the edge of town. Six or eight squat wooden buildings were packed onto a modest-size square of land, giving them the appearance of a housing project rather than homes for up-and-coming professionals. Then again, Holly Gruen had told me herself that the *Dispatch* didn't pay its reporters all that well.

I parked the Jeep halfway down the block, not wanting to call attention to the fact that I was snooping. Then I strolled back casually, double-checking the electric bill to make sure I had the apartment number right.

I found her apartment easily. It was in back, with a view of what looked like the rain forest. I could hear the roosters that live all over the Hawaiian Islands crowing, and I wondered how anybody could get any sleep with their windows open.

Stepping onto the three-foot-by-three-foot concrete square that served as the front porch, I glanced from side to side, making sure no one was around. And then, my heart pounding as loudly as the drum accompanying a Samoan war dance, I put my hand on the doorknob and tried to turn it.

It didn't budge.

I just stood there, wondering what on earth I'd been thinking. Did I really believe Hawaii was so laid back that I'd be able to waltz into a near stranger's apartment—a near stranger who also happened to be a murder victim, no less?

I was considering bonking myself on the forehead and yelping "Doh!" Homer Simpson–style, when I heard, "Can I help you with something?"

The unexpected sound of a human voice made me whirl around in surprise. Behind me stood a slender Asian-American woman, probably no more than thirty. She was dressed in a beige business suit and black high heels, and her straight black hair was primly pulled back into a bun. She was not only wearing dark red lipstick; she also had matching nails that were long enough and sharp enough that I immediately ascertained she was someone I wouldn't want to tangle with.

Figuring she had to be an authority figure, I decided to take a wild guess. "Are you the landlady?"

A look of annoyance flickered across her face. "I work for the property management company, if that's what you mean. And you are . . . ?"

"Marnie Burton was my sister. She lived in this apartment."

She looked startled, but only a moment passed before her stern businesswoman-on-the-rise look returned. "Do you have any ID?" she asked crisply.

"Of course." Without hesitation, I opened my purse and retrieved my New York State driver's license.

She glanced at it, then at me. "Your name isn't Burton."

"Popper is my married name."

"I see." She handed my license back to me. Even though neither of us was about to admit that we'd accomplished absolutely nothing by that little exchange, she pretended to be satisfied that I was who I said I was, now that I'd actually produced a government-issued document with my photo on it.

"I suppose you heard about what happened to my sister," I said, anxious not to lose the little momentum I'd gained.

"Of course," she replied flatly. "What a tragedy. I'm so sorry."

"Thank you. I flew out here as soon as I heard. As you can imagine, there are so many things to settle. One of them is shipping my sister's things back to our parents' house in Ellensburg. That's in Washington State."

I added that last part about Marnie's hometown to sound as if I knew what I was talking about. Realistically, I figured this employee of the property-management company probably didn't have the slightest idea where Marnie was from.

So I had to force myself not to show my surprise when she replied, "Sure. She mentioned that was where she grew up. I'm from Tacoma myself." I guess our little talk about common geography softened her a bit, because she added, "By the way, I'm Amy Inoke."

"Pleased to meet you, Amy," I returned, marveling over how good I was becoming at fooling people. I turned back to the front door of the apartment and sighed. "I was hoping I'd find her place unlocked, which is stupid, of course. But I don't have a key."

"I can let you in." She hesitated, then added, "I'd need you to sign some forms, of course."

"Of course." Given how promising things were looking, I was ready to sign anything.

"If you'll just give me a minute . . ."

I waited no more than five, keeping busy by

watching a tiny green gecko scramble up and down a pale pink stucco wall. To me, it was more engrossing than watching TV.

When Amy returned, she was carrying a clipboard. "If you'll just sign here and here . . ."

I wrote my real name on all the dotted lines without worrying too much about what I was agreeing to. It did occur to me, however, that it would be great if Nick could get himself through law school a little faster. Despite my initial resistance to him joining what I considered a questionable trade at best, more and more I was coming to realize that having a lawyer around might not be such a bad thing.

"There we go," I told Amy, confidently handing back the clipboard with my John Hancock scrawled all over it.

I expected her to hand over the key, turn on her treacherously high heel, and hurry off to do something useful like hassle the other tenants. Instead, she unlocked the door herself and walked in, stepping to one side to let me in.

"Thanks," I said, flashing her a smile. Underneath my calm facade, however, I was wondering how I'd ever manage to do the snooping I so desperately wanted to do with her watching me. "Uh, do you think I could get a copy of the key? I'm going to have to get some boxes and tape, then come back. I just wanted to check the place out to see how many I'll need."

"Are your parents coming too?" Amy asked.

I opened my mouth without having yet decided what words would be coming out of it just as her cell phone emitted an annoying little song.

"Sorry," she told me, without sounding at all sorry. "I've got to get this."

"Feel free. I'll just look around."

I stepped into the apartment, finding myself in a

good-size living room with sliding glass doors along the back wall. They opened onto a small concrete lanai, with a grassy area just beyond. The bedroom was on the left and the tiny kitchen was on the right. The rooms were sparsely furnished, with a sagging couch, an unmade double bed, a few low tables, and a small TV on a plastic milk crate.

I was immediately struck by the fact that Marnie's apartment reflected the same sense of chaos I'd felt by just talking to her. The sink was filled with dishes soaking in cloudy gray water, and mounds of unopened junk mail littered the kitchen counter. Her discarded clothes were strewn everywhere. A kimono-style bathrobe lay in a heap on the floor next to her bed, a bathing suit had been tossed over the towel rack in the bathroom, and a T-shirt was balled up in one corner of the couch.

The disorderliness carried over to her work area. Her laptop sat on a cheap-looking table with a Formica top designed to look like wood. It was surrounded by disheveled piles of paper, manila file folders, articles clipped from newspapers, pens without their tops, pads of brightly colored Post-its, and all the other paraphernalia of a home office.

But I also spotted signs of her love for her new island home. Half a dozen copies of *Hawaii Magazine* sat in a stack on the floor next to the TV. Through the open bedroom door, I could see a neon lamp made of green and yellow tubes that formed the outline of a palm tree. The walls of both the living room and the bedroom were decorated with travel posters featuring the islands' beaches, sunsets, and palm trees.

I was still taking in my surroundings when I heard a high-pitched cry. Instinctively, I jerked my head around. If I hadn't known better, I would have thought there was a cat in the apartment.

It *was* a cat, I discovered. A coal-black cat with large golden eyes had sneaked up behind me. He was looking up at me questioningly, and from the plaintive tone of his voice he seemed to be asking, "Would somebody please tell me what's going on here?"

"You poor little guy!" I cooed. I crouched down and waited for him to approach me, which is never a bad idea with an animal you don't know, including cats. He came right over and started rubbing against my legs. I wasn't surprised he was so hungry for human interaction, since he'd probably been completely on his own for three days. Which also meant he was undoubtedly hungry in other ways too.

"I'll get you some water and something to eat," I assured him in a soft voice, reaching down and stroking his soft black fur. He looked at me gratefully with his huge yellow eyes and mewed.

I noticed then that he wore a bright blue metal ID tag around his neck. It was etched with Marnie's phone number, as well as his name. Moose. His name implied that his kittenhood had been spent in Washington, rather than Hawaii. At least, if the availability of the animal that had served as his namesake was any indication. And that meant he had accompanied Marnie on her transoceanic trek, serving as her sidekick as she moved to a new place to embark upon the new life she so desperately wanted for herself.

"If you look at your lease," I could hear Amy barking into her cell phone, "you'll see that's not at all what it says."

Her sharp voice reminded me why I was here—and that I had to work quickly. She would be coming into the apartment any moment now, and my claim that I was about to become one of UPS's best customers aside, I knew that I'd never have the chance to come back here again. I suspected that Marnie's real relatives were winging their way across the Pacific Ocean at this very moment, bracing themselves for the heartwrenching experience of sorting through their deceased daughter's possessions.

For all I knew, they could show up at any minute.

I hadn't even had the chance to step into the bedroom before I heard Amy saying, "Why don't you call me back after you've had a chance to look at it." My heart sank when I turned and saw her standing right outside the front door, still clutching her phone as if loosening her grip on it just a tad might prove fatal.

"I've got to make a few more calls," she told me apologetically. "Sorry."

"No problem," I assured her, thinking, Yes! Let's hear it for cell phones!

It was only then I noticed that the expression on her face was stricken.

"What," she asked deliberately, "is *that*?"

My first response was to feel guilty. I assumed she'd just realized that I'd brought along a large empty tote bag and that somehow she'd figured out my intention to fill it with items I really had no right to take. But a second later I realized I wasn't the one in trouble; it was my four-legged friend.

"It looks like my sister had a cat," I replied. Trying to soften the blow of what she clearly perceived as bad news, I added, "His name is Moose."

"No animals allowed!" she shot back shrilly. "That's specifically stated in the lease."

Great, I thought grimly. Now I'm going to be fined for my imaginary sister's transgression.

But what mattered to me even more was the little guy's future.

"I'll take him with me," I promised, hoping that would get all three of us—Marnie, Moose, and me—off the hook.

"You're darned right you will," Amy barked. And then she turned her back and began punching a number in to her cell phone.

I didn't give myself a chance to wonder how on earth I was ever going to cope with caring for a pussycat, given the fact that at the moment I was living in a hotel. Not when I had much more pressing matters to deal with. I realized I'd better move fast.

I dashed into the kitchen, grabbed a bowl off a shelf and filled it with water, then opened one cabinet door after another until I located Marnie's cache of cat food. I pulled the lid off a can of a tuna and shrimp combo that seemed like something a cat living on a tropical island would like, then dumped it into a second bowl while my famished feline friend watched eagerly. He immediately got busy filling up his empty tummy. Once I was sure he was all set, I went back to work.

I decided to start in the living room, which I'd already identified as Marnie's home office. I figured it was the most likely place to find clues about what was going on in her life. I headed directly for the papers on her makeshift desk, most of which were stuffed into manila folders. Each folder was labeled with a topic that I assumed she had been researching for a possible story. Hawaii Power & Light. Governor Wickham. FloraTech. There were at least eight or ten others.

Inside, she had tucked away handwritten notes, typed notes, lists, names and phone numbers, and even clippings from other newspapers on the same subject. While she didn't appear to have followed any particular system in organizing the research materials she'd amassed, I suspected that she knew precisely what was in each and every folder.

There were also loose pages, some held together

with paper clips and some stapled together, lying among the folders. They appeared to be drafts of articles she was working on. They were filled with mentions of names and places I didn't recognize.

Marnie was a busy woman, I thought. But the revelation that she'd been working on a dozen different stories filled me with dismay. The possibility of ever reading through all her files and identifying anything that looked suspicious or pointed to any clues about her murder was looking less and less likely.

Still, this time around I had help. Maybe I could get my own recently recruited sidekick, Nick, to put some time into weeding through Marnie's endless collection of papers. He might be well on his way to becoming a lawyer, but something told me that kind of task was probably still very familiar to him from his private-eye days. After glancing at the doorway to make sure Amy wasn't watching me, I stuck the files in my tote bag.

When I'd exhausted my search of Marnie's desk without finding anything else that seemed worth appropriating, I headed into her bedroom. The clock was ticking and my heart was pounding.

"I'd hate to get our lawyers involved . . ." I heard Amy threatening.

I scanned the room quickly, wondering where to look. I darted over to the dresser, opened the top drawer, and peered inside. Nothing but practical cotton underwear and a few other pieces of no-nonsense lingerie. The other drawers didn't yield anything interesting either.

I checked her closet, but there was nothing but clothes. Then I noticed that the small table next to her bed had a drawer. I opened it, bracing myself against the possibility of finding a gun or something similarly shocking.

What I found in there was shocking, all right. But it wasn't anything that was fired by gunpowder.

It was a photograph of a naked man sprawled across Marnie's bed. A naked man with a big grin on his face, a leering look in his eyes, and an extraordinarily large penis.

Ace.

Whoa! I thought. So it *wasn't* his big blue eyes that Marnie found so irresistible!

But there was something I found even more intriguing than this potential exhibit at the Ripley's Believe It or Not museum.

Tucked underneath was a business card from Ace's Auto Artists. On the bottom was printed his name, *Ashton "Ace" Atwood,* and what was no doubt his business phone number. And handwritten on back, no doubt by Marnie, were the words, *Home: 254 Hukelani Street, Wailuku.*

Ace's home address. I jammed it into my pocket, wondering how the police had managed to miss these two gems. I supposed they were just so certain Marnie's killer had been the man she'd been seen leaving the Purple Mango with that they figured their investigation should center on learning his identity.

I rifled through the drawer, curious about what other wonders I might find in there. I found a few photographs—some of Marnie and a couple of her with Ace. I took those too, figuring they might come in handy.

Encouraged by what I'd found so far, I slipped back into the tiny kitchen. As soon as I did, my eyes lit on the short, squat refrigerator.

You can tell a lot about people by what they keep in their refrigerators.

But before I could get my paws on it, Amy appeared behind me, posing in the doorway with one hand on her hip. Not surprisingly, she still tightly grasped her cell phone in the other.

"Are you almost done in here?" she asked. She sounded exasperated, as if having one of her company's tenants get murdered was really messing up her to-do list.

"Almost," I told her. "Let me check the fridge. If there's anything in there that could spoil, it might be getting smelly." Anxious to drive the point home, I added, "Like an open can of cat food."

The look of alarm that my comment elicited told me she was already thinking about the next tenants—and the apartment's rentability. Real estate agents were famous for telling current residents to bake bread or cinnamon cookies when showing their house or apartment in order to make it more appealing to prospective buyers or renters. They rarely recommended using the smells of rotting fruit and moldering cheese and—heaven forbid—over-the-hill cat food wafting from the refrigerator as an effective means of adding ambience.

"Be my guest," Amy offered. And just in case some of that rotting and moldering and other unspeakable processes had already gotten under way, she removed herself from the kitchen instead of keeping an eye on what I was doing.

As I opened the door, I was surprised to see that the Queen of Chaos's kitchen was surprisingly orderly. Or maybe it was just that food was of so little consequence to her that a well-stocked refrigerator simply wasn't a priority. Her refrigerator told me she was one of those people who tended to eat on the go, grabbing whatever she could while darting around the island, nosing out news. Personally, I found that method worked pretty well for me too.

The painfully bare shelves of the small refrigerator

contained nothing besides three cartons of yogurt, a half-empty quart of skim milk, and an unopened package of American cheese, with each slice individually wrapped. I also found wilted salad makings in the vegetable drawer and a few pieces of fruit that were well on their way to becoming mulch.

My surprise over Marnie's relatively healthy approach to eating aside, I was extremely disappointed. I didn't know what I thought I'd find, but whatever it was, it certainly wasn't about to appear on the La Yogurt label.

I could hear Amy out in the hall, talking on her cell phone again, helping the wheels of business turn. I figured it was only a question of time before she lost patience and bodily dragged me out of there. I slammed the door shut, still discouraged over having learned little besides the fact that Marnie's meal-planning techniques pretty closely adhered to the food pyramid.

On impulse, I opened the freezer door. I didn't really expect to see it crammed with Ben & Jerry's Chunky Monkey, Phish Food, and Cherry Garcia, like mine was. So I was shocked to see that the only thing stored inside, aside from three ice cube trays and some rather large chunks of free-form ice, was a pint of Chocolate Chip Cookie Dough ice cream.

I reached for it, curious about whether Marnie had had a chance to dig into it before her dreadful demise. Somehow, the idea of someone stashing away a treat for later, then never having "later" come to pass, was extremely sad.

As I picked it up, I was surprised at how light it was. In fact, it practically felt empty.

When I pulled off the lid, I discovered that it *was* empty. At least, empty of ice cream.

Inside the cardboard carton was a sandwich-size

Ziploc bag. And inside that was what looked like an 8½-by-11-inch piece of paper, folded in quarters.

Marnie's shopping list? I wondered. Not exactly the most sensible place for her to store it, at least not if she wanted to remember to bring it with her the next time she went to the supermarket.

Maybe it's a list of the top ten reasons ice cream is bad for you, I thought. After glancing around guiltily, I stuck it in my pocket, figuring I'd find out later.

My sneakiness couldn't have been better timed. I'd barely tucked it away when Amy reappeared, cell phone still in hand.

"Jessica? Are you almost done?" she asked archly. "We have a plumbing problem in three-A, and I'd like to get up there right now and check it out."

"I'm done," I told her, even though I wasn't sure whether or not I actually was. "I'm going to need a lot more boxes than I was figuring on," I added with a sad smile.

She nodded understandingly. But before she could make a sympathetic comment, her cell phone trilled its annoying tune once again.

"Go ahead and take that call," I told her, as if there had ever been any question about her doing exactly that. "I'll come back later with some cartons."

"But you're taking that animal with you, right?"

"Definitely," I assured her. I wasn't about to leave poor Moose here for a moment longer than necessary. Especially since Amy clearly had a personal vendetta against him.

She turned away, already engrossed in her call as I slipped out, clutching Marnie's cat in one arm. With the other I patted my pockets, just to make sure the booty I was secreting away was still safe and sound.

• • •

I drove almost a mile with Moose in my lap before pulling over alongside the highway and taking out the Ziploc bag I'd found hidden in Marnie's freezer. My heart pounded as I unfolded the single sheet of paper. For all I knew, it would turn out to be nothing more than a badly written pornographic poem from her extraordinarily well-endowed lover.

It wasn't. It was a handwritten list of names, each one followed by an address and phone number. Most of them had check marks after them, followed by either *YES* or *NO*.

In the upper left corner were two big letters: *FT*.

They could have stood for a lot of things. *FT* could have been someone's initials. They could have meant *future*, as in *things to do in the future*. Or they could have been part of some code Marnie had developed for efficient note-taking. That certainly seemed like something a reporter would do.

FT could have also stood for FloraTech. After all, the new biotech firm that had just opened its headquarters on Maui was a story Marnie had been working on. It was also the subject of the one question she had asked at the governor's press conference the day she was murdered.

I scanned the list, struggling a little with Marnie's handwriting. I read one name after another, not surprised that I didn't recognize any of them.

I froze when I came across one I *did* recognize.

Alice Feeley. The woman who had found Marnie's body on the beach shortly after she was murdered.

Unlike most of the other names, there was no check mark next to it. It was also one of the few listings without the words *YES* or *NO* written next to it.

I folded up the paper, slipped it back into the plastic bag, and carefully slid it into my small flowered backpack. As I did, the name Alice Feeley echoed through my brain as if I were standing at the bottom of a canyon.

Richard Carrera had claimed she was "harmless." And the police didn't seem to suspect her at all.

Yet she had clearly been of interest to Marnie. And that automatically made her of interest to me.

Chapter 9

"Most cats when they are Out want to be In, and vice versa, and often simultaneously."

—Dr. Louis J. Camuti

Moose didn't exactly make a grand entrance into his new home. In fact, I smuggled him into the Royal Banyan Hotel in my tote bag along with Marnie's files. I even tried draping a towel over him as we made our way across the expansive lobby, but he insisted on sticking his head out indignantly—not that I blamed him. At least the bag was deep enough that he couldn't give us away by peeking over the side. He and I rode up in the elevator with three giggling teenage girls and a Japanese couple, but if they were curious about why my beach bag kept meowing, they were too polite to ask.

"Okay, Moose," I announced when we'd reached the room and I'd locked the door behind us. "This is your new home, at least for a little while."

Fortunately, the room had already been cleaned, so I didn't have to worry about anyone coming in and finding my unauthorized guest. At least, not yet. I let him out to do some exploring while I set up the kitty litter box Amy had graciously allowed me to remove from Marnie's apartment. Once again, the argument about possible smells had worked wonders. I also put out bowls of food and water along with all the cat toys I'd rescued from Palm Breezes Court.

"That should do it, Moosie-pie," I told him, picking him up and petting his soft fur once I was sure he had everything he needed. He looked at me and blinked, as if to say, *Not bad. I suppose I could hang here a while.* When I put him down, he leaped onto the king-size bed and curled up right smack in the middle. As far as I could tell, he was having no trouble adjusting to his new digs.

Satisfied that he was settled in, I trotted back down to the veterinary conference, anxious to squeeze in the session on obesity in cats and dogs.

I was genuinely interested in the topic, and I really did try to concentrate on the speaker. I wasn't surprised that he started out by saying an estimated twenty-five to thirty percent of dogs are obese, as are a whopping forty percent of cats. Obesity was a problem I'd been seeing more and more in my own practice, the result of pets getting too much food and not enough exercise. And its negative effects ranged from hypertension to diabetes to locomotion ailments like spinal problems and hip dysplasia.

But I found it difficult to focus on the talk. Instead, I chewed my complimentary plastic pen, which was printed with the name of a popular flea collar, and ruminated about Marnie Burton.

All the bits and pieces of information I'd picked up about the young reporter and the people who knew her kept whirling around inside my head like bits of confetti on a windy day. The more I learned about other people's perceptions of her, the more convinced I was that her murder had been the result of something more than a chance encounter with a stranger in a bar, no matter what Detective Paleka chose to believe.

Of course, that didn't rule out the possibility that Ace had been the person Marnie had last been seen with, coming out of the Purple Mango.

As far as I was concerned, Ace Atwood remained a bit of a puzzle. I understood why he was reluctant to admit to their relationship now, since it was bound to place him high on the cops' list of suspects. But I still hadn't figured out why he would he have acted so oddly *before* her murder. Holly had told me herself that just a few weeks earlier, he'd acted as if he barely knew Marnie, even though Marnie had specifically invited her along to show him off to her. Then there was Marnie's comment about Ace's preference for quiet, out-of-the-way places. That was another peculiar behavior that indicated he was being secretive about their relationship.

But in addition, there were so many other aspects of the victim's life that raised questions. Like her job. Just about everyone I spoke to who had dealt with her in her capacity as a newspaper reporter seemed put off by her intensity. Bryce Bolt had characterized her as "wacky." He'd also accused her of kissing up to their boss. He was clearly disdainful of her. Yet that was hardly a reason to kill a fellow employee.

The same went for Holly Gruen, Bryce's predecessor. From what I'd heard and seen, her relationship with Marnie had been complicated, at least from her end. Aside from that, she was shrouded in mystery herself—especially when it came to why she had left the paper, an unexpected move that had forced her to live on the edge financially. She didn't impress me as someone who was impulsive, yet for some reason she had suddenly decided that the situation at the *Dispatch* was intolerable. Still, the fact that she had behaved a little oddly, and maybe even been mildly obsessed with Marnie, didn't mean she had killed her.

The newspaper's editor, Richard Carrera, saw Marnie Burton's driven approach to her job as a plus. Yet even he seemed surprised by how extreme her dogged determination was. But there was something else about our conversation that stuck with me: his strange reaction when I'd mentioned the tape. He claimed to know nothing about it, yet his eagerness to hear what *I* knew led me to conclude he was lying.

And those were the people who had worked with her. What about the people on the other side of the table—the people she wrote about? Marnie's coworkers in the newsroom had characterized her as someone who always had her eye out for scandal—and who, as a result, tended to see it in even the most unlikely places. It made sense that this inclination of hers would make her a lot of enemies. They may have even included Alice Feeley, who, it turned out, had been linked to Marnie even before she found her body on the beach.

That thought led me to the other work-related notes I'd found at her apartment—specifically, the stack of file folders. Marnie had been poking her nose into all kinds of nooks and crannies. One of the crannies had obviously been FloraTech. At the governor's press conference, I'd seen for myself that it was a topic that really riled her. For all I knew, John Irwin, the governor's aide, had gotten tired of her buzzing around his head like an annoying mosquito that needed to be swatted. . . .

Now you're *really* going off the deep end, I told myself.

Glancing down at my notepad, I saw that I'd made a list of every one of the people I'd spoken to so far. Ace Atwood, Bryce Bolt, Holly Gruen, Richard

Carrera, John Irwin. For all I knew, any one of them could have killed Marnie. And any one of them could have broken into my hotel room to steal the tape she'd left behind.

The frustrating thing was that I still had no idea why.

I decided to try answering the simple questions first, starting with why Ace would continue to lie about his relationship with her. I took a moment to formulate a plan.

Once I did, I reminded myself of the reason I'd come to Hawaii in the first place. I turned my focus back to the speaker, jotting down his advice about turning Fido and Fluffy on to the joys of snacking on carrots and green beans.

• • •

It was late afternoon by the time I left the conference and went back to my hotel room. I opened the door tentatively, anxious to keep Moose from escaping.

I shouldn't have worried. Nick was lounging on the lanai, his bare feet propped up on the metal railing. Moose, in turn, was lounging in his lap, looking extremely contented.

"I see you two have met," I observed as I slid open the glass doors to join them.

"Don't tell me," Nick said with a grin. "You happened to drive by an animal shelter, and you couldn't resist going in. The next thing you knew, you'd made a new addition to your menagerie."

"Moose here certainly needs a new home, but he's not from a shelter," I explained. "He used to belong to Marnie."

"Ah." He stroked the ball of fur in his lap, meanwhile gazing at Moose sympathetically. "Sorry about that, Moose old boy. I guess you really do need a new place to live, don't you?"

"This is only temporary," I assured him. "As soon as I can, I'll find someone here on Maui who can take him. But in the meantime . . ."

"Hey, as long as he doesn't hog the pillows at night, I'm fine with this," Nick insisted.

"Great. Thanks for being so understanding. So how was your hike?"

"Spectacular. But I'll tell you about that later. At the moment, I'm much more interested in what else you found out at Marnie's apartment, aside from the fact that she liked cats. Were there any skeletons in her closet?"

"I'm not sure." I hesitated before asking, "Nick, how would you like to put some of your private investigation skills to work?"

He grimaced. "I just spent four months stuffing my brain with about eight million cases in law school. I don't know if I remember anything from my days as a P.I."

"I have a feeling that everything you learned is still in there somewhere," I returned. "Besides, what I've got in mind shouldn't be that difficult."

"Try me."

"I might not have found any skeletons in Marnie's closets, but I did find a list of names and addresses hidden in her freezer."

Frowning, Nick asked, "The other members of her WeightWatchers' group?"

"I don't think so." I took out the list and handed it to him. "Even though I hardly know anyone on Maui, there is one name on this list that I recognize."

Nick looked surprised. "Which one?"

"Alice Feeley," I told him, pointing. "Richard Carrera, the editor of the newspaper Marnie worked for, told me she's the person who found Marnie's body on the beach. Apparently people around here consider her their local neighborhood eccentric, someone who's got her share of quirks but is basically harmless."

"But suddenly it looks as if she might have been more involved with Marnie than anyone suspected," Nick said thoughtfully.

"Exactly." I was pleased that he had drawn the same conclusion I had. I guessed that saying about great minds thinking alike was true after all.

Then he pointed to the initials on top. *"FT,"* he read aloud. "What's that?"

"I'm not sure, but one possibility is that *FT* stands for FloraTech. It's a new biotech firm that just opened its headquarters here on Maui. Apparently they claim to have discovered medicinal value in the hibiscus. Marnie was working on a story on the company right before she was killed."

"And you don't think the reason her notes ended up in her fridge is that she absentmindedly stashed them there during a midnight raid?"

"Actually, I think there was a lot more to it. She'd put this list inside a Ziploc bag, which tells me she was trying to protect it. Then, to hide it, she stashed it in an empty Ben and Jerry's carton."

"Hmm. In that case, I'd have to agree." He handed it back to me. "Tell me more about FloraTech."

"I don't know much. That's why I need a good P.I. I thought you might be willing to take on the job of finding out anything you can about it. I have a folder filled with notes Marnie was gathering on the company. I also have a few folders with her notes and research materials from the other stories she was working on. I was hoping you might be able to look through those too. There might be something in one of them that would give us an idea whether anyone could have considered her passion for uncovering dirt dangerous enough to want her out of the picture."

I took a deep breath. "And if I'm not pushing my luck here, I also hoped you'd be willing to see what you could find out about another reporter at the *Dispatch,* Bryce Bolt. When I asked him about his background, he got pretty defensive. It made me think he might be hiding something."

"Sure," he agreed with a little shrug. "Glad to be of service. In fact, it'll be fun to get back into the business for a while. Sometimes I miss the thrill of the hunt. Ferreting out information, doing stakeouts, chasing after the bad guys—"

"Speaking of stakeouts," I interjected, "I don't suppose you're in the mood for one . . . like right now?"

Nick's face lit up. "Sure. What have you got in mind?"

"You mean *who* have I got in mind. And the answer is Ace Atwood. Marnie told me he was her boyfriend, yet there seem to be some questions about the true nature of their relationship. We have some time before we meet Betty and Winston at the luau, and I thought I'd use it to try to find out a little more about him."

"I'm all over it!" Nick was already on his feet, with Moose still cradled in his arms. Regretfully, he told him, "Sorry, bud. You'll have to stay here. Not that you don't have potential, but we don't need any distractions. Maybe next time."

While Nick explained the situation to Moose, I tried to put together some sort of disguise, or at least an outfit that would keep Ace from recognizing me if I was actually lucky enough to spot him. Since I'm one of those people who's obsessed with packing light, I didn't have much to work with. In the end, I decided that sunglasses and my canvas sun hat, pulled down low to cover my hair, would have to do.

I also made sure I brought along the business card I'd found in Marnie's drawer, the one with his address written on back. Just in case I lost it, I'd memorized the words, *Home: 254 Hukelani Street, Wailuku.*

"Ready?" I asked my sidekick.

Nick just grinned. I could see he was really looking forward to this.

• • •

Maui's simple road system was already becoming as familiar to me as the intricate web of highways and byways that cover Long Island. It was another beautiful day, and Nick and I rode along Honoapiilani Highway with all the windows down. I had to admit, it was extra nice having him along. I tried to remember if Ned Nickerson ever accompanied Nancy Drew in all those novels I'd read when I was young. If he had, it was no wonder she'd been so fond of spending most of her time running around, solving mysteries.

According to my map, the street on which Ace lived wasn't too far from the police station, so finding it was a breeze. I hoped accomplishing my goal of actually spotting him would be as easy.

"This is it," I muttered as I turned onto Hukelani Street. "His house is number two fifty-four."

"Not exactly the high-rent district," Nick observed.

I had to agree. Hukelani Street turned out to be a quiet road lined with half a dozen small, shabby houses. Not quite the ocean-view palaces tourists picture when they fantasize about living on Maui. Then again, Ace hadn't exactly struck me as a man who was clambering up the ladder of success.

Number 254 was at the end, the last house on the right. The condition of the place Ace Atwood called home bore out my theory. The house itself was nondescript, a single-level bungalow half hidden by the overgrown bushes and trees crowded onto the tiny front lawn. Jammed into the short driveway were no fewer than three vehicles—a dusty pickup truck with a badly dented passenger side door and two cars that might have been considered vintage if they didn't look as if a slight tap would send all the metal crashing to the ground. The sorry condition of his fleet was quite a surprise, given his line of business.

"The guy certainly seems to like cars," Nick commented. "Especially cars that have been totally trashed."

"Maybe he gets so tired of working on other people's junkers all day that he has no energy left to work on his own," I suggested.

"It sure looks that way."

Fortunately, there were a few other vehicles parked on the narrow street, much nicer ones that probably belonged to Ace's neighbors. That made my rented Jeep Wrangler much less conspicuous as I parked right across the street from his house. Still, I pulled my hat down as low as it would go, then began the arduous task of doing absolutely nothing.

Nick squinted at the side door, which was less than a hundred feet away. "Okay, now I'm starting to get curious about this guy. How will I recognize him?"

"Try to imagine the guy from *Saturday Night Fever* once he hit forty."

"Gotcha," Nick replied. Dryly, he added, "I can hardly wait."

For me, doing nothing is one of the most difficult things in the world. Within about thirty seconds, my hands start to get fidgety. My brain too. Usually, if I'm waiting in a car, I find something to do, like rearrange the bills in my wallet so they all face front, or grab the owner's manual out of the glove compartment and catch up on fun facts like what the optimal tire pressure should be.

This time I didn't dare. I was too afraid of missing my target.

"Nick," I asked, "when you did this for a living, how did you keep yourself from getting bored out of your skull?"

"Actually, that's a real problem with stakeouts," he replied seriously. "It's easy to fall asleep or get distracted by something else you've been staring at just to keep your mind working. Drinking coffee helps, although then the lack of bathroom facilities can become a problem." He reached across the front seat and took my hand. "Of course, having somebody to talk to is always useful. As long as the conversation doesn't become so engrossing that you forget what you're there for."

With that thought in mind, we chatted for a while, being careful not to talk about anything too interesting. But knowing that you're talking because you're *supposed* to be talking makes it really hard to come up with things to talk about.

Through it all, I sat with my eyes fixed on Ace's house. When Nick and I ran out of topics of conversation that were sufficiently mindless, I tried to remember the capital of each state, beginning with the East Coast and moving west.

I was starting to feel as if I'd been sitting in that spot forever, but finally, just as I got stuck on Idaho, our vigilance paid off. The side door of the house swung open, and who came loping out but Ace himself.

"That's him," I muttered, my heart suddenly pounding. Here I'd just started wondering if I was wasting my time. Yet this was turning out to be my lucky day. At least I hoped so. Part of me worried that my plan to learn more about Ace would end in disaster, since he impressed me as someone who wouldn't exactly appreciate being followed, especially by a busybody like me who he undoubtedly thought asked too many questions. Part of me was afraid of something even worse: that I wouldn't find out anything new at all.

"You were right," Nick commented. "*Saturday Night Fever,* alive and well on Maui."

Ace wasn't alone. Scampering gleefully beside him was a fair-size dog that looked as if his lineage included some German shepherd and some Rottweiler. Whether the keys in Ace's hand were responsible for his canine companion's exhilaration or it was simply the joie de vivre that ninety-nine percent of all dogs routinely exhibit, I couldn't say.

I smiled at the sight of the enthusiastic pup, then forced myself to focus on Ace. After all, it wasn't his dog that was the murder suspect.

Ace opened the passenger-side door of his pickup truck, then called, "Come on, Buddy. Climb in." Once his trusty companion was sitting shotgun, his tongue hanging out as if he were thinking excitedly, *Oh, boy! I can't believe we're going for a ride!* Ace climbed into the driver's seat and backed out of his driveway.

My heart began to pound even harder.

"Let's go," Nick urged. "Now comes the fun part."

Nodding in agreement, I turned the key in the ignition. I followed the pickup truck, driving at what I hoped anyone who observed me—Ace, for example—would consider a moseying pace. I even switched on the radio, hoping the soft rock that came floating out would help me stay in my moseying mode.

As soon as I began tailing him, it occurred to me that since Ace was a car guy, he might notice the Jeep that just happened to be right behind him looked familiar. Fortunately, scrappy vehicles like the one I was driving were common on Maui. I hoped that would keep him from peering into the rearview mirror with too much interest.

My theory seemed to hold. Ace drove at a leisurely pace for nearly two miles with his left arm stuck out the window on his side of the cab. Buddy, meanwhile, rode with his entire head jutting out the passenger-side window. Keeping up was easy. So was hiding the fact that I was following him. Since there was only one road on this part of the island, there was enough traffic on it that I could blend in, but not so much that I had to worry about losing him. Following someone on Maui was turning out to be a lot easier than it was at home. A complicated system of streets, highways, and expressways crisscrossed all over Long Island, and most of them were clogged with traffic. When it came to choosing a place whose geography was conducive to solving crimes, Magnum, P.I. clearly had the right idea.

"You're doing great," Nick commented.

"Thanks for the encouragement," I replied.

"No, I mean it. You're a natural. You're focused, you're cool-headed . . . I could have used somebody like you back in the day."

"See that?" I couldn't resist interjecting. "Turns out I'm pretty good at investigating murders."

When Ace pulled up at the front entrance of a nondescript office building, I nosed into a parking space on the other side of the lot. The good news was that from that vantage point, Nick and I could see everything he did. The bad news was that his actions consisted of nothing more exciting than sitting in his truck with the motor running.

Fool's errand? I wondered, knowing exactly who would turn out to be the fool.

As I fought the temptation to lose heart, I noticed some movement. Someone—a woman—had come out of the office building. She was dressed in a business suit, but the inexpensive-looking kind that was made of a shiny fabric. Whatever sense of authority the suit was designed to convey was pretty much contradicted by her large, flashy jewelry, which included gold hoop earrings the size of saucers and enough bracelets for an entire troupe of belly dancers. The same went for her hair, which was dyed a jarring shade of red and looked as if it had been mercilessly fluffed and teased before it was frozen in place with a frightening amount of hairspray.

In other words, she looked like just the kind of woman a guy like Ace was likely to find attractive.

"Look, he came here to pick her up," I pointed out. "Maybe I should get out of the car and go over there."

"Go for it," Nick urged. "But you need a plan. What's your excuse for being here? Even more important, what are you trying to find out?"

I thought fast, trying to decide what to do. But not fast enough. Before I could come up with a strategy, Ace and his gal pal sped out of the parking lot, disappearing down a side street before I even managed to start my car.

"Damn!" I muttered. "I missed them." By this point, I was really feeling like that proverbial fool.

"But you have some new information," Nick noted. "You know where his girlfriend works."

"How do we know she's his girlfriend?" I countered, wanting to consider every possible angle. "I mean, she could be his sister or . . . or . . ."

And then, on impulse, I retrieved the scratched and broken sunglasses I'd stashed in the glove compartment the day I rented the car.

"Where are you going?" Nick demanded.

"To find out who that woman is."

"Have you worked out your strategy?"

I just held up the sunglasses, then headed inside.

I didn't expect to be lucky enough to find any signs of life in the lobby of the building. In fact, I thought I'd simply end up perusing the directory that I figured would be posted on the wall and that my idea about how I could use the sunglasses would go to waste. So the rate of my heartbeat picked up considerably when I saw that the building actually came equipped with a living, breathing human being: a security guard.

The tall, beefy man with straight black hair shorn to a stubble was sitting behind a high counter, reading the *Maui News*.

"Excuse me," I asked him politely as I approached, "but did you happen to notice that woman who just left?"

He put down his newspaper and peered at me. "What about her?"

"I think she dropped these sunglasses." I held them up as proof, hoping he wouldn't notice what bad shape they were in. "I ran after her so I could return them, but she took off before I could get her attention."

"I'll take 'em," he offered. "And I'll make sure Mrs. Atwood gets 'em."

"Thanks," I said calmly, handing the security guard the battered sunglasses.

But I wasn't feeling calm on the inside. Bingo! I thought, as a lightbulb the size of a neon sign in the middle of Times Square went off in my head. So good old Ace has a missus!

Suddenly it all made sense. Ace was a married man who had been having a fling with Marnie. No wonder he preferred taking her to "romantic" restaurants whose main selling point was that they were out of the way. That would also explain why he got so upset whenever she was late, since whenever he was with her, the clock was ticking. It could have also been the reason he was so reluctant to show any affection for her when they were out in public with Holly.

And now that Marnie had been murdered, he was probably more frightened than ever that the truth about their relationship would come out.

I walked back to the car slowly, thinking hard. Marnie said he had something important to tell her the night she was killed. She had assumed he was going to ask her to marry him. But knowing that he was already married, it was at least as likely that he had planned to break up with her. Maybe his wife was getting suspicious . . . or maybe he was just growing tired of his duplicitous life.

At any rate, if he had broken up with her, there was no doubt Marnie wouldn't have taken the news well. That could have led to an argument, perhaps threats that she would tell Mrs. Atwood what had been going on . . .

Even though the day was warm, a chill suddenly ran through me.

I now knew that Ace had an important secret. Which raised an important question: Just how far had he been willing to go to try to keep it?

• • •

"Poor kid," Nick mused as we drove back toward the hotel. "From what you've told me, it sounds as if Marnie had no idea Ace was married."

"It seems she thought being careful not to be seen with her in public was just one of Ace's charming little idiosyncrasies," I agreed.

The fact that Ace was married—and the important something he planned to tell Marnie the night she was murdered—made me more curious than ever about what had transpired between them Sunday night.

"Nick," I said, "I'd like to check out the restaurant

where Ace and Marnie had dinner the night she was murdered."

"I'm with you," he replied. "What's the name of the restaurant?"

"I'm not sure. But I think I know how I can find out."

"Not tonight, though," Nick said. "We have that luau thing with Betty and Winston."

"Right," I replied, glancing at my watch.

I'd assumed it was getting late, since the sky was streaked with the purples and oranges of a typically gorgeous Maui sunset. But I'd forgotten that darkness falls early in the subtropics. It was actually a lot earlier than it seemed.

Which got me thinking.

"Nick," I said thoughtfully, "we're not meeting Betty and Winston until eight, and it's just after six. That gives us some time to do some more poking around. Since we're already out and all."

"What have you got in mind?" he asked.

"There's still one important spot I haven't checked out yet," I told him, "and one important person I haven't met: Alice Feeley."

"Let's go for it," he urged.

"That's my boy," I returned, flashing him a big grin.

According to the newspaper report, Alice had found Marnie's body on a remote stretch of beach on Kahului Bay, west of Kanaha Beach Park. Studying my map in the fading light, I located the park right away, a few miles away on the island's northern coast.

I hoped we'd find Alice Feeley as easily.

It was just after six twenty when Nick and I pulled into the large parking lot of Kanaha Beach Park. The park was identified by a wooden sign held in place by two concrete slabs. A thick growth of bushes and trees framed a white sand beach. It even had a rustic pavilion that, according to a sign, was the headquarters of the Lae 'ula O Kai Canoe Club.

"This park is probably beautiful during the day," Nick commented, glancing around.

"But after nightfall, like now, it's pretty darned spooky," I countered.

The fact that there was no lighting didn't help. While the three-quarter moon provided just enough light for me to make out the imposing mountains in the distance, it wasn't bright enough to make it safe to walk without tripping over a coconut or other beach debris. As Nick and I began strolling along the beach, I flicked on the tiny flashlight I always carried on my key chain, glad I was one of those people who subscribed to the Girl Scout motto: Be prepared.

Still, when a dark shape darted in front of us, I let out a yelp.

"Relax, Jess!" Nick insisted. "It's only a cat."

It was too late. My heart was already pounding and adrenaline was spurting through my body at an alarming rate.

"It looks like a feral cat," I observed, noticing with dismay how thin he was. This was one feline that didn't have to worry about snacking too much, unlike the dogs and cats I'd been learning about in the obesity lecture I'd attended that afternoon. But I hadn't brought along any food, so there wasn't much I could do to help him. At least, not at the moment. I made a mental note to come back some other time with some of Moose's booty. I hadn't even brought a stethoscope with me on this trip, but maybe I could capture him long enough to bring him to a vet here on the island.

At the moment, however, I had more immediate concerns. I took a few deep breaths to get my blood pressure back down to normal, then continued my search.

We hadn't walked very far along the beach before I spotted a lone figure up ahead. From where I stood, the silhouette I could just make out looked like a woman methodically scanning the sand with a hand-held metal detector and a flashlight. As we drew near, she suddenly stopped, bent over, and retrieved something. After studying it with her flashlight, she muttered something incomprehensible and tucked it away in her pocket.

Between her irregular halo of hair and her dogged search for treasure in the sand, I knew I'd found the person I was looking for.

"That's got to be her," I whispered to Nick. "I'm almost positive."

"In that case, let's hold hands."

"Why?" I couldn't imagine what there was about this situation that was suddenly putting Nick in an amorous mood.

"Because it will make the two of us look less intimidating," he explained. "We'll look like lovers out for a romantic stroll on the beach instead of two people who came here expressly to track her down."

"Good point." I reached over and grabbed his hand.

I waited until we had moved even closer before calling, "Alice?" in a soft, gentle voice. It was the same one I used whenever I approached a frightened animal.

She whipped around, immediately squaring her shoulders in a defensive posture. "Who's that?" she demanded in a raspy voice that was frankly a little hard on the ears. She raised one hand and began swatting at the air, as if a swarm of invisible flies was plaguing her.

"My name is Jessie Popper," I replied in the same soothing tone, "and this is my friend Nick Burby." I walked toward her slowly, holding my flashlight so it faced me. That way, she could see for herself that I wasn't a particularly threatening person. Given Richard Carrera's description of her as "eccentric," I didn't know what to expect. Besides, the last thing I wanted to do was scare her off. "We were friends of Marnie Burton's. The woman whose body you found on the beach?"

I was now close enough to get a better look at her. Alice Feeley was dressed in a long pale blue skirt, its hem decorated with embroidery and tiny mirrors. She wore a bright blue rayon shawl draped over a white tank top. Her dark red hair reached out wildly in all directions, the silver strands that were interspersed throughout glimmering in the pale moonlight.

She took a step closer and peered at me. "You're not cops, are you?"

"No, just friends of Marnie's."

"Had more'n enough of cops," she muttered, shaking her head. She looked at the sand, the sea, the sky—everywhere but at me. "Don't like talkin' to them at all. Bah, they always make me feel like I'm the one who did something wrong. All's I did was have the bad luck to come across that poor dead girl. But I guess you never know what you'll find when you're beach-hunting. Had no choice but to call 911, even though I had enough of cops when I was young. Pigs, we used to call them in those days. 'Course, they acted like pigs, beating up on kids just because they were protesting the war, exercising their right to free speech. Nothin' wrong with that, not in this country. 'Least there's not supposed to be."

She paused to take a breath, and I jumped right in. "Alice, would you mind talking to us about what happened that night? The night you found Marnie's body?"

"Well, I was just about ready to leave here. Time to

go home." She glanced around the beach. "Slim pickins tonight. Sometimes that's just how it is."

"Then maybe you'd be willing to talk somewhere else," I suggested.

"We could go to a restaurant," Nick suggested, "or anyplace else you feel comfortable."

"Tell you what," Alice replied in the same hoarse voice. "Come back to my house."

"Right now?" I asked. Not only was I caught off guard by her invitation, I was also unsure of whether going home with this strange woman was a good idea, even if she did look frail enough that I probably could have taken her on even without Nick.

"Sure, why not?" Alice agreed with a little shrug. "I don't get much company, so it's a nice change. I'll even drive you over, if you like."

Frankly, I was surprised that she owned a car. From what I'd heard and seen, Alice Feeley impressed me as someone who liked to keep her life as simple as possible. "Thanks, but it probably makes more sense for us to follow you in our car. That way, you won't have to drive us back." And we'll have the means to escape, if we have to, I thought.

She shrugged. "Suit yourselves."

"What do you think?" I asked Nick as soon as we'd gotten into the Jeep and were out of earshot.

"Don't know yet," he replied. "She seems kind of eccentric, but that doesn't mean anything. Still, it was a good idea for us to get to her house on our own steam, in case we need to make a quick getaway."

Aside from the obvious dangers of getting into a car with a stranger, I was glad I'd insisted on taking my rented vehicle. Alice's ancient, battered Ford Taurus looked as if it was likely to break down before it even got out of the parking lot. Still, after a few sputters, it ambled onto the road, with our Jeep right behind it.

We'd traveled only a mile or so before she made a left turn onto a dirt road. Only a few houses were on it, tucked behind trees and shrubs that looked as if they were purposely left untended in order to create a barrier that discouraged intruders.

Alice didn't drive very far before pulling into a driveway. I wasn't surprised to find that her house was small. It was actually a bungalow, a boxy one-story building with a peaked roof and a ground-level porch running along the front. Even though it was somewhat run-down, it was saved from looking shabby by the paint job that I suspected was Alice's own handiwork. Even in the darkness, I could see the house was a bright shade of turquoise, with huge hand-painted flowers sprouting up all around in fantastic shades of purple, orange, yellow, and pink. Along the top, she had added puffy white clouds, and a colorful rainbow arched over the front door.

"Home sweet home," she mumbled as she led Nick and me toward the front door. "You gotta make a place reflect who you are, right?"

"Definitely," I agreed. With all sincerity, I added, "I like what you've done with it, Alice. It's beautiful."

"Bah!" she snorted. "This is my home. And your home's gotta show people who you really are."

As soon as she opened the door, we were confronted with a whirling dervish of activity. I quickly ascertained that the tornado of sleek dark fur belonged to a black Labrador.

"Calm yourself, Facetious!" Alice croaked. "We got company, so behave yourself!"

"Facetious?" I repeated, amused. "That's a name I haven't heard before."

"I adopted her from the Maui Humane Society. Made the mistake of spoiling her rotten too," Alice grumbled. "Now, 'course, she thinks she owns the place. Thinks she owns *me*."

"It sounds like just about every dog I've ever met," I said, smiling. Somehow, meeting Alice's dog made me feel more comfortable with her. I had to remind myself that it probably wasn't a good idea to get too comfortable.

Once Facetious calmed down, I had a chance to look around. I immediately saw that the interior of Alice's house embodied the same spirit of creativity as the outside. The living room was painted a deep red, and the tiny kitchen at the back of the house was a sunny orange. Instead of curtains, Alice had looped lengths of sheer fabric flecked with shiny gold and silver around the windows in both rooms. Lining the windowsills were pretty shells, stones, and the occasional piece of colored beach glass. The fruits of her labors as a professional beach hunter, no doubt.

The furnishings were just as creative. The Victorian-style red velvet couch that lined one wall faced two wicker chairs, both painted with squiggles in a half dozen different colors. A huge, crude-looking drum that looked as if its roots were Polynesian served as a coffee table. Everywhere there were stacks of books, most of them tucked into corners so they wouldn't topple over.

Eccentric? Maybe, I thought. But crazy? Not at all. Just a lot more creative than your average Joe.

Alice headed straight for the kitchen. "I got two drinks to offer you: tea and whiskey. Which one strikes your fancy?"

"Tea, please," I replied.

"Same for me," Nick added.

"It's herbal," Alice called in from the other room. "My own concoction. Hope that's okay."

"That's fine," I assured her.

"I hope she's not going to drug us," Nick whispered.

"Shhh," I shot back, even though I'd been thinking the exact same thing.

"Tea for three," I suddenly heard Alice mumble. "Much catchier than tea for two. Rhymes and everything." I was about to smile at the quaintness of the moment when she suddenly added, "But none for you, Jack. Not after what you've done."

Startled, I glanced at Nick. Here I'd thought the only ones in the house were the two of us and Alice. But it turned out there was a fourth person. Or at least it seemed that way.

"Not after you went and died on me, Jack Feeley," Alice complained in her gravelly voice. "Leavin' me all alone . . . hah! You can get your own tea, as far as I'm concerned!"

I looked over at Nick again. Not surprisingly, he had the same horrified look on his face that I suspected was on mine. So much for being a good judge of character, I thought ruefully.

We stood awkwardly in the small living room, pretending to be absorbed in watching Facetious. Fortunately, the spirited Lab was putting on quite a show, nosing a rubber ball across the room, then running after it to fetch it.

"Am I crazy," Nick finally commented, "or is that dog playing ball all by herself?"

"I don't think *crazy* is the best word to use in this house," I replied in a near whisper.

Alice, however, had no qualms about making it part of her working vocabulary. "Is that crazy dog playing ball again?" she called out from the kitchen. "Tryin' to get you to join her, no doubt. Or else tryin' to make you think I don't pay enough attention to her. Leave that silly animal and come on into the kitchen so we can talk. Facetious and I don't get much company, and frankly, I'm too selfish to let her hog all the attention."

Nick and I did as we were told. After we stepped into the kitchen, I took a seat at the small wooden table and he leaned against the counter on the other side of the room so he was facing me.

I watched Alice fill a battered copper kettle with water and put it on the stove, then open one of the upper cabinets. She was muttering to herself—or maybe she was simply continuing her conversation with her dead husband. Reaching between a box of granola and a package of organic wheat crackers, she took a brown bottle down from the shelf. I figured that, like Betty, she considered whiskey a natural go-with for tea, like honey and lemon.

Then she filled a good-size tumbler three-quarters of the way full.

Once she'd placed a chipped mug of tea in front of me and handed a second mug to Nick, she sat down on the other side of the table, clasping both hands around her tumbler.

"You gonna tell me your names?" she asked, squinting at us. She looked confused, as if she'd just realized there were other people in the room.

I wasn't about to point out that I'd already made a point of introducing us both at the beach. "I'm Jessie Popper and this is Nick Burby."

"And you know who I am, right? 'Course you do. That's why you came lookin' for me. You found out it was me who discovered that poor dead girl on the beach."

I nodded. "Richard Carrera mentioned it. He's the editor of—"

"I know who he is," Alice interrupted impatiently. " 'Course I know that. I've been here long enough to know who all the important people on the island are."

"How long have you lived on Maui, Alice?" I asked gently.

"Since the late eighties," she replied in her rasping voice. I was actually starting to get used to it. "Back when real estate was still affordable. At least I managed to buy my little piece of heaven, thanks to an unexpected windfall. Lived in California before that. Got to be a bad scene, though. Bah, too crowded, too expensive, too materialistic. I was going through some messy personal stuff too, and I wanted a change of scenery. I guess I kind of ran away.

"But I realized I wanted to live a simple life, without a lot of bad stuff and bad people getting in my way," she continued. "Living near the beach—and livin' off the land, as much as I could—appealed to me. I got a nice big piece of land right behind the house, and I grow all kinds of things on it. Never regretted changing my lifestyle either. I like bein' self-sufficient."

"Nothing wrong with being independent," I commented, making a point of not meeting Nick's eyes.

"That's the truth," Alice agreed. "So you still haven't said what all this is about. You wantin' to talk to me about that night and all. You said you were both friends with that girl?"

"That's right. And we're still trying to understand what happened." Watching for her reaction, I added, "To be honest, Alice, there's nothing more I'd like than to find out who killed her and why."

"I'm sure you're not alone," she replied matter-of-factly. She paused to take a few gulps of whiskey. "But isn't that what cops are for? I suppose they do have their uses, every once in a while."

"The police are certainly working on the case. But they think she was killed by some guy she picked up in a bar. Maybe they're right." I shrugged. "But no matter what happened that night, I'm just trying to understand. Marnie and I were friends. Nick too. So we can't help trying to find out whatever we can."

"Terrible thing," Alice commented, shaking her head. "Terrible, just terrible. Young girl like that, washin' up on the beach like a dead fish or a piece of garbage somebody was trying to get rid of. Wish I hadn't been the one to find her. The image of her lying on the sand, those marks all over her neck . . . I'm doing my best to put it out of my mind. I don't even want to think about it. Still, I have a feeling it's something I'll never get over. Never."

"I'm sure that's true," I agreed. "Alice, once you got over the shock of what you'd discovered on the beach Sunday night, did you notice anything in particular about Marnie Burton? The condition she was in? Anything she was wearing or holding . . . or maybe something that washed up on the beach with her?"

Alice thought for a few moments, meanwhile taking a few more sips of her drink of choice. "Can't say as I did. I saw the marks on her neck, that's for sure. Those were as plain as day. Other than that, I can't say I looked all that close. Like I said, the sight of that poor thing was hard to bear. I never had a daughter of my own, but my heart goes out to that girl's mother. What a thing for her to have to live through."

I decided to be direct. "Alice, had you ever seen Marnie when she was alive?"

She looked surprised by my question. "No," she replied. "Never did. Which I suppose is one of the reasons I'll never get that image of her lyin' in the sand, dead, out of my head."

I glanced over at Nick, curious about what he was making of all this. But from his expression, he seemed as undecided as I was. Alice certainly sounded sincere. In fact, I probably would have been inclined to believe Richard Carrera's characterization of her as harmless if I hadn't seen her name on that list Marnie had hidden away.

"Nick and I should probably be going," I said, figuring we'd learned everything we could. "We have to be somewhere at eight." I stood up to bring my mug over to the sink and dump out the rest of its contents. "Thanks for your time—and the tea."

"You don't have to clean up," she protested. "You're my guests."

"It's the least we can do." As I stood at the sink, I zeroed in on something on the windowsill right above it. It was the color that caught my eye. While the other items lined up there were the soft grays and whites of shells and stones gathered along the shore, this one was pale blue and green and pink.

It was a single earring, made of tiny pastel-colored shells. And it perfectly matched the ones Marnie had been wearing the night she was killed.

Chapter 10

"Pet a dog where he can't scratch and he'll always be your friend."

—Orville Mars

What's this?" I asked, struggling to keep my tone casual. I could hear the blood rushing through my temples, and my head had begun to pound so loudly I hoped Alice couldn't hear it. I made a point of keeping my eyes away from Nick's, not wanting to give myself away.

"What's what?" Frowning, Alice got up from her seat and came over. I noticed that she was a little unsteady on her feet.

I didn't dare pick up the earring. Not with my hands shaking the way they were.

"That?" Alice grabbed it off the windowsill, then shrugged. "Just a piece of jewelry I found. It's not worth very much. I mean, it's not real gold or anything. But I like the colors and the fact that it's made out of shells. So I decided to make it part of my treasure collection, keep it with all those special things I found on the beach." Still holding it in her hand, she looked up at me with a puzzled expression. "Why?"

"Oh, no reason," I replied, hoping I managed to sound nonchalant. "I just thought it was pretty. Unusual too. I don't think I've ever seen anything quite like it."

I searched her face but couldn't see any reaction. "Me either. Guess that's why it caught my fancy." She put it back on the sill. "Nice to add a little color to the place, though."

Marnie's earring, in Alice Feeley's house.

My thoughts were racing. Perhaps it could provide a piece of forensic evidence that would prove the identity of Marnie's murderer, I thought. A fingerprint or some skin cells that had come from her attacker, even a stray hair that had become lodged between the tiny shells during a struggle.

But before I could give it to the police, I would have to get its current owner to give it to me. Either that or talk Detective Paleka into coming to Alice's house to get it himself.

Given the way our face-to-face meeting had gone, that didn't strike me as much of a possibility.

Instead, I filed its existence away in the back of my mind. At least for now.

"Nick, we should really get going," I said, finally daring to look at him. His forehead was tense and his eyes told me he knew something was going on. Something bad. "Thanks again for the tea."

"What was all that about?" he demanded as soon as we were safely in the car and out of earshot.

"That earring I found on Alice's windowsill," I replied in a strained voice. "It was Marnie's. She was wearing those earrings the night she was killed."

As we drove through the darkness, away from Alice's house, Nick was silent. I knew he was mulling over the piece of information I'd just delivered, trying to figure out what it might mean.

I, however, was in the mood for thinking out loud. "The way I see it," I said, "there are two possible explanations for how that earring ended up in Alice's possession. One is that it was simply something she happened to find on the beach, possibly the same night Marnie was killed. Maybe the reason she didn't turn it in to the police was that she'd found it far enough away from the body that she didn't realize it belonged to the victim. In other words, the reason Alice hung on to it is exactly the reason she gave us, which is that it was just one more pretty thing she found on the beach."

"It's possible," Nick agreed. "What's the other, as if I don't already know?"

I swallowed, hoping to alleviate the dryness in my mouth. "The other possibility is much more onerous: that just like everyone else who comes to Hawaii, Alice enjoys collecting souvenirs. Only in this case, it was something to remember her victim by."

• • •

It wasn't until I jabbed my key card into the lock of our hotel room that I realized how tired I was. It had been a ridiculously long day.

"Let's concentrate on having fun tonight, okay?" Nick suggested as soon as we closed the door behind us. "I know this was a heck of a day for you, but we owe it to Betty and Winston to forget all that and have a good time with them at the luau."

"You're absolutely right," I agreed, dropping onto the bed and cradling Moose in my arms. He looked so happy to see us that I felt bad for leaving him alone so much of the day. "I'm going to do my best to put all the bad stuff completely out of my mind, at least for the next few hours. As soon as I do one more thing, that is."

"What's that?" Nick asked warily.

"Tomorrow night, you and I are having dinner at that quiet, romantic restaurant Ace took Marnie to a few hours before she was killed. I want to find out what went on between the two of them that night."

"Okay. What restaurant?"

Leaping to my feet, I replied, "Figuring that out is my final challenge of the day."

While Nick poured food into Moose's bowl and gave him fresh water, I rummaged around in the carton I'd filled with Marnie's personal possessions from work. Reaching down to the bottom, I gathered up the stray books of matches I'd tossed in with everything else.

Then I laid them out on the bed and studied them. There were seven, six of them from various restaurants on Maui.

Only one of them interested me: the Kula Grill. Marnie had told me she was meeting Ace at an out-of-the-way restaurant that he was particularly fond of and that it was located in Kula. I dialed the number and made a reservation for two for the following night.

With that done, I silently declared myself officially ready for an evening of fun. And if it involved umbrella drinks and fresh pineapple and maybe even some more of that coconut shrimp, so much the better.

"Hey, *wahine*," Nick murmured as he came up behind me and wrapped his arms around my waist. "Want to take a quick shower before we go down to the luau?"

It took me only a few seconds to realize he meant take a shower *together.* I may have been tired, but I was still sharp enough to recognize a good idea when I heard it. And this one was even better than either pineapple *or* coconut shrimp.

By the time Nick and I wandered into the Royal Banyan's outdoor restaurant, the location of the nightly luau, I was clean and refreshed and very mellow. I could practically feel the aloha spirit in the air.

For the event, the tables at the Oceanview Terrace had been rearranged into a near circle around an open area I suspected would serve as a stage. Off to one side was a tremendous pit in which a huge slab of meat was being roasted.

"Looks like we've got some more Polynesian dancing in our future," I observed. "I hope we're not part of the show."

"This time I'm standing firm," Nick insisted. "They're not getting me up on stage unless they put me on salary. And I want benefits. Including dental."

"The food looks great," I commented, scanning the laminated menu that listed the evening's fare. "Yum. Roast pork, Hawaiian style." In addition to kalua pork, the meal included lomi lomi salmon, poi, fresh pineapple . . . True, I couldn't identify everything that was named, but what I did recognize looked mighty good.

"Aloha!"

I glanced up and saw Betty and Winston standing at the edge of our table, beaming. They looked like an authentic *wahine* with her *kane*, with Betty in a bright pink and purple flowered muumuu and Winston wearing a splashy Hawaiian shirt with his white shorts. Their cheeks were flushed, but I had a feeling the pink color had nothing to do with overexposure to the sun.

"Aloha!" Nick returned. He jumped up to pull out Betty's chair, but Winston beat him to the punch.

"What a beautiful spot!" Betty cooed. "It's so romantic here on Maui. The sunsets, the palm trees, the balmy breezes . . ."

"Very romantic," Nick agreed, casting me a surreptitious glance.

"Makes me wish I'd come here years ago," Winston added. "But I suppose that's what happens when you fall in love. You find yourself doing things you never dreamed you'd be doing."

Betty sighed blissfully. "This is just lovely, the four of us finally sitting down for a real Hawaiian dinner." Her eyes were glittering as she added, "Especially since Winston and I have wonderful news to share."

My eyes traveled downward, focusing on something else I'd just noticed that was also glittering.

Her left hand. More specifically, the ring finger of her left hand.

Before I was able to digest the meaning of what I was seeing, she announced, "Winston just asked me to marry him—and I said yes!"

While my first reaction was joy, it took only about a hundredth of a second for my stomach to feel as if someone had stored a bowling ball inside it. That is, after bonking me on the head with it.

Nick cleared his throat loudly. I had a feeling I wasn't the only one who was reacting strongly to Betty's news.

"Congratulations!" he exclaimed. "Betty, Winston, that's great news!"

"How wonderful!" I seconded, at least having the presence of mind to follow his lead. "I wish you both the best!" Somehow I managed to stand up and lean across the table to give Betty a kiss on the cheek. Nick, meanwhile, shook Winston's hand.

"Can you imagine anything more romantic than a marriage proposal on Maui?" Betty cooed. As she reached over and grabbed Winston's hand, interlacing her fingers with his, I made a point of studying the attractive floral pattern on the tablecloth. That wasn't exactly a question I was in a hurry to answer.

Betty and Winston . . . getting married? I could barely hear my own thoughts because of the buzzing in my head. When they'd only known each other for a few months? True, Betty had once commented that people their age tend to experience time differently. But they'd barely gotten used to living together!

Of course, their monumental decision also had other implications, like the fact that Nick and I were dragging our heels when it came to making a real commitment to each other. Or at least I was.

I only hoped Nick wasn't thinking the same thing.

"Have you picked a date?" I finally asked. My voice sounded only minimally strained. In fact, I thought I was doing an excellent job of hiding how stunned I was.

"Sometime this spring," Betty replied. She gave Winston's hand a squeeze. "May or June, when the flowers are blooming and the sun is shining. . . ."

"We thought about getting married here on Maui, on a secluded beach somewhere," Winston added. "It's hard to imagine anything more romantic. But in the end we decided to give ourselves enough time to plan a small, private ceremony with a reception. That way, we can include our friends."

"I was thinking it might be nice to hold it in the garden," Betty noted. Gazing at Winston with dewy eyes, she added, "Right outside our home."

Turning to me, she said, "And I hope you'll be my maid of honor, Jessica."

I gulped before replying, "I'd love to."

I was relieved when our waiter reappeared. Not that I wasn't happy for Betty and Winston. But at the same time, I was more than ready to change the subject.

"Aloha," he greeted us. Aside from the red-and-white pareo wrapped around his waist, he looked about as Polynesian as I did. In fact, his strawberry-blond hair and the sprinkle of freckles across his nose made him look more Hawaiian Surfer than Hawaiian Native. "Can I get you folks something to drink?"

"Our friends here just got engaged," Nick announced.

"No way!" Our waiter looked impressed. "How cool is that? This means the first round of mai tais is on the house."

"Really?" Betty asked. "You mean the restaurant actually has an official policy about people who've just gotten engaged?"

"Sure," the waiter replied with a shrug. "Happens all the time."

"I told you there was nothing more romantic than getting engaged on Maui," Betty commented. "I'm obviously not the only one who thinks so."

"I'd say we get at least one couple here every night who've just gotten engaged," the waiter informed us. He sounded proud of the restaurant's track record. "In fact, a couple of nights ago, we had a guy get down on one knee right here in the middle of the restaurant. When his girlfriend said yes, everybody in the place went wild. Complete strangers were going over to their table and congratulating them. It was awesome."

"How sweet," Betty cooed.

"Of course," the waiter went on, glancing around the restaurant, "half the people in here are on their honeymoon. I don't know why, but Hawaii is like the most romantic place in the world. I'll be right back with those drinks."

As soon as he left, the five-piece band that had gathered at one end of the stage area began serenading us with soft Hawaiian music.

"Ooh, let's dance!" Betty cried, jumping up and grabbing Winston's arm.

Winston allowed himself to be dragged to a standing position, meanwhile glancing at the musicians nervously. "I could be mistaken, but aren't they playing a hula?"

Betty laughed. "So they are. But it just so happens I've got a bit of hula dancing on my résumé. It was required at my audition for the Broadway production of *South Pacific.*"

Winston's expression had changed to one of alarm. I had a feeling his résumé wasn't nearly as comprehensive.

"How about you two?" she asked. "Care to join us?"

"Thanks," I replied, quickly remembering our take-no-prisoners dance teacher. "I think we'll sit this one out."

"You two kids go on," Nick agreed. "Have a blast. Jessie brought her camera. We'll take pictures."

Betty dragged Winston after her toward the stage. "Come on, Win. Let's show this audience what dancing is all about."

As soon as they left, an awkward silence hung over our table. I took a few photos of graceful Betty and panic-stricken Winston, then pretended I was so absorbed in trying to drink the mai tai the waiter had brought without getting flower petals up my nose that I couldn't possibly make conversation.

It was Nick who broke the silence.

"Those two were made for each other," he said warmly. "I'm really happy for them."

"Yes," I agreed, although the single syllable I uttered sounded more like I was choking on my drink than pronouncing an actual word.

"And Betty's absolutely right about how romantic it

is, getting engaged on a beautiful island like Maui," he continued.

"I just hope they're ready," I said, talking to the attractive tablecloth rather than to Nick. "It's such a big commitment."

"Jess," Nick said gently, taking my hand in his, "sometimes people just *know.* They don't need to think about it, they don't need to ask their friends or consult their horoscope. . . . In their hearts, they're certain it's what's right for them."

I couldn't come up with a good response. So I was greatly relieved when I glanced up and saw that Betty and Winston were already back.

"Turns out that hula business is a lot harder than it looks," Winston said apologetically as he pulled out his chair.

"Tell me about it," I replied.

Betty slung her arms around Winston. "Maybe I could interest you in a few private lessons, back in our hotel room," she offered with shining eyes.

I could only imagine what else was in the syllabus.

But my own issues with love, commitment, independence, and claustrophobia aside, I really was happy for Betty and Winston. As far as I was concerned, they were the two nicest people in the world, and I was delighted that they'd found each other.

"Betty, I'm really thrilled for you," I said sincerely. "You too, Winston. I know you're going to be happy together."

"We already are," Betty replied, smiling. "We're just making our happiness official."

"I propose a toast to the lovebirds," Nick said heartily, holding up his glass. "To Betty and Winston!"

Betty clinked her glass against Nick's. "I can't think of a better way to celebrate than with the two of you," she said. "This trip just keeps getting better and better.

Joining you on Maui was one of the best ideas I ever came up with, if I do say so myself!"

"What have you got on the schedule for tomorrow?" Nick asked after we'd toasted Betty and Winston, Nick, me, Maui, marriage, and pineapple juice.

"I'm trying to talk Winston into taking the drive to Hana," Betty replied. "It's supposed to be absolutely breathtaking." She poked him in the ribs playfully, adding, "But this old coot insists he's not up to it—even though I offered to do the driving."

"It's a pretty treacherous road," Nick commented. "Jessie and I did it the last time we were here."

I had to admit that the day trip was one of the few fond memories I had of that so-called vacation. The fifty-mile highway that ran along Maui's northern coast was filled with twists and turns and bloodcurdling switchbacks. But the scenery was spectacular. On one side was the island's breathtaking coastline, dramatic cliffs rising out of serene bays or the raging ocean, with white-foamed waves crashing at the base. On the other side was an amazing assortment of natural wonders, ranging from dense greenery with narrow paths cut through to silver waterfalls that were several stories high. I remembered stopping at one particular spot to hike and finding a group of Hawaiians sitting on the rocks alongside a stream, weaving baskets and hats out of slender green palm fronds. At the end of the long, winding road was Hana, a quiet village that consisted of a few historic buildings, a cultural museum, and a luxurious hotel that overlooked the water.

But what I remembered best was Nick and me experiencing the whole day together, our eyes wide and our mood awestruck as we took in Maui's beauty. In fact, it was one of my favorite memories of our time together.

"Maybe all four of us should go," I suggested. "Winston, how would you feel about taking the trip if Nick and I did the driving?"

"Since your eyes and reflexes are a few decades younger than ours," Winston replied, chuckling, "I suppose my nerves could handle it."

"Great," Nick said. "And we definitely have to make a stop at Waianapanapa Cave."

"Never heard of it," Winston commented. "Where is it?"

"It's right off the main road, just before you reach Hana," Nick explained. "In fact, it's in a place called Waianapanapa State Park. I read in my guidebook that the word *Waianapanapa* means *glistening waters,* which refers to the water that pools at the bottom of the cave. It's supposed to be beautiful. But what's even better is the haunting story behind it.

"According to legend," he went on, "a long time ago, a warrior chief named Ka'akea became convinced that his wife, Popu'alaea, was having an affair. He followed her to Waianapanapa Cave because he was certain the reason she was sneaking off to such a secluded spot was to meet her lover. In fact, she was merely hiding, trying to get away from him. While Ka'akea was searching for her, he caught sight of her reflection in the still waters of the cave and murdered her. To this day, the water turns blood-red every spring on the anniversary of her death, and her screams can be heard in the wind."

Just hearing the story gave me chills. "It's probably not true," I commented, "but it still makes a pretty good legend."

"Whether or not the part about the violent chief is true, it turns out the real reason the water turns red every spring is because of the red shrimp living in it," Nick said, grinning.

"But the original version makes a much better story," Betty observed. "And I'd love to see it."

"Then it's settled," Nick concluded. "Jessie already rented a Jeep. We'll find a day that works for everybody and we'll take the drive."

"How about Sunday?" Winston suggested.

"Great!" I agreed. "We can bring along a picnic lunch, and we should probably pack our bathing suits. . . ."

A day trip to Hana with Betty and Winston really did sound like a great idea. In fact, I was already looking forward to it. Maybe there was still a way that Nick and I could spend quality time together doing things that were completely unrelated to a murder investigation.

• • •

"I know it's late," I told Nick as the two of us lingered at our table on the Oceanview Terrace's patio, "but there's one quick thing I want to do before I go back to the room. If the hotel florist is still open, I'd like to arrange for a bouquet to be delivered to Betty and Winston's room first thing tomorrow."

Nick and I were among the last of the diehards. By that point, the musicians had packed up their ukuleles and gone home and the kalua pork was nothing more than a fond memory. In fact, the cleanup crew had already begun bustling around us, marking an end to the luau and what had turned out to be an absolutely lovely evening. As for the newly engaged couple, they had retreated to their room long before, anxious to celebrate on their own.

"D'you mind if I pass?" Nick asked. "I'm bushed."

"Nope," I assured him. "In fact, even though you'll be all snuggled in your bed while I agonize over roses versus orchids, I'll still sign the card from both of us."

"Okay, *wahine*," Nick replied. "But don't be long." Pulling me close, he whispered, "There's a volcano on this island that's getting ready to erupt."

"Far be it from me to interfere with the forces of nature," I replied, laughing as I leaned over to give him a kiss.

As I walked toward the string of shops that lined the hotel lobby, I realized I'd been overly optimistic. Only one store appeared to be open, the one that sold newspapers, travel-size bottles of antacid, Maui T-shirts, and other basic necessities. I made a mental note to call the florist first thing the next morning. Not quite the dramatic effect of being awakened by a bellman bearing a colorful bouquet of fragrant blossoms, but it would have to do.

Even though I was pretty tired too, I decided to use the bank of elevators at the other end of the hotel to go back to the room. Choosing that route would take me through a scenic courtyard filled with palm trees and sweet-smelling tropical flowers and even a small waterfall. The moon was shining brightly and the warm air was wonderfully soothing, and I wanted the chance to savor it all.

Especially since tonight I had it all to myself.

I strolled through the courtyard, noticing that it was so quiet I could hear the gentle sea breezes rustling the palm fronds. Aside from that, there was no other sound besides the swishing of my rubber-soled sandals as I padded across the stone walkway.

Then I heard a soft thud.

I turned abruptly, mainly because I was startled. Maybe you're not alone after all, I thought, glancing behind me.

I didn't see a thing.

I decided I was just imagining things, probably a

side effect of being so tired. I walked another ten feet, then stopped again.

This time I was certain I'd heard a footstep. Several, in fact. And when I turned, I was almost positive I saw something move in the shadows.

Relax! I chastised myself. It's not as if you're the only person who's staying at this hotel. Other people have the right to walk through this courtyard.

Still, I couldn't help feeling that I was being followed.

I quickened my pace, relieved that I'd almost reached the elevators. Up ahead I could see a few hotel shops, their interiors dimly lit. I hurried toward them, hoping someone would be window shopping at the expensive jewelry store that specialized in Tahitian black pearls or the clothing boutique that featured Tommy Bahama sportswear and rhinestone-bedecked sandals. But there wasn't a soul in sight. Not at this hour, when all the credit cards had gone beddy-bye, along with the tourists who owned them.

I finally turned in to the short corridor that led to the bank of elevators. I glanced upward to see how long it would take for one of them to whisk me off to my room. According to the numbers above, not a single one was close to the ground floor.

Frantically I pressed the up button, meanwhile debating whether to wait or to turn and try a different route. I could hear the footsteps getting closer. At least, I thought I could. My heart was pounding so loudly at that point that it was hard to tell what I was hearing.

I pressed the up button a few more times, muttering, "Come on, come on," under my breath.

And then I felt a hand grip my arm.

Chapter 11

"Some people say that cats are sneaky, evil, and cruel. True, and they have many other fine qualities as well."

—Missy Dizick

I whirled around, my hands clenched into fists as I instinctively geared up to fight. Instead, I gasped.

"Graham?" I cried. The last person in the world I'd expected to encounter in a dark alley was Graham Warner, the slick, ponytailed guy who came on to me the day before at the hotel bar.

"You sure walk fast," he replied calmly, as if the two of us had just happened to run into each other on a busy street. He let go of my arm, then used his hand to brush a straggly strand of hair out of his face.

"You were . . . I thought . . ."

He frowned. "Hey, I didn't scare you, did I?"

"I guess you could say you did." I laughed nervously, not wanting to let on how annoyed I was. "In fact, you probably took a few years off my life."

"Sorry. I didn't want to call out your name. It's so late." Glancing around, he added, "And it's kind of quiet here, since there's nobody else around."

Something about the way he made that observation sent a chill running through me. He was right; there was nobody else around. And just because the person who'd been following me through the deserted courtyard now had an identity, that didn't make me any more comfortable being alone with him in an isolated spot.

"What are you doing here?" I asked. I still hadn't decided whether I should be making polite conversation or screaming.

"Me?" He looked surprised by my question. In fact, I could practically hear the gears turning in his head as he struggled to think up an answer to what seemed to me like a really obvious question. "I hang out at the bar here sometimes. It's good place to watch the tourists."

"Right," I replied uncertainly.

"Actually," he went on, leaning in a little closer, "I'm glad I ran into you like this."

Ran into me? I thought. As if him stalking me at my hotel in the middle of the night was a coincidence.

"Really?" I looked around, a little alarmed that I couldn't see any obvious way out. I held my flowered backpack more closely against my chest, wondering if there was anything in it that could function as a weapon.

"Yeah." Grinning and attempting to exude what I imagined was his idea of boyish charm, he explained, "I realized I owe you an apology."

"For what?" I could hardly remember our earlier conversation, aside from the fact that it left me thinking he was firmly entrenched in the creep category. And given the fact that I still kept glancing around, hoping somebody—anybody—would magically appear, I wasn't in the best frame of mind to reconstruct our interaction.

"For coming on so strong yesterday," he replied. "I'm not usually like that. I guess I was just trying a little too hard, and when I saw I wasn't getting anywhere, I acted like kind of a jerk."

"It's fine," I said offhandedly. "Don't worry about it."

Just then, the elevator doors opened. Saved, I thought. At least for now. I stepped inside quickly, making a point of staying near the front so I had at least a chance of fighting him off if he decided to join me.

"Hey, let me buy you a drink." He pressed his hand against the elevator door, preventing it from closing.

"I'm pretty wiped out," I said firmly. "I've got to get some sleep."

"C'mon, one drink. You'll be back in your room in half an hour."

"Thanks, but no thanks," I told him more forcefully. This guy was actually turning out to be a lot worse than Marcus. At least Marcus eventually took no for an answer.

"Hey, I can be a pretty charming guy, if you'll just give me a chance—"

"Excuse me, I've really got to go," I insisted, raising my voice. I jabbed at the close-doors button and stepped farther back.

"In that case, at least let me give you my card." I tensed when he reached into his pants pocket. But all he pulled out was his wallet. He flipped it open and pulled out a white business card.

"Here's my cell phone number," he said, thrusting it at me. "Call me any time, Jessie. I mean it. If I can ever be of any use, just let me know."

"Okay, Graham," I humored him, reluctantly taking his card. And already planning to toss it as soon as I got back to my room.

If and when he let me do that. I was relieved that he

finally lowered his arm and allowed the elevator doors to close. "Listen, have a good night," he called after me as they separated us.

It wasn't until the elevator started moving, carrying me safely back to my room, that I realized I was covered in a thin film of sweat. Graham Warner was really starting to creep me out, and I sincerely hoped our paths wouldn't cross again.

Then again, Maui was turning out to be a very small island.

• • •

The next morning, Nick and I both awoke with a sense of purpose. From the moment I opened my eyes, the air felt charged with electricity. In fact, the atmosphere in the room reminded me of mornings at home, when we both leaped out of bed energized by the list of things we were determined to accomplish that day.

While he showered, I plopped Moose into my lap and called the hotel florist. I arranged for them to deliver their biggest, brightest bouquet of tropical flowers to Betty's room as soon as they could.

Then, over breakfast on the lanai, I studied my road map of Maui. First I checked the location of the Wailuku public library, where Nick planned to spend the morning researching FloraTech and reading through Marnie's files. Then I plotted out my own itinerary, zeroing in on two particular addresses on Marnie's list that happened to be fairly close to each other.

"Okay, I think this makes sense." I shoved the map toward Nick, which required pushing aside the bowl full of tantalizing chunks of mango drizzled with fresh lime juice that I had yet to dig into. "I'll start by checking out these two places, since they're only a few miles apart. They're both located in an area that's known as 'Upcountry Maui.' "

Nick looked up from the Hawaii Power & Light file he'd already started perusing and glanced at the map. "Looks like a plan," he commented. "Especially since the first listing has *yes* written next to it and the second one says *no*. Maybe you can figure out what Marnie's code meant."

Suddenly he frowned. "What about Moose? We'll both be out this morning when the maid comes. I have a feeling the hotel won't be very happy about us harboring a stowaway."

"Good point." I scanned the room, looking for a solution. I found it hanging on the doorknob. "How about putting out the *Do Not Disturb* sign?" I asked. "Think that will work?"

"Maybe. But just to be safe, I'll leave a note right inside the door, where the maid can't miss it. And I'll put a twenty next to it, to be doubly sure she doesn't turn us in."

When I dropped Nick at the library, we exchanged a quick, impersonal kiss, a sign that each of us was already absorbed in the day's mission. As he was about to jump out of the Jeep, he hesitated and turned back.

"Hey, Jess?" he said somberly. "Be careful, will you? You don't really know what you're getting into."

I nodded. "I'll be fine," I promised. I just hoped I was right.

After checking the map one more time, I headed south on the Haleakala Highway. The first stop I had scheduled was a place called Aloha Farm. It was located on Kula Highway, not far from the island's best-known winery, Tedeschi Vineyards. But that was all I knew about it. From its name, I figured it could turn out to be anything from a cattle ranch to a day-care center.

Even though I'd traveled this route several times before, I was still overwhelmed by the amazing scenery. To my right, the rocky shoreline tumbled downward to the turquoise waters of the Pacific Ocean. To the left, the green craggy mountains formed an irregular line against the pale blue sky. As I rounded a bend in the road, I spotted one of the clearest, brightest rainbows I'd ever seen, arcing across the horizon.

Still, the longer I drove, the more difficult it was to appreciate the island's beauty. In fact, the closer I got to the Kula Highway, the greater my sense of dread.

As was often the case, I was not only nervous about what I might find; I was also worried that I might not find out anything at all.

I located the first entry on Marnie's list with surprising ease. The street address was posted on a mint-green sign with yellow hand-painted letters. Right above it were the words *Aloha Farm*.

I pulled up in front of the sign, then rolled down the window of my Jeep to get a better look. Like Alice Feeley's house, this one was also awash in color. But there were two major differences between the two buildings. This one had been painted in soothing pastels, rather than the wilder colors Alice had opted for. But, even more striking, the condition of this house made it clear that a tremendous amount of love and care had gone into it.

The small, squat building appeared to be more than a house, however. On the front porch was a big cardboard sign reading OPEN. Beyond it, covering the hillside, stretched rows of lush trees that told me Aloha Farm really was just that: a farm.

I checked my notes. Or, to be more accurate, Marnie's notes.

"Makiko and Peter Cooper," I read aloud. *"Aloha*

Farm, two and a quarter acres." In the margin right next to it, Marnie had scrawled the word *YES*.

Not much to go on. Then again, I told myself resolutely as I swung open the car door, learning something about this place is why you're here.

Tentatively, I opened the front door, still not completely convinced that the OPEN sign meant it was okay to walk right in. I found myself in a small room that was set up like a café, complete with sunshine-yellow tablecloths printed with a whimsical coffee-cup design. Curtains made from the same cheerful fabric framed the large picture window that looked out onto the sloping fields. Three serious-looking glass cases containing displays on the history and processing of coffee lined the other walls.

So Aloha Farm is a coffee plantation, I thought, still not quite knowing what to make of that fact.

I glanced down as I felt something silky brush against my leg. A sweet-faced gray cat gazed up at me, uttering a quizzical, "Meow?"

"Hello, you precious thing," I cooed, lifting her up and cuddling her in my arms. Her fur was thick and soft, and her appreciative purrs reverberated through my chest. I nuzzled her against my cheek, suddenly reminded of how much I missed my own gray cat, Catherine the Great, as well as my tiger kitten, Tinkerbell. In fact, my heart began to ache as I thought about how much I also missed my Westie Max and my Dalmatian Lou, as well as my parrot Prometheus and my Jackson's chameleon Leilani—

"Can I help you?" The sound of a friendly female voice interrupted my unexpected bout of homesickness.

I whirled around, surprised that I wasn't alone at all. A small, slender woman about my age stood in the doorway that led into the house, smiling. She was dressed casually in jeans and a plain white T-shirt, and her straight, jet-black hair was pulled back into a low ponytail.

"I was driving by and I saw your sign out front," I said. "I thought I'd stop in and try some of your coffee."

"Certainly! Why don't you take a seat? I'll bring you a small sample of each, if that's okay."

As long as there's caffeine in it, I thought, it's fine with me. I dropped into the nearest seat with my furry new buddy still in my arms.

"I see you met our official greeter," the woman commented as she filled no fewer than five small paper cups from five different urns. "Kona is remarkably friendly for a cat. But maybe that's because she grew up in the family business."

"Really? You mean you're the owner?" I asked casually. I hoped she thought I was just another nosy tourist, making conversation.

"My husband and I have owned Aloha Farm for about twelve years. By the way, I'm Makiko Cooper."

"I'm Jessie Popper," I replied. "I'm here on Maui for a veterinary conference."

"You're a vet? So that explains why you're so good with Kona. And believe me, she loves the attention."

She turned her attention to the five cups balanced on the tray she was carrying. "Okay, this should give you a chance to taste a few varieties so you can decide which ones you like best. From left to right, we've got one hundred percent Kona Coffee, Kona Vanilla Macadamia Nut, one hundred percent Maui Coffee, and Kona Hula Pie, which is flavored with coconut, macadamia nut, and hazelnut. This last one is Kona Peaberry, which is the crème de la crème of Kona coffee. It's made with a higher grade of coffee bean."

"I didn't even realize coffee was grown on Maui," I

commented. I gently placed Kona the Cat on the ground and reached for the Peaberry, figuring I might as well start at the top.

"We grow a little here on our farm. We also roast Kona coffee that's grown on the Big Island."

"Kona coffee is generally considered the best, isn't it?"

Makiko smiled. "We get a little competition from Blue Mountain, which is grown in Jamaica. But Kona coffee is rated number one or number two in the world."

"Why is that?" I asked. I moved on to the Hula Pie variety, already realizing that picking out one or two favorites wouldn't be easy. "Or is that some kind of trade secret?"

"It's no secret," she replied, "mainly because none of it is in our control. Our coffee is of such high quality because of six factors: soil, altitude, slope, the amount of sunshine, the amount of cloud cover, and the island's rainfall." From the way she rattled off the short list, I got the feeling she'd given this explanation before.

"It sounds like a pretty idyllic life," I commented, finishing that one off and picking up another. "Living on Maui on such an incredibly beautiful piece of property, running your own business . . ."

"It's been wonderful," Makiko said wistfully, glancing around. "I really do love this place. Like you say, it's beautiful and peaceful, and I always liked the idea of owning a piece of land. It seemed so . . . substantial. Like we had something that mattered.

"And my husband, Peter, and I always loved running our own business. Especially growing coffee. There were never very many of us on Maui, but we always felt we were producing something really special."

Is it my imagination? I wondered, or is she using the past tense an awful lot?

I was trying to formulate a tactful way of questioning her when she added, "Which is why it's so sad that we're going out of business."

"Really?" I tried to hide my surprise. "Maybe I'm being too much of a busybody, but why?"

"We sold our land to a big company. They offered us a ridiculously large amount of money. Way more than market value. Peter and I discussed it for days, but in the end there was no way we could say no." Quickly, she added, "It's going to be used for a really good purpose, though."

It was time to ask the $64,000 question. "I don't suppose the company is FloraTech, is it?"

She looked surprised. "Yes. How did you know?"

"I guessed. I heard the company just came to Maui recently, and I understand they're planning to grow hibiscus." Thinking fast, I added, "Some people at the veterinary conference were talking about it because FloraTech has apparently come up with some really exciting developments in the medical field."

"That's our understanding too," Makiko said. Still sounding a bit defensive, she added, "Besides, we're not the only ones who've decided to sell our land to FloraTech. The farmers here on Maui are a pretty tight group—not only the coffee growers but also the people who grow papayas and macadamia nuts and even the flowers that are used for leis. You know, a lot of us own land that's been in our families for generations. We've loved the idea of carrying on a tradition that's been part of this island for so long. It's made us feel as if we were part of something much bigger than ourselves."

Her voice had grown thicker. Glancing up, I saw that her eyes were glassy with tears. She wiped them away, then shrugged. "But I guess it's time to move on. Progress and all that."

I tried to think up something reassuring to say. For some strange reason, I couldn't.

Fortunately, Makiko took over.

"Let me show you around," she offered. "If you're done tasting the coffee, I mean."

"I am done, and it was great. I'm going to buy a few bags to bring home."

As I followed Makiko outside, I became mesmerized. I inhaled deeply, smelling the rich, damp earth as I took in the dark slopes, the thick cover of coffee trees, and the pale-blue sky dotted with white clouds.

I couldn't remember the last time I'd been surrounded by such beauty. Or felt such a sense of serenity. For a few moments, my mind felt totally clear.

"You're right, Makiko," I told her, noticing that my voice also sounded strained. "This really is a little piece of paradise, right here on earth."

We stepped back inside long enough for me to buy several pounds of different varieties of coffee for Nick and me, figuring they'd make a great way to bring a little bit of paradise home with us. Still, a wave of sadness came over me as I paid for what I knew were some of the last bags Makiko and her husband would be selling.

As I got back in the car, I felt sobered by what I'd learned.

Maybe that was what Marnie was writing about, I thought. The idea that land that had been in the same families for generations was being sold to a megacorporation, an organization that came to Maui from somewhere else. And the fact that the farmers who had been living off the land and truly valuing the experience, people like Makiko Cooper, now had to switch gears in order to find something new to do while they left behind something they truly loved.

It was certainly a big story. Yet it didn't strike me as big enough to get Marnie killed.

I was about to beep the remote to unlock my car when I suddenly heard the rustle of leaves. Instinctively I turned. I half-expected to see Makiko's cat, Kona, emerging from the bushes.

Nothing.

"Hello?" I called, certain of what I'd heard.

There was no response. I hesitated for a few seconds, listening closely, before deciding that I must have imagined it, after all. Or that maybe the island breezes were playing tricks on me.

Still, as I climbed into the Jeep, I couldn't shake the unpleasant feeling that I was being watched.

• • •

You've got to rein in that imagination of yours, I told myself resolutely as I turned back onto Kula Highway. No one is following you and no one is watching you. Not out here in the middle of nowhere.

The real culprit, I decided, was too much caffeine.

Even so, there was definitely something to be said for the rush of energy that had come from my midmorning infusion of coffee. I actually found myself looking forward to my next stop.

Even though the second spot I planned to visit was considerably further down on Marnie's list, I'd chosen it because it was only a few miles away from Aloha Farm. According to her notes, the Spirit of Pele Plantation was owned by Wesley Nakoa and consisted of 3.75 acres. There was nothing I could see about it that seemed significantly different from Makiko's property.

One thing that was different, however, was that

Marnie had scrawled the word *NO* in the margin next to this listing. Hopefully, I'd soon find out what separated the *YES*'s from the *NO*'s.

The drive to the Spirit of Pele Plantation took me through Makawao. Thanks to Nick's guidebook, I knew it had begun as a cowboy town that served the cattle ranches surrounding it.

Sure enough, as I drove through town, I felt as if I'd stumbled upon the set for a western. The wooden buildings that lined the main street, Baldwin Avenue, were almost all only one story high, many with wooden facades that jutted up above the flat roofs, Dodge City–style. Several had wooden porches running along the entire front. I even spotted a few hitching posts.

But the quaint village had clearly moved into the twenty-first century. Makawao may have still held a big rodeo and parade every Fourth of July weekend, but it was also the home of galleries, a health-food store, and a visual-arts center.

As I turned down a side road on the outskirts of town, however, I abruptly received a harsh reminder that I hadn't come to Upcountry Maui to sightsee. Halfway down the dirt road, I was confronted by a large, crude-looking sign posted on a tree. It was made from a jagged-edged piece of corrugated cardboard covered with black handwritten letters:

HAWAIIAN LANDS ARE NOT FOR SALE!

Ten feet down the road I spotted a second sign, done in the same artistic style. This one read, KEEP OUT! PROPERTY PROTECTED BY SMITH & WESSON!

A knot the size of a papaya was already forming in my stomach. Anxiously, I checked Marnie's notes, wanting to be sure this really was the Spirit of Pele Plantation. Sure enough, this was the place.

"You can do this," I told myself. I only hoped the

reason the person who owned this piece of land didn't exactly welcome visitors wouldn't turn out to be that he was growing something illegal.

Still, it was a definite possibility. Which explained why I felt even more apprehensive as I reluctantly climbed out of the Jeep.

As I shielded my eyes from the sun and surveyed the property, I could hear the threatening bark of what sounded like a very large dog somewhere on the property. The main house, a good hundred yards back from the road, was half hidden by overgrown bushes and trees. But even the dense tropical growth didn't hide the fact that it was desperately in need of a paint job. The only other building I could see was a garage with two broken windows and a roof that appeared to be on the verge of caving in.

Spirit of Pele—or Temple of Doom? I thought.

Still, I wasn't about to let the owner's obvious need for a few hours in front of the TV, receiving some sorely needed guidance from the experts on the Home and Garden Channel, get in my way. A big, barrel-chested dog didn't deter me either, since I'd certainly dealt with my share of those. I tugged on the old wooden gate that separated Wesley Nakoa's property from the road. As I did, a chunk of rotting wood came loose in my hand.

I took a deep breath before stepping onto Mr. Nakoa's property. I was fully aware that I was violating any trespassing laws the state of Hawaii happened to have in place. If Wesley Nakoa chose to prosecute, he'd have the government on his side.

But I'd come this far, and I wasn't about to let a fear of spending the rest of my vacation in a Hawaiian jail get in my way. Not with so much at stake, including my own safety.

Cautiously I moved along the path—really a haphazard scattering of rocks that was nearly obscured by weeds—taking care not to twist my ankle. The barking continued, resonating louder in my ears with each step I took.

Once I was on the property, I saw that there was a lot more happening on this land than I'd realized. Behind the dilapidated structures were acres of farmland planted with vegetables. The even, carefully planted rows that were obviously tended with meticulous care contrasted sharply with the ramshackle buildings.

My heartbeat quickened when I spotted someone in the distance. Even from this far away, I could see he was probably in his sixties, his face leathery from both age and too much time in the sun. Beside him stood a large mixed-breed dog with matted, dark-brown fur and that big chest I could tell he had from his bark. The man's clothes reminded me of a scarecrow's. The cuffs of his loose, ill-fitting khaki pants were caked with mud, and his pale-blue cotton shirt was torn in several places. He wore his big straw hat pulled down low so that it almost covered his eyes. The crown was ripped and the brim hung limply, no doubt from years of wear. His posture was stooped and his hands were gnarled.

"Mr. Nakoa?" I called, trying to sound friendly.

But as I took a few steps closer, I saw that his eyes were filled with fire. I also realized he was pointing a double-barrel shotgun right at me.

Chapter 12

"Some people say man is the most dangerous animal on the planet. Obviously those people have never met an angry cat."

—Lillian Johnson

"Get the hell off my property!" the man demanded in a coarse, gravelly voice.

I swallowed hard. Frankly, I was finding it a little difficult to make conversation while a gun was pointed straight at me. That dog looked and sounded pretty serious too. "I'm looking for Mr. Nakoa," I finally managed. "Wesley Nakoa."

"Quiet, Poto!" he snapped at his dog. Surprisingly, the animal obeyed. At least, he did after one more sharp bark, followed by a whimper that made it quite clear he wasn't happy about doing so. The man turned his focus back to me. "You found him. Whaddya want?"

He's not really going to shoot you, I told myself. *He's just trying to scare you.*

And doing a mighty fine job of it too.

Still, clinging to the idea that this man's bark was probably worse than his bite, I forced myself to march right up to him. I tried to carry myself with dignity, along with a confidence I didn't come close to feeling.

As I got nearer, I saw that he was older than I'd first assumed. Seventies, or even eighties. His face was as dry as the arid red dirt of the Haleakala crater and crisscrossed with an even greater number of lines than the desertlike terrain. But his pale hazel eyes were bright and filled with the same fire the dormant volcano had once spewed.

I stuck out my hand. "Hello, Mr. Nakoa. My name is Jessica Popper. I live on the mainland, where I work as a veterinarian." The words kept flowing, practically out of my control, as I desperately tried to defuse some of the tension hanging in the air, especially in the small amount of space between that gun and me. "I'm here on Maui for just a few days, attending a veterinary conference. But I was wondering if you'd be willing to talk to me about a conversation I believe you recently had with Marnie Burton."

I don't know which phrase I used that turned out to contain the magic words, but he finally lowered his gun.

"You mean that reporter, right?" He pulled the brim of his straw hat down further. Not much of his eyes showed, but his scowl sure did.

"Yes. Marnie worked for the *Maui Dispatch*." I hesitated. "I don't know if you heard about what happened to her, but she—"

"She was killed, right? They killed her."

His words had the same effect on me as if he'd struck me with the barrel of his shotgun.

"What do you mean, 'they killed her'?" I demanded, feeling my cheeks grow warm. "Who?"

"How do I know you're not working with them?" he replied angrily, narrowing his eyes.

"Mr. Nakoa, you've got to trust me when I tell you I don't know who you're talking about."

"You expect me to believe that? Get off my property! I'm not afraid to use this gun! Not when somebody's trespassing on my land!"

"If you'd just let me explain—"

"Can't you people read? This land isn't for sale! Now get the hell out of here before I make you! And don't think I won't!"

I held up both hands, palms out, as if somehow that would enable me to ward off his anger if not any actual bullets that happened to come my way. "All right, Mr. Nakoa. I'm leaving. And, uh, thanks for your time."

I turned and headed back along the path, this time moving a lot faster than I had on my way in.

As I opened the car door, I realized my hands were shaking. So much for the tough-girl act.

Still, once I was safe in my own car, I began to calm down. And to puzzle over Wesley Nakoa's situation. On the one hand, it seemed to me that if the old man had a chance to unload this dump—for a tremendously inflated price, no less—he'd be crazy not to jump at the chance. There were definitely advantages to moving to an air-conditioned condo or some other modern residence that didn't require constant care, especially since he didn't seem to be up to it. On the other hand, this was his home.

Besides, maybe there was another side to it. Maybe he knew something about FloraTech. Or he could have simply been anti-progress or anti–big business or anti any number of things.

Of course, there was one more possibility: that Wesley Nakoa was just crabby and that there was no rational explanation for anything he did.

I was about to put the car into drive and take off when a loud rapping on the window made me jump.

I jerked my head around, expecting to see Wesley Nakoa's angry face. Instead, a tense-looking woman stood hunched over the driver's side of the Jeep, peering in at me.

"Excuse me?" she called. "If I could just have a minute . . ."

Curious, I rolled down the window. But only a few inches.

"I'm Lila Nakoa. Wesley's daughter. I wanted to apologize."

I could already feel myself relaxing. She didn't look much older than I was, but the fine lines in her face and the furtiveness in her green eyes gave the impression that she'd experienced a lot more than I had. She was dressed in tight, low-slung jeans and a bright orange shirt. It was made of stretchy fabric and cut low enough to show ample cleavage, as well as part of a tattoo. I couldn't quite make out what the image was, however. Her strawberry blond hair, piled up and fastened with a plastic tortoiseshell clip, was a bit too brassy to complement her dark eyebrows and medium skin tones. She'd applied makeup with a heavier hand than just about anyone else I'd encountered on the island.

"Sorry my father was so rude," she said with a rueful smile. "I happened to be standing in the kitchen, and I overheard everything he said to you."

"He seems pretty angry," I commented, opening the window the rest of the way. "But I understand him being protective of his land."

"He's lived here his whole life." Lila stood up straight, shielding her eyes with her hand as she gazed out at the field beyond the small house. "My dad's one of those independent types. Never worked for anybody else, never had a desk job." She laughed. "Could you see him selling insurance or working at Home Depot?"

I smiled. "Not really."

"I mean, just look at the name he chose for his farm. Spirit of Pele. I think that pretty much says it all, don't you?"

I shook my head to say that, as surprising as it may have seemed, I had absolutely no idea who Pele was or what the reference to his or her spirit was all about.

"Sorry. I guess I forget that not everybody is familiar with Hawaiian legends the way those of us who live here are. My dad's been telling me the story since I was a little kid. The legend goes that there were two sisters named Pelehonuamea and Hi'iaka who lived in a volcano, Kilauea, on the Big Island. Pele sent her sister to find her lover, Lohi'au. After this long, terrifying adventure, filled with battles and demons and all kinds of obstacles, Hi'iaka finally found him—and fell in love with him herself.

"When Pele found out, she killed her lover and destroyed everything her sister loved. That included burning down the 'ohi'a trees, which have bright, beautiful flowers. Then Hi'iaka learned what Pele had done and finally got the strength to stand up to her sister.

"According to legend, the fight between the two of them continues to this day. Pele is still angry, and she keeps shooting lava out of the volcano, which destroys everything it touches. But when the lava cools, it creates lava beds where new 'ohi'a trees grow. So Pele and Hi'iaka symbolize the cycle of destruction and rebirth.

"In other words, Pele is all about anger." She smiled apologetically. "Look, I know my dad comes across as a mean old goat. But don't take it personally. He acts the same way whenever those men from FloraTech come around too. Of course, they have a totally different agenda."

My ears pricked up the same way my dogs' ears do whenever they hear something of interest. Only in their case, it's usually the crinkling of the plastic wrap on food or critical words like *walk* or *ball.* "Do you know what they talked about?" I asked Lila.

"Buying his land, of course. They're desperate to get their hands on it. Apparently they discovered that hibiscus has some medicinal value, and they plan to make a bundle off it. They need as much room to grow it as they can get." She shook her head, grinning. "But when it came to my dad, they had no idea what they were dealing with."

"What about you?" I asked. "How do you feel about your dad holding on to this land? Aren't you anxious to keep it in the family?"

"Oh, I don't live here anymore," Lila told her. "To be perfectly honest, after growing up on this farm, I've had enough of it. Nowadays I got a place of my own over in Wailuku. I work at the Maui Sunrise Hotel. I'm a hostess at the lounge over there, the Silver Surf." She thought for a second, then added, "I keep telling him he should sell it. Especially with everything that's been going on around here."

The hardness in her voice startled me. "What do you mean?"

Once again, she reacted with surprise. "I guess you haven't heard about the heavy-handed tactics those FloraTech people have been using."

I wondered if I should mention that Makiko Cooper seemed to feel they were pretty fair when it came to buying her farm. But I just shook my head.

"It's hard to know how much of it's true, of course," Lila commented. "Sometimes people exaggerate, especially some of the older folks. My dad's not the only person around here who feels strongly about holding on to his land. But I heard one story about FloraTech sending a bunch of goons to drive heavy vehicles over one man's farm in the middle of the night, destroying his papaya plants. Somebody else insists FloraTech sprayed some kind of poison on their land."

Before I had a chance to exclaim with surprise, she shrugged and added, "Like I say, it's hard to separate fact from fiction. But all that aside, there's no excuse for my father to act like that." Glancing back over her shoulder at the house, "Sometimes I wonder if I should find a way to make him sell the land and send him someplace else to live. Someplace where there are people who can take care of him. If they could put up with him, that is."

"What about Marnie Burton?" I asked. "She's the reporter from the *Maui Dispatch* who was murdered. I understand she spoke to your dad just a few days before she was killed. Do you know why she was interested in your father—or why she was interested in FloraTech, for that matter?"

"Beats me," Lila replied. "All I know is that a large biomedical company like FloraTech setting up shop on Maui is a big deal for most people. It represents a lot of the stuff people live here in order to get away from. I guess she was interested in writing about that.

"Of course, it could have been something much worse," she added, sounding as if she was speaking more to herself than to me.

"Like what?" I asked cautiously.

"Maybe she was—I don't know, trying to defend them."

"I'm afraid I don't follow."

"The newspaper she worked for, the *Maui Dispatch*?" Lila said. "Over the past few weeks, it's published a few letters from readers, saying that FloraTech coming here was the best thing that ever happened to Maui, blah, blah, blah. Let's hear it for progress and big business and all that. A lot of people got angry over the way the newspaper seemed to be defending FloraTech. So the fact that Marnie Burton was working for the paper kind of made people distrust her."

"Including your dad," I observed.

"Exactly."

Of course, there are two sides to every story—which is especially important for people in the newspaper business. I wondered if the *Maui Dispatch* had really come out in favor of FloraTech or if Richard Carrera was just trying to be fair by allowing people with different viewpoints to air their opinions. After all, I'd expect that was the responsibility of a newspaper's managing editor.

Unfortunately, I couldn't say the same for Marnie. Given what I'd heard about the ambitious young reporter's determination to ferret out corruption and expose scandal, it didn't seem unreasonable to assume that that was precisely what she'd been trying to do in this instance—whether her efforts were warranted or not.

Even so, had the mere fact that she wrote for a newspaper that, at the moment, was less than popular made certain people see her as the enemy?

Or maybe even a target?

• • •

I encountered some serious traffic as I headed south along Mokulele Highway, but I was glad to have the chance to think—mainly about FloraTech. I couldn't help suspecting there was a connection between Marnie's determination to pursue a story about the new biotech firm and her death. FloraTech was more than just a new company that was setting down roots on Maui. Given the way it was aggressively buying up land, the firm's arrival was having a tremendous effect on the island's residents. And Marnie appeared to be smack in the middle of it—or at least trying to put herself there.

Besides, she must have sensed that she was in danger, I thought, speeding up to put some distance between me and a tailgater. Why else would she have hidden in the freezer her list of the people whose land FloraTech had attempted to buy?

I was still absorbed in my own thoughts when I noticed a small cluster of office buildings up ahead. The reason they caught my attention was that a half dozen cars were parked haphazardly on the grass that separated them from the road.

I stepped on the brake when I noticed that one of them was a silver BMW. And when I spotted a big sign that read PRESS stuck in the windshield, I turned abruptly and entered the parking lot.

That car could belong to only one person, I concluded, thinking back to my conversation with Richard Carrera. And that was Bryce Bolt.

On impulse, I pulled up behind the BMW, turned off the ignition, and waited, keeping my eyes glued to the doorway. There was a question that had been nagging at me for days, and I wondered if he could answer it for me.

Only about ten minutes passed before people started straggling out of the building. Some carried notebooks or laptops, others had cameras, and almost all of them were talking on cell phones.

Sure enough, Bryce was among them. I spotted him strolling out of the building, exhibiting a distinct cockiness even in the way he walked. I waited until he had made it to his car before popping out of mine.

"Bryce! Remember me?"

He glanced up, looking surprised. And puzzled.

"Jessie Popper," I reminded him, walking over to him with a big smile on my face. "Marnie's friend."

"Oh. Sure. It took me a second to place you, that's all. How's it going?" I guess he finally did remember me, because he suddenly frowned. In a much less cordial voice, he demanded, "What are you doing here?"

"I was driving by and I noticed all the commotion," I replied cheerfully, gesturing toward the last few reporters and photographers who were straggling out of the building. "Obviously something big was happening here, and I couldn't help wondering what it was."

"Just a press conference," he said, eyeing me suspiciously.

"Really? For what?" I persisted.

"The Maui Visitors Bureau. They reported the usual statistics about how tourism is up, business is booming, the environmental impact is devastating. . . . They hold these things a few times a year. Not exactly front-page news."

"Actually," I said, trying to sound casual, "I wanted to ask you something that's kind of related. To front-page news, I mean. Or at least to the newspaper business."

"Okay," he replied warily.

I hesitated. "I wanted to ask you about Holly."

He stiffened. "Holly Gruen? What about her?"

"She and I got together a few days ago. I think having the chance to talk about Marnie made us both feel a little better. But there's something that keeps gnawing away at me."

"What's that?" he asked uneasily.

"Holly wouldn't tell me why she left the *Dispatch*. I was hoping you would."

He glanced around nervously. "You know, I really

shouldn't be talking about this. In fact, I feel kind of funny talking to you at all."

I could see that he did. In fact, Bryce suddenly seemed to be having difficulty making eye contact.

"Of course you do," I agreed with the same heartiness. "Who could blame you? And I know that it's none of my business. At least, it wouldn't be if this . . . this terrible thing hadn't happened. To Marnie, I mean."

"I don't see what it has to do with Marnie," he commented, still acting kind of edgy.

I decided to go for broke. "Bryce, what do you know about the rift between Holly and Marnie? It sounds as if the two of them were close, and then all of a sudden Holly just completely shut down."

He looked stricken. "Who told you about that?"

"I've been asking around, that's all," I answered vaguely.

Bryce sighed. "Okay. What I can tell you is that from my perspective, it was all about two major egos butting heads. You know, both Holly and Marnie vying for the chance to cover the biggest stories, knocking themselves out to outshine each other, that kind of thing. And the last straw for Holly was when Marnie won that award from the Association of Professional Journalists.

"Yeah, that was the real turning point," he went on, gazing off into the distance as if he was looking back in time. "That was when Holly really started resenting Marnie. In fact, I heard it got so bad that one day they had a huge blowup, right in the office. They both acted pretty unprofessional, I guess. Screaming at each other, making all these accusations . . ."

He hesitated, as if he was considering whether or not to continue. Finally, with reluctance, he added, "I probably shouldn't go around repeating this, but apparently Holly threatened Marnie. She actually said something about how she was going to kill her." Shaking his head slowly, he added, "Right after that, Holly handed in her resignation."

It took a few seconds for the meaning of his words to sink in. "Did Marnie file a police report?" I finally asked.

Bryce shook his head. "I don't think so. I guess she figured it would just blow over. Or maybe she didn't want to involve the paper. She was pretty loyal to the *Dispatch,* always talking about how she wanted to do the right thing to preserve its integrity and all that. I'm sure she wouldn't have wanted to air two employees' dirty laundry in public."

"Bryce, how do you know about this?" I asked, thinking surely it couldn't have been Richard Carrera who told him. "After all, it must have happened before you were working at the *Dispatch.*"

"I heard about it from a couple of other employees," he replied. "After Holly left, two of the women who work in the office, Karen Nelson and Peggy Ehrhart, used to talk about it. Only when Marnie wasn't around, of course.

"According to them, their feud got even worse after Holly left. Apparently she just assumed she'd fall into some other job, maybe with the *Maui News,* the bigger paper here on the island. But for whatever reason, that didn't work out. So in the end, Marnie ended up doing just fine in the newspaper business, while Holly was left out in the cold."

"I see," I told Bryce noncommittally. By that point, most of the other cars had driven off. "Listen, I'd better let you get back to work. Thanks for your time—and the information."

"No problem," he replied, turning and heading toward his BMW.

As I walked back to my own car, I wondered why Karen Nelson hadn't mentioned the screaming fight Marnie and Holly had in the office. She had been so forthcoming, yet she hadn't said a word about that particular incident.

I was also curious about whether that final showdown between the two reporters was the reason Holly had left the *Dispatch* so abruptly. She clearly had reason to be angry with Marnie. According to Karen, she'd developed an attachment to her that bordered on pathological, then felt betrayed when Marnie grabbed the award Holly was convinced she was entitled to.

The question was whether Holly was disturbed enough to have followed through on her threat.

• • •

As soon as I walked into my hotel room, I scooped up Moose and nuzzled his soft fur. It was so nice coming home to a sweet, loving pussycat that I found myself desperately missing my own menagerie back at home.

My two dogs—Max, my eternally energetic Westie, and his sidekick, Lou, a gangly Dalmatian—gave me a hero's welcome every time I walked through the door. Even though Max's tail was nothing but a stub, a legacy of his former owner, he would wag it so hard his entire butt would shake. Lou tended to hang back a bit, since his own past, which included losing one eye, had left him on the timid side.

My two cats, serene Catherine the Great and Tinkerbell, an orange-and-white tiger kitten with attitude, were more controlled, but always just as happy to see me. The same went for my blue and gold macaw, Prometheus, who invariably started squawking some nonsense designed to capture my attention. Leilani, the Jackson's chameleon Nick and I had shanghai'd during our last trip to Maui, didn't show much emotion, but I suspected she was glad to see me too.

It was also nice coming home to Nick.

He stood in the doorway of the bathroom wrapped in a damp towel, with strands of wet hair hanging around his face.

"I have an idea," he greeted me. "Instead of holing up here in our hotel room, what do you say we put on our bathing suits, go downstairs, and act like tourists for a while? We have some time before our dinner reservation at the Kula Grill, and we can talk there while we watch the sunset. After all, that is one of the main reasons we came to Maui in the first place."

Fifteen minutes later, we were settling into a pair of comfortable lounge chairs that overlooked the hotel pool. It was actually an entire complex that looked as if it came pretty close to qualifying for water-park status. The huge operation included three pools, one of them just for kids, a half dozen twisting water slides, a bunch of waterfalls, two hot tubs, a smattering of poolside cabanas, and the usual impressive display of palm trees and brilliantly colored flowers surrounding the whole shebang. There was even a bar disguised as a tropical hut, complete with a thatched roof, tiki torches, and a bartender in an aloha shirt.

As soon as we plopped down, a waiter appeared to take our order. I barely had time to slather sunblock all over my pale face and limbs before he reappeared, this time bearing two frosty mai tais.

"This was what I call a long day," I said with a sigh. I took a sip of the cool, sweet drink and instantly felt refreshed. "And this is what I call good stuff."

Nick grinned. "There's definitely something to be said for the Magnum, P.I., lifestyle. You know that old saying: When in Hawaii . . ."

"The lying-by-the-pool part is great," I returned. "It's the investigation part that's tricky."

"Sounds like you also had an interesting day."

"Definitely interesting," I assured him. "I learned a few things about FloraTech. Mainly that the company has been pretty aggressive about buying people's land."

"Not surprising," Nick commented, "since they obviously need to grow huge quantities of hibiscus in order to produce their wonder medicines."

"True," I agreed. "But what bothers me is the way they seem to be going about it. Frankly, it doesn't sound all that businesslike."

I told him about my interactions with Makiko Cooper, Wesley Nakoa, and Wesley's daughter, Lila. "At least I was able to decipher Marnie's code," I concluded. "*YES* refers to landowners who were willing to sell to FloraTech and *NO* signifies those who weren't. Some people are matter-of-fact about making a deal with them, but others are really resentful."

"And Alice Feeley was still undecided at the time of Marnie's murder," Nick observed.

"That's what I figure," I agreed. "But that could simply mean she hadn't made a decision yet. Or even that FloraTech hadn't gotten around to making her an offer."

Nick frowned thoughtfully. "The question is, is FloraTech actually doing anything wrong? Or do the reactions of people like this Nakoa guy you met up with simply reflect the residents' feelings about an outsider coming in, especially a big company, and taking possession of something the locals don't think they have a right to own?"

"I was hoping you'd uncovered something in Marnie's files that would answer that question," I replied. "Or maybe some helpful little factoid about the company that would clue us in." My heart began pounding a little faster as I added hopefully, "Did you?"

"See, that's the strange thing." Nick sounded puzzled. "I'm usually pretty good at tracking down information. And frankly, this isn't my usual thing. But I found a librarian who really knew her stuff, and she turned me on to Edgar."

"Who's Edgar?" I asked.

"It's a what, not a who. Edgar is a service the U.S. Securities and Exchange Commission offers. It's an acronym for the SEC's Electronic Data Gathering, Analysis, and Retrieval system—in other words, the government's way of helping people get information about companies. You can even get it through the Internet. It's called Edgar Online."

It sounded simple enough. Why, then, was I hearing such tentativeness in his voice?

"It's really comprehensive," he continued. "You can search for information by company name, industry, business, even area code or zip code."

"It sounds amazing."

"It is. Which is why it's so weird that we weren't able to find out a thing about FloraTech."

"Really?" My eyebrows shot sky-high.

"Yeah, the librarian was pretty surprised too. So she suggested that I try calling the SEC's reference branch, since companies that are raising less than one million dollars aren't required to register. I thought that might be the case with FloraTech. But that turned out to be another dead end."

It sounded like another language to me. "So what does all that mean?" I asked, impatient with my own lack of knowledge.

"Only that the company doesn't offer public securities—stocks and bonds—so it isn't required to file with the SEC. Next I tried Dun and Bradstreet, which the librarian explained is one of the best sources of information about businesses in the entire world. They've been around for something like a hundred fifty years, and they collect tons of data about every kind of business you can imagine. But that didn't pan out either."

My heart was still pounding hard. But at the same time, I was starting to feel overwhelmed by a tidal wave of defeat.

"I even contacted the Better Business Bureau," Nick continued. "There was nothing on file on FloraTech."

My brain was grinding away, trying to come up with a different tack. "Could it be a foreign firm?" I suggested. "Or a division of some larger company?"

"I looked into both those possibilities, but I still came up dry. I'm afraid this company, whatever it is, remains a bit of a mystery."

"Thanks for trying," I told him sincerely.

"No problem. It was actually kind of fun, flexing my P.I. muscles." He paused. "But this librarian who was helping me agreed that it was kind of peculiar that we couldn't find out anything."

"Yet its presence on Maui is overwhelming," I mused, talking more to myself than to Nick. "I feel like I keep running into FloraTech everywhere I go."

"Or at least everywhere Marnie went," Nick noted. "Yet the question of whether or not her interest in them was at all related to her murder still remains."

"What about Bryce Bolt?" I asked. "Did you have better luck delving into his mysterious past?"

"Actually, that looks a lot more promising," he replied.

"Great!" I exclaimed. "And what professional techniques, what secrets known only to insiders in the private investigation field, did you use?"

He grinned. "I Googled his name on the Internet."

I just nodded. "That works. At least as a place to start."

"Exactly. Google led me to a few articles he wrote for a couple of other newspapers before he came to the *Maui Dispatch*—"

"Which is important," I interrupted, "because it tells us where he used to work—"

"And will therefore lead us to a bunch of people we can talk to about what he was like—"

"And hopefully tell us why he left."

"Precisely." Nick grinned. "You know, Jess, you and I make a pretty good team."

"I already knew that."

"Yeah. Me too."

Nick locked his eyes with mine for what seemed like just a little too long. Even though he and I weren't exactly on our first date, I could feel my cheeks growing warm as they erupted into what was no doubt a big, embarrassing blush.

"So," I said gruffly, anxious to change the subject, if not the entire mood, "let's get in touch with some of Bryce Bolt's old cronies and see what we can dig up about his past."

"I'm a step ahead of you," Nick replied. "I printed out the names of the current editorial staff members at the two papers he worked for previously, along with their phone numbers and e-mail addresses. Once again, we have Google to thank. And I made a few calls and sent out a few e-mails, so the wheels are turning."

"Fantastic," I replied. "Thanks, Nick." The moment of tension had passed, and we were back on the case again, playing the roles of Nick and Nora Charles. At least, that was the thought that flitted through my mind until I realized that Nick and Nora were married.

"What about Marnie's file folders?" I asked. "Did you find out anything unusual about FloraTech or any of the other stories she was working on?"

"Nothing that's going to lead us to an 'aha' moment, I'm afraid. The thickest folder was the one on Hawaii Power and Light. She did a lot of research on a controversial new power plant the company wanted to build. Tons, in fact. Interviews with people who were both for and against it, a detailed history of utilities on all the Hawaiian Islands, even a cost-benefit analysis it looked like she got from someone inside the organization.

"And the folder also contained copies of the final articles, a total of five of them. But are you ready for this? Each one was published in the *Dispatch* with Holly Gruen's byline."

"You're kidding!"

"Nope. Here, I'll show you."

As I pored over the file folder Nick thrust in front of me, my mouth literally dropped open. Sure enough, while the pages and pages of notes stuck inside proved that Marnie had knocked herself out on the Hawaii Power & Light story, the actual articles did, indeed, all begin with the words *By Holly Gruen*.

Although I finally managed to close my mouth, I couldn't keep myself from chewing my lip as I pondered what Karen Nelson had told me: that Holly was certain those articles were going to win her the Association of Professional Journalists' award. From the looks of things, her pal Marnie had done most of the work. Maybe even all of it. In fact, she might have written the actual articles herself.

Yet Holly had been the one to get credit for them.

I filled Nick in on the details, then asked, "What about the FloraTech file? What did you find in there?"

"Marnie had done plenty of research on that story

too," Nick replied. "The same kind of stuff. Interviews with people who both supported and opposed the company opening its headquarters here, a bunch of press releases about the medicinal benefits offered by the hibiscus plant, copies of letters to the editor that had run in the *Dispatch,* the *Maui News,* and even the *Honolulu Star-Bulletin.*

"The one thing that really struck me," he continued, "was how often the governor's name kept coming up. Apparently Wickham played a huge role in bringing FloraTech here. There were plenty of photos of him with Norman Eldridge, the company's founder. Formal shots, mostly. A ribbon-cutting ceremony, a few of Eldridge and Governor Wickham posing at a golf outing, that kind of thing. Obviously photo ops. Most of them were cut out of newspapers; a few were actual photos. But there were also a few shots of the two of them together that looked amateurish. From the looks of them, Marnie might have taken them herself."

"Maybe she was simply trying to expand her credentials to include photojournalism," I suggested. "The one thing everybody who knew her seems to agree on is that she was incredibly ambitious."

"I don't think so." He paused, as if he was thinking. "They reminded me of the kind of shots I used to take when I was still in the P.I. biz."

My eyebrows shot way up toward my hairline. "You mean . . . racy photos?"

"Not at all. More like . . . incriminating. Or possibly incriminating, to be more accurate. The two of them shaking hands outside what looks like a motel room. Having dinner together in a restaurant. Alone. No aides, no bodyguards, just the two of them. There was even one of them strolling around what looks like a farm."

"A hibiscus farm?"

"I guess so, given the business FloraTech is in." Nick frowned. "I can't imagine why Marnie thought any of that was interesting enough to snap pictures."

I thought about the other claim I'd heard about Marnie: that her journalistic passion sometimes strayed dangerously close to paranoia. I supposed it was possible that when it came to the controversial biotech firm, she had seen red flags everywhere she looked, finding scandal even where there was none. It was similarly possible that she'd snapped a bunch of photos that, to her, were incriminating but that anybody else would see as the usual politicking.

I was about to share this thought with Nick when someone standing no more than fifty feet away caught my eye.

"Oh, no," I groaned. "What's *he* doing here?"

"Who?" Nick shifted in his lounge chair, craning his neck to see who I was referring to.

"Don't look!" I hissed. "Maybe he won't notice us."

But I'd barely gotten the words out before I realized it was too late. Graham Warner was heading over in our direction. As usual, he was wearing sloppy cutoffs and a T-shirt that looked like it had missed a few appointments at the Laundromat. His scraggly dark-blond hair was pulled back into a ponytail.

"Who is this guy?" Nick said under his breath. "Your surfing instructor?"

"Just someone I happened to strike up a conversation with in the hotel lobby." I decided to leave out the part about our friendly little chat taking place while Nick and I were in the middle of an argument. I also chose not to mention that the location of our impromptu little rendezvous was the hotel bar.

"Hey, Jessie," Graham said breezily. "Small world, huh?"

A little too small, I thought. And here I'd been thinking it was just this island that kept shrinking. "Hey, Graham," I returned without much enthusiasm, hoping he'd take the hint.

He didn't.

"So this must be that boyfriend you mentioned." He lowered himself onto the lounge chair next to mine. I had the horrifying thought that he planned on staying awhile.

"Right," I said. Reluctantly, I added, "Nick, this is Graham Warner. Graham, Nick Burby."

"Hey, bro." With great fanfare, Graham rose halfway to his feet and extended his hand, which required him to reach over me. Nick had a wary look in his eyes as he shook hands.

"So, Jess," Graham said as he sat back down, "has the convention been eating up all your time or have you managed to enjoy the island?"

"I've done a bit of sightseeing," I returned flatly, still doing my best not to encourage him.

"Cool." Graham nodded more times than was warranted. "Hey, I'm pretty sure I saw you driving around Upcountry earlier today. That was you, wasn't it? That's a great area, isn't it? There's so much to do. Hiking in Polipoli State Park, touring the Tedeschi winery . . ."

I was barely listening. I was too busy trying to process what I'd just heard.

Graham knows how I spent the day . . . and where I went? I thought, my mind racing. The chances that he simply noticed me on one of the roads were remote, given the huge area we were talking about.

Was it possible that he'd been following me, that for

the past few days he'd been keeping tabs on my comings and goings?

Even more importantly, I wondered, swallowing hard, if he's not just some creep who goes around hassling women, then who is he?

I suddenly remembered the eerie feeling I'd gotten as I was leaving Aloha Farm. The feeling I was being watched. At the time I decided I'd just fallen prey to some of that paranoia that had apparently plagued Marnie. Now I wondered if it had been Graham Warner's deep-set gray eyes that had been peering out at me from behind the dense foliage.

For all I knew, he could even have been the intruder who'd broken into my hotel room to steal Marnie's tape.

"Look," Nick said impatiently, "I think it's time for you to move along, pal. We were having a private conversation here."

With a little shrug, Graham said, "Hey, I was just trying to be friendly. I know this island pretty well, so I thought I might be of assistance."

"Thanks, but we're managing fine," Nick insisted.

"Sure, sure." Graham rose to his feet. And then, casting me what I was certain was a meaningful look, he said, "Catch you later, Jess. And you've got my number, if there's anything you need. I'll be around."

Nick followed him with his eyes as he walked away. Then he turned to me, scowling, and said, "Who did you say that guy was, Jess?"

"To tell you the truth," I replied uneasily, "I'm not really sure."

Chapter 13

"No one appreciates the very special genius of your conversation as the dog does."

—Christopher Morley

"Now this is something I really miss from my days as a P.I.," Nick commented as we pulled into the parking lot of the Kula Grill later that evening. "I can't tell you how many nights I spent at fancy restaurants, pretending I was just another discriminating diner when I was actually doing surveillance. You know, checking out whether somebody's husband was secretly wining and dining his girlfriend, keeping tabs on some guy's wife to find out if she was really hosting a dinner with clients from out of town. . . . Of course, the person who hired me paid for my dinner, as well as my time, so I got a lot of good eats."

"Unfortunately," I pointed out as I opened the car door, "our client is in no position to reimburse us for our night on the town." I climbed out of the Jeep, being careful not to let my sundress ride up. It was a bit of a challenge, since I wasn't in the habit of wearing dresses or skirts or any other garment that didn't fashionably coordinate with my usual footwear of choice, a pair of chukka boots.

"True. But that doesn't mean we can't enjoy a nice dinner." Glancing over at the restaurant, he added, "And Marnie was right. This really is a romantic place. And it's definitely out of the way."

I had to agree. The Kula Grill was in an isolated spot at the end of a poorly paved road. The restaurant was a collection of about twenty round tables clustered underneath a green awning, which was attached to a small white building that most likely housed the kitchen. Flowering shrubs surrounded the outdoor dining room, providing lots of privacy. There were also large bouquets of tropical flowers centered on each table. Aside from the tiki torches framing the entrance, the only lighting was the flickering candles on each table. As the hostess showed Nick and me to our table and we wove among the white linen tablecloths, it was so dark that it was difficult to make out the facial features of the patrons.

"The perfect place for a clandestine meeting," Nick commented once we were seated at a corner table. "If the lighting in here was any dimmer, they'd have to print the menus in Braille."

The Kula Grill's management appeared to be putting all the money they were saving on electric bills into maintaining a large, attentive staff. As soon as we sat down, a busboy bearing a pitcher came over and filled our water glasses. Almost immediately, a second staff member came over to light our candle. Not that it did much to illuminate our shadowy little corner.

Seconds later, a pale, chubby-cheeked waiter whose wavy platinum-blond hair only added to his cherubic look glided over to our table. He wore crisp, white slacks and a tasteful Hawaiian shirt splashed with flowers in shades of blue and green that, for this corner of the world, were relatively subdued.

"Good evening. I'm Keith, your waitperson," he chirped, bowing slightly. "If there's anything I can do to make your stay even more pleasant, please don't hesitate to ask."

He seemed so sincere I was tempted to ask him for a flashlight. But before I had a chance, Nick remarked, "You should probably know that this is a very special night for us." He reached over and took my hand. "Jessie and I just got engaged."

Before I could stop myself, I let out a little yelp. I immediately feigned a mild coughing fit.

Fortunately, Keith didn't appear to notice. "Goodness, that *is* special!" he cried, clasping his hands together. "Congratulations to you both!"

"Thanks," Nick returned, looking ridiculously pleased.

"Let me tell my manager," the waiter cooed. "Maybe there's something we can do to make the occasion even more special." He fluttered off to the kitchen, so excited you'd have thought we'd invited him to be our best man.

"What did you do that for?" I demanded as soon as he was out of earshot.

"It's part of my strategy," Nick replied calmly. "Look what happened the other night at the luau when Betty and Winston told the waiter they'd just gotten engaged. He told them about every other couple that had gotten engaged or celebrated their engagement at the restaurant practically since the Civil War. And isn't that what we came here for? To find out if Ace popped the question Sunday night—or if the conversation between him and Marnie went a different way entirely?"

"Good point," I admitted. And it was. But even

though we really had come all this way to find out what had transpired between Ace and Marnie the night she was murdered, I was still having a hard time sounding enthusiastic. I was feeling pressured enough without having to play the role of the dewy-eyed bride-to-be, out on the town for the first time with the man who was officially going to become her husband.

"At the very least," Nick pointed out, "we might get a free drink out of it."

I had to laugh. "I love that you're so practical."

"Oh, yeah? Tell me what else you love about me." His voice suddenly sounded much too soft—and much too serious—for my liking. In fact, the word *mushy* came to mind.

"Nick," I reminded him, "we're here to investigate a murder. We're not really en—" I stopped myself before I choked on the word. I didn't think it would be wise to pretend to have another coughing fit, since there was a good chance our attentive waiter would summon an ambulance. "You know, the reason you told the waiter we were here. We need to stay focused."

"Actually, I'm pretty good at focusing on more than one thing at once," Nick replied teasingly. "Especially if one of them is you."

I was trying to come up with a snappy reply, hopefully one that would lead us to a safer topic like murder, when I noticed Keith gliding back to our table. This time, he was holding a tray high in the air, expertly balancing two large icy drinks decorated with huge purple orchids.

"Okay, Romeo and Juliet, these are on the house," he announced, looking as pleased as the punch in the glasses. As he placed one in front of each of us, he whispered conspiratorially, "I told Jason, our bartender, to put a couple of extra shots of rum in these.

On a night like this, I figured you two lovebirds deserve it. I'll be right back with your menus. Enjoy!"

And he was off. I glanced at Nick. "It worked. At least the drinks part."

"A very good start," Nick agreed. "The night is young. We have plenty of time to get Keith to tell us what happened between Marnie and Ace."

"And if he wasn't here that night," I added, "I'd say there's a good chance he'll do us a favor and find out who was."

"A toast," Nick said abruptly, holding up his glass. "To our future."

"To our future," I seconded, clinking my glass against his. I was grateful that he'd kept the toast fairly generic, especially since we were pretending that we'd just gotten engaged. There was no doubt in my mind that Nick and I had a future. The only question was exactly what that future would look like.

As promised, Keith soon returned with our menus. He presented them to each of us as if he was bestowing a wonderful gift upon us.

"I'll just give you a few minutes to look these over," he gurgled. "The specials are here on this separate page, right inside. In the meantime, just let me know if there's anything I can do to—"

"As a matter of fact, there is," Nick said. "Are there any employees here tonight who also worked at the restaurant Sunday night?"

"Sunday night? Let me think." Keith placed his index finger against his chin and rolled his eyes upward. "Not Steve, not Rusty . . . I think Colleen was on that night, but she's not here. . . ." Suddenly his face lit up. "I know! Desiree was here Sunday night. She's the hostess. The woman who showed you to your table."

"If it's not too much trouble," Nick added, "we'd like to talk to her. Just for a minute or two."

"Of course," Keith replied. "Do you want me to ask her to stop over when she has a free moment?"

"Maybe we'd better go to the front of the restaurant to talk to her," I suggested. "That way we won't disturb the other customers."

The idea that whatever we were up to might have the effect of causing a disturbance clearly perturbed Keith for a few seconds. But he must have realized that newly engaged lovebirds like us had no intention of causing serious conflict within the walls, such as they were, of the Kula Grill. "I'll tell her," he said. Winking, he added, "And if I were you, I'd keep away from the swordfish."

After we'd ordered and Keith informed us that Desiree had been forewarned, Nick and I wandered up to the front of the restaurant.

"Everything okay?" The restaurant's hostess was smiling, but her tone was guarded. When I'd first come in, I assumed she was in her twenties, given her pale-blond hair and her strapless cocktail dress, which looked like something the original Barbie might have worn. Now that I had a chance to study her, however, I saw that Desiree was probably in her forties. Her dark red lipstick had strayed slightly into the fine lines around her mouth, and her black eyeliner was a bit too heavy. She reminded me of Lila Nakoa, who had explained she had a similar job. Somehow, I got the feeling that being the hostess at the Kula Grill hadn't exactly been Desiree's dream of what she wanted to be when she grew up.

"Everything's fine," I assured her. "I'm just trying to find out if a friend of mine came in to the restaurant Sunday night. Keith thought you might know." I whipped out the photographs I'd brought along, the ones I'd taken from Marnie's apartment. I laid a photo of Ace and Marnie, both smiling for the camera, on the counter. "Do you remember seeing this couple come in?"

She only glanced at the photo for a second before saying, "Oh, yeah." Quickly, she added, "Wait, you said you're these people's friends, right? I mean, you're not cops or anything?"

"We're not cops," I told her. "I'm a veterinarian. And Nick here is . . . a student." My impression of Desiree the Hostess was that she wanted to stay as far away from anything to do with the law as possible, and for all I knew that included law students. I also decided not to mention that the woman whose photo she had just seen was a murder victim. "She's a friend of ours."

"I remember both of them," Desiree said, nodding.

Just then, Keith sashayed over with an empty serving tray in hand. "I hope you can help these nice folks, Desi," he said.

"I'm doing my best," she replied sincerely.

"I don't suppose you happened to overhear anything they said to each other," Nick said casually.

"I sure did," Desiree replied. "I remember every couple who comes into a fancy place like this and then ruins their entire evening by having a fight. And those two hadn't even ordered yet."

So much for a romantic evening, I thought. And so much for Marnie's expectation that Ace was about to pop the question.

Still, I did my best not to react. "They argued?" I asked in a calm voice.

"Sure did. I heard a lot of it, but not all of it. See, I started getting the gist of what was going on between the two of them while I was seating a couple at the table next to theirs. Dan and Ellen Simons. Lovely people. They come in here all the time. He's a photographer and she—"

"Get to the point, Desi!" Keith interrupted impatiently.

"Okay, okay." Desiree took a deep breath. "So I'm seating the Simons, and all of a sudden I hear the girl whisper—well, it wasn't exactly a whisper, it was kind of a hoarse-voice sound, since I could hear her even though it was obvious she was trying to keep it quiet—"

"What did she *say*?" Keith demanded.

Desiree paused for dramatic effect. "She says, 'You mean you're *married*?' "

"No!" Keith gasped, slapping both cheeks with the palms of his hands.

As for me, I simply glanced at Nick. From his expression, I could see he was thinking the same thing I was thinking.

"Then what?" Keith demanded breathlessly.

"She stormed out of here, of course," Desiree replied. "What woman wouldn't?"

"What did he do?" Keith asked.

"What do you think he did? He ran after her. But she was way ahead of him. She was just a little thing, but she was pretty fast on her feet. By the time he caught up with her, she was out in the parking lot. But I could see everything, because by that point I was back here, at the front."

"Did they continue to argue?" I asked.

"They sure did. First, as soon as he caught up with her, he grabbed her by the arm. 'Don't touch me!' she yelled. Really loud. At least, loud for this place. Good thing they were already outside by then or the other customers would have had a fit."

"That *brute,*" Keith interjected. Huffily, he added, "If I'd been here, I would have gone after him with a steak knife."

"So then I heard her say, 'I'm going to tell her what's

been going on,' " Desiree continued. "The guy went nuts, of course. So she yelled, 'Call me a taxi! I'm not getting in the car with you!' But he wasn't about to take no for an answer. He yelled back, 'You're coming with me. We have to talk about this.'

"Then, I remember, he looked back at the restaurant, like he suddenly realized he might have an audience. Which he did, of course. At least me. But I pretended I wasn't listening. I started looking through the reservation book, acting like I was busy checking off names or something.

"So then he lowered his voice. But they were still close enough that I could hear him. And he said, 'Let's go someplace where we can be alone. Someplace quiet. We have to talk.' " Desiree gave a little shrug, then concluded, "So wouldn't you know it? The fool gets in the car with him and they drive off."

I cast Nick another meaningful look, then asked, "Desiree, did you tell anyone about this?"

"Why would I?" she returned, sounding a bit defensive. "They're hardly the first couple that's had an argument here. It happens all the time."

Keith nodded enthusiastically. "That's right. Sometimes they don't even finish their dinners before they both go off in a snit. It's such a waste of food."

"So you didn't tell the police any of this," I said.

"The police?" Desiree looked at me as if I'd just suggested she join the French Foreign Legion. "Why on earth would I want anything to do with the police?"

From the horrified look on her face, I gathered that somewhere along the line, this woman had had enough interactions with the police to last a lifetime.

I thanked her for the information, adding, "I'd better let you get back to work. I don't want you to get in trouble."

Once Nick and I were settled back at our table, I observed, "So Ace and Marnie weren't exactly going hand and hand into the sunset right before she was murdered."

"Not even close," Nick agreed. "And from what Desiree told us, it sounds as if he and Marnie might have gone to the Purple Mango after they left this place."

"Which means he could have been the person the cops' witness saw her leaving with—"

"And he could also have been the person who killed her," Nick finished. "It certainly fits. First, Ace tells Marnie he's married. Maybe he even tries to break it off with her. Then she goes nuts and threatens to tell his wife. Finally, in a fit of fury, our pal Ace takes what seems like the path of least resistance, at least to him."

I just nodded. It was certainly an ugly scenario.

But Nick was right. It was also a scenario that made perfect sense.

• • •

"What's this?" Nick asked as he pushed open the door of our hotel room.

Glancing down, I saw what he was referring to: a white business-size envelope lying on the carpet. Someone had clearly slipped it under the door while we were out.

My heart immediately began to pound. What now? I thought.

"Maybe it's a bill," he speculated, bending down to pick it up. "You know how sometimes hotels slip your bill under the door."

"But that's usually the day you're checking out," I pointed out. "It's way too soon for that."

With a sly grin, he suggested, "Maybe the neighbors have been complaining about how much noise we're making. You gotta admit, we've been making the most of our 'romantic getaway.' "

I wasn't amused. "Or maybe they've been complaining about Moose. They might have noticed he'd moved into our room while you had him out on the lanai." I glanced nervously at our roommate, who was trotting toward us. He looked very happy that we were home.

I scooped him up, then cuddled him in my arms as I peered over Nick's shoulder. He slid open the envelope with his finger and unfolded what looked like a letter printed on the hotel's stationery. A smaller slip of paper was also tucked inside. Printed on top was the word *Voucher.*

"According to this," he said, "the hotel is giving us a free helicopter ride over the island of Kauai. It says here that it's a bonus for having booked the room for so many days."

"Really? That's awfully generous."

Nick shrugged. "Hey, you know what they say about never looking a gift horse in the mouth. Didn't they teach you about that in vet school?"

I laughed. "I guess I missed that lecture. When do we go?"

He studied the voucher. "It looks like we're on for—hey, that's tomorrow's date. Wow, they're even throwing in airfare to Kauai. We'll be picked up at Lihue Airport by our own personal helicopter pilot."

"Very cool," I commented. "And I thought the free tickets for the luau were a big deal. The timing is good too. The conference ends at noon tomorrow, and none of the morning lectures sounded all that interesting, anyway."

"This is so great!" Nick exclaimed. "I read all about these helicopter trips in my guidebook. Parts of Kauai are unreachable by car or even by foot, so this is the only way to see some of the most spectacular scenery in Hawaii. It's supposed to be unbelievable, with mountains and canyons and waterfalls as high as skyscrapers . . ."

As Nick babbled on, I read through the letter, looking for a catch—some fine print stating that if we opted to take the aforementioned helicopter ride, we were automatically agreeing to buy a time-share or a piece of real estate in one of the more remote corners of the Haleakala crater.

But I didn't mention my concerns, since I didn't want to rain on Nick's parade. Still, I was only too familiar with another old expression: If something sounds too good to be true, it probably is.

• • •

Nick's excitement was contagious, and I quickly put all my reservations aside. The next morning, we skipped the breakfast ritual we'd developed. Instead, after refilling Moose's food and water bowls and putting out the *Do Not Disturb* sign again, we went downstairs to the lobby to grab coffee and muffins at the hotel's complimentary continental breakfast. Before dashing out, I snatched a couple of bagels off the tray and stuck them in my backpack, figuring our helicopter trip probably wouldn't include meal service.

Then we popped into our Jeep and drove to Kahului Airport. As we pulled into the parking lot, I reflected upon how much had happened in the past five days. In fact, it was difficult to believe that such a short time had passed since we'd first arrived.

After our Hawaiian Airlines airplane rose out of Kahului Airport and Nick and I oohed and aahed over the view, I opened Nick's guidebook and read the section on Kauai. I learned that "the garden isle," as it was nicknamed, was the oldest of Hawaii's main islands, and ancient Hawaiians had lived in its green valleys centuries earlier. It still retained its spectacular beauty, most of which remained untouched by humans.

Because of its dramatic mountains and lush rain forests, it was often compared to Eden. Kauai's beautiful, untamed terrain had been featured in many movies, including all three of the *Jurassic Park* flicks. In fact, even though this particular guidebook had been written especially for "penny-pinchers" like us, its author strongly recommended that sightseers scrimp, save, or do whatever it took in order to see it all by helicopter.

The more I read, the more excited I became.

We'd barely gotten off the plane at Lihue Airport before I noticed a man in his thirties or forties waving at us. He was dressed in jeans and the usual loud Hawaiian shirt. But his face had that familiar weather-worn surfer look, with amazingly green eyes and leathery skin that indicated he was no stranger to the sun.

"Jessie and Nick, right?" he greeted us. "I'm Chip, your pilot and tour guide for the day." After we shook hands all around, he announced, "Okay, so if you guys are ready, let's hit the skies."

As we crossed the field toward the helicopter, Chip explained, "This helicopter is equipped with a two-way intercom system, so we can talk during the flight. That way, I can tell you what you're seeing and you can ask me anything that comes up."

The four-passenger helicopter, which Chip informed us was a Bell JetRanger, had huge windows that offered excellent views. It was also surprisingly comfortable, I discovered as we seat-belted ourselves in.

However, I quickly forgot all about creature comforts as we rose into the air and the island's beauty spread out before us. Chip explained via the earphones that we were starting along the north coast, heading west toward the famed Na Pali Coast. The view was amazing, and I snapped one picture after another of the treacherous volcanic mountains that edged the coastline. Just as the guidebook had indicated, I recognized those craggy peaks, jutting high into the air from dense green rain forests, from the movies—and I half-expected to see a T. rex tromping through the thick foliage.

"Pretty spectacular, huh?" Chip said. "Next we're going to head toward the center of the island. We'll be flying over Waimea Canyon, the largest canyon in the Pacific. In fact, its nickname is the Grand Canyon of the Pacific. The rivers and the lava flowing off Mount Waialeale, the island's ancient volcano, created it thousands of years ago. The Waimea River still flows through the canyon, cutting it deeper and wider every day."

Gesturing toward the guidebook he clutched in his hand, Nick asked, "Didn't I read that the canyon is over ten miles long?"

"That's right," Chip returned. "And it's about a mile wide. It's also over thirty-five hundred feet deep. Today it's part of Kokee State Park, and there are hiking trails running through it. It can be pretty treacherous going, but people do it all the time."

"Can you reach it by driving?" I asked.

"Sure, but it's a long trek. Waimea Canyon Road is about forty miles long. It's also a pretty rough road. Trust me: It's not for everybody. But you two look like you could handle a stop inside the canyon. That way, you can get out and really take a look around."

"Cool," Nick muttered. I glanced over at him and saw that his eyes were glowing.

The spiky terrain of the island's northwest coast suddenly gave way to a dramatic canyon. The dense green rain forest now covered craggy cliffs and deep crevices carved out of dusty red volcanic rock. Waimea Canyon really did remind me of the Grand Canyon.

"There it is!" I cried.

Nick was already doing some pretty serious picture-taking of his own.

"Look at that!" I cried, pointing to a silvery waterfall that looked as if it plunged hundreds of feet downward. As if it weren't dramatic enough in itself, a rainbow floated in front of it.

"Wow," Nick muttered, sounding totally awe-struck. "This is so amazing."

I reached over and took his hand in mine, giving it a squeeze. I was glad I hadn't given in to my fears about what this trip might be all about and that, for once, I'd just accepted it for what it was: a bonus for being a good tourist.

When I felt the helicopter start to descend, I peered over the side to watch as Chip slowly brought us down into the canyon. Our landing on a rocky ledge was so expertly done that I had a feeling he made this stop for all his customers.

"Okay, I'm gonna let you folks out here for a while," Chip told us. "Feel free to hike around and get a feel for the place."

"Great!" Nick exclaimed. "Thanks a lot!"

As soon as we scrambled out of the helicopter, he and I began making our way along what looked like a trail, albeit a rough, poorly traveled one. I had to pay close attention to keep from stumbling on the loose rocks that had deviously set themselves down along the path as if they were deliberately trying to trip hikers.

But I also managed to take in the spectacular view. We really were deep inside the canyon, which stretched as far as I could see in every direction. The craggy layers of rock looked as treacherous as they were beautiful. The only softness in the harsh terrain that surrounded us came in the form of the low scrubby shrubs that meandered through the rocks like rivulets.

As we walked for what must have been at least a couple of miles, the experience was so absorbing that I totally forgot to check the time. At least until I realized the sun had gotten substantially higher in the clear blue sky. It was also getting uncomfortably hot.

"Maybe we should be getting back," I suggested, glancing over my shoulder uneasily. By this point, the helicopter was no longer in sight. Not only had I lost track of the time; I hadn't realized we'd walked so far. "Chip didn't say how long we'd be staying here."

Nick shielded his eyes with his hand and gazed off. "I'd really like to get some more hiking in before we leave. This place is incredible."

"I know, but—"

I never got to finish my sentence. The thunderous noise that suddenly reverberated through the canyon made it impossible for us to hear each other speak.

For a second or two, I wondered what was going on. An earthquake? I wondered, more puzzled than afraid. Or some other type of natural disaster?

And then, as I stood halfway down the 3,500-foot-deep canyon and watched our helicopter rise into the air without us, I understood that we were in the middle of a disaster, all right.

But it was one that had nothing to do with nature.

Chapter 14

"A door is what a dog is perpetually on the wrong side of."

—Ogden Nash

"Where's he going?" Nick demanded. "What's he doing?"

"Wait!" I screamed. "Come back! Are you crazy?"

Nick shook his head tiredly. "Save your breath, Jess. He can't hear you."

"But he *left* us here!" I cried. "Stranded in the middle of nowhere! What on earth could he be thinking? How are we supposed to—"

I snapped my mouth shut. In a sudden flash, I understood exactly what was going on.

Being stranded in the middle of nowhere was no accident.

My head buzzed as I tried to wrap my brain around the incomprehensible thing that had just happened. There was only one explanation: We'd been left here to die.

The wheels in my head were turning. Whoever gave us the free helicopter trip—whoever *really* did, since it obviously wasn't the hotel that had arranged to have us stranded at the bottom of a canyon—had decided that Nick and I were getting a little too close to the truth. The truth about who had killed Marnie and the truth about why.

As I tried to digest what was suddenly so obvious, the wheels in my head weren't the only thing that was turning. All around me, the entire canyon seemed to be whirling like a merry-go-round.

"I'm trying to convince myself this is all just some ridiculous misunderstanding," Nick said in a strained voice. "Unfortunately, I'm not doing a very good job."

Suddenly he snapped his fingers. "Hey, what about your cell phone?" he suggested. I heard a distinct note of optimism in his voice. "I didn't bring mine, since I figured it was just one more thing to carry. But did you bring yours?"

"I did!" I cried. But when I pulled it out, I saw that there was no signal.

"Look, I'm sure we won't be stranded here for long," I insisted. "I mean, they've got to patrol this whole area from the air. Don't you think so?"

"Sure," he agreed, sounding as uncertain as I had. "They probably come by every few hours to make sure no hikers or campers get left behind."

"Right." I could barely get the word out. I was too busy looking around at our wild and treacherous surroundings. Steep mountains, shaped like canine teeth and edged with sharp, forbidding-looking rocks, that towered above us into the sky and dropped just as far below. A waterfall the height of a multistory skyscraper, thousands of gallons of water shooting downward with alarming force. Thick ground cover everywhere, making it hard to move around and hiding who only knew what kind of wildlife.

I had a feeling there weren't a lot of hikers or campers who came this way.

"But in the meantime," I suggested, "maybe we should look around for a way out of here." I tried to keep my tone light. It wasn't easy, given the fact that a lump the size of a small boulder had lodged itself in my throat.

"Definitely," Nick agreed. "And we're going to think positive. There's got to be a way out of here. There's no way we're stuck. I mean, gazillions of tourists come to Kauai every year. How would the island's biggest industry survive if they lost a couple of visitors in their canyon every now and then?" Glancing around, he added, "We're going to find our way out of here. The question is, which way should we head?"

Like him, I looked to the right, to the left, and behind. My spirits plummeted even further. There was no logical answer to his simple question, since there was clearly no easy way out. Not unless your idea of an afternoon stroll was struggling a few thousand feet up out of a canyon. As for which direction to proceed, I didn't have a clue. We could move west, with the sun, or east so it was behind us, but I had no idea which way was more likely to get us out of here and back toward civilization.

"You decide," I finally said.

He glanced around a few more times, then began walking. I didn't know what factors he'd considered in making his decision, but I suspected he didn't have any better idea than I did. Still, doing something seemed a whole lot better than doing nothing. So I followed.

We walked in silence for a very long time, with Nick leading the way and me just a few feet behind. I tried to find comfort in the steady way he marched along, sticking to what could loosely be defined as a path. I concentrated on the rhythm of his footsteps, the soft thuds that were the only sound I heard aside from the manic chittering of birds.

The longer we walked, the harder the blistering sun beat down on us. The merciless heat made me wonder why people actually paid good money to come to hot, sunny places like this one.

Nick and I walked for hours. I kept glancing at my watch, each time figuring a very long time must have passed since I'd last checked. Instead, I discovered that the day was crawling by. Two fifty, three o'clock, three ten.

The sun was getting low enough to cast sweeping shadows on the west side of the canyon, meanwhile illuminating the east side so the red portions looked as if they were on fire. But that didn't mean the air was getting any cooler. It was disheartening, realizing that it would be hours before the sun's rays stopped working so hard at draining away the last bits of energy I possessed. I berated myself for not having had the presence of mind to bring along a bottle of water. Still, I couldn't stop thinking about those frosty glass pitchers of ice-cold pineapple juice I'd noticed sitting casually on a white linen tablecloth at the hotel's breakfast. At the time I'd barely glanced in their direction.

I reminded myself that baking in the sun was better than trying to make our way through the pitch-black of nightfall. Which I knew would be the situation all too soon.

"Are you okay?" Nick called back over his shoulder. I'd already become so used to the silence that the sound of a human voice made me jump.

"Huh? Oh, I'm fine. How about you?"

"I'm okay. A little thirsty, but fine." We walked another few feet before he added, "I'm trying not to think about the mai tai that I keep telling myself is waiting for me at the other end of this adventure."

Two mai tais, I thought. At least. And a tall glass of ice water. One that's about as high as that waterfall way off in the distance, the one that doesn't seem to get any closer no matter how far we walk. Frankly, I didn't know if fantasizing about cool liquids I wasn't likely to encounter ever again only made things worse.

"You know," he went on, sounding almost chatty, "we're kind of lucky, in a way."

I couldn't wait to hear where he was going with this. Especially since I was starting to find his Boy Scout cheeriness a tad irritating.

"I mean, we're getting to see some of the splendors of the Hawaiian Islands that most visitors never get to see."

"Certainly not this close," I mumbled, stepping around a large rock that looked like it had just moved into my path on purpose.

"It's one thing to view Waimea Canyon from a helicopter," Nick continued with the same hardy cheerfulness. I knew he meant well, but frankly, at this point he just seemed to be making things worse. "And you've got to admit, the views from the helicopter were pretty amazing."

"Absolutely spectacular," I agreed. But I was thinking, Too bad we'll never be able to show any of our friends all the great pictures we took.

"But being down here," he continued, "right in the middle of such an incredible natural wonder . . . that's really something."

"This is certainly an experience I'll never forget," I assured him. I just hope I have more than a day or two to look back on it, I thought. The image of the mai tais, the mile-high glass of ice water, and the refreshing pitchers of pineapple juice was gone. In its place I pictured a slew of vultures flying overhead, licking their lips, at least metaphorically, as I took my final breaths in one of the most spectacular spots on earth.

All of a sudden, Nick stopped walking. I did too, although I came this close to bumping into him.

"Jess?" he said, turning around to face me. "I just thought of something. Don't pilots have to log in information like how many people they left with—and how many people they returned with? There's got to be some regulatory agency that makes sure things like this don't happen."

My mind raced as I debated whether or not to point out that this *was* happening. We had been stranded here, so obviously our helicopter pilot had no fear of paperwork. But by that point I was so hot, thirsty, and tired that it just seemed easier to agree.

"I'm sure you're right," I told him. "Besides, I'm certain we'll find our way out soon. In fact, we'll probably be laughing about this by nightfall."

"Between someone spotting us down here and us getting ourselves out, I don't think you and I really have anything to worry about," he concluded.

His innocence made me want to lean over and hug him. He reminded me of a little kid, begging for some sensible explanation that had the power to banish the ghosts and monsters from underneath his bed.

As we started trudging along again, I became aware of an uncomfortable rumbling in my stomach. As if being hot and thirsty weren't bad enough, I could now add intense hunger to the list of things I yearned to complain about but didn't because I was afraid of lowering our morale even further.

I guess Nick's stomach was on the same schedule as mine, because he suddenly glanced over his shoulder and said, "I don't suppose you brought anything to eat, did you?"

I was about to say no in as upbeat and positive a way as possible when I remembered the two bagels I'd squirreled away at breakfast that morning. At the time, I'd wondered if it was worth the trouble. Now I wished I'd stuck donuts and bagels and anything else that was edible into every pocket I could find.

"I have bagels!" I announced triumphantly, unbuckling my backpack and pulling them out. Even though they'd been stuck in there with everything else I routinely carried around, they were bearing up well. Certainly much better than the donuts and Danish pastries I was fantasizing about would have.

"Great," Nick said breathlessly. "Thank you for being such a good planner."

"Maybe we should split one," I suggested. "Then we could split the second one later."

Nick looked at me woefully. While my idea made sense, I realized that making even small admissions about one's vulnerability was a horribly effective way of making a bad situation even worse.

Even so, he willingly accepted the half I offered him after tearing the bagel into two equal pieces.

We started walking again, chomping on our bagels. I assumed I was coordinated enough to do both those things, walk and chomp, while returning the second bagel to my backpack. But somehow, when I thought I was slipping it back inside, I instead managed to slide it past the bag's opening. Before I even realized what was happening, the second bagel—our only form of nourishment—went tumbling down, bouncing off several big, craggy rocks before disappearing deep inside the canyon.

"No!" I cried, tempted to run after it but knowing that hurtling into a rocky abyss was probably an even less savory way of ending my life than starving to death.

If I ever get out of here, I thought mournfully, I'm never going to take a bagel for granted again.

I glanced at Nick, and the expression on his face made me want to cry. I was sure there were plenty of things he would have liked to say to me, but mercifully he just sighed and continued walking.

We'd gone a few hundred feet farther, meanwhile finishing up our pathetic half bagels, when Nick proposed, "Maybe we should just find a comfortable spot and wait for someone to rescue us."

"Don't you think we should keep going?" I asked halfheartedly. I hadn't given up hope that somehow, amid the canyon's twenty-seven million square feet, we'd find a magic door marked EXIT. By this point, I'd come to believe that scenario was the only way we'd ever survive the ordeal.

"We could find someplace that's easily visible from the air," Nick suggested. "Someplace shady."

"Let's walk a while longer," I said. Trying to make it sound as if I'd adopted at least a little of his optimism, I added, "We might as well enjoy the view while we're waiting to be rescued."

As if to emphasize what a great idea I thought it was to keep moving, I resumed striding along the rough path, this time taking the lead. But I hadn't walked more than five or six feet before I took a step and, before I understood what was happening, felt the earth beneath my right foot crumble.

"Ahhh!" I yelled as I stumbled. It felt as if everything was suddenly moving in slow motion as I sank down a slope. Because I was so badly off balance, my right leg twisted under me. "Owww!" I added as I slid downhill, my butt and my shins scraping against the sharp-edged shards of volcanic rock that were scattered everywhere.

"Jessie!" I heard Nick cry in the background.

My eyes opened wide with terror as I continued plummeting downward. Right in front of me stretched the canyon, opening up wider and wider as if it couldn't wait to swallow me up.

And then I felt all the air in my lungs shoot out of my body as I abruptly made contact with a small bush, its branches pushing against my chest as if someone strong but clumsy was performing the Heimlich maneuver on me.

Everything suddenly seemed strangely still. I couldn't breathe, my ankle was in excruciating pain, my butt felt as if someone had shredded it with a paring knife, and my entire leg, the one that was still folded beneath me, was scraped raw. But at least I'd stopped sliding.

"Oh, my God, Jessie!" Within seconds Nick had scrambled down the incline far enough to reach me. Clinging to another one of those small bushes with his left hand, he reached for me with his right. "Are you okay?"

"I think so," I gasped. By that point, I was back to breathing and speaking, and my ability to feel pain seemed to be increasing every second. "Ouch! My ankle is killing me, but otherwise I'm fine."

With Nick grasping me by the wrist and dragging me upward, I managed to climb back up to the path by putting all my weight on my good foot. The other one, meanwhile, was so badly twisted I couldn't put any weight on it at all. I had to hold my leg in the air like a wounded animal.

When I finally got to the top, which returned me to the same spot I'd been in when I fell, I felt as if I'd achieved something really worthwhile. But my feeling of triumph only lasted about two and a half seconds. My ankle was absolutely throbbing with pain. In fact,

I recognized that if I'd been the type who cried easily, this would have been a good time to do so.

However, being practical by nature, I realized it wouldn't do me any good to lose even more moisture than I already had. Now, more than ever, I would need every drop of water I possessed, even tears, to get through this ordeal.

Aside from still being horribly thirsty, I would have traded my clinic-on-wheels for a hose to wash off the fine red dirt that now covered most of my body. I had rust-colored dust in my hair, in my eyelashes, even under my fingernails.

I swept the dust off my right foot and studied my ankle.

"How bad is it?" Nick asked anxiously. "Do you think it's broken?"

"Let's just say that my tap-dancing career may well be over," I muttered.

"Jessie, I can't believe you're joking around!"

"Sorry." I examined the injured spots, wincing whenever I touched it. From the way it looked and felt, I suspected it was just a bad sprain. Good news, I supposed, even though I was still going to find it close to impossible to walk.

Now we'll never get out of here, I thought, blinking hard in a last-ditch effort at holding on to those tears.

I glanced up at Nick, feeling truly sorry that I'd gotten him into this situation. If I hadn't been so nosy our first day here, barging into the ballroom at the Royal Banyan to see what all the singing and cheering was about, right now I'd be sitting by the pool or snorkeling instead of languishing in a hot, dry canyon with a useless foot that felt as if someone had just tried to snap it off.

I would have forgiven him for anything he might have said to me at that moment, no matter how terrible his accusations. Instead, he looked around and said, "I don't suppose you saw that other bagel down there, did you?"

I actually laughed. It felt good, as well as very strange.

Unfortunately, our moment of levity lasted exactly that long: one moment. "What do you think we should do now?" I asked Nick. My own decisions had turned out to be such bad ones that I no longer felt I deserved to take on a leadership role.

"I don't think we have much choice," he replied. "If you can't walk on that ankle, we'll just have to wait for someone to find us."

I nodded. My eyes were burning and my throat was so thick I didn't think I could speak. As if I hadn't done enough by getting us into this awful situation in the first place, now I had made it even worse by getting hurt. If we'd ever had a chance of getting out of here on our own, it was pretty much gone.

And even though I felt horribly selfish for even thinking it, I was glad that in one of the worst hours of my life, at least I had Nick at my side.

• • •

Darkness came early, just as I knew it would. By that point, thirst and exhaustion had become old news. In fact, they both paled beside the hunger that now gnawed at my stomach. Nick and I sat huddled together on a large ledge we'd found three or four feet below the path, not far from the place in which I'd taken that fateful step. While it wasn't exactly cold now that the sun was gone, the air felt uncomfortably cool and damp, especially given my sweat-soaked, red-dust-covered clothes.

We'd tired of talking about our situation long before. In fact, I was pretty sure we'd entirely run out of things to say to each other, not to mention the energy with which to say them, when Nick suddenly said, "You know, Jess, you and I never really talked about what happened the last time we came to Hawaii."

And this is a good time? I thought irritably. We're stranded in a canyon in Kauai without water, food, sunblock, flashlights, Ace bandages, maps, or any chance of ever getting out of here, and you decide it's time for a heart-to-heart we've put off having for nearly a year and a half?

"I'm talking about the time I surprised you when I asked you—"

"I remember what you asked me," I replied, surprised by the way he'd been on the verge of breaking our unwritten rule of never directly addressing the actual event. As a result, my words came out a lot sharper than I'd intended. But it wasn't only Nick's timing—or even the subject itself—that was responsible. The incessant pain in my ankle was also to blame for turning me into the person most likely to get voted off the island on one of those reality shows.

Nick was silent for a long time before he said, "You really hurt me, Jess."

The rawness of his confession instantly rendered the pain in my ankle irrelevant. "I know I did," I said in a much softer voice. "And I'm sorry, Nick. Really sorry. I know it's kind of late to be saying this, but—"

"You don't have to apologize," he insisted. "I understand that what happened was simply the result of where you were at that point. Besides, I probably shouldn't have surprised you like that. I had this idea in my mind that you'd fall into my arms, like we were in some movie or something, and the two of us would go off hand in hand into the sunset. . . ."

I had to admit, the guy really was quite a romantic.

I supposed it was a good thing that at least one of us was.

"But I think we've both come a long way since then," he continued. "Don't you?"

"Definitely," I agreed, not sure where he was going with this. But I'd read *Lord of the Flies* and seen the movie about those poor people who were stranded in the Andes and had no choice but to resort to cannibalism, so I figured I'd better do everything I could to stay on his good side, just in case. After all, we were talking dire straits here.

"I've really enjoyed these last three months," Nick went on in a strained voice. "The two of us living together, I mean. I really love you, Jessie."

"I love you too, Nick," I said sincerely.

"You know, you might not want to admit it, but just by agreeing to give that a try, you were making a commitment."

The C word. I should have known it would pop up sooner or later. The only good thing was that just hearing it sent enough adrenaline rushing through my entire body to seriously ease the pain in my ankle.

Nick continued, "Do you think—if we ever get out of here, that is—that maybe you and I should get married?"

"Is that an actual proposal?" I asked lightly.

"Yes," he replied. He pulled away just enough to turn and face me. His voice sounded anything *but* light. In fact, even in the dark canyon, I could see that his eyes were filled with a startling intensity. "That's exactly what it is. Jessie, I love you. Will you marry me?"

This time around, he didn't blush or stutter. Instead, Nick was asking me this all-important question from a place of complete confidence, sincerity, and love.

In fact, this entire scenario was a far cry from his

fumbling attempt at cementing our relationship the last time we were in Hawaii. And it had nothing to do with the two of us being stranded in a canyon that we'd probably never manage to get out of alive.

It wasn't only Nick who was different. I realized I was different too.

The main thing that struck me was that I wasn't suddenly overwhelmed by a surge of panic. Then again, I couldn't ignore the fact that, at the moment, the chances that I'd ever see the inside of a wedding dress seemed slim indeed.

I don't know what was responsible for the way I felt. But I really did mean it when I said, "Yes, Nick. I'll marry you."

And then, as we sat halfway up from the bottom of a huge hole in the earth, miles from civilization, with my ankle throbbing and my clothes smelling and my pores clogged with red dust, he leaned over and gave me the longest, sweetest kiss of our entire life together.

When he finally pulled away, his eyes were glassy. "Hey, Jess?"

"Yes?"

"Now that that's settled, you do think we'll get out of here, don't you?"

I didn't answer. In fact, I held up my hand in a silencing gesture.

"Did you hear that?" I asked, blinking. I was almost afraid to say the words, figuring the sound I'd just noticed was merely the result of sun poisoning or red-dust poisoning or some other dreadful syndrome that was about to finish me off.

"No," Nick replied thoughtfully. "I mean, I don't hear anything. What does it sound like to you?"

"It's a rushing sound. Far away. It sounds like . . . like water."

He listened for a few seconds, cocking his head in

the same way I was cocking mine. It was something I'd learned from my dogs, who were true hearing experts. "Hey, wait. I do. At least, I think I do." He scrambled across the rocks, ducking out of sight and disappearing somewhere below.

A few seconds later, he reappeared, poking his head over the edge of the flat rock that had become our home away from home. This time, he was wearing a huge grin.

"A stream!" he announced. "It's about fifty feet below us. And running alongside it is a bona fide hiking path. I can help you down, and we can follow it and maybe get out of here! Or at least I can, and I can get help."

"Thank you!" I cried, although exactly who I was thanking wasn't clear to me. It could have been Nick, it could have been some higher power—heck, it could even have been Pele, although I found it hard to believe a female deity would ever put two ordinary people like us through such an ordeal.

I crawled across the rock, telling myself the excruciating pain would soon be over. Sure enough—on the other side, down at the bottom of a hill, was a stream with a path next to it. Nick helped me make my way down along the rocks, which didn't seem nearly as treacherous now that I knew we'd actually stumbled across a way of getting out of this canyon.

As soon as I reached the rushing water, I stuck my ankle into it. It was surprisingly cold, instantly making my ankle feel a hundred times better.

"Hey, check this out!" Nick pointed to what, to me, looked like nothing more than an unsightly mess that someone had left behind. Then I realized the implications of what I was looking at.

"Campers!" I exclaimed.

"Even better: really sloppy, inconsiderate campers."

Gleefully, he held up a bottle of water that was still half full. "Look! They even left some of their gear behind!"

Either that or they were eaten by giant lizards that no one knows inhabit this canyon, I thought. But I didn't care what had happened to the last group of adventurers who'd come this way. I was too giddy over the sight of that bottle of water.

Nick tossed it over to me, then continued taking inventory. "Granola bars!" he cried. "And beef jerky! Take your pick!"

He could have been offering me filet mignon and a pint of Ben & Jerry's. I grabbed a granola bar and wolfed it down in about six seconds flat.

"Early tomorrow morning," Nick said, "as soon as the sun comes up, we can follow this path and find our way out of here."

"We could also follow the trail of granola bar wrappers," I added, giddy with my newfound sense of hope.

By this point, the cold water from the stream had melted away most of the pain in my ankle. I glanced around, trying to find something I could bind it up with. Nature's version of an Ace bandage. I didn't see anything that looked suitable, especially since ideally I needed something with some elasticity. I racked my brain, trying to imagine something that was lightweight and stretchy, yet still strong. . . .

Got it, I suddenly thought. Necessity really is the mother of invention.

I began taking off my T-shirt. Nick, meanwhile, stared at me as if I'd gotten delirious from weather exposure.

"What are you doing?" he asked, sounding alarmed. As I pulled my sports bra off over my head, he added, "You're not going skinny-dipping, are you?"

I wriggled back into my T-shirt, this time braless.

Grinning, I dangled my bra in front of him. "I found a way to wrap up my ankle so I can walk on it. Now that the swelling is going down, I think I'll be able to manage."

"You're a genius," he returned. "Then again, I've always said you were somebody who plays your cards close to your chest. Or plays your chest close to your feet. Or something like that."

"Ha-ha," I said. I was amazed that we were actually joking around. Funny how access to a few basics like food, water, and a way out of the Canyon of Death could make things look so much brighter.

I wrapped up my ankle with the sports bra, twisting the stretchy straps over the top of my foot to hold it in place. Then, holding my breath, I took a few tentative steps. It worked. I could walk.

"Good as new!" I announced. "In fact, I'm beginning to believe that we're actually going to get out of here alive."

Nick looked surprised. "Did you ever doubt it?"

I decided to save my honest answer for another time. "Let's try to get some sleep," I suggested. "I have a feeling tomorrow's going to be another long day."

• • •

The following morning, Nick and I sat in silence as we drove back to the Royal Banyan Hotel, with me in the driver's seat and him sprawled out beside me. By that point, both of us were too grubby, too exhausted, and too stupefied by our arduous adventure to make conversation.

On a Saturday morning, Maui was strangely quiet. There were fewer cars on the road than usual. It was difficult to believe that Nick and I had already put in a long day. As soon as the sun's first tentative rays had begun illuminating the canyon, we started walking, following the river. I had to admit, the jagged red walls of the cliffs rising up alongside us, glowing like hot coals as the golden sunlight hit them, were beautiful. So were the signs that other hikers before us had followed this same route. While we didn't find any more caches of water and granola bars, we occasionally came across a piece of the shiny wrapper from a candy bar or even a footprint. It wasn't much, but it went a long way in encouraging us.

When we finally made it to the mountain road, I knew the worst was over. We kept walking, marveling over how much easier it was to tread upon pavement. My makeshift Ace bandage worked wonders. Even so, the sun was getting pretty hot by then, so we were pleased when a man in his pickup truck stopped for us. He even made his golden Lab move to the back so Nick and I could take her place in the front seat. Just like her, I stuck my head out the open window, luxuriating in the cool air and the warm sunshine and the knowledge that we'd survived.

The driver dropped us at the airport, where we booked seats on the next flight to Kahului Airport. I was thankful that Nick and I both routinely carried our credit cards, even on sightseeing expeditions. But when it came to buying out half the food at the concession, we stuck with cold, hard cash. Coffee and a couple of fried-egg sandwiches went a long way toward restoring both our energy and our good humor.

In fact, as we drove along the now-familiar roads of Maui, grateful to be back in one piece, our night on Kauai felt like something that had happened long, long ago. But that didn't mean I was planning to forget it.

Or that I wasn't more anxious than ever to find out who had arranged for Nick and me to be stranded at the bottom of a canyon.

Chapter 15

"The more I see of men, the more I admire dogs."

—Jeanne-Marie Roland

By the time Nick and I rode up in the hotel elevator, all I could think about was a hot shower. As for our discussion about getting married, it remained unacknowledged and undiscussed now that we'd been thrust back into our real lives. As far as I was concerned, the entire episode was simply the result of our shared fear that we'd never again see Betty or Winston or any of our friends and relatives, much less a justice of the peace.

Besides, I had more immediate problems to think about—like how I was ever going to wash off all the sweat and grime and red dirt that coated every square inch of my body. I was so focused on what would be required to feel like a normal human being that I even forgot we had a houseguest.

I remembered as soon as we stepped into our room and found Moose standing right inside the door, mewing at us crossly.

"You poor pussycat!" I cooed, crouching down and scooping him into my arms. It felt wonderful to hold his warm, furry body, but it also made me miss my own menagerie terribly. "I'm so sorry, Moosie-pie. We didn't mean to leave you alone for such a long time."

"Is he okay?" Nick asked.

"He's fine. Just hungry. And maybe a little lonely." Stroking Moose's silky black fur, I added, "I've got to find him a home. He doesn't belong in a hotel room. Besides, we'll only be here for a few more days. There must be somebody on this island who'd be willing to make Moose part of their family."

"You'll think of something," Nick said. "Maybe you can call a local vet and ask if—hey, look. The light on our phone is blinking. Somebody called."

He sat down on the edge of the bed and dialed the code required to retrieve messages. He listened, frowning, then grabbed the pen and pad sitting on the night table and scribbled something down.

"It was Rob Kourvis," he informed me after he hung up, "one of the newspaper editors I tried to contact on Thursday. I left my cell number and the hotel number on his voice mail. Yesterday he called me back at this number."

"What did he say?" I asked anxiously.

"That he'd be happy to talk to me about Bryce Bolt," Nick replied. He hesitated before adding, "It seems he's got plenty to tell me. In fact, he left me his home number."

Before I had a chance to comment, Nick began punching numbers into the phone. "He's on the West Coast," he told me as he waited for someone to answer. "It's a bit early for a Saturday morning, but—"

He held up his hand to indicate that he was listening. After a few seconds, he said, "Hi, Mr. Kourvis. It's Nick Burby. Thanks for returning my call. I'll try you again later today. In the meantime, I'll leave my phone numbers again . . ."

After he hung up, he looked at me expectantly. "Now what?"

"A hot shower," I replied. "And once I feel like a human being again, I'd like to pay another visit to Ace Atwood."

Nick's eyebrows shot up. "What for? To tell him you found out he and Marnie had a big fight a few hours before she turned up dead?"

"Actually, that's not what I'm curious about. There's something else Ace mentioned that's been nagging at me. He's about to make a career change. I want to find out if the corporate ladder he's about to climb has an *FT* on it."

Nick frowned. "Wait a minute. You think Ace might have ties to FloraTech?"

"It's just a theory," I told him. "And even if he does, it still might not mean anything. But I intend to find out."

With that, I headed into the bathroom to make that shower I'd been fantasizing about a reality.

• • •

As I walked into Ace's plastic surgery establishment, I saw that his operation was in full swing. I had to admit that his team of Auto Artists seemed to do good work. At least, if the gleaming Mercedes, Toyotas, and Saabs scattered around the shop, with their perfect paint jobs and not a scratch or a dent or a ding anywhere in sight, were any indication. Surrounded by all that machinery, I had to wonder if his interest in metal and motors extended to helicopters.

I spotted Ace in his office, talking on the phone. He was wearing the same tight T-shirt as last time, and his hair looked just as perfect. I slunk over, then stood behind a stack of cans of something called "body filler" so I could eavesdrop.

"Listen, it's gonna be fine," he was insisting. "Can't you trust me on anything? Hey, I know it's a big change, but I'm somebody who knows a golden opportunity when it comes knockin' at my door. . . ."

I got the feeling he was talking about the very subject I'd come all the way over here to discuss: his impending career change. And while I had no idea who he was talking to, I suspected that whoever it was had the same impression of Ace Atwood I did—that he wasn't someone who worked well with others.

But he'd told me himself he was looking forward to the predictability of a nine-to-five job. And given what a small world this was turning out to be—or, more accurately, what a small world Marnie Burton's world was turning out to be—I was pretty sure I already knew whose time clock he'd soon be punching.

"You again," Ace greeted me crossly as he hung up the phone and I emerged from the shadows. His mouth twisted into a scowl, and his brilliant blue eyes had a guarded look.

"This time I'm here on business," I told him, refusing to be intimidated by his clear dislike for anyone who had any ties to his philandering past. "I noticed some scratches on my car. Since it's a rental and all, I wanted to get an idea of what it would cost to fix before I return it, so they don't scam me." I couldn't resist adding, "You know how those car rental companies are."

He snorted to show how strongly he agreed. "Tell me about it." As he strutted toward my Jeep, he added, "I did some work for one of 'em once. A place called Makai Rentals. I did the work, but then, when it was time to collect, they had all these sob stories about their insurance and their suppliers. In the end, they stiffed me."

Like Ace, I recognized a golden opportunity when I

saw one. "I guess that kind of experience is what made you decide to get a regular nine-to-five job."

He glanced over at me so quickly I wondered if he'd given himself a case of whiplash. "Who told you about that?" he demanded, his left eye giving a telltale twitch.

"You did," I said, plastering on the most innocent expression I could manage.

"Oh, yeah. Now I remember." Still looking doubtful, he added, "I'm tellin' you, I'm not sorry I'm gonna be giving all this up soon."

I decided to take a chance. "And I've heard FloraTech is really great to work for."

"That's what they say." As soon as he said the words, he looked over at me, his expression shocked. "Hey, how did you know—"

"You mentioned that last time," I said quickly. "That you were going to work for them, I mean."

"Yeah? I don't remember sayin' anything about them."

I gave a little shrug. "How else would I know?" Before he had a chance to respond, I added, "From what I understand, FloraTech coming to this island is the best thing that's ever happened to Maui."

"Hey, they got great benefits. Medical and life insurance and all that. Frankly, that's all I care about." He hesitated before sticking his chin a little higher in the air and adding, "I just found out my wife is having a kid."

The announcement this proud father-to-be had just made caught me entirely off guard. Even so, the wheels immediately began turning in my head.

Thanks to what Nick and I had learned about the argument Ace and Marnie had a few hours before she was killed, Ace had already moved higher on my list of suspects. But throw in his wife's announcement that she was pregnant and the stakes suddenly got even higher.

Especially since Marnie had threatened to tell Mrs. Atwood all about their affair just a few hours before her body washed up on a beach.

It was such a likely scenario, one that was practically a cliché, that I found myself wondering if I'd been wasting my time by putting so much effort into trying to find out about FloraTech. I fixed my eyes on Ace's, trying to see inside him. Even though I lacked the sixth sense I so desperately wished I had, I couldn't help thinking that I might have been foolish to let myself get so distracted. Detective Paleka was probably right that Marnie had been murdered by the man she was seen with at the bar. As Marnie's boyfriend, Ace was the most obvious suspect.

The more I learned about him, the clearer it seemed.

Still, I couldn't just ignore the fact that FloraTech had resurfaced once again, this time as Ace Atwood's soon-to-be employer and financial savior. The company popped up everywhere I went. Even though the answer to the question of who had killed Marnie and why might have been staring right at me—literally—I couldn't let go of the idea that it was no coincidence that so many of the strands from Marnie's life were connected to the biotech firm.

"Congratulations," I said. "On the baby and all."

"Thanks," he muttered. He seemed to have already lost interest in that particular topic of conversation. "So where are these scratches?" he asked, scanning the side of my Jeep.

"Uh, right there. Under the mud . . . ?"

Frowning, he brushed at the streaks of dried mud with his sleeve. "I don't see anything."

"Gee, you're right." I did my best to sound surprised. Thinking quickly, I added, "I guess that guy was just teasing me."

"What guy?" he asked suspiciously.

"The guy at the gas station. The one who, uh, filled my gas tank. He's the one who told me the door was all scratched up. Or maybe the mud made it look that way."

He looked at me as if I was so dense that I was destined to spend my entire life being the butt of blonde jokes. And my hair color is close enough to brown that it barely puts me into the blonde category.

But I didn't care. Not only had I gotten confirmation that Ace was one more person in Marnie's circle who had ties to FloraTech, I'd also learned he was on the verge of becoming a daddy, another solid reason for him to suddenly feel his paramour was a liability.

• • •

As I drove away from Ace's Auto Artists, my mind drifted back to the problem that had confronted me earlier that day. Moose needed a home. And he needed it sooner rather than later. I ran through the list of people I'd met on Maui, trying to decide if any of them was a possibility.

Ace Atwood, Holly Gruen, Richard Carrera, Bryce Bolt, Alice Feeley . . . Considering the fact that most of them are suspects in Marnie Burton's murder, I thought grimly, they're hardly candidates for adopting her cat.

Then, in a sudden flash of inspiration, I thought of someone else, somebody whose character I'd never considered the least bit questionable.

I pulled into the first parking lot I spotted and dialed information. Not surprisingly, it turned out there were several listings for *Nelson* on Maui. I jotted them down, figuring I'd try them all until I located Karen.

When I punched in the first one, it rang a dozen times without anyone answering. I moved on to the next number on my list. As soon as I heard a pleasant "Hello?" I knew I'd found her.

"Hi, Karen," I began. "This is Jessie Popper. We met a few days ago at the *Dispatch* office. You gave me Holly Gruen's phone number, remember?"

"Of course I remember," she replied. With a little laugh, she added, "Seems to me I also gave you a lot of advice. All of it completely unsolicited, as I recall."

"It was very helpful," I assured her. "But I'm calling about something else entirely. I'm trying to find a home for Marnie's cat. His name is Moose, and he's very sweet. I wondered if you might be willing to take him."

"Sure, why not? I've already got a cat, so adding a second simply means putting out another food bowl. Why don't you bring him over this afternoon? Grab a pen and I'll give you my address. . . ."

"Yes!" I cried after I'd hung up the phone. Not only had I found a home for Marnie's cat; he was about to be adopted by someone I felt really good about.

At least there's one thing I've managed to resolve, I thought, pulling back onto the road and heading toward the hotel. But my sense of accomplishment lasted only a few seconds. After all, finding a place for Moose to live was small potatoes compared to the enormous questions about his former owner that, at the moment, I didn't feel even close to answering.

• • •

This time, as I unlocked the door of my hotel room, I was prepared to find Moose waiting for me. However, I didn't expect to find Nick. But he was sitting on the lanai, talking on his cell phone.

From his tone of voice, it sounded serious.

"I see," I heard him say as I slid open the glass door to join him. "Okay, thanks for being so straight with me, Mr. Kourvis—I mean Rob. . . . Yes, I realize that, but you've still been extremely helpful."

"Anything interesting?" I asked as soon as he ended his call.

"Definitely in the 'interesting' category," he replied. "I just spoke to Bryce Bolt's former boss at the *San Diego Times*. Just as he promised, he had a lot to tell me."

"What did he say?"

Nick frowned. "Apparently the reason Bryce left his last job wasn't that he was dying to live in paradise. He was fired for journalistic fraud."

My jaw dropped to the floor.

"It seems our buddy Bryce won quite a bit of acclaim for a series he wrote on sex offenders who were released into the community after serving time," he continued. "It sparked a lot of debate and he was quite the media star for a while. Then it came out that he had fabricated almost all of it."

"He made stuff up?" I asked, incredulous. "In a newspaper?"

"In a very fine newspaper, in fact," Nick replied. "One of the most highly regarded newspapers in the country. Bryce used fake names for the sex offenders and the members of the community he wrote about, he made up quotes—he even made up most of the incidents he wrote about.

"His defense was that the people in his articles were composites and that he'd changed names to protect the people he'd interviewed. He also claimed he'd combined quotes from several different people to voice what he called 'common sentiments.' "

"You can't do that!" I cried. "Newspapers are supposed to report the truth!"

"Bryce's boss, Rob Kourvis, felt the same way. So did all the other higher-ups at the newspaper. Not only was Bryce fired; the *Times* printed an apology. A whole bunch of other newspapers picked up the story too. So Bryce Bolt's name was mud."

"At least on the mainland," I observed. "I suppose it's possible that the scandal didn't travel all the way to Hawaii."

"That must be the case," Nick agreed, "since Rob insisted that after word spread, no newspaper would touch him."

"So it sounds as if Bryce Bolt is someone who'll stop at nothing to achieve the success he wants," I commented.

"That's what Rob Kourvis seemed to think. Along with just about everybody else in the journalism business."

The severity of Bryce Bolt's transgression left me reeling. He had not only betrayed the newspaper he worked for; he had broken every rule of journalism. He had also compromised himself in ways that would make it impossible for most people to look at themselves in a mirror ever again.

Yet from what I had seen, he'd remained unfazed. He still thought of himself as an ace reporter, someone who belonged at a high-quality newspaper like the *Honolulu Star-Bulletin*.

I felt as if my gut reaction to the arrogant Bryce Bolt was justified. I hadn't liked the man from the start.

Still, the fact that he was ambitious enough to let poor judgment come close to ruining his career didn't necessarily mean he was ruthless enough to commit murder.

• • •

After lunch, Nick went to the beach to enjoy some well-deserved downtime. As for me, I gathered up Moose, his toys, and all his other worldly possessions and headed off to Karen Nelson's house in Wailuku.

Thanks to the directions she'd given me on the phone, I found it with ease. As I pulled up in front of the modest one-story ranch, I noted that it was surprisingly similar to the homes that covered Long Island. It was painted pale yellow, with a small porch edged with a white wooden railing. The property even included a tiny lawn, so narrow that it stretched only about ten feet from the road. A neat row of bushes was planted along the front of the house, although they were so sparse and fragile-looking I suspected they hadn't been there very long.

The front door was open, and Karen appeared in the doorway before I'd even climbed out of my Jeep. As if wanting to prove her claim that she was already a cat owner, she was carrying a white Persian in her arms.

"How were my directions?" she asked cheerfully, coming out to greet me. Instead of the business attire she was wearing the other time we'd met, she was dressed in beige Bermuda shorts and a pink and green plaid shirt.

"They were great," I assured her. "Moose and I found you without any problem."

I also held the cat in my charge in my arms, not sure how he'd react to his new surroundings. I shouldn't have worried. As soon as he saw the lawn and realized he'd been freed from the confines of hotel living, he began squirming and meowing, telling me in no uncertain terms that he was ready to be let loose.

"Okay, Moose," I told him. "I can see you're anxious to check out your new home."

"I'll hold on to Eudora here until Moose gets the feel of the place," Karen said.

But it didn't take Moose long to start acting as if he belonged here. After being cooped up inside for so long, he probably felt he was in heaven. Karen introduced Eudora, and after the two cats checked each other out for a minute or two, Moose found a shady spot, plopped down on the grass, and cast me a look of great satisfaction.

"Come on inside," Karen offered. "Can I get you something to drink? Lemonade, iced tea . . . ?"

"Iced tea sounds perfect.

"Thanks for taking Moose," I said as Karen plunked down a tall frosty glass in front of me.

"Glad to have him," she replied, sitting down next to me with a glass of her own. "In fact, it's kind of nice to have something of Marnie's. It's a way of keeping her with me. I know the guys in the office used to complain about how pushy she was—and how ambitious—but she wasn't any different than they were. It's just that she was a female, so they had different expectations. I thought she was a great kid. Full of energy, full of life . . ."

She stopped, pretending the reason was to sip her iced tea. Before speaking again, she cleared her throat. "By the way," she asked, "did you ever get in touch with Holly?"

"Yes, thanks to you," I said. "I used that number you gave me. We had lunch in Lahaina a few days ago." I hesitated before adding, "You were right. There were definitely some issues between her and Marnie. I'm not sure I understand all of it." Thinking out loud, I added, "Maybe I should call her again to see if I can find out anything more."

"You'd better hurry," Karen advised. "She's leaving the island."

"What?" I cried.

"That's right. She stopped by the *Dispatch* office yesterday afternoon to say good-bye."

"But I just talked to her a few days ago," I said, still in shock. "She didn't say a word about it."

"I had no idea either. Not until she came in to say good-bye to Peggy and me."

"Not Mr. Carrera?" I asked, surprised.

Karen grimaced. "They're not exactly on the best terms. I don't think he ever forgave her for quitting so abruptly and leaving him in the lurch."

My eyebrows shot up. "I didn't realize there was tension between Holly and Mr. Carrera."

"Sure. When Holly quit, she hardly gave any notice at all. If I remember correctly, she announced on a Thursday that she was leaving and that the next day would be her last. Mr. C was in such a panic to find a replacement that he started going through all the résumés he had on file. We get a lot of them, since it seems just about everybody in the universe wants to live on Maui. Anyway, Bryce Bolt was the first person he contacted who said he could start the following Monday. He hired him sight unseen."

So that's how he landed another reporting gig, I thought, despite the scandal that drove him away from his previous job. But I decided not to mention anything about Bryce's past.

"Do you know where Holly's going?" I asked.

"Back to the mainland," Karen replied. "Florida. That's where she's originally from. But I believe she's flying out this weekend, so if you want to talk to her, you'd better not wait. If you'd like, I can give you her home address."

"Had she been planning this for a long time?" I persisted. "Do you know if she has another job there or her family wants her to come home . . . ?"

Karen shrugged. "As far as I know, it's something she just decided on the spur of the moment. Yesterday was certainly the first time I'd heard anything about it."

I hadn't intended to contact Holly again. But the fact that she'd suddenly decided to take off made me anxious to talk to her one last time.

Especially since I couldn't help thinking that her decision to leave Maui less than one week after Marnie had been murdered was more than a coincidence.

Chapter 16

"A dog is a man's best friend. A cat is a cat's best friend."

—Robert J. Vogel

Like Marnie, Holly Gruen lived in an apartment. But her complex looked considerably older than Marnie's, with its shabby white stucco buildings and its dense growth of bushes in desperate need of trimming.

According to the mailboxes, the Gruen residence was located on the third floor. I tromped up two flights of open-air steps, which were covered in terra-cotta tile. When I reached the landing, I was surprised to see that the door of Apartment 3B was wide open.

"Holly?" I called softly. "Anybody home?"

I peered inside, scanning the empty bookshelves, the cleaned-out kitchen cabinets with their doors wide open, and, through an open door, a bed stripped down to the mattress. Two giant wheeled suitcases lay on the floor, packed so densely that zipping them up promised to be a real challenge. The three cardboard cartons that sat on the kitchen counter were just as full. Two of them were crammed with dishes, pots, and other housewares, while the third one was stuffed with file folders, envelopes, and papers.

"Holly?" I called again, this time more forcefully.

She appeared in the doorway of the bedroom. Even though it was warm, she was wearing jeans, a baggy black T-shirt, and scruffy sandals. Her dark-brown hair was tucked behind her ears but stuck out haphazardly in a few spots.

"Jessie?" she asked, looking surprised. "What are you doing here?"

Ignoring her question, I said, "Karen Nelson told me you were moving this weekend. I can see you're already halfway out the door."

"My plane leaves in . . ." She glanced at her wristwatch, an oversize model with a clunky stainless-steel band. "Four hours and twenty minutes. So if I'm going to make it, I've really got to get busy."

I glanced around. From the looks of things, she'd already packed away every possible sign that she'd ever inhabited the compact apartment in the first place.

"I understand you're going back to Florida."

"Yup." She gave a careless little shrug, meanwhile pushing her black-framed eyeglasses up the bridge of her nose. "I've had enough of paradise. In fact, I don't know why I didn't leave months ago."

"Holly, did your decision to leave Maui have anything to do with what happened to Marnie?" I asked gently.

"Why, do you think I'm next?" she returned sharply.

Her words surprised me. "No," I insisted. And then, doing some fast thinking, I added, "Do you?"

She stared at me for a long time, her eyes burning into mine. At first I thought she was angry. Then I realized she was thinking. Thinking hard.

I stepped toward her slowly, approaching her as if she was a frightened animal. "Holly," I said in a soft voice, "I think it's time for you to tell me what you know."

Her eyes immediately shifted to the box of papers sitting on the counter, a reaction that verified what I'd suspected almost from the beginning.

"It's all about the work you and Marnie were doing at the *Dispatch*, isn't it?" I said. "The fact that you found something. Both of you, working together."

"What did she tell you?" she demanded, her voice shrill.

I decided to take a stab at it. "She told me all about FloraTech," I said simply, hoping she'd fill in the blanks.

Holly's reaction told me I'd struck gold.

"She was such a fool," she mumbled, shaking her head hard. "I tried to get her to listen. But Marnie was so ridiculously headstrong. She thought she knew it all." Laughing coldly, she added, "Or else she was so naive she never believed they'd make good on their threats."

Her words struck me with the force of a physical blow. I walked over to the couch, a red plaid upholstered monstrosity that looked as if it belonged in Hawaii about as much as an igloo. I sat down, my way of communicating that I wasn't going to leave until I got the whole story.

"Tell me everything, Holly," I said in a low, urgent tone. "I want to hear your version of what happened."

"Oh, boy." Rubbing her forehead, she sank onto the couch beside me. "I knew from the start that those people from FloraTech were ruthless," she said in a dull voice. "I could tell they meant business. They'd been watching us, so they knew from the beginning what we were doing."

"What were you doing?" I asked.

"What reporters do," Holly replied. "Talking to

people, working our butts off to find out the truth. . . .”

She let out a deep sigh before continuing. “It was Marnie who figured it all out. Of course, she was the one who’d been suspicious right from the get-go.” With a strange little laugh, she added, “This was one time when what we were all in the habit of thinking of as her paranoia turned out to be a real nose for news.

“And at first it was great, working on the story with Marnie. We felt so cool. I mean, here we were, barely out of college, and we were uncovering the hottest story of the decade. It was fun. At least, until they realized what we were doing. They found out we were talking to some of their employees, and they weren’t happy about it. That was when they approached each of us—Marnie and me—and offered to pay us to keep quiet about what was going on. A lot of money too. More than either of us was making working for the *Dispatch*. The deal was that as long as we agreed not to go public with what we knew, they’d keep paying us hush money.”

She looked at me with dull eyes. “That’s why I left. It wasn’t a deal I could live with. But Marnie kept on going. Not only did she refuse to believe they were serious; she pushed even harder, determined to follow it through to the end.”

“But what was it that FloraTech was so anxious to keep under wraps?” I asked.

Lowering her eyes, Holly muttered a single word: “Cocaine.”

“What did you say?” I demanded, my voice a hoarse whisper. Just hearing the word sent a chill more powerful than a blast of the strongest air-conditioning on the island through my entire body.

“Cocaine,” she repeated. “Snow, C, blow, flake,

whatever they're calling it these days. Coca plants are being grown here on Maui, right under our noses."

I was still having trouble taking all this in. "And no one's noticed?" I asked. "Not the police, not the DEA, not even the nosy neighbors next door to wherever they're growing it?"

"That's the whole point," Holly replied, her eyes boring into mine. "It doesn't look like coca."

Whatever she was trying to say didn't make sense. "Tell me what you know," I insisted.

Holly took a deep breath. "There's this new plant FloraTech developed, a crazy hybrid. It looks like an ordinary hibiscus. As far as anybody can tell, the fields that are covered with it look like regular hibiscus fields. But by using genetic engineering, they've invented a hibiscus that produces cocaine."

"How?"

"I'm no scientist, so I don't understand all the technicalities," she continued in a low voice. "But somehow they take the genes from the coca plants and stick them into a hibiscus. The DNA gets mixed up so they end up with a flower that looks like a regular hibiscus—except it has the same chemical the coca plants make on their leaves. That's the stuff they process and turn into cocaine. Here, I've got the name written down in my notes."

She strode over to the box on the kitchen counter and shuffled through the file folder until she located the piece of paper she'd been searching for. She handed it to me.

Written on a sheet of paper in a handwriting I now recognized as Marnie's was a single word: *benzoylmethylecgonine.*

I knew enough chemistry from my four years of college plus another four in veterinary school to recognize it. She was absolutely right. This was, indeed, the chemical compound that most people knew as cocaine.

If what Holly was telling me was really true, I thought, my mind racing, if this cocaine-producing hybrid had actually been genetically engineered and was growing right here on Maui, then the two reporters were on the verge of uncovering one of the biggest stories to come out of Hawaii since the bombing of Pearl Harbor.

It also explained why Nick couldn't find any information on FloraTech, I realized. It wasn't a legitimate company at all. It was a front for an illegal drug-producing scheme—not some innovative biotech firm using the science of botany to advance medical science.

"Holly, how did Marnie figure all this out?" I asked.

"A secret source," she replied. "Some guy who worked for FloraTech started getting nervous about working for such a sleazy operation. In fact, he's the one who approached her, not long after FloraTech arrived on the island. Seems he was having second thoughts about being involved in what they were doing, even though the money they were paying him was phenomenal. She wasn't sure whether or not he was being straight with her, but she taped their conversations on this little tape recorder she had. After she did some nosing around and verified what he was telling her, she planned to use those tapes as proof. Not only for the newspaper articles she intended to write, but also for the cops."

I could practically hear a snapping sound as one more piece of the puzzle fit into place.

The audiocassette. The faulty tape, the one she had left behind in my hotel room—the one that somebody else wanted badly enough to break in.

"Who was the person who offered you this . . . this

deal, Holly?" I asked. "Who told you FloraTech would pay you hush money to keep the truth under wraps?"

"I didn't know the first guy, and I never saw him again," she replied. "I think he was somebody from FloraTech. A guy in a suit. He never told me his name.

"But he wasn't the only one," she continued. "Someone from the governor's office came to my house."

"The governor's office!" I cried. "Who?"

She looked surprised. "It's nobody you'd know. He's just an aide. I mean, it's not as if he's in the public eye or anything."

"What's his name?"

"John Irwin."

I gasped. "What did he say?"

"That if the truth about FloraTech ever got out, the governor's political career would be ruined. He said it was his job to make sure that didn't happen."

I thought about the photographs Nick had found in Marnie's folder, the ones of Governor Wickham with Norman Eldridge, FloraTech's founder. He had described them as the type of photos he took when he was a private investigator. The two men outside a motel room, shaking hands. Dining in a restaurant, alone.

And walking through a hibiscus farm.

Is it possible even the governor is in on this? I wondered, a sick feeling suddenly descending over me. *Could the story that Marnie was about to expose be that big?*

My head buzzed as I tried to think of who else might be involved.

"What about Bryce Bolt, the reporter who replaced you?" I demanded. "Do you think he's taking money from FloraTech?" By that point, my brain felt as if it was on fire. As the magnitude of what Holly told me really started to sink in, I was beginning to understand the possible ramifications. Not only in terms of what was happening right here on this idyllic island, but also in terms of Marnie's murder. "And what about Richard Carrera? How does he fit into all this?"

"Look, what goes on with Bryce and Mr. Carrera is really none of my business." Within seconds, Holly's entire demeanor had changed. She was suddenly so closed off it was as if someone had slammed a door shut. "If I'm going to catch my plane, I have to get moving. And believe me, I really want to catch that plane. The truth is, I can't wait to get out of here."

She jumped up off the couch and crouched down in front of one of the overstuffed suitcases, pretending she was absorbed in rearranging the contents so she could eventually zip it shut.

"Holly," I persisted, "you have to finish this story. Aside from Marnie, you're the person who was the most involved. The person who was closest to her and what she was doing. You must have some idea of who killed her."

"I don't know anything about that," she mumbled. But from the way she kept her eyes down, refusing to meet mine, I knew she was lying.

"Holly, please," I begged. "You're getting on a plane in a few hours. You're about to leave all this behind. But there are so many other people who won't be able to come to grips with what happened to Marnie until they know the truth. The whole truth. Surely you must have your suspicions."

She stopped moving. Instead, she simply stared at the bunched-up sweater she clasped in both hands. I held my breath, waiting for what seemed like an eternity.

My heart was racing when she finally looked up at me.

"You want answers?" she asked with a cold smile. "Go ask Alice."

• • •

As I drove away, I realized I was gripping the steering wheel so tightly that my hands ached. It was an indication of just how frustrated I was over Holly's unwillingness to tell me the whole story.

She'd shooed me out right after she made her enigmatic comment, insisting she had nothing more to say and that she had too much to do to spare any more time. Yet I finally knew the truth about FloraTech. And what she'd told me about Marnie's involvement made me determined to follow through on the one clue she'd been willing to give me concerning her murder.

In a way, I wasn't all that surprised that my search was bringing me back to Alice. I kept thinking about that earring I'd spotted on the windowsill behind the kitchen sink. I even wondered if Holly had known about it and if that was why she'd pointed me in her direction.

Alice Feeley's neighborhood seemed eerily quiet as I pulled up in front of her bungalow in my Jeep. In the fading daylight, her tiny house looked even more garish than the last time I'd been here. The turquoise exterior seemed almost luminescent, and the bold pinks and purples and yellows of her handiwork, the giant flowers and the rainbow that curved over the front door, popped out like the brightly painted decorations on a day care center.

Going there in the daytime also gave me a chance to get a good look at her entire property. I was surprised at how far behind the house her land stretched.

No wonder FloraTech wanted it, I thought grimly. The fertile soil that Alice used to grow vegetables would undoubtedly be ideal for growing the company's genetically engineered hibiscus.

There were no signs of life coming from her house. As I walked purposefully toward the front door, I heard nothing but the occasional chirp of a bird and the soft rustling of the bushes on the front lawn. In fact, I wondered if I'd even find her at home.

But as I grew closer, I heard music drifting through the open windows, James Taylor crooning about fire and rain. I didn't see a doorbell, so I knocked on the door loudly.

As soon as I did, Facetious began barking from inside the house. Alice opened the door seconds later, clasping the black Lab's collar in an only partially successful attempt at restraining her. She was dressed in a long batik dress splashed with the deep greens and blues of the sea. It looked like the type of garment Betty would wear, except that on Alice, it seemed to hang slightly off center. Her dark red hair with its silver glints was pinned haphazardly around her head, with loose strands falling around her face and neck.

But it was the distracted look in her eyes that grabbed my attention.

"Who are you?" she demanded, her voice coarse and a little too loud. "Do I know you? What do you want? Quiet, Facetious! I can't hear myself think!"

"It's me, Jessica Popper," I replied calmly over the noise. "Do you remember me? I was here on Wednesday with my friend Nick."

I studied her face, searching for some sign of recognition. There was none.

"We talked about Marnie Burton," I tried again. "The reporter whose body you found on the beach."

"Poor girl," she said, shaking her head.

"Alice, I'd like to talk to you about her a bit more."

I didn't know if she'd finally remembered me or if

she'd just decided I was harmless. But she opened the door. As soon as I walked in and starting scratching Facetious's neck, she quieted down. Her tail, however, went into high gear.

"I hope I'm not interrupting anything," I said, stroking the dog's sleek head to keep her calm.

"Nope. I was just talking to Jack." She let out a ragged laugh. "That's Jack Feeley, my husband. I need advice, and I don't know who else to ask."

I couldn't help wondering what she was consulting a dead man about. "Advice on what?"

"What to do about my land."

My ears pricked up like Max and Lou's ears do at the sound of the refrigerator opening.

But before I got the chance to ask for more details, she said, "Bah! That's family business. You're not interested in that. You came here to talk about that poor dead girl. Come into the kitchen. I must have something cold to drink."

I was only too glad to follow her toward the back of the house, into the kitchen. This time, instead of sitting down, I headed straight for the sink and leaned against the counter.

"So where's that good-lookin' boyfriend of yours?" she asked as she studied the contents of her own refrigerator as if they were a complete mystery to her. "He looked like he was worth holding on to."

So she did remember. "He's enjoying the beach today," I told her.

"Good for him. Much better than spending the afternoon talkin' to a crazy old lady."

"This is very important to me, Alice," I said. "I'm still trying to figure out what happened the night Marnie was killed. But there's still so much I don't know. I was wondering if there was something, anything, you remember from that night that you didn't think to mention when we last talked. Something you noticed, maybe something you found . . ."

"I got nothing more to tell," she said with a little shrug.

"I see." I stared out the window behind the sink, acting as if I were lost in thought. And then, lowering my eyes to the collection she'd assembled on the windowsill, I focused in on the single earring made of tiny pastel-colored shells that was displayed with all the other stones and shells Alice had found on the beach.

"There's that earring again," I commented, trying my best to sound as if I was just making casual conversation. "It's so pretty. You're so lucky to find such wonderful things on the beach."

"Oh, I didn't find that piece on the beach," Alice said offhandedly.

My mouth was suddenly dry. I couldn't remember exactly what she'd said about the earring the other time I was here. But I'd just assumed it had come from the same place as all the other pieces on display.

Struggling to keep my voice even, I asked, "Where did you get it?"

"I found it in my car, under the seat."

"Your car?" I repeated, surprised.

"That's right," she replied. "It was just a few days ago. Early this past week, Monday or Tuesday."

Monday or Tuesday, I thought. And Marnie was murdered Sunday night.

I studied Alice's face, looking for some reaction to the conversation we were having. Yet she seemed completely unaffected.

My mind clicked away. Had I been wrong in assuming there was no way Alice Feeley could be crafty enough to have committed murder, then act completely innocent when asked about it—even though she was caught with an earring the victim had been wearing at the time she was killed? Was she someone who had managed to fool me as effectively as she'd fooled Richard Carrera and, from the looks of things, the police? Was Holly the only one who'd seen through her—and was that what she'd been trying to tell me before she got on a plane and disappeared forever?

It was certainly possible. Yet it seemed just as possible that Alice had no idea the earring had belonged to Marnie.

By that point, my heart was thumping so loud that I desperately hoped it wouldn't give me away.

Trying to sound casual, I commented, "I'd like to get a pair to bring back home as a souvenir. But they're obviously one of a kind, not the type of thing you can pick up just anywhere. Do you have any idea who might have owned these earrings? I'd like to ask her where she got them."

"Nobody I know," she said. "I haven't given anybody a ride lately."

She frowned slightly, as if she was thinking. "Then again," she added pensively, "my son could have given someone a ride."

"Your son?" My mouth was suddenly so dry I was having difficulty forming words. "I didn't know you have a son."

"Oh, yes. My baby. He borrowed my car a few days ago." She laughed, her voice filled with affection and warmth. "Of course, he's not even close to being a baby anymore. Funny how mothers never stop thinking of their kids as 'their baby,' no matter how old they get. And he's my only child, so that makes him even more special."

"I don't suppose you have any pictures," I said in what I hoped was a chummy voice. "I love family photos."

"I sure do!" Alice was already loping out of the

kitchen to retrieve a picture of her son. Just as there were undoubtedly few mothers who ever stopped thinking of their children as their "babies," there were few who could resist showing photos of their offspring to anyone willing to take a look at them.

She returned seconds later, her cheeks flushed. In her hand was a stack of glossy photographs of different sizes. There were snapshots, wallet-size school photos, even one that somebody had thought deserved to be blown up into a five-by-seven print.

With trembling hands, I reached for them.

When I saw the photo on top, electricity shot through me as if I'd been standing on a tin roof in the middle of a thunderstorm. The picture had been taken at Christmastime, probably anywhere from five to ten years earlier. Standing in front of a slightly misshapen evergreen festooned with the usual assortment of ornaments and lights was Alice, looking a bit younger and much more relaxed. There were fewer lines in her face and fewer silvery hairs woven through the dark red strands. She was dressed in loose-fitting green velvet pants and a gauzy bright red top that was draped across her torso.

However, it was the person standing next to her who grabbed my attention. Alice's son, her only child. Like his mother, he was smiling at the camera, looking happy and carefree. As was typical for a young man in his twenties or thirties, he was dressed for the family holiday celebration in comfortable-looking jeans and a button-down shirt. His casual clothes, his grin, and his attractive features made him look like any other dutiful son who was spending Christmas with his mother.

But what I'd just learned about where Alice had discovered the earring, combined with common sense, told me that the man who had killed Marnie was the man in the photo.

Chapter 17

"One of the most striking differences between a cat and a lie is that a cat has only nine lives."

—Mark Twain

I didn't realize Bryce Bolt was your son," I remarked in a strained voice.

"You know Bryce?" she asked, surprised.

"Yes. I know him through Marnie."

"Of course, the dead girl." Alice had already turned her attention back to the photographs, which clearly interested her more than Marnie Burton. Distractedly, she added, "They worked at the *Dispatch* together, didn't they? If you and that girl were friends, it makes sense that she would have spoken about him." She studied the holiday photograph, then smiled. "Maybe she even had a crush on him. Not that I could blame her. Of course, I'm not the most objective person in the world, but you've got to admit that my Bryce is quite a good-looking fellow. Charming too."

I was at a complete loss for words. I knew I was supposed to agree, but I couldn't bring myself to speak, much less to lie. Fortunately, Alice was a million miles away, lost in her own reminiscences.

"Funny that I had three husbands but just the one child," she continued, gazing off into the distance as if she were looking backward in time. "My first marriage was to my college sweetheart, Danny Lucas. That lasted only a few months. Plenty of passion, but we were both too young. My marriage to my third husband—that was Jack Feeley—was also short, but that was because he went and had a heart attack after we'd been married only a couple of years.

"The husband I had a child with was the middle one. Arthur Bolt." With a hoarse laugh, she added, "Looking back, I think he's the only one I ever really loved. I mean the way people fall in love in books and movies. But I was stupid enough to let that marriage slip through my fingers. Didn't know a good thing when I had it."

She sighed deeply. "Funny, I still miss Arthur. Jack was the practical one and Danny was special because he was the first, but Arthur was my real soul mate. That's the one that should have lasted.

"But Bryce makes up for it. Every day I thank my lucky stars that he's living here on Maui now. Gives me a chance to make up for all that lost time."

"Lost time?" I repeated, not understanding.

"Arthur and I got divorced in the late eighties. I got a chunk of money, thanks to California's divorce laws—community property and all that—so I moved here. But Bryce had just turned fourteen, old enough to decide which parent he wanted to live with. He chose to stay in California, with his father. But now, after all those years of me and him living in different places, he ended up coming to Maui to work at the *Dispatch*." Her eyes glowed with an almost alarming intensity as she added, "He's the light of my life, that boy."

I tried to maintain a neutral expression as she spoke. But the wheels in my head were turning. The pieces of the puzzle were suddenly fitting together in a way that should have been satisfying but was instead horrifying.

Sunday night, the night Marnie was killed, Bryce Bolt had borrowed his mother's car, preferring to use hers instead of his own to carry out the despicable deed he had planned. He undoubtedly knew about his mother's reputation as an eccentric, one of those people who hover in the background while everyone else pretty much ignores them. He also knew the area's residents were used to seeing Alice's dilapidated old Ford Taurus at Kanaha Beach Park at all hours, so no one who spotted it in the area late at night would have raised an eyebrow.

Using his own car, meanwhile, would have immediately identified him with the heinous crime. After all, Richard Carrera had told me himself that Bryce Bolt was always bragging about his BMW.

The rest of the details suddenly seemed painfully clear. Some time Sunday night, Marnie had met up with Bryce at the Purple Mango. Maybe their rendezvous was prearranged, or maybe he had been keeping tabs on her closely enough that he managed to make their encounter look accidental.

But at some point, he got Marnie into his mother's Taurus. He drove to a secluded spot and strangled her, not noticing in the heat of the moment that one of the distinctive shell earrings she was wearing fell onto the floor of the car. He threw her body into the ocean, then returned the Taurus to his mother. As he drove back home in his own car, after picking up the silver BMW wherever he had left it, the cocky reporter undoubtedly believed he'd committed the perfect crime.

I wondered how he'd felt about involving his mother—not only by using her car to commit the crime but also by practically guaranteeing that she would be the one to find Marnie's body on the beach.

Alice was still talking. Even though I felt dazed, I forced myself to focus on what she was saying.

"Of course, Bryce is all grown up now," she went on happily. "He doesn't want his mother hangin' around him all the time. So I keep my distance." Her voice softened as she added, "But I get to see him often enough. And I always know he's close by."

Suddenly I thought of one of the other unanswered questions that still hovered in the room.

"Alice, I'm curious about this 'family business' you mentioned," I said. "The question about your land that you were discussing with Jack. That has something to do with Bryce, doesn't it?"

Alice sighed. "Bryce is so certain I should sell my property to those people. Been workin' on me for weeks. But I don't trust corporations. Especially those drug companies. They're always selling us expensive drugs that turn out to be bad for us. And then the drugs that really work cost so much that people have to go without food just to get the money they need to get 'em."

"FloraTech," I said. But I didn't need her to tell me what I already knew.

"That's right," she muttered. "Doesn't matter if they're supposed to have found some magical way that hibiscus can cure people," she went on, shaking her head. "Still don't trust 'em."

"I think you're very wise, Alice," I said. "If I were you, I'd hold on to your land."

"What's he expect me to do, go live in one of those communities for senior citizens?" she continued. But she no longer seemed to be talking to me. In fact, I wondered if her words were meant for Jack Feeley's ears, wherever they happened to be. "Bah! Who wants to hang out with a bunch of old people all the time? Especially when I've got my own house, my own garden. . . . Maybe Bryce is too young to understand, but that means a lot to me."

Or maybe he'd get a piece of FloraTech's profits if he got his own mother to sell them her land, I thought angrily. Who knows how deep his loyalty to them was? Especially loyalty that came with a price tag.

"Hey, look at this photograph," Alice croaked happily. "This one's from Bryce's high school graduation. He looks so handsome in his cap and gown! I always knew he'd be a success. And that's exactly what he turned into."

Alice's eyes were shining brightly as she paused to leaf through the rest of the photos. I suspected she was reliving some of the most meaningful moments of her life, most of which happened to involve her son.

The look of joy on her face made my heart wrench. If I was right, if the scenario that I'd constructed in my head really was correct, this loving mother was soon going to have to face the fact that her only child had turned into a coldhearted killer.

• • •

As I drove away from Alice's house, I felt completely washed out. I was also sick over what I now knew lay ahead for her. It was tragic that such a devoted mother was about to embark upon what would undoubtedly be the most difficult chapter of her life.

As for me, I still had some important work to do. And the most daunting task ahead of me was convincing Detective Paleka that I'd figured out who killed Marnie Burton.

I tried calling the police station, but as I expected, he wasn't available on a Saturday evening. Despite my attempts at getting another number at which I could reach him, the best I could do was leave a message. Other than that, the most I could get out of the officer who answered the phone was that I'd be able to contact him on Monday morning.

As I pulled into the hotel's underground parking lot, I pondered the fact that it may have been just as well. It probably made sense for me to pay him another in-person visit, rather than trying to explain what I'd learned over the phone.

Still, I had a feeling the rest of the weekend was going to pass very, very slowly.

As I shuffled into the hotel room, the way I felt must have been written all over my face. The moment Nick saw me, his expression contorted into one of alarm.

"Jessie!" he cried. "What happened?"

I sank onto the bed. It was funny: At that moment, I really missed Moose. I desperately wished I could cradle a warm, furry animal with ridiculously soft fur in my arms.

"I know who killed Marnie," I said in a flat voice.

Nick sat down beside me, then listened, wide-eyed but silent, as I told him everything I'd learned that afternoon. When I finished, he leaned over and put his arms around me.

"We have to tell Detective Paleka," he said.

"I know. I've already tried calling him, but it looks like it's going to have to wait until Monday." I couldn't resist adding, "I guess the Maui police aren't used to having the tourists do their murder investigations for them."

"In that case, it's good that we have a long, busy day ahead of us tomorrow."

I looked at him blankly. Right then I couldn't remember a single thing about my real life. My head was still too full of what I'd just learned about Marnie and the events that had resulted in her death.

"The trip to Hana," he reminded me. "With Betty and Winston. I think it'll be good for both of us to get out and forget about all this, at least for a few hours."

I couldn't have agreed with him more. A change of scenery, as well as the chance to spend some time relaxing with our friends, sounded like a welcome refuge.

• • •

My mood was considerably better the next morning when Nick and I met our friends in the lobby. Betty's face was as pink with anticipation as her bright pink sundress. She wore a big floppy straw hat, and she was carrying a wicker picnic basket brimming with goodies.

Winston also looked prepared for a day of sightseeing. He was wearing crisp navy blue Bermuda shorts, a white polo shirt, and a New York Yankees baseball hat that he somehow managed to make look dignified. A camera with an impressively large lens hung from his neck on a thick nylon strap.

"All set?" Betty greeted us brightly.

"I think we've got everything," Nick replied. "Bathing suits, towels, a change of clothes, and, just in case, a couple of bottles of water and a big bag of macadamia nuts." Casting me a wary glance, he added, "I don't know about you, but I'm never going anywhere without bringing my own food and water again."

We piled into the Jeep, with Nick and me in front and Betty and Winston in back. After a few miles of familiar roads, we reached the Hana Highway, which meandered along Maui's spectacularly beautiful northeastern coast. It felt good to cruise along with the windows open and the cool ocean breezes wafting in.

Guided by Nick's *Penny-Pinching Traveler's Guide to Maui,* we made our first stop at Puohokamoa

Stream, where we admired the pools and waterfalls. We did some hiking at Kaumahina State Wayside Park, then dug into the picnic lunch Betty had brought at a picnic table before getting back on the road.

But we'd driven only a mile or two before I started to fidget.

"Nick," I said uneasily, glancing into the side mirror, "have you noticed that the same car has been following us ever since we stopped at the state park a while ago?"

He cast me a strange look. "It's a two-lane road, Jess. Whoever gets on the road right after us has no choice but to follow us."

"True." But I kept my eyes on the car behind us. The fact that it had tinted windows made me uneasy. And while the driver wasn't exactly tailgating, something about the dogged way he consistently maintained the same distance behind us made me suspicious.

I tried to convince myself that Nick was right, meanwhile concentrating on the view. But even though it was spectacular, I wasn't doing a very good job of appreciating it, much less having fun.

I was relieved when we got off the road for our third stop, the Keanae Arboretum, where we took another short hike. Strolling beneath the dense green canopy was refreshing, but I was glad when Betty and Winston apologetically explained that they'd done enough hiking for one day. Frankly, I'd had enough hiking myself, and my right ankle was starting to hurt. But I didn't want to be a spoilsport.

In fact, everyone's energy was starting to lag. After a quick stop at the Keanae Overlook to ooh and ah and take a few photos, we decided to drive straight through to Waianapanapa State Park, which was right before Hana. I was actually feeling pretty mellow by the time we got into the car.

At least until I glanced at the side-view mirror and saw that the same white vehicle was still behind us.

I opened my mouth to ask Nick again what he thought. But I snapped it shut, realizing there was no point in bringing it up a second time. Instead, I joined Betty in singing "Bali Hai" from the musical *South Pacific,* pretending to enjoy myself even as I kept my eyes fixed on the mirror.

We had just passed Mile Marker 32 when I spotted a sign that read WAIANAPANAPA STATE PARK.

"Everybody up for another stop?" Nick asked, sounding as if he was getting his enthusiasm back.

"This is where that famous cave is, isn't it?" Betty asked excitedly, leaning forward in her seat to get a better look as Nick slowed down to turn into the parking lot.

"That's right," he replied. "Remember the cool legend I told you, about the princess hiding in the cave to get away from her jealous husband . . . ?"

I was only half-listening. I was too busy watching in the mirror as the white van followed us into the parking lot. As it did, I finally got a good look at the driver.

My mouth went dry as I saw that it was Bryce Bolt, the man I was convinced had murdered Marnie Burton.

Chapter 18

"Lots of people talk to animals. Not very many listen, though. That's the problem."

—Benjamin Hoff, *The Tao of Pooh*

"Nick," I said uneasily, keeping my voice low in the hopes that Betty and Winston wouldn't hear me, "I don't think we should stop here."

"Why not?" he asked. I got the feeling he was too distracted by the sudden traffic jam to listen very closely.

"Because you know that car I thought was following us?" I replied, trying not to sound as panicked as I felt. "I was ri—"

The sudden bleating of a horn sent me jumping out of my skin. Wrenching my head around, I saw that the offender was a gigantic tour bus lumbering into the parking lot, right behind the white van.

"We'd better hurry," Betty called gaily from the backseat. "This place is about to be inundated with tourists."

Ordinarily, I would have thought the disdainful way she referred to "tourists" was cute, given the fact that she was practically the poster girl for the tourism industry. However, at the moment I was much more worried about the man in the car behind us. A man who had obviously followed me all the way out here to the remote edges of Maui.

"Nick," I tried again as he pulled into a parking space, speaking softly so Betty and Winston wouldn't hear me, "we can't stay here. We might be in danger."

Apparently I spoke so softly that even he didn't hear me. He and my other two traveling companions had already opened their car doors and were climbing out, chattering away happily about the sightseeing opportunities that lay ahead of them.

Great, I thought miserably. Now not only does Bryce know Nick and I are here; he got a good look at our two friends. Our two elderly, vulnerable friends.

"Bad timing," Winston muttered. "Let's see if we can make it into the cave before all these visitors get off their bus."

No sooner had he said the words then dozens of tourists began oozing out of their vehicle, swarming the parking lot like ants at a picnic. As I anxiously surveyed the crowd, I realized they were primarily senior citizens, many of them using canes or walkers to get around.

"You're right, dear," Betty observed. "It looks like we'll have plenty of company. Oh, well, this is still a beautiful spot. Just look at that black sand beach! I can't wait to take some pictures."

"I'd like to check out the cave first," Nick said, glancing over in that direction with interest. "How about you, Jess?"

"Uh, maybe later," I told him. "Why don't we follow Betty's suggestion and take a walk along the beach first?"

And *stay* on that beautiful black sand beach, I thought—in fact, let's keep as far away from the cave as possible. Especially since it looked as if most of these tourists weren't about to go inside to wade in the cold, brackish waters that flowed into the volcanic caves, and the last thing I wanted was to find myself alone in nature's version of a dark alley. We were much better off remaining completely in view, with as many people around us as possible.

Besides, I desperately wanted to get Nick alone for a minute so I could explain that the four of us needed to get out of there *fast.* But Betty had taken Nick's arm and was chattering away happily, admiring the fine sand and the deep blue-green ocean and the clear blue sky.

I looked around frantically, trying to see where Bryce had gone. I finally spotted the van, parked close to the exit. It was empty.

The getaway car, I thought grimly, realizing that Bryce had done more than follow me here. He had also planned a strategy.

And then I saw him slip into the cave.

"Nick," I said, trying to sound calm even though my stomach was doing flip-flops, "there's something I want to show you." My mind raced as I tried to come up with a convincing reason. "It's, uh, a really cool plant I saw over there."

My ploy worked. "Sure, Jess."

"Nick, we have to leave—now!" I hissed the moment Betty and Winston were out of earshot. "Bryce Bolt followed us."

He stared at me in disbelief. "Are you serious?"

"Of course I'm serious. I saw him go into the cave just now. If he really is doing FloraTech's dirty work, all four of us could be in danger."

"In that case," Nick said evenly, "let's find Betty and Winston and get out of here."

Desperately I searched the crowd of wandering

tourists, trying to pick out the bright pink fabric of Betty's sundress. It turned out she wasn't the only traveler with a taste for loud clothing. I latched on to four or five different people I thought might be her, two of whom turned out to be men.

When I finally spotted her, I let out a cry.

"Nick, she's going into the cave!" I exclaimed. "And Winston is with her!"

He nodded. "Okay. I'll go grab them so we can get out of here."

"No!" I insisted. "I'll go."

He glanced at me quizzically. "But—"

"Look, I'm the one who got us all into this mess. I feel responsible."

"Then why don't we both go?"

"It makes more sense for you to call the police," I told him. "And get the car!"

"Jessie—"

I began jogging toward the cave, not wanting to waste any more time discussing our strategy. As I drew near, I saw that I'd been right in my assumption that there weren't a lot of sightseers going inside today. In fact, there was no one around as I stood at the edge, my voice cracking as I called, "Betty? Winston?"

Nothing. At least, nothing aside from the sound of my own voice bouncing off the hard black walls of the volcanic rock formations arching over the ocean.

I had no choice but to go inside.

Cautiously, I stepped into the shadowy cave, creeping along the edge and hoping I was managing to keep out of sight. I was struck by the sudden change of atmosphere. There was a dramatic difference between its cool, dimly lit interior and the warm, inviting sun I'd just left behind. I also discovered I could barely see in the darkness.

I blinked hard a few times. Gradually, my eyes

adjusted well enough for me to see. What I saw froze the blood in my veins.

Betty and Winston cowered at the opposite end of the cave, their eyes bright with terror.

Right behind them stood Bryce Bolt. Even in the dim light, I could see he had a gun in his hand.

Oh, my God, I thought, quickly stepping backward in an attempt at disappearing into one of the cave's craggy alcoves. My heart was pounding so loudly I suspected Bryce could hear it even from where he stood.

At least he can't see me, I thought.

But my relief lasted only a moment. Almost immediately, I remembered Nick saying that, according to the legend, when the wife of the jealous chief fled to this very cave, she also tried to hide by standing close to the irregular cave wall, but he spotted her reflection in the water.

Slowly, I lowered my eyes. And saw my reflection in the clear, smooth water below.

The unmistakable feeling of defeat crept over me. He knew I was in here. And even though he was holding Betty and Winston at gunpoint, they were only his hostages. It was me he wanted.

Even before I'd made a conscious decision about what to do, I leaped out of my ineffective hiding place.

"Let them go, Bryce!" I cried. "It's me you want, not them. They have no idea what's going on!"

"But you do," he returned nastily. "You've got it all figured out, haven't you?"

"Just let them walk right out of here," I told him. I was astonished by how calm I sounded. "If you do, I'll do whatever you want. I'll go with you right now, I'll leave the island—whatever you say. Just put that gun away."

I saw the glint of metal in his hand as he moved, positioning it to fire. Only this time, it was pointed directly at me.

I knew I had to do something—anything. I couldn't just stand there, waiting for him to shoot me.

Without thinking, I plunged into the water. As I hit the surface, I heard the loud splash, its sound amplified by the hard walls of the cave. I hoped the noise would bring people running. At the very least, I hoped my unexpected action would buy me some time.

I stayed under as long as I could, wanting to remain as difficult a target as possible. But I couldn't keep myself submerged forever. Finally, desperately in need of air, I popped my head above the surface. My eyes were wide as I blinked away the salty water, trying to see if my surprise move had made any difference.

It had. Bryce had stepped closer to the water's edge, temporarily releasing Betty and Winston. I saw them scurrying as far away from him as they could. His attention was now focused on me. So was his gun.

Time seemed to stop as I heard a click.

"No!" I cried, then instinctively dropped down beneath the water's surface.

As I did, the sound of a gunshot exploded in my ears.

For the next few seconds, I heard nothing but the gurgling noises of the water bubbling around my ears. Even though I didn't feel any pain, I assumed I had been shot. I also assumed these were my last moments on earth.

But I didn't want to spend them underwater. Some primitive urge propelled me upward, toward the air and the light and all those basic things that suddenly seemed so important.

As I burst through the water's surface, gasping for breath and struggling to see, I expected to see Bryce standing at the water's edge with his recently fired gun still pointed at me. As soon as I blinked a few times, I discovered that he was in front of me, all right. But I felt my eyes widen as I watched the gun slip from his hand, landing on the rocky ledge with a thump before it plummeted into the water. And then Bryce's entire body crumpled. He dropped to the ground and slid into the water.

Slowly, the pool of water inside the cave began turning red.

I was vaguely aware of screams and the chaos of people running, their footsteps falling hard against the rocky floor of the cave.

"What—?" I cried, still unable to figure out what had happened.

I wrenched my head around, looking for something, anything, that would explain what was going on.

It was then that I spotted Graham Warner. And saw the gun in his hand.

"Graham?" I cried. "What are you—?"

Three or four others, people I didn't recognize, emerged from behind him. Their sudden presence only added to my confusion.

"Pull his body out of there," Graham commanded. He spoke in a gruff voice that I'd never heard before, using a tone I never would have thought a laid-back Hawaiian transplant like him would have been capable of producing.

"You—you *shot* him!" I cried.

"Thanks to you having the presence of mind to surprise him by jumping into the water," he replied grimly. "Once he released those two people he was using as a shield, I was able to move in."

He extended his arm downward, offering to help me out of the water. I did a much better job scrambling up the side by myself.

"But—but it's not as if you're a cop!" I cried, swatting at my wet clothes once I stood steadily on the ledge. My voice wavering uncertainly, I added, "Are you?"

Despite the seriousness of the situation, Graham laughed. "Let's just say things aren't always what they seem."

Especially on Hawaii, I thought, remembering Marnie's prophetic words.

"Jess?" I heard Nick cry as he came rushing into the cave. "What happened? I heard a gunshot! Are you all right?"

"I'm fine," I replied. "So are Betty and Winston. Thanks to Graham."

"Graham?" Nick repeated, puzzled. "The creepy guy from the hotel?"

"See, that's what I meant about things not always being what they seem," Graham replied with a wry smile. "I'm not the burned-out surfer dude I was pretending to be. I'm with the Drug Enforcement Agency. I've been working undercover, investigating FloraTech. We suspected they were using genetic engineering techniques to produce cocaine. We got involved in the investigation of Marnie Burton's murder because we figured they were behind it, although we weren't sure who was actually doing their dirty work for them. Since you came on the scene, Jessie, we've been keeping an eye on you. We thought you might find out something useful."

"I did," I told him breathlessly. "Graham, Bryce Bolt killed Marnie. He borrowed his mother's car that night to do it. But he didn't know that one of the earrings Marnie was wearing fell under the seat. When I found out that Bryce was Alice Feeley's son—and that she'd found the earring in her car—I knew it had to be him."

"Makes sense," Graham said, nodding. "We knew all about FloraTech paying him off to keep quiet. They paid off the newspaper's editor too. Richard Carrera."

That explains the strange way Mr. Carrera reacted when I mentioned Marnie's tape, I thought, as well as his interest in learning what I knew about it.

"We thought it was probably either Carrera or Bolt who killed Marnie," he continued, "since they were both on FloraTech's payroll. It made sense that the folks at FloraTech wouldn't have any qualms about throwing in a few extra assignments."

"That probably included getting hold of Marnie's tape," I mused. "The audiocassette that was supposed to contain Marnie's interview with her 'secret source.' It must have been Bryce who broke into my hotel room, trying to destroy every piece of evidence he could get his hands on. In fact, it was probably him who paid the helicopter pilot to strand Nick and me in Waimea Canyon after I started poking around the properties FloraTech was buying."

"And today," Graham added, "he followed you all the way out here with the intention of getting rid of you, once and for all."

"I survived, but poor Marnie didn't," I said, shaking my head. "FloraTech tried to buy her silence too, but she didn't understand just how badly they wanted it. In fact, she blithely went ahead with her plans to expose them."

"Sounds like she was kind of an innocent," Graham commented. "In the end, it cost her."

An innocent. That was exactly what she was. Thinking back to the lively young woman I'd met my very first day on Maui reminded me of something else: the incident with John Irwin that had brought us together in the first place.

"Graham," I asked, "how high up does this go? Allowing FloraTech to do what it's doing, I mean?"

"Pretty high, I'm afraid."

"As high as the governor's office?"

He looked surprised. "So you knew about that too. We've had someone working there undercover. And we learned that John Irwin, one of the governor's aides, had worked with Wickham to bring FloraTech to the island. They were both getting a big fat piece of the pie."

Marnie had found that out too. She even had the pictures to prove it—the photographs of the governor and his new best friend, the biotech firm's founder.

For the moment, I'd heard all I could stand about FloraTech. I was sopping wet, badly shaken, and totally wiped out. I was also worried about Betty and Winston, who were nowhere in sight.

"Where are our friends?" I asked Graham anxiously. "Are they all right?"

"They're fine. They're outside, talking to one of our people. But we can get statements from everybody later. I suspect that right now the four of you just want to go back to your hotel and start trying to put this behind you."

That sounded like the best idea I'd heard all day.

• • •

It's over, I thought, feeling dazed as I wandered out of the cool, damp darkness of the cave and back into the sunlight. Marnie's murderer has been caught. The truth about FloraTech is going to come out, and everyone who was part of it will pay for what they've done. Most importantly, the people I care about are safe—and so am I.

I spotted Betty and Winston standing near our

rented Jeep. Betty's eyes were bright and her hands fluttered excitedly as she related the details of her harrowing experience to a man in a suit. Winston stood beside her, looking as solid and supportive as the dramatic volcanic rocks jutting out of the dark blue-green water just beyond. I was glad to see how well they were handling this. Then again, given how strong they both were, I supposed I shouldn't have been surprised.

"Are you okay, Jess?" Nick, who was walking beside me, asked solicitously.

"I'm fine," I assured him. "And I'm glad you're all right, Nick. I don't know what I'd do if anything ever happened to you—" My voice had suddenly become too choked for me to go on.

"Exactly how I feel," he returned, putting his arm around my shoulders and pulling me close. In a near whisper, he added, "But it's finished."

"Yes," I agreed, leaning my head against his chest as we walked. "Thank goodness."

"Think of it this way," Nick said lightly. "If it hadn't been for this little adventure the two of us fell into, we never would have gotten to see Waimea Canyon."

I glanced up at him and grimaced. "Thanks, but I think next time I'll do my sightseeing with a reputable tour company."

"But that little side trip gave us a chance to have a very important conversation. One in which I was able to ask you a very important question. I asked you—"

"I remember what you asked me," I assured him.

"You do?" he returned. He tried to sound as if he was only teasing, but the huskiness of his voice gave him away. "Does that mean you also remember how you answered?"

"Yes."

"And now that we're out of harm's way, would you still answer the same way?"

I stopped, turning to face him. I reached up and put my hands on Nick's shoulders, meanwhile looking earnestly into his eyes.

"Yes, Nick," I told him. "I'll marry you."

About the Author

CYNTHIA BAXTER is a native of Long Island, New York. She currently resides on the North Shore, where she is at work on the next *Reigning Cats & Dogs* mystery, *Who's Kitten Who?*, which Bantam will publish in fall 2007. Visit her on the Web at www.cynthiabaxter.com.

READ ON FOR AN EXCLUSIVE SNEAK PEEK AT CYNTHIA BAXTER'S NEXT MYSTERY!

Who's Kitten Who?

A *Reigning Cats & Dogs* Mystery

by

Cynthia Baxter

On sale October 2007

Who's Kitten Who?

On sale October 2007

Chapter 1

"Man is the most intelligent of the animals—and the most silly."

—Diogenes

"Ouch!" I cried. "Stop, I'm begging you! You're torturing me!"

"Hold still!" my attacker insisted.

I glanced around desperately, wondering if there was any way out. But I was afraid that continuing to resist would only anger my assailant—who was armed, dangerous, and clearly determined to make me her next victim.

"You are moving too much, *Signorina*!" she exclaimed. "I cannot make the neckline straight if you will not stop—what is the word?—fidgeting!"

I have every right to fidget, I thought crossly. First, I get roped into spending my Saturday morning standing on a ridiculous pedestal in the middle of a bridal shop, surrounded by enough ruffles and veils to make me break out in a rash. Then I get turned into a giant pincushion. As if that's not bad enough, I'm periodically forced to twirl around like an Olympic ice skater to make sure the skirt of this preposterous dress swirls just the right way.

But I knew I'd get no sympathy here. In fact, from the relentless way Gabriella Bertucci kept sticking me, you would have thought she was a voodoo priestess instead of a fashion designer whose wedding dresses were well known all over Long Island.

"Take a look in the mirror, *Signorina,*" Gabriella said with a sigh. "You look so beautiful, no?"

I screwed up my face before forcing myself to peer into the three-sided full-length mirror. When your idea of sprucing up is putting on a freshly washed Polar-fleece jacket and a sparklin' new pair of chukka boots, being encased in a Barbie Doll frock that reaches down to the floor (and is cut nearly as low) is about as much fun as changing a tire on a twenty-six-foot veterinary clinic-on-wheels. In the dark. In the rain. And sleet.

But after all the time, energy, and emotion I'd invested in having this dress made, I figured it was time to check out the results. Maybe, I hoped, I would even look something close to *nice*. . . .

"E-e-ek!" I cried.

"Signorina!" Gabriella sounded as if she was about to burst into tears. "You don't like?"

I stood a little straighter and forced myself to take another look. An objective look. Even though my dark blond hair hung limply, and even though, as usual, I wasn't wearing any makeup, I was startled by what I saw. The dress Gabriella Bertucci had custom made for me fit beautifully, making me look more like Cinderella than I ever would have thought possible.

The dress was made from a silky fabric that draped around my various body parts in a surprisingly flattering way. It skimmed over my torso and waist and hips, giving me a womanly shape that a comfortable pair of jeans just didn't capture. Even the low-cut neckline looked good on me. At least, once I finally stopped tugging at it after remembering that the petite *fashionista* had a sharp pair of scissors in her possession and that even she had a breaking point.

The only problem was the dress's color.

Mint green.

When it came to planning her wedding, my dear friend Betty Vandervoort was turning out to be a real traditionalist. Instead of an edgy event with, say, a justice of the peace who did a rap version of the ceremony or a hippie minister who recited the poems of Charles Bukowski, she surprised me by insistng on something out of a fairy tale. And it included a bride in a long white gown accompanied by bridesmaids in pastel shades like baby pink and pale yellow and my own mint green, colors that made us look more like dishes of candy than grown women.

I'd pleaded with Betty to let her bridesmaids wear a more dignified color.

"How about black?" I had suggested hopefully. "These days, a bridesmaid dressed in black is considered the height of sophistication."

"Black is for funerals," she returned with a frown. "When I married Charles longer ago than I care to admit, we eloped. This time around, I want the kind of wedding I've dreamed about since I was a little girl. And that means a maid of honor who looks like an angel, not the Grim Reaper!"

The other details of Betty's spring wedding, now just three weeks away, were equally traditional. She was even demanding that the canine guests come formally attired.

In fact, it seemed as if she had put more thought into deciding what my snow white Westie, Max, and my black-and-white Dalmatian, Lou, would wear on the big day than she put into choosing her own dress. She'd finally decided on red bow ties for both of them, and for Winston's dog, a wire-haired dachshund named Frederick, she'd selected a bright yellow bow tie that would complement his soft fawn-and-tan fur.

Personally, I thought all three dogs looked just fine naked.

But it wasn't my wedding. Betty had already pointed that out several times. And a few of those times, she'd suggested that I'd have much more leverage if I'd consider making it a double wedding. That certainly put an end to my complaining.

Now that I was officially engaged to Nick, ideas like that probably shouldn't have surprised me. Yet becoming engaged had been a big enough step, one I was still trying to adjust to. I hadn't quite gotten used to wearing the small but tasteful antique diamond ring that had belonged to Nick's grandmother, so the idea of shopping for caterers and squealing excitedly over bridal shower gifts and enduring fittings for my own white dress—not to mention contemplating actually *being* married—was way beyond me.

For the moment, the role of maid of honor was about all I could cope with.

"What you don't like?" Gabriella asked hopefully, studying my reflection with the same intensity I was.

"The dress is beautiful," I assured her. "It's just that it's so . . . so *green*."

The tiny native of Milan, Italy, with the build of Pinocchio and the determination of Julius Caesar, folded her arms against her chest. *"Signorina,"* she replied crisply, "is not me who choose the color. If you no like, you talk with *Signora* Vandervoort and see if she change."

Fat chance, I thought. There was no reasoning with a woman who, in her eighth decade of life, was suddenly subscribing to magazines like *Over-the-Top Bride*.

Still, Betty had promised to meet me at Gabriella's shop this morning so she could see the dress. I supposed this was my big chance to make whatever constructive criticisms I could come up with, but I was torn. Up until a few minutes ago, I'd believed I was willing to do anything in the world for her.

I was pondering the possibility that the one thing I *wasn't* willing to do was risk being arrested for impersonating Scarlett O'Hara when I heard a car door slam outside the shop. Seconds later, the bride-to-be—and the person responsible for my transformation into a life-size after-dinner mint—came dashing through the door.

From Betty's fringed, lime green Capri pants, lemon yellow linen blouse and orange espadrilles, no one would ever have guessed that at that moment Gabriella was busily stitching up a wedding dress for her that had enough satin, Belgian lace, and tiny beads to make my dress look like a military uniform by comparison. Just looking at her was enough to provide me with the day's minimum requirement of vitamin C.

I was mustering up the courage to register my concerns over the dress when I noticed the expression on Betty's face.

"Betty, what's the matter?" I demanded. "You look like you've just lost your best friend!"

"Simon Wainwright may not have been my best friend," Betty replied seriously, "but that doesn't make the fact that he was murdered last night any easier to take."

It took a few seconds for the meaning of her words to sink in.

"Someone you know was *murdered*?" I cried. I lifted my skirt and started to step off the pedestal.

"Scusi, Signorina," Gabriella burst out, sounding completely exasperated. "We will never finish the dress if you do not stop moving around like a . . . a puppy!"

"Let's take a break," I suggested, more calmly than

I felt. Apparently, the dress designer's English vocabulary didn't include the word "murder."

But mine did.

"Sit down," I instructed Betty. "Take a few deep breaths and tell me exactly what happened."

"*Signorina!* The pins—"

"I'll be careful," I assured Gabriella. Suddenly, getting poked with a few straight pins didn't seem to matter at all.

As soon as Betty and I perched on the brocade-covered couch that graced one corner of the shop, I turned to face her.

"First of all, who is Simon Wainwright?" I asked.

"He's a member of the amateur theater group I belong to," she replied. "He just joined us recently after the Port Players' executive director heard about a fabulous play he'd written. It's called *She's Flying High*, and it's based on the life of the famous aviator Amelia Earhart. It was going to be the world premiere."

"So he is—was—a playwright."

"He was also the male lead. He was playing the part of Amelia's husband, George Putnam." Betty sighed. "Simon was one of those 'triple threats,' a rare individual who was an amazing actor, singer, and dancer. But he was also an extremely talented writer. There was even talk of *She's Flying High* being produced on Broadway!

"He was so charismatic, someone who would light up a room the moment he walked into it," she continued, wiping away a tear. "Yet he never let any of it go to his head. Everyone loved him. He was one of the kindest, most charming, most down-to-earth people I've ever met."

"And now he's dead," I said softly, still trying to take it all in.

Betty nodded. "His body was found in the theater early this morning. The police won't know the actual cause of death until an autopsy has been performed, but the detective I spoke to said it looked as if someone had struck him in the head from behind with something hard."

"Who discovered his body?" I asked.

"The costume designer, a young woman named Lacey Croft. She was poking around the storage room, checking to see if there were any costumes left over from some other play that would be suitable for this production. She opened an old trunk that had been pushed into a corner and..." She swallowed hard. "Simon's body was stuffed inside."

"That's awful!" I cried. "You must be so upset, Betty. What a horrible thing!"

She covered her face with her hands. "Simon was such a dear friend!" she cried in a choked voice. "I thought the world of that young man. I'd only known him for a few weeks, but I was already starting to think of him as a son, much the way I think of you as a daughter, Jessica."

I just nodded. "I'm so sorry," I said. "If there's anything I can do—"

She lowered her hands into her lap and looked at me intently. "As a matter of fact, there is."

• • •

Theater One in Port Townsend had begun life as a button factory a hundred years earlier. Since then, the freestanding red brick building had also been a warehouse, a vaudeville house, and a movie theater. Its last incarnation was still in evidence, thanks to the big marquee jutting out over the glass-and-wood front doors, the large glass-covereed displays with posters publicizing the next production, and the old-fashioned box office in the middle of the tiled entryway.

I must admit, I felt a little flutter in the pit of my stomach as Betty and I walked through the side entrance marked "Stage Door." I knew the circumstances that were responsible for my being here in the first place were tragic. But I couldn't help feeling a twinge of excitement over getting a behind-the-scenes look at a theater company.

True, the Port Players was only a local group, run by amateurs. But theater had always held a certain mystique for me, mainly because I couldn't fathom anyone actually having the guts to go onstage in front of an audience and perform. Personally, I was one of those behind-the-scenes people. Of course, the only real theatrical experience I'd had was in college, when I'd worked backstage at the Bryn Mawr College Junior Show.

Inside, the lights were low and the air was somber. It seemed fitting that the entire stage was black, not only the floor, but also the tremendous backdrops hanging behind the stage. As we walked down the short set of stairs off to one side, I glanced out at the audience. At least twenty-five people were scattered throughout the first four or five rows.

As Betty and I sat down in dark red velvet seats, a tall, gangly man rose from the first row and turned to face the audience. He had gaunt features, piercing dark eyes, and dark brown curly hair so thick I wondered how he managed to get a comb through it. It kept falling into his eyes and he resolutely kept pushing it back.

He was wearing black pants and a white turtleneck, an outfit that screamed "director." At least to me, who'd learned most of what I knew about the theater from the movies.

As if she'd read my thoughts, Betty leaned over and whispered, "That's Derek Albright, the Port Players' executive director."

"This is truly a sad day," Derek began somberly. "We have lost a man who was more than a member of our troupe. Simon Wainwright was our spiritual leader. Yet even in this time of deep despair, it's imperative that we continue," he went on. "The expression 'the show must go on' has never been more true. I don't think any of us doubts that that's exactly what Simon would have wanted. Jonathan, who's been playing Charles Lindbergh, has agreed to step into Simon's role of Amelia Earhart's husband, George Putnam. I'm hoping you'll all agree that the best way we can remember Simon is to bring his work off the page and into this theater. Let's work together to honor the man who was our friend and mentor by finishing what we started—"

"How *can* you?"

The high-pitched female voice that rose up from the back of the theater startled everyone, cutting through the somber mood. As I craned my neck to see who had spoken, I noticed that everyone else in the audience was doing the exact same thing.

Halfway back, a young woman stood up. She was dressed entirely in black, wearing a long dress that looked as if it was from another era. Either that or it was one of those bridesmaid's gowns I'd been wishing Betty would opt for.

Still, there was no way I would have traded my mint green frock for her getup. Not when the dress was accessorized with a dramatic black velvet cape edged with silver sequins and a black felt hat that swooped down over one eye and was decorated with a huge feather that some poor ostrich was undoubtedly still looking for.

Once I managed to get past her startling look, I saw that her features were pretty enough, if not particularly outstanding. That is, except for her green eyes, their striking emerald color no doubt the result of tinted contact lenses. Even though her eyes were ringed in thick black eyeliner, I could see that they burned with fury.

"How *can* you?" she repeated, gliding down the aisle. "How can you possibly go on as if nothing has happened?"

"That's Aziza Zorn," Betty whipered. "Simon's girlfriend."

"Does she always dress like that?" I asked.

But Aziza had reached the front of the theater by then. She planted herself firmly next to Derek, then, throwing her arms out dramatically, she cried, "Simon is dead! He's gone! Some vile person has taken his life. And with that cruel act, he's taken a part of our lives too! So how can we be expected to proceed as if . . . as if life could possibly go on in exactly the same way?"

"I agree with Aziza," a male voice added. I turned in time to see a tall, lean man with sandy colored hair rise from his seat. "If you ask me, the best way to honor Simon would be to admit that we can't possibly continue without him."

Instantly, the entire theater erupted in chaos. I had to admit, this was turning out to be much more interesting than I'd expected.

"People, please!" Derek finally yelled, his voice loud enough to rise above the racket. "Take your seats. Please, we must discuss this reasonably!"

Once everyone had quieted down, he held up both his hands. "I hear what you're saying, Aziza. Kyle too. When you come right down to it, we all have to mourn our loss in our own private way. But for me, that means continuing the work Simon started. Those of you who agree with me, I invite you—no, I *beg* you—to stay. Those of you who don't, you're welcome to leave, with no hard feelings."

Aziza bobbed up from where she'd sat in the front row. "You all know what I think," she said, turning to address the audience. "I'm just too sickened by what happened to go on."

With that, she squared her shoulders and stalked out of the theater.

"Anyone else?" Derek asked.

The room was so still you could have heard one of Gabriella Bertucci's pins drop.

"Good. Then, I suggest that we all go home and try to get over the shock of the terrible news we received this morning," Derek said firmly. "As for our production, we'll stick to our schedule and meet for our next rehearsal Monday evening at seven."

As the cast and production crew stood up and the room buzzed with their conversations, Betty turned to me. "Well?" she asked anxiously. "What did you think?"

I just shook my head. "I'm sorry, Betty. I didn't really get a sense of anything aside from what a terrible loss this is for everyone who knew Simon."

"Of course you didn't. How could you have?" Betty frowned. "I knew this wouldn't be an actual rehearsal, but I didn't think Derek would end it so quickly. Would you be willing to come back another time?"

"Of course," I assured her.

"Oh, thank you, Jess! Let's check with Derek to make sure he's comfortable with having you at the next rehearsal."

We walked over and waited while Derek continued the conversation he'd been having with a slim, forty-something woman.

"We've lost our Amelia!" he wailed. "I can't believe Aziza is doing this to us!"

"We'll figure something out," the woman assured him. "Elena Brock is the obvious person to take over the lead. I'll start working with her right away."

"Then who'll take Elena's role?" he asked, sounding just as woeful. "Who'll play Anita?"

The question remained unanswered as he let out a loud sigh, then turned and noticed Betty and me.

"Derek," Betty began, "if you have a moment, I'd like to introduce a friend of mine, Jessica Popper. Jessie is interested in coming to Monday night's rehearsal—"

I stuck out my hand to shake, expecting him to do the same. Instead, he just stared at me, his face lighting up as if Greta Garbo herself had just walked in.

"Perfect!" he cried.

Something about his sudden burst of enthusiasm made me nervous. "Uh, what's perfect?"

"You are! You're perfect for the role of Anita Snook, the aviation pioneer who gave Amelia Earhart her first flying lesson."

"But I never—"

"I won't take no for an answer," Derek insisted. "Whoever you are, *please* say you'll join the cast!"

• • •

I was still trying to reconstruct exactly what had gone on in that theater as I steered my little red Volkswagen off Minnesauke Lane and bumped along the quarter-mile driveway leading to my stone cottage. After an afternoon that had left me in a fog, I was even more anxious than usual to surround myself with all the elements in my life that really mattered.

As I let myself into the cottage, I heard the water running in the bathroom, a sign that Nick was showering. Fine with me, since it gave me a chance to reconnect with my loved ones from the Animal Kingdom.

In fact, I was instantly smothered in dog kisses as my two dogs rushed to greet me, both so happy I was home that their claws skittered across the floor as if they were the Keystone Kops.

"Hey, Louie-Lou!" I cooed, throwing one arm around my one-eyed Dalmatian. Max, my tailless Westie, jumped up and down as if he was a marionette rather than a crazed terrier. "Hello, Maxie-Max. Were you afraid I'd forget to say hello to you?"

As soon as he realized his favorite playmate was now available for fun and games, Max sprang across the living room to retrieve his favorite toy, a pink rubber poodle that was eternally covered in saliva. I dutifully wrested it from his jaws, then tossed it back to the other end of the room. Both he and Lou scampered after it, their body language communicating "Don't you just love playing Slimytoy?" The fact was, I loved it as much as they did.

All this commotion prompted my blue and gold macaw, Prometheus, to start squawking his own greeting "*Awk!* Who's the pretty birdy?"

I went over to his cage and stuck my hand in so he could climb on.

"Welcome home, Jessie," he greeted, mimicking my voice perfectly "*Awk!*"

"I've got a special treat for you," I told him, running my hand along the bright, silky-smooth feathers along his back. "I'll get you a piece of apple as soon as I get my bearing."

"*Awk!* Prometheus loves apple!"

As I put him back in his cage, Catherine the Great, better known as Cat, crept over. My lovely gray kitty was clearly feeling her arthritis. Even so, as she made her way toward me, she carried herself like a *grand dame,* someone along the lines of Queen Elizabeth—or perhaps her namesake, the enlightened Empress of Russia during the 1700s.

Cat's quiet dignity was emphasized even further by the appearance of the latest addition to my household, Tinkerbell. The spunky tiger kitten had joined our household a few months earlier, after Nick found her abandoned in a cardboard box in a field on his university's campus.

"Hey, Cat!" I crooned. "Hi, Tink!" I flopped on the

couch with Cat in my lap, just as Nick emerged from the bathroom, drying his dark hair with a white towel. A second towel was wrapped around his waist, giving him a sexy beach boy look I kind of liked. "Hey," he greeted me. "I didn't hear you come in."

"You're never going to believe what I did today," I returned, stroking Cat's fur distractedly.

But from the stricken look on his face, I got the feeling he hadn't heard me. Not when he clearly had something much more pressing on his mind.

"What's the matter?" I asked, sitting up straighter. A hundred different possibilities flashed through my head: He'd failed an exam at law school, something terrible had happened to one of his friends....

"It's my parents," he announced, plopping down on the couch beside me.

"What about them?" I asked cautiously.

He cleared his throat. "You know they've been anxious to meet you for a really long time," he said. "And now that we're engaged, they can't wait."

"I can't wait to meet them either." My own parents had been killed in an automobile accident years earlier. All the more reason I was looking forward to getting to know Nick's, even though he'd been warning me for years that his mother was—what was the word he always used? Oh, yes: difficult.

"No, they *really* can't wait," he continued. "They're coming here to meet you. All the way from Florida. Soon."

Something about the way he said the word "soon" made my stomach tighten. "How soon?"

"Monday. The day after tomorrow."